PRAISE FOR

LOIS LANE FALLOUT

"Readers are in for a treat. A spectacular prose start for DC Comics' spectacular lady."
—*Kirkus Reviews*, STARRED REVIEW

"It's not a bird, it's not a plane, it's Lois Lane, boldly following clues wherever they lead, taking readers along for a thrilling ride." —*Chicago Tribune*

"Bond cleverly reimagines star reporter Lois Lane as a teenager today. . . . delightful."
—*Booklist*

"Lois Lane is your new YA fiction hero." —*Yahoo! Movies*

"Step aside, Katniss: it's time for a teenage journalist to take over." —*The Hollywood Reporter*

"So it's basically Lois Lane in a Veronica Mars-esque plot, which sounds like all kinds of awesome." —*Entertainment Weekly*

"This project should appeal not only to YA readers, but fans of the heroine who may have felt neglected with 20 page comics lately." —*The Examiner*

"This is a story with a strong female protagonist. Lois is smart and gutsy . . . an enjoyable ride."
—*VOYA*

"Gwenda Bond concocts an intelligent novel that moves faster than a speeding bullet . . . May this be the first of many more." —*Shelf Awareness*

"A perfect read for anyone who loves a good mystery, with some romance, and a tenacious lead character." —*SupermanSuperSite*

"*Lois Lane: Fallout* is an innovative and overdue revitalization of Lois Lane, and stands on its own as a stellar YA debut for the character." —*The Comics Journal*

Lois Lane: Double Down is published by Switch Press
A Capstone Imprint
1710 Roe Crest Drive
North Mankato, Minnesota 56003
www.switchpress.com

STAR38239

Superman created by Jerry Siegel and Joe Shuster.
By special arrangement with the Jerry Siegel family.

Library of Congress Cataloging-in-Publication Data is available
on the Library of Congress website.

ISBN: 978-1-63079-039-4 (paperback)

Summary:
Lois Lane has settled in to her new school. She has friends, for maybe the first time in her life. She has a job that challenges her. And her relationship is growing with SmallvilleGuy, her online maybe-more-than-a-friend. But when her friend Maddy's twin collapses in a part of town she never should've been in, Lois finds herself embroiled in a dangerous mystery that brings her closer to the dirty underbelly of Metropolis.

Cover design by Lori Bye
Book design by Bob Lentz

Printed and bound in China.
9996S17RRD

LOIS LANE
DOUBLE DOWN

GWENDA BOND

SWITCH
PRESS
a capstone imprint

CHAPTER 1

"You lost?" the man asked. He had a zillion wrinkles, and he was wearing a hat that would suit an old-fashioned detective. He perched on a stool beside the stairs out of the subway station, ready to launch into a guitar solo. The guitar's case lay open on the ground in front of him.

I doubted he was going to rake in much cash. But this was his turf, not mine. I'd never been to Suicide Slum before.

So I tossed a few dollars into the case. "I'm never lost," I said, hoping it was true.

The first twangs from his guitar followed me up the stairs to the street. I felt somewhat conspicuous even though I'd purposely dressed down today, pairing a blue T-shirt with a robot on the front with jeans and my comfiest boots, my long black hair scooped back in a loose ponytail. As soon as I stepped out into the light, I knew I wasn't anywhere near the relatively posh digs my Army general dad's salary got us. Okay, I knew that already—it had taken three different subway transfers and a good forty-five minutes to get here from school.

Most of the buildings I passed looked abandoned. Boarded-up windows, layers of graffiti, padlocked doors. So I seemed to be in the right place.

Then I spotted who I was looking for.

Ahead at the corner, a slender boy my age slicked a roller of light gray paint across the broad surface of a wall that stretched high above him. He had a scaffold set up and some other supplies, a sketchpad and a selection of spray paint cans and brushes among them.

"You must be the artiste," I said in greeting, emphasizing the "eest" at the end.

He glanced over his shoulder and finished up the swipe before lowering his arm. "I hope not. Because if I am, I sound terrible," he said, and mock-shuddered.

He set down the roller carefully on a drop cloth and stuck out his hand. Black hair hung to his jaw, his brown eyes taking in everything. He wore an old T-shirt and baggy jeans, both paint-splotched, and had the kind of open, welcoming expression that makes it impossible not to like someone.

"I'm Dante Alvarez," he said. "And you must be the journaliste." He drew out the pronunciation of the word to mimic mine.

I snorted. "You're right. That does make us sound terrible."

My fellow *Scoop* staffers had guilted me into spending my

Friday after school on this human interest story. Real, serious news about the strange and nefarious things I was certain must be happening all around us had eluded me for the two weeks since my first articles, and they'd presented a united front at our staff meeting the day before. Everyone *else* had done a story like this, of the regular old day-to-day variety, with no mind-control bullying or secret evil corporation angle. My new friends insisted it was my turn.

Like it wasn't hard enough keeping on Principal Butler's good side at school and my dad's at home, juggling homework with *Scoop* business, and also continually trying to figure out my relationship with SmallvilleGuy.

Having friends was a new enough development that I was forced to say yes. But it was also Friday, and that meant I had a date . . . or what *I* thought of as one, anyway . . . with SmallvilleGuy later that evening. My cheeks warmed.

Get it together, Lois. It isn't a date.

"Hello?" Dante said.

"Sorry. I'm Lois Lane, here to write your story." There was a short stool among Dante's equipment, and I sat down on it to rummage in my messenger bag for my small notebook.

When I looked up, pen at the ready, it was into the face of one amused artist. "It's not *my* story," he said. "It's the story of how art can help revive a neighborhood that needs to be reminded it matters."

He waved his arm to encompass the environs around us. While the block I'd walked up had seen far better days, from this vantage at the corner there were visible signs of liveliness on the other streets. Neighborhood shops—rundown but open—dotted the next block, along with some apartment buildings, and there were plenty of adults and children out and about.

"Is art enough?" I resisted mentioning the time I helped bust an art forger. "This is clearly a neglected area of the city. Not getting a lot of attention from City Hall." I paused, struck by an idea. "Wait. Is the problem mainly neglect, or is there corruption causing the neglect?"

"You make it sound like that would be a good thing," he said.

"Sorry, nose for news." Oops. Maybe I was getting a little *too* desperate for a big story. "Tell me why you're doing this."

I scribbled notes as he talked about his project. A nonprofit had awarded him funding to design and paint the first of a planned series of murals throughout this section of town, and he'd spend the coming week completing it. He was in a special art magnet program at our school, and he took those same three trains I'd taken today every morning to get there. Ideally, he said, there'd be a school with decent art classes closer to home, but his mom hadn't been able to locate one.

There wasn't much mural yet to speak of other than a base layer the gray of rain clouds, but I'd passed so much graffiti on this street alone I had to ask. "Do you worry about someone vandalizing your art?"

"No, I don't. Taggers here respect other people's work."

"There is a lot of crime in this area, historically speaking."

"That's controlled crime. I don't think the Boss cares about murals."

That was an odd way to put it. "The Boss?"

Dante looked right and left before he answered. But there was no one close to us, hadn't been the entire time we were talking. "The one who controls the crime," was all he said. I waited, but he didn't elaborate.

"Okay," I said, underlining the word *Boss* in my notes, but moving on. "You still haven't answered my first question. Is art enough?"

"No," he said, tilting his head to one side, considering the blank wall where his mural would go. "But it's a start. There's that waterfront project people are saying will help too, but . . ."

"But what?" I prompted.

He smiled. "Sometimes people need a reminder that they are connected to each other, to something greater than themselves. That there is beauty in the world, and if they look they'll see it. That they can create it. That it's possible to change things yourself."

"On that we agree. So, what's the mural going to depict?"

"I'm not exactly sure yet—waiting to be inspired."

"Here's to inspiration showing up soon if you have to finish it up this week," I said, then closed my notebook. "I think that's all I need. Thanks."

I snuck a peek at my phone as I replaced the notebook in my bag. If I hurried, maybe I wouldn't be late to virtually "see" SmallvilleGuy in the real-sim holoset videogame *Worlds War Three* after all. We'd been meeting there on Friday evenings for the last two weeks, a new tradition in addition to our weeknight chats.

I really didn't want to be late. And I really *did* want to know if I was the only one of us who thought of it as something more than our chats had been before, who thought that our relationship was changing. That it might be becoming a *relationship*. And yet, so far I couldn't bring myself to ask.

"What do you think that's about? Is she lost?" Dante pointed across the street to a taxi.

I did a double take when I saw the girl getting out of the car. She was clearly not a neighborhood local, and she was holding on to the door with a death grip, like she might tumble to the ground if she let go. With obvious effort, she released it and took a few steps toward an abandoned building. Then she stumbled.

I recognized her. And I was already halfway across the street when she fell.

I darted around the taxi and reached her just in time to slow her descent to the ground. She lay flat, collapsed on the sidewalk. Dante had followed me, and he lowered to a crouch at her side.

An unhealthily red-faced taxi driver opened his door and shouted, "You haven't paid me yet—" He broke off, frowning down at his passenger's crumpled form and then at me.

I held my finger up to him. For all I knew, he was considering harvesting his pay from her wallet and leaving her there. My kingdom for the taxi driver I trusted when I needed a ride somewhere. But I'd have to deal with the one in front of me.

"Wait right where you are. We may need you to take us somewhere." I put my hand to the neck of the girl's prone form to check her pulse. She was down like a prize fighter after a knock-out punch.

"Should I call nine-one-one?" Dante asked.

"Ye—"

But her eyes popped open then, big and blue, accentuated by picture-perfect makeup. "No, don't call anyone," she insisted. She blinked. "You're Maddy's friend," she said to me. "Lois."

"And you're Maddy's sister." Maddy—my new best friend and colleague at the *Scoop*—had a twin sister. But I realized that Maddy had never said her twin's name in front of me, and I had never asked. That was awkward.

Dante helped the girl into a seated position, earning a frown from her instead of a thank you.

"I don't have all day," the cab driver said.

"Or much of a civic spirit," I said. "I'll pay. You can keep the meter running." I put my hand on Maddy's sister's arm. "I'm sorry, I don't know your name."

With a wince, she lifted her nose in the air. "What do you mean? How can you not know my name?"

Her tone was affronted, not hurt. What offended her wasn't that Maddy hadn't mentioned it, it was that I hadn't heard of her otherwise. "I'm new here," I said.

"Oh," she said, as if that explained it. Sort of. "I'm Melody."

Dante leaned close enough to me to say, probably without her hearing, "Queen of the school."

Aha. To her, I said, "Melody, I feel like we should get you to a doctor."

"No." She began to struggle to her feet, and when she reached out for help, Dante supported her. "I need to go over there. It's why I came here." She gestured at the abandoned building.

That was a command, like she was in charge, even here. Dante obeyed, with a shrug to me. I got out my wallet to give the grumbling cabbie some money, but as I passed it to him, I said, "But wait a sec, all right?"

When I turned back, Melody had hooked her arm through Dante's and wobbled the rest of the way to the building. Boards with a giant graffiti tag that looked like a B almost concealed the front entrance of the place, which might have been a decent office building at some point. The top glass of the door behind one plank was visible, with broken, sharp shards jutting out from the edge.

Melody shook off Dante's arm and tried to peer in past the boards and broken glass. She pressed her forehead against a piece of wood.

"Watch out for splinters," I said, crossing the sidewalk to them. Though what I wanted was an explanation of what she was doing here, not to be giving safety tips. What was she desperately looking for in a building that housed nothing?

She angled her face toward me. Even after fainting, her makeup and hair were barely mussed. "It's gone," she breathed, her voice as shaky as her legs had been earlier. "Gone. What am I supposed to do now?"

"What's gone?" I asked.

"The guy, the lab, all of it. It's gone. What am I going to do?"

My nose for news metaphorically twitched, catching the scent that had been eluding it. "There was a lab *here*? And you came back to it. Why?"

"Because he said to. He said I should let him know if . . ." She trailed off and frowned.

"If what, Melody? You can trust me."

"I don't trust anyone."

Not even her sister? I raised my eyebrows at that. "Trust me."

"I would," Dante said, "if I were you." Nice of him, considering we just met.

Melody still hesitated, but not for long. "He said to tell him if there were side effects. There haven't been, not until now. But I don't know what else it could be. And it's gone. He's *gone*."

"Side effects? Sounds like you need a doctor." I looked at her, hard, and she returned the favor. We were sizing each other up.

"No," she said, voice thin and breathy again. "I need to find *this* particular doctor. Fast."

"What other leads do you have on where to look for this particular doctor?"

She shook her head, eyes landing on the building.

"This can't be it," I said.

"It is."

And I thought she might collapse again, her shoulders dipping as one of her legs gave.

Dante saw the same thing, and he stepped in to offer his arm again. She grabbed it. Which told me something important about Melody Simpson: she might not ask for help, but she clearly needed it. I made a decision on the spot.

"Good thing I happened to be here. I'll help you."

She blinked at me. When she didn't respond, I added, "I'll have to interview you, get more information, in order to track him down. Especially if you need to find him fast. So, you want my help or not?"

It was a gamble to press, and if she said no, I'd have to try some other way to convince her. I was new to this friend stuff, but Maddy would want to know about this. She would want me to help her sister. Wouldn't she?

"Yes," Melody said. "I need help. Badly enough to accept yours."

"I'm choosing not to take that as an insult." Though it sounded like one. I asked Dante, "Can you help her into the taxi? We'll go to the *Scoop* office."

"Wait a second," Melody said, as if something awful had occurred to her. "What will people say if they see me?"

"You look fine," I said. "No one would have a clue you almost fainted."

"No," she said, with a dismissive head shake. "What will they say if they see me with you guys?"

She's Maddy's sister, I told myself. *Be nice.*

"Probably something less awful than if they saw you collapsed on the sidewalk?"

And we were back to sizing each other up.

Dante ignored the tension and said, "I'll stick with you guys, just in case."

I didn't miss how Melody continued to lean on him. She needed the support. I gave him a subtle nod, and he eased her into the backseat, then asked, "Where are we headed?"

I told the driver, "You're taking us to the Daily Planet Building."

"Hold on. I'll stash my stuff," Dante said, jogging back across the street. He was truly a nice guy, tagging along with the supposed queen of the school and me. Despite her looks, it was tough to believe Melody was related to Maddy.

I took out my phone and signed in to the custom-made hyper-secure messenger app SmallvilleGuy and I used. Then I tapped out a note.

SkepticGirl1: *I'm going to be a little late. Duty calls.*

SmallvilleGuy: *Hurry if you can. I have something important to tell you.*

"Let's not take the scenic route," I told the cab driver.

CHAPTER 2

The scenic route must have been the only one, because it felt like it took forever and an age to get across town. But when I checked, a mere twenty minutes had passed. Still, by the time we reached the sleek mirrored column of the Daily Planet Building, topped by its giant globe, I was obsessing as much (okay, more) about what SmallvilleGuy might have to tell me as I was about Melody's story.

Anyway, she seemed to have recovered. She was acting completely normal—except that she kept circling the wrist of her left arm with her right hand absently, then dropping it with a jerk a few seconds later like she'd realized what she was doing. It was a strange tic. On the trip from the curb to the revolving doors, she did it again.

"You're really all right?" I asked her. "You seem jumpy."

"I'm not jumpy," she said, turning to look at me. "It's just unsettling that you're the best option I've got."

Her self-confidence level was annoyingly high, yes, but her confidence in me was less than inspiring. I'd have to change that. She was wrong about whether she was jumpy, but right about the other part. I would've helped her with her missing lab and mysterious side effect problem, annoying or not, but it was more important now because she was Maddy's sister. So I'd force myself not to be distracted or irritated—for the next few minutes, at least—and focus on her.

She made it inside without needing to clutch on to Dante, further proof of her recovery. I slowed to watch their reactions to the buzzing grandeur of the lobby—Dante's was an impressed double take and Melody raised her eyebrows in what might have been approval as she turned her head to take in the entire space.

"Your first time here?" I asked, a little surprised she wouldn't have visited Maddy before. But then I'd never seen her at the *Scoop* offices.

Melody nodded, and for once didn't add a prickly remark. *Huh.*

"Well, don't let this splendor fool you. We're going to the basement." I waved to the guard and signed in my guests, then led us into the grim gray service elevator. Juggling the various parts of my new life was a work in progress, but the most shocking thing was how normal it felt for me to stride in here, like I owned the place, after a few short weeks.

I'd waited to ask more questions of Melody, giving her the

ride over to regain her strength. Plus, Maddy would want to know what had happened, I figured.

But truth was, I wasn't sure. Navigating friendship waters was tricky for me. I wasn't used to it—I was brand new to it, in fact—and the only thing I really knew about Maddy and Melody's relationship was that it was stormy. Now that I'd gotten an unhealthy dose of Melody's attitude, I understood why.

Neither Melody nor Dante said anything when we reached the gloomy lower level. But Melody raised her eyebrows again, this time with semi-alarm at the framed front pages shouting about old catastrophes and corruptions. They stayed up as we reached the office proper.

I'd thought it was dire down here on my first visit too, but now there was no place I liked better in the world. The Morgue might be, well, the *Morgue*, surrounded by endless tall cabinets packed with crumbling newspapers, but it was also the *Scoop*'s office. It was home.

My family had spent our whole lives moving constantly to wherever my Army general dad had been assigned. When I walked in here, knowing we were in Metropolis to stay, that this was *my* place in *my* city, I felt more at home than I ever had.

Especially now that I had the scent of a potential story.

The other *Scoop* staffers were at their ancient, oversized wooden desks. Cool and collected Devin was deep into some design project on one of his two giant monitors, while prepster James frowned and typed away at his keyboard, and Maddy head-bopped to whatever was blasting through her space-age headphones.

Devin noticed us first. He had a short afro and an ever-present air of calm, and he nodded to me. "I thought you were finally out doing a story, superstar."

When James raised his head, his face lit up. "Melody!" he said, fairly leaping out of his chair and crossing the room. Oh, right, he and she ran in the same crowd. He was in one of his usual collared-shirt-and-khakis ensembles. But he looked tired, and his hair—usually glossy and perfect—was almost rumpled.

Before I could ask if he was okay, Maddy chimed in. "*Melody?*" She blinked at us from across the room and slipped off her headphones. I couldn't help being reminded how her sister had blinked up at me from the sidewalk. They truly were identical, if completely different in style and mannerisms.

While Melody was the perfect princess with full makeup and bouncy blond hair, Maddy was punk-rock pretty with a crimson-streaked chin-length cut and a never-ending supply of band T-shirts. The one she had on today read Tyrannosaurus Hex, and I alone knew that the band almost certainly didn't exist. Maddy secretly longed to be in a band, so she made up new band names and created T-shirts for them daily.

"Have a seat," I said to Melody.

"Hi," Melody said to Maddy, taking the chair beside my desk. And circling her wrist with her opposite hand yet again.

"What are *you* doing *here?*" Maddy demanded, heading over.

I internally cringed. I'd never heard that tone from Maddy before. She sounded nearly as affronted as her sister had when I'd revealed I had no clue what her name was.

Oh, sibling-hood. This was going to be complicated.

And then I saw something else that could get complicated. Dante was looking at Maddy. Like, *looking* looking at her. Like he might have to pick his jaw up off the floor looking at her. He smiled at her, a wide-open smile, and I thought her jaw might hit the floor too. She shyly nodded to him.

"They're good?" Dante asked her. "I've never heard of them."

"Who?" Maddy asked.

"Tyrannosaurus Hex," he said. "Great band name."

Maddy's cheeks went as red as the streak in her hair. "Yeah. Um—they're pretty underground."

I rescued her. "Maddy, this is Dante. He's the artist I was interviewing and he helped me get your sister here. I'm guessing you want to know why I brought your sister here? So do I. Melody, you up to telling me a little more about what you were looking for?"

"Should I talk in front of him?" Melody asked, ticking her head toward Dante. "He's technically not one of you."

Graceless, but a fair point.

I had the same sense about Melody I'd had with Anavi, the subject of my first big story. The *Scoop* staffers and SmallvilleGuy and I had rescued her from a corporate experiment using videogame technology that had turned her into part of a badly behaving hive mind. Anavi and Melody were worlds apart personality-wise, but there was a story here, I could feel it—a weird one.

One that Dante might not be up for believing.

"That's cool," Dante said, preventing further awkwardness.

"I don't want to get in the way. I should head back. You got what you need on the mural already."

"One thing before you go," I said. "Do you remember the tenant in that building?"

Dante squinted. "I live nearby. I remember there being some business, and one time I saw a weird guy in a suit going in. No one bothered him, so I assume he was good to be there. But that's about it. Been a long time."

"Thanks," I said, but he barely seemed to hear. His attention had settled on Maddy and stayed there.

"I might look for you at school next week to check in," he said. "Let me know if you need anything."

"Will do," I said.

Dante turned toward Maddy, but Maddy wasn't paying attention. She was watching James wheel the chair from his desk over to sit beside Melody. That meant Maddy missed Dante's wave to her as he left.

James was oblivious to Maddy's crush on him in a way that made me want to smack him sometimes. He had eyes only for her sister. I didn't see him as the right type for Maddy, but that was beside the point. Once Dante was gone, I turned back to Melody. I needed to get home as soon as I could. SmallvilleGuy didn't usually have "important" things to tell me.

"You were saying?" I prodded the queen. She wasn't making this easy.

"It's okay to talk to all of you? No one will blab?" she said.

James put a hand on her arm, and Maddy watched, her eyes narrowing. "Of course," he said.

"James," I said, sitting down at my desk, "you don't usually hang around on Fridays. Why are you here?"

"I work here," he said. "Including sometimes on Fridays."

Devin's desk was beside mine, and he gave my foot a tap with his sneaker. I glanced over, where he clicked the mouse to bring something up on one of his screens, ever the soul of discretion. It was the *Planet* home page, which I hadn't seen since earlier in the day.

A headline blared across the top: *Ex-Mayor's Homecoming From Prison Bittersweet.*

Oh, riiiiiight.

James's dad, James Worthington, Jr., had gotten his good-behavior release from prison today, after a year's time served for various corruption and embezzling charges. That's why James was here. He was avoiding going home.

Which meant I couldn't tell him to leave. I nodded slightly at Devin and his screen changed to another site.

"You can talk freely," I reassured Melody, while I excavated my notepad. "We've all seen some pretty strange things, so we'll believe you. And we'll keep it quiet."

"I'm trusting you." Her eyes skated over to Maddy, then down to her lap as she began to spill. Her voice was soft, and it was the first time I'd seen her less than confident. That included coming back from unconsciousness. "A couple of years ago, there was an ad asking for identical twins, preferably between the ages of thirteen and seventeen, to give blood and DNA samples for some research. They paid in cash. Only two visits required. So I did it. I went to that building."

Maddy was gaping again, for an entirely different reason than before. "Are you stupid? Why did you need money? Mom and Dad would have given it to you."

"Mad," I said, "not helping."

She sat down on the corner of Devin's desk. "Sorry," she muttered, not entirely convincingly.

James was rubbing Melody's arm in shallow circles that were obviously meant to be soothing, but looked annoying. But Melody didn't seem to mind. "Where was this?" he asked.

"It was in Suicide Slum. Or just outside it," I said. "That's how I ended up running into her today."

"Oh," Maddy said, but nothing more.

James frowned at the news of the unsavory destination. He'd probably never been anywhere near that part of the city.

I needed to take control here, if I wasn't going to stand SmallvilleGuy up. And I wasn't. "Melody, do you remember anything about the company? A name?"

"It was called Ismenios," she said, pronouncing it slowly. She spelled it too, before I could ask. "There was a logo with a man fighting some kind of monster on the front door. The guy was weird. It was just him, I never saw any staff. I almost backed out when I got there the first day, but he told me it would be easy, painless."

"So was it?" I asked. "What did he do?"

"That part was true. It was painless. I barely felt a thing. He took a couple of little vial things of blood and rubbed a big Q-tip on the inside of my mouth each time. After the second time, he told me there might be a sense of disorientation that could manifest. I remember he used that word, manifest. He said that there shouldn't be, but there might. If I ever had any side effects, I was supposed to inform him."

This guy sounded like Dr. Shady. "This was two years ago, you said?" I asked. "What kind of side effects are we talking—why do you think they're related?"

"Because the list of side effects he gave, it was specific. I do feel disoriented. Just in the last week. I . . . It's like I'm seeing through someone else's eyes. He said I might feel things like they were happening to someone else. And I have been."

"I don't understand," Maddy said. "How can you have side effects from having blood drawn?"

I could feel a story here. I tried not to show it, though. Because I didn't want to scare Melody off. And because Maddy was scowling at James's hand on her sister's arm. "How vivid are these feelings?" I asked.

"Vivid enough that I think they're real. I'm seeing through someone else's eyes. Literally."

It took us all a moment to absorb that.

"Whose eyes are we talking about?" James asked.

Melody shook her head. "I don't know. But someone's. It's a man, I think. I see a lab, like the one I went to but not exactly the same . . . This one has a big glass tank in it. Once I saw streets—that was today, right before Lois found me. I see him messing with this bracelet thing around his arm." She lifted her hand, ringing her wrist with the fingers of her other hand. That automatic gesture she'd been doing. "It's gray, with a few lights on it, a black clasp. Almost like one of those fitness trackers, but more high tech looking. Bulkier. He's always messing with it."

"Like some kind of prison tracking device?" James asked.

"I've never seen one," Melody answered, and James dropped his hand from her arm. Embarrassed, if I was guessing right, that he'd reminded everyone about his dad. But Melody went on, "I get woozy too, like he said I might. Dizzy. I was trying to push back, to fight it, when I fell today. And afterward, I feel drained. But then it goes away. Mostly."

Maddy had placed her own fingers around her wrist, as if in sympathy with her sister's movements. I doubted she realized she was doing it. That was interesting.

But interesting or no, I needed to get out of here. But not just yet.

"Let's back up for a sec," I said. "For these samples you gave, how much cash are we talking? What kind of resources did this place have?"

She swallowed. "Five hundred dollars."

"Wow," Devin said. "That's not pocket change."

"It was a real lab," Melody said.

"Even if it was in a bad part of town. And the guy was weird," Maddy said dryly. "It wasn't the dumbest thing ever for a girl who knows nothing about that part of town to traipse into it and offer up a blood sample. Twice."

Melody made a face at Maddy.

"Tell me about Ismenios Labs," I said, attempting to head off further conflict, even if Maddy wasn't wrong. I was also mentally tallying how late I was to meet SmallvilleGuy. I was pretty sure our date—or non-date, who knew?—was supposed to have started a half-hour ago. And he'd asked me to hurry.

"The building was clean and nice, no boards or broken windows or graffiti. The upstairs was fancy, but . . ."

"Weird?" I supplied. She nodded, and I asked, "What was weird about it?"

"For one thing, the doctor or lab guy, whatever, never used anything electronic. I mean, there was electronic equipment—spotless—all around, but he took notes on paper. There were stacks of file folders and filing cabinets. He took notes in writing, not using a computer. Kind of like here, and you," she said, gesturing at my notebook.

"I'm a reporter, not a creep," I said.

"She can't help it," Maddy said. "She's judgy."

Melody tossed her hair over her shoulder. "I am *not* judgy. Whatever that means. If it's even a *word*."

"Judgy," Maddy said. There was a real tone of anger in her voice.

Devin met my eyes, and his were wide. We both had little sisters, but we did not have twin sisters. This spat could easily get out of hand.

"Anything else?" I asked.

"He was a whistler," she said.

Maddy recoiled. "Only serial killers whistle."

"Serial killers and creeps," I agreed.

"Are you serious?" Melody asked, leaning forward with wide eyes. She wasn't playing it calm anymore.

I attempted to calm them down. "There probably has never

been a study definitively linking whistling and serial killers. Anyway, you're alive, if not exactly well. We know the lab's not there now, but this Ismenios should be easy enough to track down now that you've come to us."

"I tried searching online, but I didn't find anything," Melody said. "Look, you can't just talk to me at school, if you need to update me. People will see."

"Who cares?" I asked. I legitimately meant it.

"*She* does," Maddy said. "Nothing's more important than Melody's popularity."

Granted, I'd been aiming to make one friend here, and to have a few now was a big deal for me. I understood the need to fit in. But I was mystified. "Doesn't being popular just mean that a lot of people like you? Won't they still like you no matter what you do?"

"Did you move here from outer space? No, that's not what it means." Melody sighed. "Maybe it was a bad idea coming to you for help."

"Or maybe it was a bad idea going to some random lab," Maddy said.

"You didn't come here for help," Devin said. "Lois found you and offered to assist. Most people would say thanks."

His arms were crossed over his chest. He was one of the so-called cool kids, not like Melody and James in the popular crowd, but the sort of effortless cool kid who migrates between groups. But I'd never heard him say a word about maintaining that status, not like Melody. I'd have to get him to explain it to me. Later.

"Don't worry," I said. "I'll find your missing scientist and we'll see what he was up to. We'll make sure your side effects get taken care of, with no harm to your precious popularity. If he told you to tell him about them, there must be something he can do."

Not that we can trust the guy, of course. But there was no need to scare her. Her problem seemed straightforward enough, even with the complication of her personality. Of course, I'd probably doomed myself by thinking that. Life rarely unfolded according to any plans I made. Speaking of which . . .

"I really have to go." I got up, stowing my notes and grabbing my bag.

James had his hand on Melody's arm again. "I'm happy to see you home," he said, like some olden times gentleman caller.

"No need," Maddy said. "Since we live at the same place, I can handle it. She'll just have to get over being seen with me."

But Maddy trailed me on my way to the door as James and Melody continued to chat. She stopped me before I could leave. "She's not a story. She's my sister."

I didn't try to hide my surprise. "She may be both."

"I know she can be hard to take. But she's my sister first."

"Okay," I said. "I get it."

And I hoped it was true. I hoped that I did get it. Because if I didn't, I could fail at friendship—and lose Maddy.

CHAPTER 3

Lucky for me, Mom and Dad were scheduled to attend some sort of work function, and they had told us that morning they'd leave money for pizza. When I got home, a red and white box was already sitting on the kitchen table. My sister, Lucy, must have ordered it after school.

I snagged a slice, folded it in half, and wolfed it down on the way upstairs to my room. Lukewarm pizza wasn't my favorite variety—piping hot or next-day cold both ranked higher—but it wasn't bad. I heard Lucy in her room talking, which probably meant she was playing *Unicorn University* with her renegade posse of unicorn friends. And I was en route to visit *Worlds War Three*, with its real-time conflict between the worlds of aliens, fantasy creatures, and humans. The Lane sisters, spending their Friday nights in real-sim holoset games.

I swallowed a drink of water and tried to calm my breathing as I hooked the device's shell over my ear and sat down on the bed. My heart was beating faster. Maybe because I'd been running around and was late, or maybe because I was on the trail of a new story. But something told me that I'd have felt the same combination of anxiety and anticipation even if I was right on time.

We were about to see each other. By the only means we had available, as long as SmallvilleGuy insisted I couldn't know his real identity.

I powered up the holoset. My bedroom fell away, the spray of lights in front of my face becoming an altogether different landscape. It felt as real as my room had, grass tickling my always-bare-in-the-game feet.

Two low red moons presided over a mostly quiet night. There were the sounds of distant gunfire, normal, and a few closer screeches from night creatures, also normal.

A familiar stone tower loomed above me on the sloping hill I hurried up.

The turret was part of Devin's castle, which he was slowly and surely rebuilding. The Warheads had destroyed it—before we'd turned them from a psycho squad back into normal gamers. He'd basically given this section to SmallvilleGuy and me a week ago, jokingly calling it the Lois Annex. Since I hadn't killed him for designing my game character as a pointy-eared and curvy-bodied elf named Princess Lo, it seemed a fair trade. Having a quiet, somewhat private place to meet meant SmallvilleGuy and I weren't constantly interrupted by random attacks from other players who were here to war, not have maybe-date night.

SmallvilleGuy stepped out of the tower's shadowy entrance, his light green skin casting a soft glow in the moonlight. He was a standard-issue alien here, in contrast to my elf princess.

"Finally," he called out, walking to meet me. "I thought you weren't coming."

He'd designed his character to be tall, but not over-the-top muscle-bound like some players' avatars, and he wore a pair of glasses with black frames. I had no idea if any of this corresponded to his appearance in real life, though. I'd never seen him.

We'd met on a message board called Strange Skies two years earlier. The Strange Skies website was a haven for people who had seen or experienced unexplainable things, or for people who claimed they had, in some of the less-than-believable cases. I had first posted there after almost being pummeled by falling rocks one dark night outside Wichita, Kansas. A person flying through the air had saved me from disaster—along with my dad, who'd forbidden me to ever talk about it. SmallvilleGuy and I had quickly progressed to DMs, and then to chatting; we even had a special secure app to talk privately. He knew my name, not just my handle. But for whatever reason, SmallvilleGuy wouldn't tell me who he really was; he said it wasn't safe for me to know.

I used to ask him at the end of every one of our nightly chats, but I'd stopped weeks ago, after he revealed that he'd told his parents about me and they'd forbidden him to divulge his identity. He promised that he *would* tell me, as soon as he was able.

I hadn't even considered the possibility that it might be tonight.

"Sorry," I said when I reached him. "I got here as fast as I could. Some news showed up. What was, um, that important thing you had to tell me?"

"I thought you were out on a puff piece." I must have frowned at that, because he added, "That's what you called it. Not me. What news showed up?"

And though I wanted more than anything to know what he'd wanted to say to me, I was struck with the shyness that attacked without warning around him more and more often of late.

I was *not* shy. I'd *never* been shy.

But he hadn't answered when I'd asked about the important thing. So I didn't insist he go first. I didn't ask what he wanted to tell me again. Not yet.

"I told you Maddy has a twin sister, right? The one James has a crush on?"

"You said you got the feeling the twins were really different," he said.

"You can say that again." I related the whole afternoon to him, sounding more confident than I was about managing to fix everything, get a story out of it, and not alienate Maddy in the process.

This is what we always did—told each other everything. The thing was, usually when we swapped stories about our day, we were both completely engaged. I was perfectly capable of forgetting how much time had passed and what day of the week it was when we were in the game together or chatting back and forth on our laptops. And I thought it was the same for him. But tonight he hardly seemed to be paying attention. He was restless instead, lanky alien body meandering around the hillside while I talked.

"And then the ceiling fell in and it turned out the entire Daily Planet Building had collapsed under alien attack," I said. "Everyone died, the end."

"Huh," he said.

"And I'll be starring in a musical version of these dark events."

No reaction.

It stung that he wasn't listening to me. Maybe this had to do with the important something. Although I'd assumed the something was good. That could have been a way overly optimistic assumption. After all, my luck tended to be bad.

I snapped my fingers near his face, not loud or obnoxious but enough to get his attention. "I just told you that the *Daily Planet* blew up and everyone died and I was going to be in a musical about it. You're a little distracted tonight."

He kicked the ground. "I'm sorry."

"So, what was it you wanted to talk about?" I asked, my heart speeding up again. Stupid heart.

What if it *was* bad news?

Or what if it was news that would tell me once and for all whether he thought of these meetings as dates?

He came closer, his restlessness evaporating, transforming into smooth, deliberate motion. His hand landed on my elbow, and he led me inside the turret.

"I don't want anyone to overhear," he said.

"I'll bet you use that line with all the girls," I quipped. But I was ridiculously aware of his hand on my skin.

You're really sitting in your room, alone, remember? I told myself. But the game always felt so real, like it might as well *be* reality. The present moment was no exception. We were in this moment, together, and the rest of the world might as well not exist. It could be fake.

"What? No, of course I don't. I'm sorry," he said. "I'm being mysterious, I know."

"More mysterious, you mean."

"Right. More mysterious."

There was a hint of the humor that came naturally to us, our state of equilibrium with each other.

The torch-lit turret's interior was brighter than the moon-light outside had been. In here, the flickering shadows from the flame dappled his green skin, showed off the blue eyes behind his glasses. He offered me his hand.

"What's this?" I asked. I put my hand in his and my heart sped up again.

"A maybe-surprise that I hope works," he said. "To make up for before?"

His hand closed lightly around mine, and then—

I gasped. Our feet left the ground and we floated up and up and up, into the tall turret, through the air.

"I've got you, but don't let go," he cautioned.

"I won't," I said, marveling at how safe it felt to float through space with my hand in his, high above the ground. I laughed. "How are we doing this?"

"Aliens can develop the ability to fly in here. I wasn't one hundred percent sure I'd be able to bring you with me, so I didn't want to spoil it in advance."

"Good surprise, Smallville."

He flew us over to a narrow window about halfway up the wall, with a ledge and a bench cut into the stone beside it. We smiled at each other, still holding hands. I'd already forgiven him forever for being distracted.

We sat down on the bench, and his hand left mine. I spread my fingers on the rough stone beside me, like I didn't mind that he wasn't holding it anymore.

Stupid, ridiculous heart, I thought again. Mine was beating so hard I could barely hear myself think over the racket.

The window gave us a view of the landscape outside, a squad of mercenaries crossing it then, black-clad and toting heavy artillery. A bat with red lasers mounted on its wings flew by.

"So the flying was what you had to tell me?" I asked.

"Sort of," he said. "But not that flying. Have you been on Strange Skies since this morning?"

I shook my head. "No, why?"

"A new user registered today, with the handle Insider01, and he or she is claiming that they know details about a 'flying man,' and they'll be posting them on the boards."

His expression had changed to show his emotion. His skin pulled tight over the angular bones of his character's face, eyes darkened with worry. It never ceased to amaze me how realistic the effects were in here.

"What am I missing? That's definitely strange, but why is this a huge deal?"

When SmallvilleGuy first private-messaged me on Strange Skies after my first post, he'd assured me I wasn't crazy and that I had seen what I thought I had that night. But he couldn't tell me how he knew or who he was or explain any more. It was the only gulf between us, and it seemed narrower or wider depending on the moment. It was always, though, a gulf filled with secrets.

Sometimes I almost forgot it was there, but it never really went away. He raked a hand through his avatar's short black hair. "People on the boards are freaking out over it. They want whatever this person knows."

"I know you . . . know or knew something about the person I saw," I said carefully. "Someone else could too, couldn't they? And if there's one flying person, could there be another?"

I could feel the gulf of secrets spread between us, wider than ever.

"I don't know what to think. The whole thing feels off. What if this person does know something?"

"About the flying man I saw?" I didn't understand what about this was making him so upset.

He nodded sharply. "But . . . do you think there could be another one? Like . . . maybe it wasn't the same man?"

There was a quality to his voice I'd never heard before. I couldn't tell if that possibility made him feel better or worse, hopeful or scared. I couldn't decode it from his expression, because he shifted to look out the window. I didn't have a good enough angle to play interpreter of his features anymore, or enough information to translate his reaction without more to go on.

I followed his gaze and saw the bat with red-laced lasers along its wings that had flown by earlier. It hovered in the air outside the opening, barely an arm's length away. Like it was watching us.

"Is it eavesdropping?" I asked.

"Not for long." SmallvilleGuy removed his glasses and shot laser vision to the left of the bat. It took off, flapping away into a sky a deeper red than the lines on its wings.

Once it was gone, he scooted so he was facing me again. "What do you think the person plans to post?"

"No clue," I said, "I guess we'll just have to wait and see. That'd really be something if it *was* good information. You know I've always been curious . . . but I'm not getting my hopes up. It'll probably turn out to be someone who's mad no one takes their probe stories seriously, having some fun with the rest of us. They'll probably post that the flying man's from the moon and only eats green cheese."

I was sure that would make him laugh. But it didn't.

"I'm sorry," I said finally. "I can tell this is bothering you. Do you want to tell me why?"

"More than you know." But he didn't say anything else.

I nodded. "You can't. I get it."

I expected him to apologize; that's what he would have normally done. Instead, he asked, "You really think it's nothing?"

He was acting so strange. But I wanted to make him feel better. "If that's what you want, then I'm going to say yes. It's probably nothing."

His shoulders relaxed a fraction. "You're probably right—as usual." We smiled at each other, but his didn't last. "But, Lois, it just doesn't feel right. It feels like a threat. Like a trap."

A trap for the flying man? Well, after all, I owed the flying man one. He'd saved me and my dad from certain rock-doom.

I chose my words with great care. I knew I was treading in dangerous territory. I just didn't know why it was dangerous. "Maybe there's some way to alert him. I know you can't tell me how you knew I was telling the truth about seeing a person flying that night. But wouldn't it make you feel better if you could get this off your chest and warn the guy?"

I had no way of knowing if SmallvilleGuy could contact the flying man or not. But I knew he knew more than he could—or would—tell me.

"It would," he said. But nothing more.

I'd never seen him like this. He was always the mellower one, the calm to my chaos. His restless unease was contagious. "Like I said, it'll turn out to be nothing," I said. "I'll bet you."

I put enough challenge in my tone to make it clear the offer was literal.

"What's the bet?" he asked, intrigued.

"Hmmm." I searched for something good. He had asked a few days ago if I'd seen the Metropolis Monarchs, his favorite baseball team, like they'd just be strutting around town tossing balls in the air and catching them. "If you're right and this is truly something to worry about, then I have to go to a Monarchs game and take pictures for you."

"And also wear a Monarchs T-shirt *and* a cap," he said. "Like I would."

I rolled my eyes. "Fine, I'll wear the whole costume and take a selfie."

"It's not a costume," he countered, "it's showing team spirit."

"The whole costume," I repeated. "And if *I* win, which I will, you have to . . . take a picture of Nellie Bly and send it to me every day for a week. Bonus points if Shelby the wonder dog is in it too."

Nellie Bly was a baby cow a few weeks old that we'd named together. Shelby was his golden retriever.

"Deal," he said. "As much as I want those game photos, I hope you're right. It just feels . . . off. Sorry again about before and being so . . ."

"Space cadet-y? Ancient history. Don't worry about it—and try not to worry about this boards stuff so much either, okay?" I grinned. "I hope I win too."

"I'll try not to worry, Princess Lo."

"Funny—" but I stopped when I heard a noise from outside the game, the sound of a door shutting.

I knew it was outside the game because SmallvilleGuy gave not one single sign that he heard it. And it was followed by the distant but distinct jingling clatter of keys being placed on the table by the front door downstairs.

"My folks just got home," I said. "I better go."

I wasn't ready to leave, and I didn't think he was either. "Thank you," he said. "Talking to you always makes me feel better."

Double stupid heart, it *beat-beat-beat* like it might burst.

"My pleasure, sap."

In the game I gave him a wave, and outside it I reached up to depress the holoset power button. I closed my eyes so I wouldn't come out too quickly.

Which meant I barely had time to leap off the bed and stow the holoset in my desk drawer before a knock sounded at my bedroom door.

"Come on in," I said, faking a yawn.

The door hinged in and my parents stuck their heads in the door. Mom looked beautiful, with her honey-blond hair in a schmancy party updo, and Dad was beyond polished, decked out in his dress uniform with all its ribbons and medals. Lucy stood behind them in unicorn-covered pajamas. She had a dot of chocolate on one cheek.

"You guys are back early," I said.

"We just went to the reception," Mom said. "Didn't see the point in staying for dinner."

"Too bad you only left us one slice of pizza," Dad added.

"Whoops," I said.

"Night, Lois," Mom said, and eased my door shut again.

I waited until I heard their steps go the rest of the way up the hall to their room, then opened up my laptop and navigated to Strange Skies.

The post SmallvilleGuy had been talking about wasn't hard to find. It was in priority placement, the most popular new thread, nestled right below all the sticky "Introduce Yourself" and "Ground Rules" posts. There was a flaming fireball next to it that indicated a lot of activity. Even though the timestamp was only a few hours old, it had six hundred views and seventy comments. For Strange Skies, that was a ton of action.

I clicked to open it, feeling a resurgence of SmallvilleGuy's contagious worry.

Posted by **Insider01** *at 3:30 p.m.:* I know many of you have witnessed a flying man and posted accounts here. I am pleased to tell you that I have many important details to share about a flying man. And I will be sharing those with you here in the coming days. Keep one eye on the skies and another eye here. You won't want to miss this.

CHAPTER 4

I wasn't typically an early riser on Saturdays, but dreams like I'd had all night would roust anyone out of bed. About flying men toppling from the sky while I watched, helpless, and bats with lasers coming straight at me, and weird labs filled with paper files whose pages went blank as soon as I opened them. I didn't need to consult an oracle to know I was feeling stressed about everything that had happened the day before.

My laptop hummed to life with a press of the spacebar. I swung by Strange Skies first, where the Insider01 post had garnered another four hundred views, bringing it over one thousand, and had a slew of more comments. None of them were from SmallvilleGuy. He wasn't in our chat app when I signed in either, but I left the window open as I navigated to my browser and did a basic search on "Ismenios laboratory, labs, company."

I clicked through a page of unpromising matches. The only mentions of the word Ismenios were mythology-related, not a lab among them. The dragon Ismenios, named for where it lived, had fought and lost to a guy named Cadmus in Greek myth. He planted its teeth in the ground, because . . . myth reasons, I guess, and they became warriors who helped him found some ancient city. Melody had said a guy fighting a monster was the logo for her company, so it was probably the inspiration for the name. But not what I was after.

I added "Metropolis" to the search and retried it.

Still nada.

I located my phone and selected Maddy's name from my contacts list. I could have texted, but if she *wasn't* up yet, the blaring punk that was her ringtone would serve the function of an alarm.

"Lois?" she growled.

Not up, then.

"Um, hi, is Melody handy? I have a question for her."

The phone landed on a surface with a *kerplunk* and Maddy called, "Melody! Come here, please. It's Lois."

A few quiet moments and then, "Could you keep it down, please? Do you want Mom and Dad to find out about this?"

These two were masters of swapping the sarcastic "please." I wondered if they'd ever gotten along. Twins were supposed to have a special connection, weren't they?

I heard a noncommittal grunt that must have been Maddy's response to her sister. A second later, Melody's voice sounded in my ear. "Yes? Did you find something?"

"Good morning to you too," I said. "Not yet. How did you hear about the offer? An online ad, or something in a magazine or the newspaper? Craigslist?"

"Oh," she said, "no. There was a flyer on the announcements board at school. It had those little squares you tear off with the phone number."

An honest-to-goodness lead. "Do you still have the number?"

"No, I didn't save it in my phone. And I tossed the paper ages ago. That's why I took the taxi out there yesterday, obviously. Why?" Her voice got strained then. "Are you running into trouble?"

"Nothing major," I said. "It would have made things easier, but hard is fine too. The hard way and me go way back. How are you feeling?"

"Perfect as usual. Maddy—stop it, I'm still talking—"

"That all you needed?" Maddy asked.

"Yep." I didn't think it was a lie. I drummed my fingers on my desk.

She lowered her voice. "You are going to be able to help her, right?"

I hope so.

"Maddy, you can trust me."

"I know," she said. "I'll talk to you again at a decent hour when normal human beings have conversations."

"Hilarious."

She hung up. I crossed my fingers that she wasn't actually mad. I had no idea if I was doing the friend thing right or utterly screwing it up.

So. Perfect-as-usual Melody had found out from a flyer posted in the school, which meant zero potential to track down an online ad. The weird science guy might not even have hung it up himself. He could have paid a student to do it, if he was doling out $500 left and right and maintaining a top-secret lab far under the radar.

One detail drifted back to me: that he had avoided anything but paper for recordkeeping.

Besides the name Ismenios, I had the address. Pulling up a map site, I plugged in info for the mural's location, then dragged the cursor across the street and jotted down the address for the building directly opposite.

If science guy didn't leave a paper trail, the property owner could be a place to start. I pulled up Metropolis's property information search and plugged in the address . . . and came up with nothing.

Now, that *was* weird. Weirder than Ismenios Labs not having a website. A big fat zero results for any existing properties on that block. Nobody owned it?

My news nose was tingling again. I'd been to the address, and it showed on the map, therefore it existed. Just not in this online database. There had to be a paper trail somewhere, but it would take a visit to City Hall to rifle through records and locate it. And the property and business registration offices' page informed me there were no Saturday hours due to budget-saving measures.

I'd have to take a field trip there after school on Monday.

I clicked over to our chat app. SmallvilleGuy remained MIA.

But when I went back to the Strange Skies tab on my browser, there was a new post on the Insider01 thread.

Posted by **Insider01** *at 8:20 a.m.:* I'm pleased, if not surprised, by your clear interest in what I have to share. I'll post the first exclusive details about the flying man at precisely 8:05 p.m. UTC. Stay tuned.

What in the world was UTC? I looked it up. It stood for Coordinated Universal Time, which had more or less replaced Greenwich Mean Time decades earlier, aka the international standard everyone else set their time zones by. The acronym didn't match the term exactly because the French and the English had some sparring match over it and had to compromise. It was five hours ahead of us, which meant the post would be up this afternoon at 3:05 p.m. my time. It also meant the poster had left no clue about where he or she might be located. I closed my browser and keyed in the uber-long password for our secure chat program. SmallvilleGuy still wasn't online, but I typed out a message he'd see when he logged in.

SkepticGirl1: *Talk to you at 3:06 p.m. Eastern, I guess?*

I waited a couple of minutes, but he didn't show. And I couldn't just sit around here all day doing nothing, waiting and making no progress on my story and Melody's problem.

I couldn't let Maddy down. Finally, I had friends, and I was determined to be the best friend anyone ever had. That this resolution was perhaps a little pathetic wasn't lost on me.

It didn't matter. My friendship with Maddy was worth more than my pride.

I closed my laptop, picked up my phone, and texted her: *I'm coming over later.*

First, I needed to borrow an item from my dad.

★

I wanted to pay a visit to the scene of the crime, as it were, and to do that, I needed to raid the stash in Dad's locked cabinet. Alas, I wasn't the only early riser. Dad was in his study, a major complication to my day's developing itinerary.

As a foil, I lugged the homework I had to do at some point this weekend (better now than never) down to the living room. I'd wait for him to do something—anything—else, and leave me free to access the cabinet.

An entire hour after I set up camp, he emerged. He was in his day-off casual clothes, no uniform in sight, and yet he exuded a sense of unquestionable authority. A general was always a general was always a general.

"Homework this early on a Saturday?" he asked. "Wait. Is it the apocalypse? Did someone forget to tell me?"

"Haha, Dad. Very funny," I said. "I guess if you don't *want* me to care about school . . ."

I flipped my notebook shut on a series of short answer responses for English. The sexists of Hawthorne's New England and their dark red letters could wait.

"Lois," he said, with a long-suffering sigh, "I was kidding. It's good to see you working so hard. At school and even your job."

"Even my job," I deadpanned back. "That awful thing."

"I mean it," Dad said.

I gave him a salute. "I'm sure."

"Lois, I really do. I'm glad you're settling in here. Principal Butler says you're behaving better at school."

I hadn't realized the two of them had become so chatty. Figured.

He stood there, looking at me and waiting for some kind of response.

I rolled my eyes. "Right. Butler is a reliable source. He's a man who deeply cares about the students of the school. Especially the one who publicly embarrassed him."

Butler had taken some heat over his non-response to the bullying of Anavi, which had been the subject of my very first story for the *Scoop*. That he'd been seemingly unaware of the extent of the illegal experiment his students turned out to be subjects for didn't help him out any either.

"I'm aware of your thoughts on the man, but he's been perfectly nice to me, and if you didn't notice, that was favorable feedback about you."

He was right. I should be glad the loathsome Principal Butler had given me a good report. But I wasn't going to admit it out loud.

"At any rate," Dad said, and sighed, "I came out here to tell you I'm going for a run."

He headed upstairs, presumably to change. As soon as he was out of sight, I scurried into the study.

Waiting until he was officially out of the house would be better. But the "even your job" comment rankled. The *Scoop* was important to me and he knew it, and he also knew that I'd knocked it over the wall for a home run—was that how that worked? I'd ask my favorite sports fan later—with my first stories.

"The *Scoop* is the most important thing I'm doing." Muttering under my breath, I hurried through his study, with its thick books about wars and big desk with rarely used computer and comfy leather chair, making my way to the framed family photograph on the top of the bookshelf. My face scowled out at me from amid my parents' and Lucy's smiling ones.

Dad's job for the military involved a lot of heavily classified activities. I wasn't exactly sure what they entailed, but it meant he kept a veritable treasure trove of handy items under lock and key here at home.

I plucked the key from where it was stuck behind the frame of the family photo and moseyed over to the tall wood cabinet. I'd made a thorough inventory of everything in it, so I didn't hesitate, just bent to retrieve the lock pick tools I needed. Door closed, lock re-locked, key re-stowed.

Dad came down in his running clothes and sneakers just as I hit the hallway, pocketing the tools.

He stopped at the bottom of the stairs. "Sorry about before. I just wanted to let you know that I'm proud of you. You've been trying hard since we got here, and I've noticed."

This was why Dad inspired such loyalty among the soldiers he'd commanded and the people he worked with. Winning his approval wasn't easy, and he parceled it out scarcely, which made it all the more gratifying. My palm itched around the tools I'd borrowed from his office.

My guilty conscience itched too.

"I maybe overreacted before. Sorry," I said. "Homework and I never did get along this early in the morning, so I'm going out to have lunch with Maddy and her sister. I'll be back before dinner."

Before 3:05, in fact.

Upstairs, I gathered my phone and bag, and checked chat one last time. SmallvilleGuy wasn't currently logged in, but he *had* responded to my message.

SmallvilleGuy: 3:06.

SmallvilleGuy: *I'm afraid you're going to win our bet.*

His terseness was worrisome, particularly after his reaction last night.

But there was no way to fast-forward to later this afternoon for a sneak preview of what Insider01 had in store for us all. So I might as well try to get a lead on the missing lab in the meantime.

Given how much what was happening on the boards upset SmallvilleGuy, even if this person did have information about the flying man, I didn't want to win.

CHAPTER 5

I had no idea what Maddy and Melody's parents did for a living, but it was clearly lucrative. They didn't have the kind of money James Worthington the Third's family had (before his dad went to jail anyway), but they lived in a modestly ritzy apartment building in a modestly ritzy section of the island of New Troy. It wasn't that far from our nice (if actually modest) brownstone, but it was a world apart. A world with cheerful uniformed doormen. Theirs had already been given my name, and he admitted me with a smiling flourish toward the first door to the left of the marble lobby.

My welcome would probably have been less effusive if the doorman had known I was here to invite the Simpson twins on a field trip to Suicide Slum. I'd dressed down again, wearing jeans, my trusty boots, and a slightly faded houndstooth-patterned button-down from a vintage shop Maddy had dragged me to the week before.

I rang the bell, and the door immediately opened to reveal Maddy. She must have been waiting there. Her T-shirt today was for a band called Snoozer Loser.

"Did you invite James?" she asked, raising her voice enough to be heard over the dulcet tones of classical piano music emanating from inside the apartment. None of this was expected—not the question or the sonic environment.

"Uh, no," I said. "Why?"

"Because—" she motioned for me to follow her up the hall. The music got louder with each step we took, and we entered an elegant living room with tall ceilings and a grand piano. "—this," she finished.

James and Melody were in the room, she at the baby grand and he watching in rapt attention from a dainty brocade settee as she played a piece. She finished with a polished, clearly practiced stroke of the keys, and James burst into applause.

Then she saw us. I expected an imperious command of some kind for us to applaud too, but instead she blushed.

"So, you guys have music in common," I said to Maddy.

"Not really," Maddy said.

"Maddy's taste is too cool for me," Melody said, making it sound like an insult. "She stopped taking lessons when we were twelve."

Maddy didn't counter, so I assumed it was true. Interesting.

"What are *you* doing here?" James asked me, and got up from the dainty sofa.

"I could ask you the same question," I said. "But I'm going to caper out on a limb and go with . . . avoiding your father."

"Got it in one." He ducked his head and considered his shoes with a thoughtfulness that obviously wasn't about his footwear.

I probably shouldn't have brought up his dad.

Great job, Lane, proving you really get this whole friendship thing.

I resolved to do my best to be nice to him. Mostly. Even if he was inadvertently distressing Maddy with his clueless fixation on her sister, he was my friend too.

"You guys game for a little espionage?" I asked.

"Yes," Maddy said, clasping her hands together under her chin in eagerness.

"What sort of espionage?" Melody asked.

James frowned, the expression he almost always deployed in response to my plans.

"I thought we'd take a field trip to get a closer look at the building with your phantom lab. See if we find anything there to point the way. It might refresh your memory. You up for it?"

Melody hesitated, doubtless worrying about us all being seen together. I was prepared to argue her into it, but she nodded. "Anything that will make this nightmare end."

Of course, that was officially too nice, so she had to add something. "Besides, James will be there. Being seen with James is fine."

"Yuck," I said. Then, to James, "Sorry. You know what I mean."

"Don't mind me," he said.

He was officially acting weird too. There was none of the usual peeved tone he responded with whenever I inadvertently—or advertently—insulted him. Boys. Who could understand the mysterious workings of their minds?

"I'll arrange a ride." I whipped out my phone and sent a text to my favorite trusted cab driver: *Available to pick up four of us?* I added the address.

Be right there, came the response.

Melody left the room, presumably going to get her stuff, and Maddy came closer. James did too. "She had another episode," Maddy said. "After you called this morning. It didn't last long but . . . She looked so weak afterward. She didn't even yell at me to get out of her room."

"This whole situation is bizarre," James said. "Why did she need the money?"

Maddy said, "She didn't. My parents would give her the moon if she asked for it. Maybe literally."

Unfortunately, Melody returned in time to hear this. "No, they wouldn't," she said, her cheeks still pink. Being embarrassed about playing the piano made about as much sense to me as having to obsess over what people thought of everything you did because you were popular.

It was pretty clear that Melody and I didn't have a lot in common.

To prevent the sisters from resuming their starring roles as the lead players at the bicker twins theater, I made for the door. "That's settled, then. Let's get moving."

True to his word, my cab-driving, um, acquaintance—
friend seemed a bit strong—pulled up to the curb moments
after we stepped out the front door and onto the sidewalk to
wait. He waved a beefy, blinged-out hand, rings on every finger, as I climbed into the front and let the others take the back.

"Where are my favorite reporters headed to? Daily Planet
Building?" he asked. "Can I expect one of your famous tips?"

"Sorry," I said, "this is a normal tip kind of day."

He snapped his fingers. "Can't win them all. Where to?"

I fished out my notepad and showed him the address I'd
harvested off the Internet.

"Good thing it's daytime," he said. "Not the best
neighborhood."

I remembered Dante's conviction that it was just a neighborhood that needed to feel like it mattered again. "Not the
worst either."

He grunted. "Close enough to it, though. For a story?"

He was as nosy as my parents. "Maybe. But only if we get
there this year."

"Fine, fine," he said, and put the car in drive.

James surprised me by staying quiet and not chatting up
Melody. And Maddy and Melody weren't going to gab with
each other, so it was a silent ride. I did note that Melody had
her wrist cradled in her opposite hand, but she didn't drop it
periodically, like she had the day before. The tic was changing.
Who knew if it meant anything?

When we reached the site, I saw Dante deep into painting
across the street from our target. He'd finished up the base

for the background of his mural and had started roughing in a city skyline.

I pulled out some money and turned to collect the rest from the back seat. Maddy looked at Melody, who said, "I forgot my card. Can you cover us both?"

"I didn't bring mine either," Maddy said.

"I'll cover it," James said, taking out his wallet and passing over half the fare in cash.

I doubted he could afford to throw in that much. He'd told me that his family took a big financial hit when his dad went away, all outward appearances to the contrary. But I held my tongue.

"You want me to wait?" the cabbie asked.

"Probably better if you aren't hanging around. I'll text when we're done and you can come back? It should take an hour or two."

"Sure thing, unless someone willing to give the big tip calls first."

"Touché," I agreed.

We got out of the car, and I gave a pointed look in Dante's direction and fake-fanned myself. "Is it hot out here or is someone just going to be happy to see you?" I murmured to Maddy.

In seconds, she wore the same blush her sister had before. They did have a few things in common.

Dante spotted us and began *beaming*. Not just in our general direction, but right at Maddy. With a smile that could rival the sun. He stowed his paint roller and loped over to join us.

"I'm like some kind of psychic," I told her.

"Stop," she said. But she bit her lip against a smile.

"Hi there," he said when he reached us. "I didn't think I'd be lucky enough to get to see you again before Monday."

Melody choked out a cough, but Maddy's reaction was so intense she didn't seem to notice. She froze in nonverbal blush mode.

"Did I say that out loud?" Dante said, laughing at himself. "I meant it. But I didn't mean to scare you off. I'm normal, promise."

I was certain Maddy wouldn't be able to respond. She was always so reserved around James whenever he paid even the smallest amount of attention to her. And her judgy sister was watching.

But she smiled at Dante. "What if I'm not normal?"

"Tell me more," he said.

James raised his eyebrows when I looked at him. Melody slipped her arm through his.

"Looks like I'm the only one who forgot to bring a date," I muttered.

But, then, I always was. How could I be anything other than a fifth wheel when the only person I was interested in was 1,200 miles away in Kansas—not to mention hiding his real identity?

What would it take to have a world where we both live in Metropolis and know each other?

Maybe someday.

Maybe someday I'd know his first name.

I was pretty sure I sighed out loud. So before they could

tease me about it, I sped up to get out front of the others, extracting the tools I'd brought.

"I figured we'd look for a back entrance," I said over my shoulder. "Otherwise we'll have to clear these boards away. And given my luck, the cops would probably cruise by at just that moment."

"This might not be such a good idea," James said.

"We're not going to break anything. Not even bend. We just need to poke around inside. It's abandoned and we'll leave everything just as we find it. Promise."

"Right," James said, unconvinced. "So then how do we get inside?"

"There's something else," Dante said, and pointed to the graffiti on the boards. "Those tags have a meaning. They mean, essentially, no trespassing, orders of the Boss. He's a big part of why this neighborhood needs reminding that it matters."

The Boss again. I wanted to know more, but it could wait until we were inside. I swept my arm to indicate the mostly deserted street around us. "I don't see anyone, and especially not a boss. We'll be okay."

"Back door is smarter," Dante said.

He stuck with us as we traveled up an alley and around back. There were more tags, similar to those up front—variations on the stylized B—along the back wall, the door, covering the two dumpsters. But the heavy metal door bore only a single impressive padlock.

"B is for bingo," I said. "Let me get out my lock picks."

"Lois—" James started.

"Oh, ye of little faith," Maddy cut him off.

But James rolled his eyes. "It's not locked," he said. He pointed at the padlock, which was, in fact, not quite closed.

"Great work," I said. I carefully removed the lock and swung the door open. Uninviting darkness awaited us within.

"You're sure this is a good idea?" James asked.

"This does kind of look like rusty nail heaven," Maddy said.

I swapped the lock pick set for a compact flashlight I feared would be no match for the lightless interior we were about to enter. At least there were several of us? Not that I'd confess it to any of my companions, but I might have hesitated to go inside alone. Maybe.

I flicked on the flashlight. "It's the best idea I've got today. I want Melody to get a look around. See if being here jogs any more memories. We need clues."

Melody met my eyes, level, challenging. "I thought you liked the hard way."

"I do," I said. "That's why we're here."

She raised her chin in a nod. "Lead on."

The rustle and scurry that preceded us into the building was the opposite of comforting. "I don't think the mice got the memo about trespassing," I said.

"You *hope* those are mice," Dante said. "Probably our own special Suicide Slum rats."

I heard a gentle whimper from Maddy's direction, and Dante quickly said, "It's okay. The rat thing was a joke." That seemed unlikely, but I kept quiet. He went on, "I looked up that band, by the way. Tyrannosaurus Hex? But I couldn't find anything about them. I dug your review of Library Riot in the *Scoop*, though . . ."

Dante was staying close to Maddy, distracting her by complimenting her reviews. Oh, they were too adorable. She deserved someone who was into her. Not someone like James, who continued to frown—as usual—and had Melody's arm looped through his. With her perfect hair and flowery sundress, she looked as out of place as possible in this abandoned locale.

Melody shrugged James's arm off to come up beside me. "He was on the top floor," she said.

We navigated in silence except for Dante's low and continuous stream of conversation directed at Maddy, and the occasional scurrying in front of us. The elevators were obviously out of commission, and a light switch I tried in the hall did nothing. But we found a set of fire stairs, and they were remarkably tidy except for a thin film of dust.

"Why did I have the impression buildings like this became squats and things?" I asked no one in particular. "Is this a stereotype I have about bad neighborhoods?" I might have moved around a lot, but I was under no illusions about the level of privilege I had. I wanted to be called on it if I was making bad assumptions based on watching too many movies and not knowing enough about the actual neighborhood we were in.

"It probably would be a squat," Dante answered, breaking off his Maddy distraction mission. "But the Boss controls that kind of thing."

"Who is this Boss?" I asked.

"The Boss rules this area, for better or worse. Mostly worse. When he says to stay out of a building, people stay out."

Yesterday Dante had said something about the Boss controlling crime. "So he's a crime boss then?"

"He's *the* crime boss," James said. "Moxie 'Boss' Mannheim. He's been remaking his image as a respectable businessman for years, but rumors persist. Don't you read the *Planet*?"

"Of course I do." The name had rung a vague bell when James said the whole thing, but clearly I had some homework to do.

I pushed open the door to the third floor and let Melody go in first.

This *had* been the lab. That much was clear from what lay in front of us. There were a handful of waist-high counters, a few filing cabinets left around the edges. Some test tubes and syringes. But it was a shell of a lab. These remnants were all there was left. I checked out one of the filing cabinets, opening the drawer to reveal a whole lot of empty inside. I tried another one. Same.

"This was the place," Melody said.

Standing by one of the counters, she reached out to touch a small rack. "I don't remember anything . . ."

I started looking around the edges of the room. Maybe there was a clue for me here outside her head.

I did see a slip of paper on the floor, the size of a sheet from a small notepad, and bent to retrieve it. The words written on it in pencil were too faded to read, but there was a signature. It was two Ds though, hardly a name.

Something I could keep in mind when I went down to City Hall on Monday. I pocketed it, and jumped when a crash and clatter sounded behind me.

"Melody!" James called.

When I turned, he had a grip on one of Melody's arms and Maddy had the other one. Melody was pale, eyelids fluttering, her legs wobbly enough that she'd have been on the ground if James and her sister weren't holding her up. Just like the day before.

"Mel," Maddy said, a tremble in the word. "Mel, what is it?"

Melody wrenched her hand from James and put it to her forehead. She mumbled something under her breath.

We waited, and I knew everyone was as scared as I was. We stood in a dark abandoned ruin, where something inexplicable had happened to Melody, completely powerless to help her.

If I'd convinced myself that this was anything like Anavi and the Warheads, and that I'd solve it with relatively little problem, that dream evaporated as we waited to see if she'd recover.

I had no idea what was going on here, no idea who was behind it.

No clue, except a possibly meaningless DD signature on a scrap of paper and a phantom address for a phantom company.

Melody's eyes fluttered once more, then popped open and she was with us again. Sweat was a sheen on her cheeks. "Can I speak to you alone?" she asked me, only slightly imperious. She looked at Dante.

I couldn't speak for Maddy and James, but I'd forgotten that Dante wasn't one of us. He had no real idea why we'd wanted to get into the building badly enough to force entry. But he'd come along anyway.

"Of course," I said, and I helped her walk with me to the nearest corner. Dante didn't say a word, giving us privacy. Maddy and James hung back too.

"I saw something," she said, fingers circling her wrist. "When it happened. I was trying to remember being here before and instead . . . All I could see clearly was that gray wristband, him touching it. And I saw stairs. A lot of stairs, in the dark."

"Any hint where this was?" I asked.

She shook her head. "Not here." Then, "You still like the hard way?"

"Less and less all the time," I said. "Try not to worry."

I was telling people to do that a lot lately, even when I had no evidence it was sound advice.

"I'm trusting you, so of course I'm worried," she snapped.

Oddly, the intended insult was a relief. It reminded me what I was, no matter how out of my depth I felt, no matter how new to it I was. I had found my calling. I was a reporter.

"Don't. Finding things out is what I do. I'll get to the bottom of this. You have my word."

★

By the time we got the lock on the door and our cabbie had arrived at my summons, Melody had recovered. And remembered nothing else new. Dante had stayed to work on his mural, and James, Maddy, Melody, and I headed back uptown to the sisters' address. I forked over the cab fare when we arrived, not wanting James to have to shell out again.

"Thanks, girl reporter," the cab driver said, and I realized I'd never bothered to learn his name.

"It's Lois. What's your name?"

"Taxi Jack," he said, and then waved and took off.

I could easily walk home from Melody and Maddy's place, but I was in danger of running late again. I didn't want to miss SmallvilleGuy at 3:06.

"You're sure you don't want us to come in?" James asked them as we stood on the sidewalk outside their building. Both twins shook their heads no and disappeared inside.

I was about to tell James I'd see him Monday, but he said, "Can I talk to you for a sec?"

Employing my stealthiest discretion, I checked my phone for the time. It was almost three. The poster would be putting up his revealing details about the flying man any time now.

"It'll only take a minute," he said, raising an eyebrow at my phone.

So much for my stealthiest discretion.

"What's up?" I asked, heading east up the street of tall, mostly residential buildings. We passed a small grocery store, the inside crowded with shoppers stocking up for the week.

James followed me without so much as a peep of a question about where we were headed, which was in the direction of my brownstone.

The two of us hadn't hit it off when we'd met, though we

now mostly got along fine. But I still didn't feel like I could get very close.

With James, there was that whole business with his dad, the ex-mayor of Metropolis, being sent away to prison on charges that included embezzlement, blackmail, and other unsavory activities. James Worthington, Jr., had lost the public's trust. A golden boy toppled from the greatest of heights, his family left in the shadows of his fall.

"My dad came home yesterday," he said.

"I know, as does anyone in town with eyes and ears," I said, but gently. Trying to lighten his solemn mood.

"Right." He paused to let a couple towing two crying children pass us. "You know that I thought Dad deserved what he got. But now I'm not so sure."

Wait a second. This was a big deal. James had told me that he *agreed* with the reporters who'd helped take his dad down, that what his father had done was wrong. That was why he wanted to work at the *Scoop*.

"What do you mean?"

"Lois," he said, and paused. He began to walk along the bustling sidewalk again, before I could even ask what was wrong. "He told me he's innocent."

"*What?*" I said. It was too loud, but I couldn't keep it in.

He steered us out of the direct path of other people, glanced around, and lowered his voice. "Me and my mom. He turned on some music really loud last night and pulled us in close and then he told us that he was innocent. But that we couldn't say anything about it to anyone."

"And you're telling *me*?" I wasn't at all convinced by his dad's post-jailhouse confession, but I had to admit I was touched that James had come to me about it.

"Do you think it's possible?" he asked. "Is it wrong that I want to believe him? He's not like he used to be. He was always a good mayor, but he was cocky. He thought no one could be smarter than him. He's not cocky now."

"Well . . ." I said, buying a moment to think. "You know him better than I do. What do you think?"

"That's just it," he said. "I gave up thinking I knew him years ago. When he got caught. When he went away."

"You're a good reporter." The me of three weeks ago could never have imagined saying this, but it was true. "Perry would say you should trust your gut."

"What would you say?" he asked.

The answer he needed wasn't mine. "James, I can't tell you how to feel about this. You don't have to decide today, do you?"

"Nope, but I have to go home and look him in the eye. I was hoping you'd tell me how to feel."

"Sorry," I said, and that was true too.

He nodded, and we stepped back into the flow of movement on the sidewalk. I couldn't shake the feeling I was letting the people I cared about down by not having all the answers.

Yet.

CHAPTER 6

I was ten minutes late. I didn't take the time to hit Strange Skies first, just went straight to chat. The message came as soon as I logged on.

SmallvilleGuy: *Did you see it?*

SkepticGirl1: *Not yet. Give me a sec.*

SmallvilleGuy: *Hurry. I need you to calm me down. I might be freaking out.*

Posted by **Insider01** *at 3:05 p.m.*: The flying man will be sighted tomorrow night near Omaha, Nebraska, at precisely 2:30 a.m. UTC, or 8:30 p.m. local time. The coordinates are as follows: 41°22'04.59"N, 96°04'22.73"W. This is not a prank, a joke, or a hoax. I have information that this will definitely occur. I expect someone here to report back and confirm that it did.

I tried to wrap my head around what this meant and why

it had SmallvilleGuy so freaked out, failed, and clicked back over to chat.

SmallvilleGuy: *Did you read it? Do you think it's legitimate?*

SkepticGirl1: *I don't know. Those coordinates are pretty specific.*

SmallvilleGuy: *So you think it's true? That whoever this is knows there will be some kind of appearance of a flying man?*

I was shaking my head before I remembered he couldn't see me. That was a habit I hadn't been able to break. Sometimes it felt like we were sitting across from one another.

If only. Then maybe I could see more about what he was thinking.

SkepticGirl1: *I don't know. I guess? We'll have to wait and see.*

SkepticGirl1: *Um, can I ask something and you won't get mad?*

SmallvilleGuy: *Always.*

I hesitated, but I trusted him. I trusted that he meant it.

SkepticGirl1: *Why are you so worried by this?*

He didn't respond right away, but when the message came it didn't look like I'd offended him.

SmallvilleGuy: *It must seem like I'm overreacting.*

SkepticGirl1: *Maybe a little. ;)*

SmallvilleGuy: *I promise I'm not. I don't know what this means for me.*

I stayed careful.

SkepticGirl1: *I've never asked you how you knew what I saw happened, but I've always assumed that you've seen him too. Or you know him.*

No response.

SkepticGirl1: *I don't know who I saw that night. I only know that it's not a surprise to me that there might be another person like him.*

I expelled a breath of air in relief when I saw that he was typing a response. I felt like I was balancing on a bridge over that gulf of secrets between us.

SmallvilleGuy: *They said "the" flying man this time.*

SkepticGirl1: *I noticed that too.*

SmallvilleGuy: *Seems like there must be only one.*

SkepticGirl1: *One flying man seems like a lot.*

He ignored that.

SmallvilleGuy: *There's no way they could know this information. What do you think they want?*

I drummed my fingers on the desktop and thought about it. The most obvious answer would be that the poster either was the flying man or had firsthand knowledge of his movements. But SmallvilleGuy seemed positive they couldn't be posting honest intel, and I trusted him more than some random poster. Oh, how I wished I had more answers for the people who wanted them from me.

Having people you cared about and who cared about you in return wasn't easier than being lonely. It was a different kind of hard. A kind of hard that could hurt someone besides yourself, if you weren't careful.

SkepticGirl1: *I can't know that without knowing if it's true—or assuming it's not, as you think—without knowing who is doing the posting.*

SmallvilleGuy: *Good point. I'm going to contact TheInventor.*

TheInventor was another member of the message board—perhaps its creator, though I didn't know that for sure. I did know that he'd made the chat software we were currently using, and the messaging app on our phones. He'd also helped SmallvilleGuy infiltrate a developer's circle to provide an assist with my first big story.

Maybe he *could* help with this too, uncover some detail that would make SmallvilleGuy feel better.

SkepticGirl1: *It makes sense, though. That someone's looking for the flying man . . . I suppose I have been too, in a way, that's why I came to the boards. Why we met. If there really is a man out there who can fly—and I think you and I both agree that there is—then I bet I'm not the only person who's been looking for him. We know other people who've seen him and posted about it.*

The little flashing ellipses that meant he was typing a response popped up and stayed there. Flashing and flashing. But when the message posted, it was short. Which meant he'd probably deleted whatever he'd been typing and typing. More thoughts I'd never get to see.

SmallvilleGuy: *I liked your other bet better. This feels . . . dangerous. The post feels dangerous.*

The gulf between us felt like it widened, the bridge across ever shakier under my feet. I wanted to keep from tumbling off it, and so I didn't ask what he'd decided not to tell me. I joked with him instead.

SkepticGirl1: *I'd better go buy a T-shirt, it sounds like. And a cap. The whole costume.*

I wanted to bring us back to *us*. Everything felt too serious, too heavy. I wished he could tell me the whole truth, so I could understand *why* he was so worried.

But the thing was, I didn't need any more information to share the feeling. He wasn't going to explain why, not tonight, that was clear. I knew that, after our exchanges. But I wasn't offended by the secret-keeping, not right now. That wasn't what bothered me.

It bothered me that I couldn't ease his worries. That *he* was so obviously rattled made me feel rattled too.

I was sympathetically rattled—which, I realized, is what it means to care about someone. Which was scary, considering I still didn't know if he felt the same. But from the lack of response, I could tell he wasn't up to joking around and pretending normalcy.

I could do serious honesty, if that was what he needed.

SkepticGirl1: *The flying man, he saved my dad's life and mine. He changed the way I see the world.*

I took a deep breath. Did I have the guts to type this next part? My shyness didn't kick in. I typed and hit enter, putting it out there where he could see.

SkepticGirl1: *He brought me to you. We'd never have met otherwise. If your worries are right, he could be in danger. You should warn him if you can. I owe him a debt. Let me know if I can help.*

He didn't reply for a long moment.

SmallvilleGuy: *It's still not a costume. And thank you—you helped me. You always do. I have to go.*

SkepticGirl1: *Talk tomorrow, right?*

He was already gone.

My message hung there, unanswered; his username gray.

I didn't delete my question. I could have. But instead I left it there for him if he returned later. I might have been thrown by a lot of things that day, but I had faith we would talk the next day. We always did.

★

Almost always.

Twenty-four hours later, he hadn't returned to chat. He hadn't posted on the message board. I left my app signed in on my phone, kept it at my side the entire day on Sunday. Nothing. Not one word from him.

He'd vanished.

I had no other way to contact him. I had to wait.

If there was one thing I sucked at, it was waiting. Being patient? Not happening. I brought dinner up to my room, much to my mom's disapproval. And I waited at my computer, impatiently checking chat and then the boards and then my phone in a clockwork rotation.

Now it was evening, fast approaching the designated hour of the "sighting." I went back to Strange Skies and stared at the message. *"Near Omaha, Nebraska . . . at precisely 8:30 p.m. local time."* Omaha turned out to be in a time zone an hour behind us, so it was after nine here—and in Smallville.

The post had twenty-five hundred views, and fourteen comments like "No way!" and "Wish I could make it!" and, finally, one from a poster I recognized:

I knew her. Not in real life, just from the boards. QueenofStrange was a waitress in rural Nebraska. Over the years she had posted about lots of stuff, including her belief that she saw the flying person one night herself but also about a woman coming into her diner who claimed to have as well. She usually shouted out to me, aka SkepticGirl1, when she talked about the flying person, convinced we'd seen something similar. Though in my case it had been more up close and personal, and potentially deadly.

My entire family had been driving cross-country on our latest move, and I'd asked Dad to pull over when I spotted something strange outside Wichita. A rock tower, stacked and teetering high into the air, in the middle of a flat plain, revealed by the clear night and the ambient light from the city. Dad and I had approached and the rocks had begun to tumble down at us. At the last possible second before they crushed us, someone had appeared and *flown* the rocks away, saving us. The flying man. Was he going to make an appearance tonight?

Finally, at 9:30 p.m., there was a post from QueenofStrange: *It was true.*

That was it. That was the only thing she said. Her posts were usually gabfests, full of asides and little details.

It was true.

I checked the circuit again. Nothing.

There was a light knock at my door, and Lucy came in. Her blond hair was pulled back in a ponytail, and she was wearing her unicorn pajamas. In the game she played, she wouldn't be caught dead in pastels. But she couldn't tell Mom that, and so she had to wear the unicorn pajamas she'd gotten for her birthday.

"Hey, Luce, what's up?" I demanded. That came out harsher than I wanted.

She recoiled, then took a few steps farther in. "Would you mind reading over this paper I had to write?" She paused. "You can ignore the spelling. I can do that part."

I hadn't even noticed she had a sheaf of papers in her hands. I glanced at my computer screen again, confirmed the nothing and no one in chat, and shut the lid. Lucy didn't know about my secret long-distance friendship.

"No problem," I said. "But don't you usually get Mom to read for you?"

"I thought you might like this one," she said. "For, uh, reasons."

"All right, I'm intrigued. Hand it over." I stuck out my hand and accepted the papers.

While I read, she sat down on my bed, waiting for the verdict.

The paper was a short history of journalism in the United States with a focus on women and cultural views about women journalists. It included sections about Nellie Bly and Ida B. Wells, mention of an old movie called *His Girl Friday*, and even a reference to work for the *New Yorker* and *Vanity Fair* by a writer Lucy knew was one of my favorites because I had a quote of hers on my bedroom wall, sharp-tongued member of the Algonquin Round Table Dorothy Parker. And the entire thing ended with a big finish, calling the *Scoop* the next part of the story.

I'd have thought it was good even if I wasn't the perfect audience for it, but . . .

Lucy stood when I looked up. "You liked it, right? Your story was so good. Everyone at school was talking about it. The teacher asked us to write about a larger topic that we had a personal connection to, and I wanted to show off a little. I guess that I . . . I guess I'm . . . proud." She sounded slightly disgusted when she added, "You know, of you."

Lucy and I had been through a lot together. We'd packed many suitcases in the same room, said goodbye to many of the same schools and all the same towns. She'd called me the worst many times, but later recanted. She'd also always had an easier time than I did fitting in, even if she'd never been able to put down roots either.

It occurred to me that journalists consulted experts. I was a good sister, but Lucy was winning the race, especially tonight, with her sweet gesture. She could be my expert.

"Thank you," I said. "I'll never tell anyone you said it."

She snorted. "I better get a good grade on this."

"You will," I said. "I have another question for you. It's related to a story."

Her eyes grew big and interested. "Shoot."

"Is there anything you could imagine me doing that would be so bad we wouldn't talk to each other anymore? Ever?"

Lucy took her pages back, her face pinching as she thought—if I had to guess—about every slight I'd ever slighted her, and vice versa. "No," she said. "We'd still be sisters. No matter how mad I was. I'd get over it eventually."

"Me too. That's what I thought, but thanks. And for the essay."

Whatever had driven Maddy and Melody apart must be bad, but it couldn't be insurmountable. Maddy still cared or she wouldn't be concerned about how Melody fared. Or maybe she would, because that was the sister deal. Argh.

Lucy closed my door on her way out. I murmured, "They're still sisters, so don't mess this up."

I hoped to make some progress on Melody's problem the next day after school. But it was all a distraction, and I was already reopening the laptop lid. Mostly, I hoped SmallvilleGuy would show up to tell me what he'd found out from TheInventor.

I just wanted him to show up. Period.

I opened my computer and logged in to chat. His name still wasn't there.

SkepticGirl1: *I'm starting to worry about you.*

SkepticGirl1: *Please let me know you're okay when you get this, mystery boy. Otherwise, I'll have to hunt you down.*

SkepticGirl1: *;)*

The winky emoticon was an attempt to disguise how worried I was. We'd never gone this long without communicating, not since we met.

I checked the boards one last time. There was still no SmallvilleGuy anywhere I could locate. So I signed in to the app and turned my phone up to max volume before I went to bed, in case he messaged while I was asleep.

The *ding* of a new message woke me from a repeat of one of the nightmares from the other night, a shadowy form tumbling out of the sky and to the ground as I watched, unable to do anything to save him.

I fumbled for my phone.

SmallvilleGuy: *Catch you up tomorrow. Got in touch w/ TheInventor.*

SmallvilleGuy: *I'm okay.*

SmallvilleGuy: *& I'm glad we met too. You and me, I mean. I owe you more than one.*

I wasn't even sure if he'd read that part of what I said the night before. He'd taken off so quickly, without acknowledging it. I put my hand over my heart. It *thump-thump-thumped* and I had so many questions to ask him. But he'd said tomorrow.

Still.

SkepticGirl1: *Where have you been all day?*

But he'd already signed out again. My message went nowhere.

That was all right, now that I knew he was. I'd ask him again tomorrow. Asking questions was something I was much better at than waiting patiently.

CHAPTER 7

I strode into the outer part of the principal's office at the beginning of first period and waved a white paper bag at my office assistant pal Ronda. Behind her gatekeeper desk, she wore a red and black flowery ensemble and approximately half a tube's worth of mascara. She smiled when she saw me.

"For me?" she asked.

I gingerly placed the bag in front of her. "Who else? They're your favorite."

It was less a white bag of surrender, more a bribe to keep us on good terms. Powdered sugar donuts from the bakery up the block from my school subway stop. I'd been running a few minutes late, but keeping Ronda on my side was important. And I wasn't *that* late.

Not that I cared about timeliness for this particular

appointment. Yes, it was an abhorrent fact: I had a standing Monday morning session with Principal Butler. It was penance for the story I'd written about the Warheads and the scrutiny it had brought him and the school. Why did *I* have to do penance when all I'd done was uncover a shady research partnership that shouldn't have been taking place, ever, period, and definitely not under Butler's nose? It only made sense in Butler logic. Too bad for me, East Metropolis High operated on that.

Ronda fished out a sugary white donut and took a bite, eyes closing as she chewed. "Go on back. He's waiting."

"Thanks, I guess. Onward to victory—or, more likely, a painful half-hour."

I marched past her, up the short hall, and straight into Butler's lair, with its dark wood paneling and bookshelves filled with thick leather spines and reproduced paintings of fox hunting. Everything was perfectly in its pretentious place.

"Lois, welcome. I do so like our chats," Principal Butler said.

He sat behind his desk. His shark-silver hair was neatly arranged, and today's crazy-expensive suit was a light plum that might have been dapper on someone I loathed less.

He'd been waiting for me. His hands were folded one on top of the other over the enormous file that contained my "unique" permanent record.

Much to my frustration, I had never been able to sneak a peek inside it. Though he'd given me some out-of-context highlights at the first of these excruciating tête-à-têtes. I had *not* led teachers on a high-speed foot chase off campus, I'd been helping find a kid's lost little sister in the woods. And if helping a bullied boy fill someone's lockers with some harmless feathers as payback on his last day at that school was wrong, I didn't want to be right.

He leaned back in his chair when I plunked into my usual seat opposite him.

"For a minute there, I thought you were going to stand me up," he said.

Ew. But I tried not to let it show on my face.

"Never," I said. "Not in case of rain or sleet or snow or the zombie apocalypse."

"Oh, really?" he said.

"Maybe not the zombie apocalypse. Unless they're slow zombies."

We sat, looking at each other in awkward silence. During last week's meeting, he'd started off by asking me how I was enjoying P.E. Like physical education, with its mandatory polyester shorts and sweating, wasn't the worst thing he'd done to me yet. I didn't have the patience for sports.

"So," Principal Butler said.

"So," I returned.

Apparently he hadn't come up with a topic of conversation for us this week. I thought back to James's revelation about his dad's possible innocence. Principal Butler had known him, at least in the capacity of a small-fry donor to the ex-mayor's campaigns, and imagined them to be friends.

"Hey," I said, "you used to know Mayor Worthington, didn't you?"

"I still do," he said. "I'm thrilled that they released him. I can't imagine such an accomplished man in jail. He was the best mayor we ever had. You've never met him, I suppose, but he's just a delightful human being. Everyone loved him."

Coming from Butler, that was less than convincing.

"Huh," I said.

He went on. "You and James are colleagues, aren't you? How's he doing? I should send flowers . . ."

Trailing off, he hit a button on his desk phone. It rang once before Ronda answered, her "Yes, sir?" sounding suspiciously like it came from a mouth filled with donut. I liked Ronda.

"Send Mayor Worthington and his wife some welcome home flowers from me. Don't be stingy either." He paused. "But not too pricey. Something just right."

"Of course, sir."

He clicked the phone again to turn the speaker mode off.

I didn't envy her having to decipher his vague directive. "That's nice of you."

Putting my hands on the arms of the chair, I considered what else I might be able to find out from him, if he didn't have an interrogation planned for me.

"Do you think the ex-mayor did it?" I asked. "Did the things he was accused of?"

He stared at me in surprise. Then, "What do you mean? Is this a trick question?"

"No trick, just curious about your opinion."

He raised both well-groomed silver eyebrows. But he must have decided I was asking sincerely, because he answered.

"He must have. Good men can fall subject to bad influences, corruption, and the schemes of others."

"And some not-good men," I muttered pointedly. I had no proof he'd known what Advanced Research Laboratories, Inc., had been up to with the Warheads, but I had plenty that Butler hadn't intervened even though it was obviously unsavory and hurting a student.

His eyebrows came together in a scowl. "Be careful, Miss Lane. We've been getting along so well. But I am the authority figure here."

Because the world is an unfair place filled with horrors.

"You're right," I said sweetly. "I'd better get on to AP Lit. If you don't have anything else."

He didn't stop me when I stood, and only when I hit the door did he say, "Give James my best. Tell him to drop by and see me if he needs to talk about anything. It must be hard for him."

"Will do."

Did Butler have a soul? Or did he just think James's dad—who everybody had loved—might be back on the rise now that he wasn't behind bars?

I wasn't the one who'd solve that mystery. At least not today.

*

Maddy had saved my seat in AP Lit with a notebook, which she moved for me when I slipped in. Everyone in class knew the reason for my delay, which I considered less embarrassing for me than for Principal Butler. We could meet on Monday mornings until all his sins came home to roost, or whatever. It would never stop me from pursuing a story.

I studied Maddy's profile as we listened to our teacher, Mrs. Garrett, outline the virtuous sub-themes of the famous scarlet A. I wondered what would be off limits to report on at the *Scoop*, if anything. There were obviously still some things I couldn't write about without the larger world (not to mention Perry) calling me crazy—like flying men. And Melody was Maddy's sister, not just a story. I couldn't forget that. But it was time to focus on finding some break in her case. It would save me from mini-obsessing over SmallvilleGuy's weird behavior.

I was officially counting every second until I could get an explanation for his sudden MIAness in response to the flying man's rumored appearance. Our Monday schedules didn't match up well, so it wouldn't be until tonight's chat. And today we'd be at risk of missing each other more than usual, even, given that I had to go to City Hall first thing after school. I was torn about whether to hit the property office first to look up the address or try the business registration records to check for Ismenios. It was a tossup . . .

At the end of class, the first thing I asked Maddy was, "Anything new on the sister front?"

"Same old perfect self, now with added drama." Maddy shrugged a shoulder. When she stood up, I could see that her T-shirt today was for a band called Sibling Rivalry.

Ha. But I also took it as a warning. She was worried about Melody, but only showed it to me.

"No more episodes?" I asked as we walked down the hall.

She shook her head. "Not that she told me, anyway. She might tell you."

There was something about the way she said it. She wouldn't look at me. The bright red streak in her hair draped forward to hide her expression. That was deliberate. She hadn't used her hair to hide her face from me since we first met.

"Whoa," I said. "Hold up. Talk to me."

"It's just . . . It's stupid." We'd reached her locker and she opened the royal blue door to use as a shield.

"You're never stupid. Maddy, tell me what's wrong."

I glanced over my shoulder, and there was Melody, swanning through the hall behind us in a red dress like a very popular devil, in the company of the same clump of friends she usually traveled with. Only James was missing. She must have seen us standing at Maddy's locker. In fact, I knew she had, because her nose lifted fractionally. But that was the only acknowledgement we merited, being in public and all. Her fingers absently circled her wrist, though, and I couldn't help wondering if she was seeing the gray wristband she'd described through the unknown man's eyes.

After Melody walked by, Maddy sighed and began rifling through her locker.

"Talk," I told her.

"It's just . . . Melody's the perfect one, okay? I know you've heard me say that. James fawns all over her, and now . . . Now she's even interesting to you. She gets everything she wants in the end. I was the interesting one, you told me that, and I can't believe how I hung onto that. It had been so long since I felt not invisible, compared to her. I told you it was stupid."

Ohhhh.

"Maddy, look at me." I stepped in front of her and prayed that I was about to say the right thing. "You're my friend. Your sister is someone I'm helping—and not in small part because she's your sister. You are the interesting one. And the nice one. Not to mention, you're *you*. Melody's afraid to show anything of herself. You aren't." When her face and shoulders relaxed, I added, "Pretty sure a certain crazy-hot art boy thinks you're more interesting too."

I lifted my hand to indicate she should look over her shoulder, and she turned. Dante was the one passing by this time, *and* he was mooning at Maddy in the sweetest possible way. She smiled before she could stop it.

He beamed back and waved to her.

She tried to school her expression, but it was too late. I'd seen, and I was smiling too. "Like ships passing in the hall. You guys are so freaking cute."

"Shut up," she said, and started to her next class.

Before she was out of earshot, I said, "Mad?"

"Yeah?" She stopped.

"I've got Melody's back for now, even if she doesn't like it. But I'll always have yours."

She made no attempt to hide the smile that crossed her face. I took that as a win.

★

After last period, I waited for Devin on the steps out front of the long brick behemoth that was East Metropolis High. The sun beat down on my bare arms and the top of my head as I sat and squinted down at the screen of my phone.

It would be hours before I could really talk to SmallvilleGuy, and I'd done a pretty good job not obsessing all day. But I signed in to the secure messenger app on my phone. In case he happened to be signed in too.

The message came immediately.

SmallvilleGuy: *Sorry I worried you yesterday.*

SkepticGirl1: *You better be. If you were in front of me, I might punch you. Never do that again.*

SkepticGirl1: *Why did you?*

SmallvilleGuy: *Farm emergency. & TheInventor summoned me to chat. & other reasons. You'll be around later?*

SkepticGirl1: *I'll be around later. But I want the truth, not excuses.*

No response for a long moment, then . . .

SmallvilleGuy: *Okay.*

SkepticGirl1: *Gotta dash. Hitting City Hall with Devin.*

"Okay" was a more noncommittal response than I wanted, but I could tackle that later.

I stowed my phone and looked up at Devin.

He gave me a teasing grin. "Did you know I was here?"

"Of course I did. I'm a reporter, remember?"

Devin was the *Scoop*'s master of data and computers, and

so I'd asked him to come with me to City Hall. He might see something in the records that I didn't.

"You looked like you were deep in conversation. The rest of the world tuned out." He offered me a hand and pulled me onto my feet.

I'll admit it. When I first came to Metropolis, I had the tiniest bit of a crush on Devin. He was smart, cute, and *here*. But as it turned out, I was only interested in one mysterious person. The two of us were a lot alike, though.

"I was," I said. "But it's time to get deep into the research for this story."

CHAPTER 8

The Metropolis Municipal City Hall was a daunting stone palace of a building. A variety of flags hung from the tops of the third floor in front of the grand center dome and along both broad-windowed wings. Suited people with an air of importance about them arrived and exited via the wide granite staircase.

We started up it too, Devin a little behind me.

"This is going to be exciting, spy-filled intrigue kind of stuff, right?" Devin asked. "I'm ready to get my James Bond on."

I bit back a smile. "Glad to hear it. You're right—getting this information isn't going to be easy."

He rubbed his hands together jokingly—well, half-jokingly.

This was going to be fun.

We paused on the terrace at the top of the stairs, which led to a row of grand arched doorways, only one of which was open. "After you," he said. "Oh, wait, what do we tell them we're here for?"

"Leave that to me," I said. "I'll fill out the destination. Just copy it."

I hoped he had a sense of humor about the minor trick I was playing on him. But, in fairness, he had provided too great a set-up to ignore.

Once inside, I assumed we'd have to put our bags through a metal detector and go through an old-school security check-point. Wrong. The system had been updated to the latest and greatest: a holoscanner. A solemn guard behind a nearly transparent display only he could read waved me forward first. "Next," he said. "Sign in with your destination and then proceed into the scanner."

I flashed an ID at the second guard behind the old-school sign-in book, scribbling in our time of arrival and destination: 3:45, hall of records. Then I walked forward to stand in the center of a person-sized circular sun inlaid in the marble. "Do you have any items to declare?" the solemn guard asked.

"Not that I know of," I said.

He didn't react, other than to touch a spot on the transparent panel in front of him. A column of pale yellow light sprayed up from the floor, surrounding me, scanning my body for any forbidden items.

"Next," he said, and Devin completed the same process.

The property records were on the second floor, in the same wing as the suite that housed the mayor's office. We had to pass it to reach our destination, the propped-open doors at the entrance flanked by two flags and two suited members of his security detail.

As we navigated the marble halls, I thought of James. I imagined that he felt as at home here as I did at the *Scoop* offices. He must have visited this palace of government and the mayoral suite about a million times. That was, until his father began to act like it *was* a palace and he was an untouchable king.

Assuming he was guilty.

He must be, right?

Probably the ex-mayor wanted a clean slate to start over with his family, and I could be sympathetic to that. But if he was lying about his innocence, that might prove nothing had changed.

We reached a sign that read Hall of Property Records, and went into a long, high-ceilinged room filled with rows and rows of files that reminded me of library stacks. An older lady with penciled arches in place of eyebrows was the clerk on duty at the front counter. "May I help you?" she asked.

"I'm looking for information on this property," I said. I handed a sheet of paper with the address on it to her. She entered it into a computer, clacking away at the keys.

Devin coughed, then asked under his breath, "What are you doing?"

I softly shushed him in return.

The woman stopped typing and frowned. "That's odd."

"You couldn't find it?" I asked. "Me either. I don't think it's in the online database. Can we maybe check the paper files? We verified it exists."

"How did you verify that?" she asked.

Devin and I looked at each other. "I stood in front of it," I said.

She stared at us both, then nodded. "If you're sure. Unusual to find kids these days who are willing to put in this much work."

"We don't give up easily," I said.

"Lois doesn't, anyway," Devin said, the truth of the boring nature of our search sinking in.

I gave him a sheepish shrug, trying not to enjoy the moment too much. "I told you it wasn't going to be easy."

"That was mean, Lane." He shook his head. "I will get you back."

But he flashed me a grin, so I knew he wasn't mad. *Whew.*

The woman got up from her desk and led us through the maze of long rows of shelves packed with thick three-ring binders with labels that indicated the blocks where the properties were located. Back and back and back we went, passing by every street address in Metropolis.

"Here we are," she said finally. "I'll be up front. Let me know if you need to make a copy of anything."

"Sorry," I said to Devin as she walked away. "I know public information isn't exactly James Bond material. Next time."

"Don't make promises you can't keep." Devin ran his finger along the spines, checking the labels, then stood on tiptoe to pluck a slipcase free. "It should be in one of these boring dusty old binders. Seriously, Lane, you brought me to a room full of *binders*."

"You are the best of us at data research." There were no chairs or comfy seats on offer, so I sat on the rough carpet in the aisle. A little cloud of dust puffed up as I sat down. "I'm not going to think about the last time this was cleaned."

"Probably the seventies, but it doesn't seem high traffic." He joined me, and I reached up to accept one of the binders from him.

The items inside were visibly aged, faded ink on yellowed papers. There were dozens of documents included, along with some crammed inside without being hole-punched. Whatever was in here, not only had it not been digitized, it hadn't been touched in a very long time.

I flipped through the contents, increasingly weirded out with each sheet. There were addresses, but not the one we were looking for. It wasn't where it should have been, and not anywhere else either. "It's not in here," I said.

"Hmm," Devin said. "We should check the other ones nearby. Could be in the wrong place."

So much for the excitement of reporting, but legwork was part of the job. He handed me another binder, and took one himself, replacing the set of papers I handed back. I was running out of hope that we'd turn up anything when—finally, after a good half-hour—I found a sheet almost stuck to another at the back of the last binder on the shelf.

I checked twice before I said anything, in case it was a mirage. I'd almost given up hope.

"This is it," I said.

"No kidding." Devin blinked. "We might get out of here someday after all."

He scooted over next to me. The document had the right address and location, and even better, an owner. And the name listed as the most recent property owner—since the early 2000s—was familiar.

"Moxie Mannheim," I read aloud. "That *is* quite a name, isn't it?"

"An *infamous* name," Devin said.

"James mentioned yesterday. Crime boss?" I hadn't gotten to do my homework on him yet. Looked like that would be getting a priority boost.

"Yeah, better known as Boss Moxie. You know that controversial waterfront property that's been in the paper lately, some people upset that a crime boss is going to profit from the city's purchase?" Devin asked. "And the mayor's into it? I know you're new to Metropolis, but . . ."

"Definitely answers a few questions. Like how this property record magically doesn't show up online."

Dante had brought up the land deal the other day too, among the other things he'd said about the Boss. He'd told us that the tags outside meant stay out—orders of "the Boss," in fact. No wonder, if he owned the place.

"Why is he not in jail? If he has the nerve to go around calling himself 'Boss'?" I asked.

"That part is a nickname," Devin said. "He's known by Boss Moxie. The crime boss stuff is all rumors. Somehow, he never goes down for anything. He supposedly owns a lot of property. These days, the mayor makes him out to be a legit businessman."

"But you don't think so?"

"My mom doesn't." Devin removed his phone and snapped a photo of the document I held. "Remember, she's a public defender—director of the office actually."

"I didn't realize she ran it. Impressive," I said.

"Yeah. And over the years, she's had to represent a lot of people Moxie has forced to do things they wouldn't have done otherwise. The feds and the DA have gone after him a few times, but he manages to always come out clean."

This situation smelled so newsy my nose ached, but I couldn't figure it out. "Why would a mobster have a property being used as a lab for shady research purposes?"

"A lab located in Suicide Slum, no less," Devin said.

"It doesn't make any sense."

I handed him back the document and he replaced it in the binder.

"We should check out the business registry too, make sure Ismenios isn't similarly buried in their documents." I climbed to my feet.

He followed suit, slipping the binder back into its hidden row. "This isn't looking good for Melody. Mixed up with Moxie Mannheim?"

"She's going to be fine," I assured him—and, perhaps even more importantly, reassured myself. "She has to be. She's Maddy's sister."

Maddy's sister, who had managed to cross the tracks once and end up at a secret business in a building owned by an untouchable mobster. Her luck was as bad as mine. We still didn't know what had made her answer that ad in the first place, not with Maddy insisting it couldn't have been for the money.

"You have any idea what the story between those sisters is?" Devin asked as we started to wind our way back out of the file maze.

"Not yet." But I wanted to know. It would help me understand Maddy. "Melody and her popularity thing—what's that about? You're my expert resource on that. Explain it."

"Me?" he asked. "Why?"

"Maddy always says you're a cool kid. You must get it, why Melody's so attached to it," I said.

"Not really." Devin hesitated, and then gently said, "But maybe more than you. So, there are two kinds of popularity. The kind that comes naturally, and so you just do what you do and people take notice of you and that's about it. I guess that's me? But I don't think of myself that way. If I did, I would *not* be cool."

"That's you," I confirmed with a wink. "What's the second kind?"

"The kind where you work hard to maintain a status, because it seems like everything will be easier if you have it. It's not mean girls and queen bees and bullies and jocks in charge these days, not like it used to be, but there are still hierarchies. A lot less likely to come in for criticism if you're at the top of one," he said. "But if you do, the claws will come out. So you have to work hard to stay where you are."

"Sounds exhausting. I still don't get it."

"Clearly." Devin grinned, and I knew he was sort of making fun of me, sort of not.

I deserved it, after my teasing earlier. And with Devin, I felt more sure than I did with my other new friends that I wasn't going to put my foot down wrong and mess up.

We went from the property stacks to the business registry office further up the hall. I told the clerk, a thin boy who must have been barely out of high school, "We're looking for information on a business named Ismenios Labs." I spelled it, and then added, "Or any variation of that name."

He disappeared for a few minutes and then came back, shaking his head. "Nothing."

"You're sure? Could we look—"

"I know the alphabet." He shook his head again. "There's nothing."

I prepared to argue, but I was interrupted by the blaring of an alarm. It shrieked again and again, punctuated by a robotic recording that said: "Evacuate the building in an orderly manner. There has been a reported threat. Evacuate the building in an orderly manner."

"Sorry," the registry kid said. "We have to go now."

I assumed the alarm was nothing. Well, not *nothing*. It was inconvenient, because it would prevent me from poking around more in the files. But Devin and I did as we were told anyway.

In the hallway, my phone buzzed in my pocket. I'd forgotten to sign out of the messaging app.

SmallvilleGuy: *Did you end up going to City Hall?* Daily Planet *breaking news popped up with a security alert there.*

I pulled Devin to the side of the hall as the clerk and other people streamed by so I could tap a response back. He might have left me hanging the day before, but I wouldn't do it to him.

SkepticGirl1: *I'm sure it's nothing. We're leaving now.*

I replaced my phone in my bag and stood in place for a moment. Devin said, "What is it?"

"There was already a news alert posted about this alarm. That's weird, isn't it?" I asked him.

He nodded. "Even I couldn't have posted it that fast."

"Which means someone must have tipped off the *Planet*," I said.

Some uniformed security guards appeared at the end of the hall and bellowed: "Everybody out. Come on."

At the end of the hall, who should we meet emerging from an office but the peeved-looking current mayor, accompanied by a woman in a pantsuit, and an earpiece-wearing security detail? The guards made us stop again, waiting as they ushered Mayor Ellis past. He had thinning blond hair and a tan he'd probably picked up on a golf course somewhere. And he was in a low-voiced conversation with the woman, but they were too far away for me to make out any of it except a stray expletive or three.

"They should nickname him Mayor F-word," I told Devin.

We followed the detail out, the mayor cursing to the person beside him the whole time. He didn't look frightened or worried, more in a bad mood.

We passed through the front doors, and I glanced down the steps. *Wait a second.*

I grabbed Devin's arm and pointed down the stairs, not quite able to speak.

On the sidewalk below, about to disappear into the regular sidewalk traffic, was a man in an anonymous-looking gray suit. He stopped, fidgeting with a wristband on his left hand. A gray wristband. With some spots that might be lights.

I raised my phone and snapped a photo of him.

"What are you doing?" Devin asked, frowning. Someone beside him was pointing. "Was that the old mayor?" he asked.

The other people were murmuring the same thing.

Because the man who was disappearing—fast—up the sidewalk? It was James's dad.

A dark-haired woman stopped to chat with one of her colleagues. "Did I hear this alert was a possible threat from Mayor Worthington? That he was spotted around the building?" she asked.

A man among the murmuring people said, "I think we just saw him," and hurried down the steps to where some security guards were clearing people back from the sidewalk, presumably to tell them.

Security guards who'd shown up on the scene just in time to miss the man in the gray suit.

A City Hall guy in a button-down and loafers told someone,

"I don't know if it was him. Isn't he on house arrest? I thought everyone liked him. Until, you know."

"Everyone except Mayor Ellis, who said he shouldn't be released early," the woman replied. "He may have been right."

The other person joked, "For once."

Speaking of which, the current mayor and his detail were setting up camp on the sidewalk, about ten feet from the bottom of the stairs, in the opposite direction of the way the man in the suit had gone.

The man with the gray wristband like Melody had described. Reporters were already gathering around the mayor and his goons.

Hmmm.

Devin was squinting at me. "What?" he asked.

"Shhh," I said, and steered us down to where the press corps was lining up to listen to the mayor speak.

Our boss at the *Scoop*, Perry White, rushed up, his tie loose around his neck and a question on his face when he spotted us. But before he could ask what we were doing, I said, "How'd you get here so fast?"

Perry was our boss, but his main job was as a reporter at the *Planet*. He shrugged. "When someone calls in and tells you the former mayor, who's supposed to be on house arrest, may have just been spotted at City Hall, you get moving."

Everyone quieted, and we turned toward the mayor. "Mayor Ellis will give a brief statement about the alarm and take a few questions," said the woman he'd been cursing at.

Perry fished out a recorder and a notepad. I could tell he

was done talking to us. After all, he was here to cover the security alert story.

I stepped away and pulled up the photo I'd taken on my phone, squinting to see it better in the sun. Was it possible? There was the way he'd stroked his wrist . . . and the way the wristband was exactly as Melody had described. His fingers on it had eerily evoked how she circled her own wrist.

I pulled Devin away as Mayor Ellis began to speak. The mayor now seemed visibly shaken, as opposed to his furious nonchalance when we'd seen him on the way out.

"The building has been evacuated without incident after a troubling report from security that someone on a classified list was seen near the premises and reported to security," said Mayor Ellis. "No name will be released unless more information is confirmed. At this point, the incident should be treated as potential only. Questions?"

Perry called out, "The rumor mill says it was Mayor Worthington. Care to comment?"

"I think you mean *ex*-Mayor Worthington," said the new mayor, earning a laugh. "No name will be released unless the identity of the person is confirmed. But I think *he's* otherwise occupied."

Oh, really. Easy enough to find out.

But I had another hunch to check out first. I looked back down at my phone and called Maddy.

She picked up right away. "It's happening," she said. "Right now."

"For the last ten minutes or so?" I asked.

"Yeah," she said, shaken. "She seems to be coming out of it."

"Put her on," I said.

I heard two brief, shaky puffs of inhale and exhale, and then a breathless, "Yes?" from Melody.

"What did you see this time?" I asked her.

A pause. "I was outside. I mean, he was outside. Stairs and . . . a sidewalk. A blaring noise. I was . . . I mean, *he* was excited."

"And you touched your wrist?" I said. "Like you'd seen before?"

"He did," she said, her voice becoming more stable. "He was touching that wristband, like he always does."

"I'll have more for you later," I said.

I hung up, then texted James: *Are you at home? Is your dad there?*

He texted back: *Yes. And the cops are here too.*

I responded: *Send your address. Devin and I are on our way.*

CHAPTER 9

If City Hall was a palace, so was Worthington Manor.
When Devin and I climbed out of the taxi and stared up at its
looming edifice, there was no question from either of us that
we were in the right place.

"Wow," I said.

"Yeah." Devin shaded his eyes to get a better view of the
three-story brownstone manse in front of us.

The houses on either side were also incredible real estate
showpieces. But there was something about the gothic architecture of this one. Ivy tendrils crawled along the front of it,
and fearsome gargoyles gaped down at us.

James had told me that part of the reason his dad had been
embezzling was because they were short on funds. But the
family home had to be worth millions, and they'd held on to it.

So they must not be experiencing fund shortness on anything like the scale of normal people.

I rang the doorbell and we heard its echo inside. I half-expected a butler to appear, but James opened the door. He admitted us with a soft, "Come in."

His movements as he led us into the showplace he called home were slow and deliberate, not infused with his usual relaxed confidence.

But it was easy to see why. Two police officers in uniforms, along with a detective in a suit, occupied the formal parlor, where James's dad was being questioned.

The ex-Mayor Worthington sat on a straight-backed leather chair, the left sleeve of his pristine white shirt rolled up to reveal a thick black band around his forearm, which the detective was peering at closely. The ex-mayor was stiff, his cheeks a little red. Embarrassed, if I was reading him right.

The detective punched a series of digits on a panel along the wristband's top and waited for the result. It wasn't the wristband I'd seen earlier. Besides the difference in color, this one was far more substantial. Mayor Worthington wasn't in a gray suit, either; his white shirt was paired with ironed khakis and a pair of leather loafers—or maybe they were fancy slippers. He wouldn't have had time to run home and change after leaving City Hall.

The man I'd seen hadn't been Mayor Worthington. But it had been his exact double.

I inched closer to James. "How long have they been here?"

"Since about five minutes before you texted me."

So they'd been dispatched as soon as City Hall was evacuated.

One of the officers glanced up. "Social calls can probably wait," he said to James.

"It looks like you're finishing up," I said. "James, have you been home with your dad the whole afternoon since school?"

Lines emerged on James's forehead, but he answered me. "Yes, I came home right after school. Mom had to go out. She and I—we've been taking shifts. We didn't want him to have to be home alone yet."

"Good," I murmured, thinking.

I was pretty sure James was telling the truth.

"Do you have any evidence the ex-mayor hasn't been here all afternoon?" I asked the cops.

"Who's she?" the detective asked, shooting a skeptical expression my way. Funny that he hadn't asked me directly. I'd noticed that there were some men who treated girls and women like they were invisible. He must be one of those.

James's dad tilted his head at me in curiosity. "We already told the police all this. James has been with me for the last two hours." He turned to the officers. "Do you have anything else?"

"Okay, Mayor Worthington, settle down, just doing our jobs. Your monitor seems to support your story," said the detective, rising from his seat. "But please be aware that if you violate your release terms, you will be back in jail before you can pass go. If you think you can get away with any infractions or attempts to bend the rules, let alone any threats against the current occupant of your old office, I assure you that you are incorrect."

James's dad lowered his chin. "Understood."

There was shame in the reaction. And suddenly I got it. This whole episode was orchestrated purely to rattle James's dad. But . . . why?

The detective and one of the cops left. The other officer lingered until they were gone, then said, "It was a real shame what happened to you, Mayor. But he's right. The people who don't remember working for you will throw the book your way. Be careful."

Maybe everyone *did* love him before.

The ex-mayor responded to the officer's kindness. "I promise I did not leave the premises," he said. "I'm too grateful to be home with my family."

The cop nodded to him and left too. James followed to show them out—and lock the manse door behind them. We needed to have a private conversation.

Mayor Worthington turned toward Devin and me with a frown. I knew he wanted us to explain who we were, but I wanted to let him wonder. I wanted to observe him for these stolen moments before we were introduced.

He and James were obviously related to each other. He had the same brown hair as James; his was shorter, but just as glossy. He had dark brown eyes; a few wrinkles, but not so many for a man in his late forties; and a sense of poise in his posture that likely came from being accustomed to respect. To being in charge. To having people watching him.

James returned, and I looked away from his father. "Were you telling the truth about being home with your dad for the past two hours?" I asked.

"Yes." There was no hint of hesitation or lying in the answer or his face.

"Who are your friends, James?" his dad asked.

"We're his colleagues from the *Scoop*," I said, still watching James. "I'm Lois Lane and this is Devin Harris. We came by here because we have something to show James."

James waited while I pulled out my phone and found the photograph I'd taken. I held it up where he could see. His mouth dropped as wide as the gargoyles' out front.

Only then did I pivot to show the photo to his dad.

"Devin and I were at City Hall earlier, looking into some documents for a friend," I said, to cover the silence of their reaction. "We happened to be there during the evacuation. It was pretty crazy."

James's dad reached out and took the phone from my grip. He gawked at the photo of the man. If he'd looked into the mirror and seen the man from the sidewalk staring back, he likely wouldn't have known the difference either.

"I know," I said.

James's dad leapt to his feet and grabbed my arm. He pressed my phone back into my palm. Then he lifted his hand, the tracking device snug around the bottom three inches of his forearm above his wrist, and placed his index finger in front of his lips.

He wasn't going to speak. He didn't want me to either.

I'd figured that much. And I thought I knew why.

"Sorry we're here with such bad timing," I said, as casually as possible. "We didn't want to be late for our study date with James. You still have that music you were telling me about? Could we maybe listen to it while I get your notes? And I think you and Devin have some *Scoop* stuff to discuss, don't you?"

The resemblance between James and his dad was even stronger when they were both frowning. "Sure," James said, and he and his dad led Devin and me from the room.

We traveled down a long hallway lined with a thick rug, and into a salon-type room edged with a variety of potted green plants. A deluxe stereo system waited in front of a sitting area and a table.

None of us said a word as James turned on some music— overblown mellow eighties stuff, like my own mom and dad occasionally pulled out—and cranked the volume to a moderate level. This must be the room where his dad had made his confession to James and his mom.

"So, Dev, what story did you say you were working on this week?" I prodded Devin.

"Oh, not so much a story as some new design features," he said.

James said, "What kind of features are you thinking?"

"I'm going to use the bathroom," I said, but I didn't get up. I winked at them instead.

Devin and James nodded and continued to talk, while I

motioned for James's dad to take a seat on the couch. I did the same, a couple of feet away. I pulled out my notepad and wrote my first question down on a fresh sheet of paper.

He watched me, still frowning.

You think the house is bugged? I held up the pad to show him what I'd written.

He nodded.

James and Devin's conversation faltered for a moment, but then they continued smoothly. "If we didn't have to moderate all the comments," Devin was saying, and James agreed, "Yes, it's so very time consuming. But you know what they say about the comments."

I wrote another question, and held it up for James's dad to see. *Were you innocent?*

His nod was measured, and convincing.

Okay, next question. *Have you ever seen the man in the photo before?*

He shook his head.

Do you have a brother, a twin? Any idea who the guy is?

He expelled a sigh. None, he mouthed, shaking his head.

James and Devin were managing to keep up their fake conversation, but barely. If this place was bugged, the listeners would start to question why my voice or James's dad's were never heard, so I needed to finish up here. But I was certain of one thing: the man at City Hall, James's dad, and Melody's weird side effects were somehow connected to each other.

But what could I ask him to prove it?

Oh, wait. I added a new question, based on the property revelation Devin and I had turned up:

Do you think Boss Moxie framed you?

His frown lines deepened around his mouth and eyes, but he didn't move to respond otherwise. I'd take that as a yes.

That was fine. I had another question anyway. Two, to be precise.

Did Boss Moxie associate with any scientists?

Does the name Ismenios mean anything to you?

James was peering down to see what I was writing, and he and Devin were silent for a moment as I held up the notepad.

The ex-mayor's head tilted again, curious. He held out his hand.

I forked over my notepad and pen and he accepted them. He hesitated, but then wrote something and handed it back.

Yes, actually. Dabney Donovan. Scientist at Ismenios.

The ghost of the double D signature on the bottom of the paper I'd found at the original lab location came back to my mind. I wrote another question:

Do you know where this person is now?

He shook his head. A short, sharp no.

I held up one finger to indicate one more question. For now.

Do you have any way we can prove your innocence?

He stared at me, then his gaze flicked to the pad in my hands. There was such a longing reflected in his face. He reached out his hands, and I placed the notepad and pen into his again.

He flipped the page over and began to add something.

The ex-Mayor Worthington passed the notepad back to me. He'd written:

Too dangerous.

There was only a single logical rationale for the events of this afternoon: They were a message that he wasn't really "home free," and that there were people paying attention to him who could and would set him up again if they so wished.

Say, if he tried to clear his name, now that he was outside.

And the warning had worked. He was scared.

"I think we're just about finished with this, Lois," Devin said.

James agreed, "Looks like it."

My mouth opened and I barely kept an argument from spilling out. He didn't get to decide what was too dangerous.

But this would do for the time being. I'd convince him when I had to. Someone else deciding what was too dangerous for me to be involved in or pursue had never stopped me yet. This would be no different, especially since Melody needed help too.

I jolted in shock at the completely normal sound of my phone ringing.

I knew that ringtone. Yep, the word HOME flashed on the screen.

I was done with investigative work for the night. My parents would be wondering where I was, and SmallvilleGuy still owed me a full report on his whereabouts.

"Hi, Mom," I answered. "Oh, no, Devin and I were working

at James's and I lost track of time. I'm headed home right now. You guys go ahead and eat."

I hung up and faced the others. "I really do have to go. We'll talk tomorrow."

I stashed my notebook and tapped out a message on my phone. It was to data-master Devin. James's dad confirming the association between Moxie and Ismenios Labs might prove extremely helpful: *Do some thinking about how we might be able to make a list of Moxie's properties? Esp in Suicide. Ismenios could still be hiding in one.*

He took it in and began tapping a response as we started up the hall to the door. My phone buzzed: *Won't be easy.*

I returned: *Easier than going through each one of those binders by hand.*

He nodded to me and mouthed: *I'll try.*

I turned when we reached the front door and tapped out a group message, watching Devin and James's phones light up with it. Maddy would be getting it too.

It was simple, and Devin and James probably could have figured it out on their own: *Let's meet first thing in the a.m. Melody's problem and what happened today are connected. Not sure how yet.*

But I vowed that I would know before long.

CHAPTER 10

"Lois, is that you?" my mom called from my parents'
room when I hit the upstairs landing at home.

There was nothing for it but to go see them. And seeing
your parents lounging in bed would never not be weird. But
there they were, tucked in under a turquoise-and-black plaid
blanket in their room at the end of the hall, doing their usual
winding-down-before-an-early-bedtime things. Dad was reading a thick biography of the military variety, and Mom was
watching TV and playing a game of solitaire on her tablet at
the same time.

"Sorry I'm so late," I said, leaning against the doorway. "I
grabbed a slice on the way home."

"Woman cannot live on pizza alone," Mom said.

"Girl can try," I countered.

"Touché," she said. "But tomorrow go nuts and add a vegetable of some kind?"

"Deal." I swung away from the door, preparing to head to my own room and a waiting SmallvilleGuy.

"Did we see you on TV earlier?" Dad asked, stopping me in my tracks.

This had taken a turn I had no idea how to map in advance. "Um, I doubt it . . ."

Dad didn't let the matter drop. "I thought I saw you in the background during a story about some disturbance at City Hall. Something to do with the mayor's office?"

"Oh, yeah, probably," I said. "Sounds like it was just a false alarm, rumor mill working overtime because the old mayor's out on good behavior now. Devin and I went there to do some shoe leather reporting, looking up some documents. The building got evacuated just as we were finishing up."

"You should be careful," Dad said.

As if I'd known the building would be evacuated.

"Always," I said, and they both rolled their eyes in tandem. Thanks for the vote of confidence, parental units. I made my escape, saying, "Good night."

In my room, I logged in to chat while changing into my pajamas. A message awaited me there.

SmallvilleGuy: *I'm in* Worlds. *I think it'll be easier to talk than type, if you don't mind?*

It was from fifteen minutes earlier.

The entire day had been one loopy event after another. I didn't know what to make of the appearance of the double of James's dad, or the connection I thought he had to Melody, and what role the timing of all this played. I didn't understand what could possibly link a random student at East Metropolis with the ex-mayor. Or why Mr. Worthington hadn't fought the charges if they were false. Not to mention why he'd been framed to begin with.

I didn't know what to make of any of it.

But I'd puzzle all those things out eventually.

And I knew one thing. Talking to SmallvilleGuy would make me feel better.

I locked my door and slipped my holoset over my ear, easing down onto the bed. I pressed the power on and blinked to find my room replaced by the holoscape as it rose up in front of me.

Nighttime had come again in the game, with the sounds of distant gunfire and the eerie repetitive melody that sometimes accompanied spaceships with their sequences of glimmering lights. The red sky also contained a purplish hue this evening, and a million pinprick stars shone down in various colors: red, white, blue, green.

Night was never exactly the same twice in the game. But it was always lovely.

"There you are." His familiar voice greeted me. "I am so sorry about yesterday. Were you really freaking out?"

He left the shadow of the turret. Guilt tinged his question, and it was so sweet, if I hadn't forgiven him already I would have in that moment. I never could hold a grudge against him, it seemed. Which was inconvenient, but in a nice way.

"I was," I answered truthfully. "I'm not used to not being able to get in touch with you. I mean, not during times when I expect to be able to. We've always known each other's schedules. And then there was all the weirdness with the boards and our new Insider."

I couldn't quite bring myself to say it was because it felt like I *should* know. And yesterday, I hadn't.

"I was trying to get to the bottom of that," he said.

I frowned. "No farm emergency?"

"There's that too. Bess . . . she was sick. Still is."

"Oh no!" I laid my hand on his arm before I realized I was doing it. Bess the cow was Nellie Bly the baby cow's mother, and a fixture at the farm. I was pretty sure he thought of her as a giant pet.

"My thoughts exactly," he said, putting his hand on top of mine. "Shelby was beside himself."

The dog worshipped the cow as his giant idol, from all reports and photographic evidence.

"And how's she doing now?" I asked, afraid of the answer. I imagined farms could be as life-and-death as a battlefield.

"Much better, but it was hard to see her so sick. To not be able to do anything to make her feel better."

"I can only imagine." Poor Bess.

"The good news is Dad was able to get the vet out and now she's on antibiotics and responding well. Just an infection." He steered us inside the tower, where we were heading by habit and silent agreement. "But we're having to bottle-feed Nellie, and she is a hungry baby. Dad needs sleep more than I do.

So when I wasn't checking into the Insider thing, I was out in the barn playing fake mama."

I didn't have any idea what he looked like outside the game. So my mind conjured an image not that far off the form in front of me, sans the green skin; a boy with black hair and blue eyes behind glasses, cradling the small, adorable Nellie as she gulped down sustenance.

It was a nice image. I was diverted from it by a glimpse of what I thought was a pair of red-lined wings drifting through the sky nearby. But I wasn't positive it was the bat, and then whatever I'd spotted was gone. If the possible spy showed up again, though, I would officially have to start to worry about that too.

"I have a lot to tell you," I said. "After your news."

His hand slid down my arm, and I felt the touch in every cell and molecule along the way. He took my hands in his, and mine warmed instantly. I hadn't noticed the chill before. We floated up in flight through the hollow tower, parallel with each other, hands clasped tight. He guided us to the bench by the window, more smoothly than the other day—as if his flight skills were improving—and we sat down beside each other. Was it my imagination or were we sitting closer than we had the first time?

I missed you, I wanted to say, about the day before. But I didn't.

He said, "You first."

"Well, I do have a favor to ask. It's a long story, but that alert at City Hall gave us a lead on Melody . . ." I related the main events of the afternoon, gratified by his surprised reactions.

"What happened to her is mixed up with James's dad the ex-mayor, who I now believe might be innocent after all."

He blinked. "Busy day. Okay. What can I do?"

"Nothing for now. I have Devin figuring out if we can make a list of places owned by Moxie where Ismenios and this Dabney Donovan guy might be holed up, assuming he's Melody's guy." My gut sensed that he was—and I was curious about how and why James's dad had met him, and known he was a scientist at Ismenios. But that could wait. James's dad seemed too spookable to push before I had to. "You just take good care of Nellie Bly."

"I'd never let anything happen to our Nellie on my watch."

I brushed my hair back over my bare elf shoulder. The words "our Nellie" made me want to grin like crazy, but I forced myself to focus. He still had news to tell me, from consulting his genius friend.

"Did TheInventor have much to tell you about our mysterious Strange Skies poster?" I asked.

He turned to face me, his knee touching mine. I tried not to be distracted by the light contact.

"So, I don't know if I ever told you this, and I wasn't sure until now, but TheInventor didn't just build our chat software. He built Strange Skies too."

"Interesting," I said. "Not shocking, but interesting."

"He's paranoid about protecting user identities, apparently for a reason, and flushes IP addresses automatically. Which unfortunately means he doesn't have any way of finding out who the new person is. They didn't respond to a DM from him."

"Sorry," I said.

"Don't give up hope yet." But his expression had gone grim. "He reached out to QueenofStrange. She did go to the 'sighting' and says in reality there wasn't one. She agreed to post that there was."

I had never even considered that her terse message might have been a lie. I sat straighter, knee pressing more firmly against his. "Agreed why? With who?"

His grim expression got grimmer. "With the federal agents who were waiting there to interview her when she showed up. They asked her all about the flying person, what she knew about him, when she'd seen him. She told TheInventor the whole thing rattled her so much she won't be back on the boards anytime soon."

"What kind of federal agents?"

"You and I are great minds. You're asking all the same questions I did. They showed zero ID and she didn't press for it, but they convinced her they were definitely some kind of investigators. FBI maybe?"

"FAA concerned about the airspace issue?" I offered. "NSA? CIA?"

"Right," he said, serious as I'd ever seen him. "Who knows? It could be anyone."

"You think Insider01 will be back to post again? Queen can't have had much to tell, not beyond what she's put on the boards."

"I do," he said. "I wouldn't be surprised if there's another post when we leave here."

SmallvilleGuy's instincts had trumped mine on the new poster being something to worry about. I was going to lose the bet we'd made, and I didn't care anymore.

This was bad news.

"Any theory what they want?"

"I think they're hunting the flying man."

The words sent a shiver through me. He said nothing more.

Here was something else to stay worried about. So, the list now included: the scope of my story and whether it *was* too dangerous like James's dad had said; how to track down Melody's lab and this scientist, the elusive Dabney Donovan; *and* an unnamed official threat to the boards and the flying man, from some nebulous federal agents.

"I should probably get going in a couple," I said. "I have to meet with everybody else in the morning. I need to think about Melody and Worthington and this Ismenios guy, come up with a theory."

"I know you do. You're always thinking, Lois Lane."

I gave him a small smile. "It's the only way things get figured out."

"I should go too," he said.

But neither of us moved. The torchlight flickered over our faces as our eyes met.

The thing I hadn't listed that I was worried about, of course, was whether we *were* becoming more than friends. Or whether the gulf of secrets was too wide for us to cross.

When he spoke, I understood we hadn't left because we were *both* aware there was more left to say.

"There was another reason I didn't answer yesterday."

I was on a date, my traitor brain imagined him saying. *I was making out with my new girlfriend.* Not that I could fault him. We had no agreement otherwise, and we weren't *in* each other's lives, not in a daily, real-world way.

But it felt like we were. Like we were as important to each other as anyone else, as the people who we *did* see every day, right in front of us.

"I don't like having to hold things back from you," he said. "I can't tell you the whole reason I'm so concerned about this stuff on the boards. And that bugs me. A lot. It's not because I don't trust you."

My traitor brain—and my traitor heart—might want to know his every secret. But it found this way more acceptable than the other explanations it had supplied.

"I'd rather you just tell me that than disappear," I told him. "It'll be okay as long as we can talk. Promise me you'll always show up so we can talk, and we're good."

We stared into each other's eyes and I didn't know what was going to happen. Then he raised his chin. "Promise."

"Good. We'll talk tomorrow then."

"Until tomorrow," he said.

I reached up to turn off my holoset. He rarely left before I did, waiting until I was gone before he switched his own set off. A little thing that held greater significance to me, but which I couldn't be sure wasn't a random or regular nicety on his part.

You could ask. Ask whether you mean more to him than just a friend.

And I would. Just not today.

I sat on my bed returning to the real world for several long moments. I did need to think. I had to come up with some plan of attack for the giant story of giantness. A story growing so big in one short day that I could barely wrap my head around it.

But I crossed to my laptop and navigated to Strange Skies first. SmallvilleGuy's ominous prediction had come true. There had been a new message posted while we were in chat.

Posted by **Insider01** *at 10:05 p.m.*: The flying man will be sighted tomorrow night outside Medford, Oklahoma, at 3:30 a.m. UTC, or 9:30 p.m. local time. The coordinates are as follows: 36°46'04.52"N, 97°41'05.20"W. Like the previous sighting, this will occur at the precise time and location noted. If you intend to be a witness, do not be late.

CHAPTER 11

I knocked at the door of study room C in the silent-as-a-tomb-or-temple library before first bell the next morning. Over the past couple of weeks, Maddy had gone out of her way to befriend the librarian. Now, she let her use this space whenever it was free and the school was open, whether we needed it for homework or reporting business.

It came in handy.

The door slivered and Maddy's eye appeared at it. "Password?" she asked.

Of course. Always, she liked a password. I never managed to recall it right away. She usually set it for the next time when we were leaving the room.

"Still can't remember," I admitted.

Maddy sighed. "Finc."

The door opened. She muttered, "It was Nellie Bly this time."

The other two of my fellow *Scoop*ers were already in attendance, seated around the long study table.

"You've called us all together here today for reasons which you will now reveal," Devin said, deepening his voice. Maybe these were the booming tones he used when he was playing his King Devin, Ruler of Ye Olde Troy, character in *Worlds War Three*, and needed to command his griffin soldiers.

"Does this mean you didn't have any luck with the property list?" I asked.

"Nothing in the public search, obviously," he said. "But I'm working on something with a program I wrote to look, and we'll know after school if it panned out. Cross your fingers."

I lifted my right hand and stagily crossed them. "Did anyone else have any bright ideas on how we tackle this?"

James was sitting with his hands carefully folded in front of him. He said, "Does that mean *you* don't?"

I ignored him and turned to Maddy. "They brought you up to speed on where we were as of last night, I take it?"

Maddy nodded thoughtfully. "I have many questions and concerns."

"Don't we all." I dropped my messenger bag onto the table and slid up to sit beside it. "First things first, if anyone wants out of the loop on this one, I understand. We're talking about—at a minimum—tangling with a mobster who has in the past been accused of all types of unsavory things." I'd done a little Boss Moxie research, and it seemed he was the model for a famously murderous movie role. Something that had been less than wonderful to discover. Unlike his movie version, he never got linked to anything directly enough to visit a jail cell or even be questioned. He was smart.

Too smart to get caught, so the wisdom went.

And yet I had to try, to press, to keep pushing to find some weakness, or he'd win. The disturbing truth I avoided dwelling on was that he might win anyway. I still had no idea why Mayor Worthington became his target in the first place, but big city mayors were powerful enough that might be all the explanation required.

I went on. "*And* some associate of his named Dabney Donovan who took Melody's DNA, but whose name also turns up nothing on a search. Along with *another* associate who looks a lot like James's dad."

"About that," Maddy said. "Can I see the picture?"

I pulled out my phone and scrolled to the photo. Her eyes widened as she took in the uncanny resemblance.

James rose out of his seat to peer over Maddy's shoulder. "Still just as freaky as the first time."

"They must be identical." Maddy squinted as if she could tease some answer out if she looked hard enough. Then, "But why would Melody be having mental flashes from a person who looks just like James's dad? Have you figured that out?"

This was the main thing I'd been rolling around and around *and* around the night before, the place I'd focused my thoughts and pushed and pushed *and* pushed trying to make a breakthrough.

"So," I said, "yes, I came up with a theory, which you probably won't like. I think that the research, the harvesting of Melody's blood sample, was used in some way with the doppelguy who looks like James's dad, and it created a twin bond between them."

There was silence.

"Come again," James said, finally.

"Look, I know it sounds crazy, but a few weeks ago we'd have thought an experiment creating a group consciousness using holoset tech was completely nuts too." But that's exactly what we'd uncovered by helping Anavi with her bullying problem.

"You have a point there." Devin's hand went involuntarily to his ear, where he frequently had a holoset looped. Probably remembering the brief period when he'd been in danger of personality erasure via the Warheads himself.

"I know," I agreed. "It seems too convenient that suddenly there's this guy who looks exactly like James's dad showing up when it'll create the most speculation—just as he's released. He's identical enough to be a twin. The way Mayor Worthington reacted when I asked him about Moxie, I think we can assume that if he was framed then Boss Moxie was involved. And we know that this Dabney Donovan character is a known associate of the Boss and has something to do with Ismenios. Maddy, can you check with Melody and see if she recognizes the name?"

Maddy made a face. "As soon as I can get her alone where no one will see."

I rolled my eyes at the ridiculousness of Melody's concerns.

"Maybe I'll do it."

"No," Maddy said, fast. "I will."

I felt in danger of treading on sisterly toes, so I went on. "We also know the experiment Melody was involved in took place two years ago, which is awfully close to when the evidence against James's dad turned up and he went to jail. It happened so speedily because he didn't fight. At all. Which now makes slightly more sense."

"Where has this Ismenios guy been since then?" Devin asked.

"Living out his days in splendor? Looking like some poor schlub who they decided to target?" I shrugged. "I honestly don't know. But I'm hoping you can find me an address, as you know, that might fit the profile of the last one."

"My dad's not a schlub," James said.

"You know what I meant."

"Don't forget that there were incriminating recordings and photos of Mayor Worthington back then," Maddy said. "That was part of the case against him."

I nodded. "That's more evidence for the link between all these different elements, even if the nature of the link itself isn't clear. And so let's just say that this blood sample was used in some way to make this guy better able to mimic James's dad. And through whatever weirdo presto change-o process that was, it made this connection between him and Melody. A twin bond. Which we'll need to break somehow."

Maddy was radiating skepticism, but it was Devin who spoke up. "Explain the twin bond thing."

I knew Maddy would be the toughest sell on this, so I turned toward her. "Everyone knows that twins have a special bond with each other. There are all these stories of, say, two sisters separated at birth who live in different cities, and then one of them has a heart attack or falls off a cliff or whatever—" Maddy's eyebrows inched higher as I went on, but I didn't let it stop me. "—and the other one senses it, knows something's up without any physical contact whatsoever. They also tend to develop secret languages and just have this . . . connection. I think whatever this dirtbag scientist did made a more elaborate form of this happen between Melody and the guy who looks enough like James's dad to fool everyone. He knew it was a risk, so he warned Melody about the side effects. He needed a twin because she was primed for it."

"Except," Maddy said.

"Yes?" I prodded, gently, when she didn't continue.

I'd never seen Maddy truly upset before, but she appeared to be getting there. Her face was tinted pink all over, not a blush but a flush, and her expression had a near-angry quality that reminded me to proceed with extreme caution.

She still didn't speak.

"Except what?"

"*Except*," she said. "That's not a real thing. It's complete nonsense. There's zero actual scientific evidence of any of this stuff and as Melody's actual twin, I can tell you *we* do not have a special bond. Not of any kind. And the guy doesn't look like Melody, he looks like Mayor Worthington."

"Oh-kay," I said, scared I'd pushed too far. But I was equally scared that she'd be way more upset with me if her sister's problem didn't get resolved. "I hear you. But are you willing to be open to the idea that maybe *some* twins at *some* point in history had one? And that maybe that's what's happening here? It would explain Melody's symptoms. Like I said, I think Melody's DNA was used in some way to make him look right. If there's something special about being a twin, maybe it can be copied. It's a leap, I know, but it feels like the right one to me."

I expected pushback, and I waited and watched for its arrival. I didn't dare look to Devin or James for support. I wanted Maddy to know her answer mattered to me. Hers alone, in this moment.

Her T-shirt today was for a phony band named Worst Crush. I wanted to ask her if it was a reference to Dante and meant she was starting to like him back, or to her sadness over James's continued fixation on her sister.

I also wanted her to concede on my theory so we could move forward. And, obviously, to not hate me.

"Unless we come up with a better idea to explain it . . . all right," she said. "Working theory. But please note for the record I am extremely skeptical that twin bonds are a thing. Ever, in history or now."

Weak agreement, but I'd have to take it.

"Good." I finally looked away from her and to James. "Anything to report from your dad?"

He must have been focusing on Maddy's verdict as closely as I'd been, because he said, "What?"

"Your dad—anything relevant last night after we took off?"

James took a second to think over what I'd asked. "Paranoid. After you left, he combed through every room, silently, like he was looking for the bugs he's sure are planted in the house. I tried to ask him questions, like you did, on paper, about the evidence or whether he had any way to prove his innocence and he . . ." His jaw tightened. "He burned the paper."

"We don't need him cooperating more yet. It's okay," I said. "He must be afraid for you and your mom. I think you should hold on to the fact that he told you. He wants you to know the truth. Be patient."

I was telling someone to be patient? But James seemed to relax a bit.

"To sum up," Devin put in. "We've got an untouchable mobster mastermind, a missing lab to locate, some dude with a twin bond with Melody running around causing trouble, and a disgraced politician to unframe. No sweat, right?"

I also had a government agency investigating the flying man on my agenda, but that was a completely separate matter. "No, I'm sweating."

The group did a double take, like it was choreographed. "You are?" Maddy asked, surprised.

I wasn't willing to put them on. The situation felt so . . . big. I wasn't able to shrug that off. I *was* worried that I'd finally bumped into something *too* big for me to handle, even with help. That my place in the world was about to vanish in a puff of failure if I screwed this up, along with my friendship with Maddy.

"What's our next move?" James asked.

"We'll have to figure that out this afternoon. And hope Devin has some answers for us on properties that belong to Boss Moxie."

"Hope hard," Devin said.

"I am. Otherwise we may be walking around Suicide Slum looking for tags like the ones on our old building."

"Not ideal," James said.

"There's another issue you didn't mention," Maddy said.

"What's that?" James asked.

To my fascinated surprise, Maddy trained her eyes to the front. She didn't immediately turn toward James like he was the sun she was starved for, like she usually did when he deigned to notice her.

"Are you sure Mayor Worthington is innocent?" she asked.

James said, "I asked myself the same question. Lois knows I did."

"I think he must be," I said.

"You're sure?" Maddy asked again.

I shrugged one shoulder. "As sure as I can be without uncovering the evidence that proves it. The rest of this doesn't add up, and he says he's innocent, so . . ."

"It's just, you know Perry did those stories," Maddy said.

My jaw dropped open. *Oh god. She's right.*

Perry and his Pulitzer-nominated stories. I had completely forgotten that he was the one who'd really taken James's dad down. The authorities hadn't had enough to go on until Perry started digging and publishing his findings. *Crap.*

Maddy continued. "Have you read them? I did, last night, after James texted me. There were not just photographs of the mayor, there were recordings voice-analyzed by the FBI, fingerprints that matched those on file. Even identical twins don't have the same fingerprints. There were also records of wire transfers. Extensive evidence. Really extensive. Perry never revealed his sources of info, either."

James had texted her? But I snagged on one other thing she'd said—well, besides Perry's name and the fact I was engaged in actively planning to overturn his finest hour of reporting. "The fingerprints are hard to explain. Though I guess they could have been planted."

"Perry's going to need more than we have to tell him," Maddy said, "to believe any of this."

She was right. He deserved to know if he'd been tricked. But a vision of telling him all this in the *Scoop* offices materialized in my mind. He'd explode. And what if I was off base? I was a rookie, and even I suspected I was in over my head on this. I'd rather deal with something less dangerous first. Like a murderous mobster.

"Let me handle Perry," I told them. "I'll wait until it's the right time."

"No argument here," Devin said.

The others must have agreed too, since the *brinnng* of first bell interrupted no contrary opinions. Or maybe they sensed that the right time was a mirage, and we might never arrive there. In which case, Perry would never have to know and he'd never go nuclear reaction on us.

CHAPTER 12

I was the first to arrive at the *Scoop* office after school. Which was part of my plan for the day all along, and the reason I'd brought my laptop with me that morning.

I tromped over to my desk and, without delay, opened my computer and joined the network. I logged in to chat. The entire process took less than a minute, even with the hassle of keying in the sixteen-character alphanumeric password.

SmallvilleGuy showed up as "currently in chat," and his first message popped up in seconds. A sense of relief flooded through me.

SmallvilleGuy: *Whew. I can't stay long and I was afraid I'd miss you.*

We didn't have any more leads, not unless—or until—we had a verdict on Devin's mysterious "working on it." I feared this was going to be a long, frustrating evening of beating our heads against the Morgue walls to figure out our next move. So the official reason I'd been so eager to log on was to check out SmallvilleGuy's reaction to the latest Insider01 post, in case I didn't get to chat with him until way later. But I had also wanted to test his promise. He'd said he wouldn't go MIA again, and I was relieved by the proof: he was here. Now.

SkepticGirl1: *But you're here, which . . . Thank you.*

SmallvilleGuy: *And I come bearing gifts.*

SkepticGirl1: *You shouldn't have.*

SkepticGirl1: *Now gimme.*

SmallvilleGuy: *Nope. I'm saving it for the end. You know what they say: good things come to those who wait.*

SkepticGirl1: *"They" are evil, and don't understand that the pleasures of instant gratification trump the delayed kind. I hate waiting.*

SkepticGirl1: *But I'm intrigued.*

Oh, this was nice. We were behaving like us again, us as a unit of quips and banter and, most of all, trust. It muted the in-over-my-head, gulping-for-air feeling I had with this ex-mayor/mobster/bad news situation.

SkepticGirl1: *So . . . you were right about there being a new post. What's your take on the latest supposed sighting?*

The little message popped up that said he was typing. More waiting. I truly was the worst at it.

Devin came in then. I cringed when he flipped on the overhead fluorescents, bathing me in their ghastly glow. I'd been so eager to sign in to chat, I had neglected to let there be light when I got to the office.

"Hey," Devin said, "time to see what we've got."

SkepticGirl1: *BRB—don't go anywhere, okay? Gotta talk to Devin.*

I hope I didn't miss getting to discuss SmallvilleGuy's reaction. He'd said he was in a hurry. And the revelation about government agencies being involved in this somehow had made me feel bad that I hadn't been able to share his concern over the posts from the start.

Devin slid into his chair and tapped the spacebar to bring his computer to life. Then he waved his hands around in a gesture that was half spirit fingers, half preparing to attack the keyboard. "Here comes . . . hopefully something. Nothing would suck."

I wheeled my chair out so I could see what he was doing. "What is this, anyway? Did you figure out a way to search?"

His fingers clacked and clicked while he responded, typing a query into a box on a page that had a black background and a single box on it. "I did try querying the property records database by owner, but got nowhere. So then I thought we could try a speedier variation of what you did with the paper records."

I glanced at my laptop, but this was important. "Which was?"

He stopped working and looked up at me. "I pulled every street address in the zip codes in Suicide Slum out of the mapping data, and then I wrote a program that's been working all day, checking them against the database."

I still didn't quite get it. "But if there's nothing in the database . . . ?"

"You IDed an address you knew existed in real life, but which was removed from the database—presumably because Moxie's the owner. The program has been looking for other addresses in our target zip codes that exist but don't show up in the database. Seems like we can work under the assumption they'd be Moxie's too."

"Devin, you're a genius," I said, slapping him on the shoulder.

"Maybe. Let's find out if it worked." He hit enter and sent his query and we both watched the monitor. A few seconds later, a list of addresses began to fill the screen.

"Okay, I'm a genius," he said, grinning. I high-fived him.

"Now I also found out that the city keeps a database of supposedly vacant properties, sans owner listing, to make it more efficient for the police to identify possible trespassing and illegal squats when they get complaints. I should be able to cross-reference these two . . ." he trailed off, typing again. "And find out which properties Moxie owns that are occupied in the neighborhoods we think are likeliest and we can check them out."

"I'm impressed."

"You should be," Devin said, smiling, but not looking away from his monitor.

Content to let Devin work his tech magic, I returned to my laptop and opened chat with SmallvilleGuy. And frowned. He hadn't posted a response yet.

I decided to test the waters by wading back in.

SkepticGirl1: *Hey, I'm back. Devin thinks he may have figured out a way for us to find some likely spots for the un-findable Ismenios to have holed up. Places we can go check out.*

This did get an immediate response.

SmallvilleGuy: *That should make Maddy happy, though it sounds dangerous. Potentially.*

I ignored the danger comment, and thought back to Maddy's reaction to my twin bond theory. That seemed way more dangerous at present.

SkepticGirl1: *Actually, I think Maddy's afraid I'm going to betray her and her sister or something. And that I'm not that great a friend.*

SmallvilleGuy: *Then she doesn't know you like I do.*

My heart liquefied.

SmallvilleGuy: *I may not be around later. Bess is better, and I'm close enough to drive to the sighting tonight. That's my reaction to it. I'm going.*

He must have guessed how I'd feel about this plan, because he rushed on before I could respond.

SmallvilleGuy: *That way I can get some visual intel to share with you and TheInventor. Maybe we can figure out what's going on. Who exactly these searching people are.*

I frowned at the screen in reflex. My immediate reaction *was* negative—whether he'd anticipated it or not.

SkepticGirl1: *I think this is a bad idea, and I'll tell you why.*

SmallvilleGuy: *Listening . . . But how will we find out anything otherwise about who they are, confirm their motives? It's what you'd do, isn't it? If you were me?*

Okay, he wasn't wrong about that. I'd have hopped a bus or bummed a ride. Technically, I *could* drive, after a couple of lessons in a jeep on base, and while someday I wanted to get a license, at the moment it wasn't exactly legal—or safe—when I got behind the wheel. But if I had been close enough to get there, I'd definitely go.

But I didn't tell him that. We were two different people. As far as I knew, he'd never been in trouble a day in his life.

And I was about to behave uncharacteristically for the second time in a day. I was going to tell him to proceed with caution too.

SkepticGirl1: *1) If you can see them, you run the risk of them also seeing you.*

This next part was harder to get myself to type, but I had to spell it out. Make it plain enough for him to understand that my concern was real. I wanted to protect him.

SkepticGirl1: *2) You're always telling me to be careful, but you're the one who should in this case. I am not asking the who-are-you question. We agreed to table it for now. That agreement stands, like I said last night.*

SmallvilleGuy: *You know I wish I could tell you. But, Lois, I can't just not do anything in this situation.*

SkepticGirl1: *2 continued) You can't just not do anything in this situation, but you also can't tell me . . .*

I paused and thought about how to word what I had to say. The sound of Devin's fingers clacking at warp speed on his keyboard reached me, and then it became muted as I typed at a warp speed of my own.

SkepticGirl1: *. . . you also can't tell me, who you say that you trust, why that is. If you can't tell me who you really are and how you could confirm what I saw two years ago, then you should tread lightly until we know more about who it was that cornered QueenofStrange and why. You don't know who TheInventor even is. You know me.*

SmallvilleGuy: *I'll keep it in mind. I'll be careful.*

SmallvilleGuy: *And TheInventor has only ever helped us.*

I sighed. Using caution was the smart move here, but it wasn't fair to expect him to behave any differently than I would myself.

I hated it, but I had to cede the point.

SkepticGirl1: *Keep your phone with you. Logged in to the app so I can reach you and vice versa. You let me know when you're out of there, minimum.*

SmallvilleGuy: *Deal. I won't be leaving for another hour or so.*

I stared at the screen. I probably looked like a confused lab experiment myself. "Girl, dying of worry, trapped in newspaper office," the notes of that particular mad scientist would say.

"Uh-oh," Maddy said, "you have that expression."

She and James had apparently both arrived during my chat, and were at their desks. Devin remained deep in tech mode, eyes fixed on his screen and hard at work on the list. He didn't look up at our voices.

"What expression is that?" I asked.

James was listening in, and he answered instead of Maddy. "The one that makes us think things are about to get more complicated than we ever thought possible."

"Oh," I said, "*that* expression. Well, yeah. I am wearing that expression." I moved to log out of chat and shut my laptop, but he'd posted again.

SmallvilleGuy: *Maybe this will make you feel better. Your gift.*

I'd forgotten all about it. And I was powerless not to smile at what was on the screen in front of me. It was a photograph of Nellie Bly, devotedly and adorably sucking at a bottle, and cradled in what looked like a strong arm against an equally strong T-shirted torso and chest. His other arm was extended to take the shot.

What I could see of him was nice. Very nice.

If the frame of view was a smidgen bigger, I'd be able to see the face that went with it.

SkepticGirl1: *It does. But be careful.*

SmallvilleGuy: *I will. I'm not you. ;)*

SkepticGirl1: *Funny. Talk soon.*

I closed my laptop just as Devin broke out of his work, raising his hands over his head and cracking his knuckles before again spirit-wiggling his fingers.

"Who's the king of the newsroom?" he asked. "Ultimate and supreme ruler because he rules?" He put a hand up to his ear, to better hear the response.

"We're not in *Worlds*, King Devin," I countered, getting up to go see what had brought on this burst of self-satisfaction. It must be list-related. "This newsroom is a democracy."

"So declares newsroom queen Lois," James said, walking over to Devin's workstation too. I stuck my tongue out at him.

Dante had called Melody queen of the school. I had no designs on royalty.

"She's a princess, actually," Devin said. "Princess Lo. I thought about making her a queen in the game, but I didn't want to imply something about our relationship." He winked at me and added, "Not that I wasn't interested. I was."

Maddy came over and stopped beside me, crossing her arms. "That was an unmomentous way to make a pretty momentous declaration. Are you two a thing? Why didn't you tell me?"

Her voice trembled with hurt. *Oh no.*

"Nah," Devin said, tone light. "I saw early on that there was another guy in the picture. I even gave them a spot to meet in *Worlds.*"

Maddy's voice stayed trembly. "Who is this mystery man? Why haven't you told me about him?"

"It's um, complicated," I said. "But I want to."

She gave me a tight nod.

I had to get better at this friend stuff.

"He's a mystery, all right," Devin said, trying to defuse the tension, which I appreciated. "An alien, that's about all I know. He—"

"Okay, okay, your highness," I interrupted, "show us what you found. You can gossip about my mysterious love life later." My cheeks felt hot. How could I explain to them that I didn't know who he was either? But I did want to tell Maddy. I wanted her advice.

Did I have a love life? Or was I kidding myself? Why was

getting what you wanted so much harder in real life than they made it out to be on TV and in the movies?

"So," Devin said, letting me off the hook. He twisted his chair around to face us, playing to his audience. "After I ran the ghost addresses against the vacant property database, there are still a lot left. All twenty-three, to be exact. It would take us a while to check them all on foot."

"Why is all Moxie's real estate vacant?" I said. "I don't understand why you're so happy. This is not good news. But give me the list. Foot check it is." Traipsing around these properties might not be the smartest move, but it was beginning to sound like the only one.

"I'm only half-following this," Maddy said.

"Same," James agreed.

Maddy gave him a tiny smile. At least she was still smiling at someone around here.

"It will all make sense and be less dire. Hang in until the end," Devin said. "And that was not the end." He waited until we were listening politely enough for him again. "Thank you. So, I thought it was weird that they'd *all* be unoccupied too. So much so I wasn't convinced this wasn't more bad data—the property listings were missing, but they all turned up in this vacant property set? Weird."

"And?" I asked.

"And it turns out the power company—with all that nice data about what buildings are drawing on the power grid and how much—has really old software and a weak firewall to go with it."

"That's not publicly available information," James said. "The firewall is to keep people out. We're trying to prove someone *didn't* break the law, so it seems like not a good idea to be doing it ourselves."

James, the stalwart and predictable. This time, for once, I sympathized with his impulse. He really didn't want to be like his dad.

But maybe not. For a long time, James had assumed his dad was a criminal, and now he might not be. That kind of sudden shift had to be tough to deal with, even if the result was positive.

"We are trying to find a missing mad scientist who was obviously breaking laws," I said. When James started to interrupt, I went on, "And to figure out who this double guy is so we can prove that your dad didn't. But point taken."

"Anyway," Devin said, "that part's all done. Tell yourself it required no bending of any code to achieve. I matched the supposedly vacant addresses we believe are owned by Moxie up against the properties the city detects as receiving juice from the power grid. There are three out of the twenty-three that do not appear to be vacant at this time, despite reporting they are. All in Suicide Slum, though different areas."

Devin reached down and hit a button. The ancient printer we'd inherited from upstairs hummed into action and a sheet of paper rolled forth. I snatched it off. Three neat addresses waited there, none familiar.

"Excellent work," I murmured, considering them. "I do love a lead."

"I should come with you," Maddy said.

"Hmm? Where? I'm not going anywhere," I said, playing innocent.

Maddy didn't buy it. "I know you and you'll be going to those three places. I should come too."

"Maybe we all should," James said. "Safety in numbers."

I wasn't sure that was the best idea. The last thing I wanted was to put Maddy in harm's way when her sister already was. And if I was going into enemy territory, James being spotted could put him and his dad in greater danger than they already were. But how to say that without making them angry at me?

But as it turned out, I wouldn't have to.

"Hey, sorry to interrupt. Hi there."

The interruption was courtesy of Dante, freshly splattered with paint, who distracted Maddy immediately. She began to blush and develop a serious interest in her shoes. He had to have noticed her reaction, because he gave little indication he knew the rest of us were in the room.

"What are *you* doing here?" James asked, and it came out brittle. I frowned at him.

"Yes," I said, upping my niceness level to counteract James's cool welcome. "What brings you to us? Did you just want to see someone, perhaps?"

Dante smiled at Maddy, and then—finally—looked away from her, to me. "Busted," he said with a smile that contained the tiniest amount of chagrin. "It could have waited until school tomorrow, but I figured I'd make a trip. I'm collecting some visual references for my mural anyway."

"What could have waited?" James asked, sounding like he wished it *had* waited. There was nothing for him to hold against Dante. They'd seemed to get along fine when we'd bonded over breaking and entering.

Dante ignored James's attitude. "I saw a guy poking around the building across the street. He didn't belong in the neighborhood. He was peeking into the door, and then when he saw me, he came over. He started asking me questions about the mural. And then about a girl—I'm pretty sure he meant Melody," he said.

"Why?" Maddy asked, but before he could answer, Melody wobbled in through the *Scoop* office door. Her steps were shaky. Maddy flew to her side, Dante with her. I was surprised James didn't vault over to replace one of them, but he stayed put, brows drawn together.

Dante and Maddy had their arms around Melody and brought her closer to us. Her face was pale, her lips devoid of any hint of the bright pink lipstick she'd had on when I'd seen her at school earlier in the day. She chewed on her lips as she neared, anxious. She looked more like Maddy's shadow, like some ghostly reflection, than like her more confident twin.

Melody wasn't getting any better. If anything, she was getting worse. And so fast—this hadn't been going on long, and we'd barely started investigating.

"Melody, are you all right?" I asked, afraid of the answer.

"No. It happened again." She sucked in a breath. "I barely got away before my friends saw."

For her sake, I was going to need to pick up the pace.

CHAPTER 13

I wheeled my desk chair out into the unoccupied center area of the office between our desks so Melody could sit in it. She gratefully sank into the seat, nearly collapsing, with a heavy, dramatic sigh.

"Water?" I asked, and Melody nodded.

Devin got up to fetch Melody a bottle of water from our mini fridge. But James stayed put, standing beside me.

What was up with him? Until today, he'd been all eyes and ears fawning over Melody.

"You did the right thing, coming here," I said.

Melody looked at me, and then pointedly at Dante. But I'd already done that math.

This entire situation was complicated by the fact that Dante was still something of an unknown quantity to us. (Though an unknown quantity with excellent taste in crushes, in my opinion.) But if Melody didn't want to spill what she'd seen in front of him, I needed to get whatever else he knew that could help us out of him fast. And then brush him out of here without screwing up the flirtation between him and Maddy.

"Dante," I said, "the questions the man asked you, what were they?"

"The thing is," he said, "he asked if I'd ever seen a pretty blond girl hanging around here. But there was something more out-there than that." He was suddenly uncomfortable, shifting his weight from foot to foot. He looked at Melody. "It might make you feel weird."

"I'm the queen of feeling weird lately," Melody said with a hoarse cough of a laugh.

Her fingers circled her wrist, and I wondered if the motion was automatic now. Devin handed her the water, and she dropped her hand to take it, with a disconcerted glance at her wrist. That answered that question. She hadn't known she was doing it.

"Go ahead," she said, unscrewing the top on the water.

Dante went on. "So I hadn't even answered his first question. It was like he knew I must have seen her. Um, you. He asked if I'd been working at this spot for a few days and so I nodded. You can tell that from the state the mural's at. It's really coming along . . ." He looked evasively at his shoes. "But then he asked if the girl, the pretty blond girl, if she seemed happy. He asked me if you seemed happy," he repeated to Melody. "That's weird, right?"

"Anything else?" I asked, saving Melody from having to answer.

"Yeah," Dante said. "He asked me her name." Maddy gasped beside him, and he put a reassuring hand on her arm. Her eyes went to it, widening. "I didn't tell him. I told him that people might get the wrong idea with him asking questions like that in this neighborhood and that I had to go. I told him he should stay away from the Boss's property."

Oh, that was good. "How'd he react?" I asked, exchanging a look with James.

"He laughed," Dante said. "He said that wasn't possible."

Hmmm. More evidence he worked for Moxie in some way. And his whole line of questioning to Dante further strength ened the connection to Melody's situation too.

Somehow.

There was only one more question I had for Dante, mainly to confirm my suspected answer was correct. "What'd he look like? Can you describe him for me? Or sketch him?"

"Don't have to," Dante said.

He pulled a phone out of his pocket and tapped at it. Then he held it out.

It was the *Daily Planet*'s mobile site. And the story he'd found was one of Perry's stories about James's dad and corruption. One of the stories that got him sent away to prison.

"It was that guy," Dante said. He expanded a photo of ex-Mayor Worthington's face. "He looked like him."

I didn't look at James, but it took effort. I heard Devin say, low, "Don't stress, man, we're on top of this."

"Thanks," I said. "Look, I need to talk to Melody alone, do you mind . . . ?"

"That's all I had to tell you." He angled his body so he faced Maddy. "Walk me out?" he asked.

She clearly wanted to say yes, her mouth opening to form the word, but James cut in. "She probably wants to check on her sister. I'll show you the way," he said.

"No need," Dante said. Without turning away from Maddy, he added, "See you at school. You want to get coffee tomorrow, after last period?"

"I'd love to," she said, with zero pause. "See you tomorrow."

That made him happy. It made me happy, too.

He smiled at her, and then headed to the door. "Thanks, Dante, we appreciate it," I called after him, and he waved a hand in acknowledgement before he disappeared into the dim hallway.

James was still frowning after Dante left. Now *that* was the disapproving scowl I'd come to know.

"What'd you see?" I asked Melody, but once again, I could have guessed. An uneasiness, like standing on the deck of a boat rocking on waves, passed through me. I could already guess because we'd gotten the report from the other side of the twin bond already from Dante, courtesy of the guy who looked like Mayor Worthington. I believed Dante's account of what he'd said, of his interest in her.

And Melody confirmed it. "The building, the old one we went to, I saw the outside of it. I was messing with the wristband." She touched her wrist. "He was, I mean. And then

I—he—touched one of those keep-out B graffiti tags that guy, um, you know—"

Her eyes skated to the door.

"Dante is his name," Maddy supplied.

"Do you like him?" Melody asked.

"Why would you care? So you can insult my taste or so you can steal him?"

Maddy flinched at her own words. I could tell she hadn't meant to say that. She carefully did not look at James, only at her sister. "Sorry. Finish your report," she mumbled.

I made a mental note to ask Maddy if she and her sister had always been like this with each other, and to press her for a real answer. This felt like a rift, and rifts were created by an event.

But rifts could be bridged. And I was confident (er, mostly) that was what a friend would do.

"I saw him. Dante," Melody said, more timid than usual. "And the mural behind him. No wonder the guy thought to ask him about me."

So the stories matched up, as I'd suspected. This had taken place this afternoon. Dante and Melody had both come straight here.

"Why's he looking around the abandoned building, though? Do you think he's having side effects like you are?" I asked. But I didn't expect an answer.

"What he asked Dante about her being happy," Maddy said—to me, not to her sister, sitting right in front of us—"Can she feel how the guy's feeling? Is that part of the twin bond thing?"

I turned a questioning gaze on Melody. "Do you feel anything?"

Melody sniffed. "No . . . He feels empty. Like he's pulling on me, to fill himself up. If that's not crazy . . . Wait. What twin bond?"

I did not want to reopen that can of worms. "Mad, did you get a chance to ask if she remembered the name Dabney Donovan?"

"Not yet," Maddy said. And to Melody, "Do you?"

Melody was nodding. "Doctor Donovan, yes, I think that was him. Tall and weird. I never heard his first name, though."

Excellent. "That much is great."

"So, what's the twin bond thing?" Melody asked, curiously eyeing her sister.

"A theory," I said. "Maddy can fill you in."

Maddy scowled at me. "I will not—"

Perry strode through the door, his dress shoes clicking on the tile beneath our feet. He had on one of those knock-off suits he wore. Once again, I was saved by an interruption. Sort of.

"Hello, cub reporters," he said, looking around. "I thought I'd better check to make sure you're working on news stories. You are, correct? Working on *news* stories? Because I'm seeing a lot of *features* go up. They have their place, but expectations are high, and . . ."

He stopped, blinking at Maddy and Melody.

"This is Melody, Maddy's twin sister," I said.

"The one that James . . ." Perry started, but then obviously remembered that if he did know James had a crush on Maddy's sister he shouldn't mention it out loud. I wanted to kick him.

"Is friends with," James said.

"Right," Perry said. "James's friend."

Maddy was scowling more.

"What are you working on, though?" Perry asked. "That's why I came by. You set expectations and so far, you're not living up to them."

Ouch. I had to bite back the urge to counter with the truth. Instead, I went with almost-truth. "Um, I'm working on a hot take . . ." Perry's eyebrows lifted, interested. ". . . on street art, a mural in Suicide Slum."

Perry's eyebrows fell. "There is news to be had in Suicide, but the hot stuff is hardly the art scene. Prove the waterfront project's a sham and we can talk." It was a joke, and one that judged us—me—as not up to snuff.

If he only knew cracking the waterfront project story might not be that out of reach. We might do it as a corollary to the story he definitely could not know we were working on yet.

There had to be something in it for Boss Moxie, his elaborate scheme to get rid of Mayor Worthington, and now that Perry mentioned it that lucrative project might be the reward in question.

I was prepared to take the disappointment bullet from Perry for the moment, but of course, he wouldn't leave it at that. "What else?" he asked.

"I actually have to . . . go," I said. I still had the sheet with the three addresses in my hand. I waved it around with no explanation. "To check out a lead on something that might just be . . . something."

"Ooh," Perry said, tone flat, "*something*. My, that does sound exciting. I'll tell them to hold page one for 'something.'"

"'Sarcasm is the refuge of the weak,'" I said. "That was Dostoevsky."

"Russian writers, such optimists," Perry said. "Bring me a story, Lane. A real one."

"Can do. But right now . . ." I gathered up my laptop, shoving it in my bag. "I have to go. I'll see you tomorrow, guys."

Maddy started to shake her head, as did James. Devin gave me a look of the "I know I can't stop you, so I'm not bothering to try" variety. He was right.

"Wait," James protested.

"Can't," I said, and none of them would stop me, not with Perry standing right there. I tried to imagine his mood if he found out where I was really going, what story I was really working on.

"I'll let you all know tomorrow what I find out," I said.

I hurried up the hall to the fire stairs, stopping inside to text my favorite cabbie. I took the stairs two at a time, and jetted out of the building's front doors before anyone could catch me.

The cab squealed up to the curb. Rings shone on every one of Taxi Jack's fingers, and I thought he might have added another gold chain to the mix around his neck. Probably paid for by my tips.

"Howdy, partner. You look like you're in a big spender mood today," he said, flashing a gold tooth. "Where to?"

I climbed into the backseat and flashed a handful of twenties I'd saved for this kind of special occasion. After I saw his be-ringed fingers tighten on the wheel in eagerness at the sight, I passed him the list of addresses.

"I told you already that a nice young lady like you should avoid this section of town."

"But I need to drive by these three addresses." I smiled at him. Innocently.

"Just drive by?" he asked.

I rubbed a twenty between my fingers, holding it up to show him. "There's a great tip in it for you."

"I don't know," he said. "I don't usually go there after dark."

It was still a while until sunset. "We're just driving by. We'll be done before darkness falls." He wasn't convinced, because we hadn't started moving yet. I added, "Partner."

"This for the big story you're working on?" he asked. "Same as the other day?"

"A reporter never reveals her sources or her secrets," I said.

But he clearly took that as a yes, because he put the car in gear and careened into traffic. "I'll have to be snappy if we're going to make it out before dark," he said.

"Whatever makes you feel better."

"You want to hit these in this order?" Jack asked.

"Whatever makes sense," I answered.

I stared out the window at pre-sunset Metropolis: so many people were walking around, hurrying out to dinner or back to the office to finish up that one last thing before they went home for the night. Kids sighing at overprotective parents, people going in and out of stores, no one worrying about the truly bad guys out there—villains as extreme as any made-up ones, willing and able to play with people's lives like we were all just small movable pieces on a chess board. So light, so easy to move.

I wondered if the scientist I hoped to find would even remember the pretty blond girl he'd experimented on, if he would recall telling her to contact him about any side effects.

Probably not. It wouldn't surprise me if he'd forgotten her entirely.

I looked forward to surprising him, though.

Doctor Dabney Donovan made the mistake of having luck worse than mine when he experimented on my friend's sister. On someone who'd come to *me* for help.

He'd made the mistake of teaming up with a person who moved another of my friend's father into jail.

Two strikes. I wanted to knock him out.

Soon enough, Taxi Jack's cab left bustling innocent territory and we entered the darker, more cramped, more threatening streets of Suicide Slum. That the city allowed a neighborhood to get stuck with such a name was bad enough. That it wrote this place off was worse.

The first so-called vacant address was occupied, all right. There were shiny sedans parked in front, and guys who looked like extras from a mob movie. They wore slick suits, more expensive than Principal Butler's even, if not as dapper.

These were all black, and tailored to fit their giant muscled arms and torsos. One had a gun tucked into his waistband and made no attempt to hide it as we glided past.

"Driving by," the cabbie said, and he didn't so much as turn his head.

It was sketchy. But nothing about the tableau led me to believe there would be a lab coat inside. "Next," I agreed.

The next place was several streets over and blocks away, and more of the same, sans sedans. No one fancy enough to merit such an automobile on the scene, I supposed. But there was a distinctive mix of guys in suits and guys in tracksuits coming in and out of the building, and two women in business suits who carried lawyer-esque briefcases. It still didn't feel like the right address. My news nose refused to tingle.

"Third time's the charm," I said to the cabbie.

"Sun's getting low," he said, driving away.

"Just one more to go," I promised.

He kept driving, slowing finally before we'd left Suicide Slum. We weren't that far away from Dante and his mural; a few blocks at most.

I knew we were at the right place the moment I saw the three-story building. There was an image on its tinted glass door. It depicted a man in Greco-Roman-style warrior garb, armor and a short white tunic, wielding a sword against a dragon, fire flowing from its mouth. Ismenios versus Cadmus.

Melody had described a similar design on the door at the other place. Ismenios's logo, I supposed.

"Pull over to the curb," I said, and he stopped across the street. There were other buildings around of varying heights, a few alley openings, and the sidewalk was deserted.

My first story had involved a project called Hydra, named for a monster. And now here was another monster, that fire-breathing dragon.

I was a little tired of monsters, to be honest.

"I'm in a hurry," Jack said, "to get us out of here."

The building looked deserted, aside from how clean it was. Except, when I rolled down the window and stuck my head out for a better look, for a light on at the tippy-top third floor, shining like a discreet beacon advertising nefarious activity.

I passed the twenty over the seat. "Give me five minutes. I just want to get a picture with my phone."

I moved to open the door.

"Wait," Jack said.

And I saw why. The double—the man who was identical to James's dad—strutted up the street from the other direction. He wore a long-sleeved black shirt and black slacks today. He paused for a second on the sidewalk, gazing up at the building, reminding me of a pet who'd escaped its leash but had nowhere to go except back to its terrible owner. I picked up my phone and snapped a photo, quickly checking to be sure I'd gotten him.

"We'd better get going, big tipper," Jack said. The photo was clear as clear could be. I watched while the double opened the tinted glass door and went inside. I was sure he hadn't seen us. This might be my only chance to observe him—not that I intended to apprehend him or anything, or even to speak to him. But this was an opportunity to check out this part of the situation closer up.

Melody needed us to break this case. To find a solution.

Maddy needed me to, too. And James. That double was the key to the ruination of the ex-mayor's life, I knew it, and Boss Moxie and whoever else was involved in this wouldn't hesitate to turn it in the lock again. Whatever was happening inside that building, it was a huge part of constructing an ironclad corruption case against one of the most powerful men in the country.

I couldn't sit here and do nothing. I couldn't tell Jack to hit the gas.

"I'll be right back," I said, stepping out of the car before my cabbie friend could leave.

He started to protest, but his objections were silenced when I shut my door. He didn't roar away, abandoning me. I appreciated that. He killed his headlights and let the engine idle.

My phone was still in my hand. I tapped out a message in the app.

SkepticGirl1: *You there?*

SmallvilleGuy: *Just about to leave.*

SkepticGirl1: *I'm about to do something really stupid. If you don't hear from me in 30 minutes, start to worry. Here's my last-known location.*

I sent my location, then stowed my phone in my bag and slung the strap over my shoulder.

It wasn't fair play, but maybe this would keep him from going to the sighting.

I also trusted him to get word to my parents or the authorities, should that be necessary.

But it won't be, I told myself. *You'll be careful.*

Whatever reply SmallvilleGuy sent made my phone buzz as I crossed the street and paused in front of the monster on the door. I didn't bother checking. I didn't want to lie to him the way I had to myself.

Nothing about this was careful.

CHAPTER 14

I pressed my face close to the tinted glass. The building was dark inside, but not entirely. There was a thin glow coming from somewhere above, enough that I could see that the lobby was empty. It was too dim for me to see any other helpful details, but I was confident enough there was no movement in there, no one waiting just inside to grab me.

Not if I hurried.

I considered my options. The door probably had an automatic lock. Maybe the double had a key or a code or a card or something that scanned him in.

Probably I wouldn't be able to follow, even if it was a good idea. Which I knew it wasn't.

I tested the metal handle, cool against my fingers. It resisted.

My phone buzzed once more in my bag, but I continued to ignore it. The only result that could come from reading the messages was to abort this mission. So, instead, I dug out the lock pick tools I'd borrowed from Dad, which I hadn't exactly returned yet. I unfolded the end into its longest skinny tool form, then slipped it up the side of the door and then back down. If the catch didn't let go easily, I'd take it as a sign to turn tail and get back in the cab.

I felt it give within seconds. That was a sign too.

But . . . was I really doing this? Following this strange doppelmayor into a crime den?

I was in so far over my head already one more inch of hot water wouldn't matter. That was what I told myself.

The answer was yes. I was doing this.

"Open sesame," I said, tugging the handle.

I went inside quickly, guiding the door gently shut behind me.

After all, what choice did I have? *This* was my job, whether it was hard or easy—following a lead wherever it went, bringing Perry the *something* I'd promised, something that would allow me to tell him the whole story and be believed. If I was lucky.

Which I wasn't.

Ever.

I blinked, letting my eyes grow accustomed to the low light.

Two sets of grand stairs wove between the three floors, almost like a double helix of DNA, with one wood-and-frosted-glass door at the center of each landing where they met.

This must have been an artsy deco paradise in its heyday. It still possessed plenty of rundown glory; brass and dark wood, stained glass, and probably whispering ghosts.

There was no sign of the double down here. But then, the third floor was where the light had been on.

An elevator waited on one wall, but it was dark. And even if it had been working, someone above seeing the lights or hearing the noise as it traveled would have been too much to risk. Instead, I hesitated between choosing the left or right staircase, and made a quick examination of each side.

The one on the left had traces of dirt up the middle of the wood and more scuff marks. The one on the right was coated in a light film of dust.

Right side it was. If someone came down while I was here, hopefully they'd stick to the other staircase. I crept up the stairs like *I* was the quiet ghost haunting this shell. I placed my feet with care on each step, moving up and up and up as soundlessly as I could manage. At the landing, I scurried to the next set of steps, limiting how long I'd be exposed if anyone stepped out of the top floor's entrance.

The closer I got to the top, the more an antiseptic, almost hospital-like smell wafted down to sting my nose. The bright chemical scent layered on top of whatever decay it was meant to cover up.

The odor wasn't the only thing I noticed.

There were voices coming from the third floor. But I forced myself to stay slow, steady, quiet. And, finally, I was close enough to make out the words.

"Here, take your meds, they'll make you feel better. Keep you fit and fine." The voice was a man's and gruff.

"They always do." The next man's voice was flat, even, average—nothing distinctive about it per se—and also familiar. I tried to place it and then realized it was like James's dad's voice, but with all the emotion ironed out of it, all the politician inflections gone. The voice sounded tired.

There was a series of beeps and a brief sound like rushing water. Then the conversation resumed.

"I looked at your tracking data. You went somewhere you weren't supposed to today." The gruff-voiced man indulged in a lengthy pause, before demanding: *"Why?"*

"Well," said the voice that I thought belonged to the double.

"'Well' is not an explanation," the other man countered.

"I went right where you told me. But when I was reporting back, I got confused. I went to the old place. Then I had to come back here."

I leaned forward, afraid I'd miss the response. My ears strained.

"We'll run a cognition test tomorrow. Sleep now."

There was the sound of a glass being set on a counter, after a moment, and then a series of others I couldn't identify as easily. The slide of something opening, the click of a closure, the rustle of paper against paper.

The shadow appeared in the door seconds before the man it belonged to caught up.

I hurried back down a few steps as quietly as possible.

The man walked through the doorway and stood there, at

the top of the landing, like he was listening. I couldn't see his face, not a single detail. I lowered myself to a crouch on one of the wide steps, burrowing into my jacket and staying as deep in the shadows pooled there as possible. My foot thudded softly against the wall, and I held my breath.

Please don't let the sound carry. Why did I risk this? What was I thinking? How quickly could someone get here? How far am I from the thirty-minute alarm mark? How long will SmallvilleGuy wait before calling the cops?

The man standing framed in the dim doorway began to whistle, and I was convinced he'd spotted me. He'd seen some movement in the dark, or heard the impact of my shoe.

The jaunty serial killer tune kept up, but as he whistled he traipsed down the opposite staircase. In the glimpse I caught before he was out of sight, I could tell he held something under one arm, and he moved swiftly down, not pausing to seek out an intruder. I tracked each dull tap of his shoes on the stairs, and I pretended I was a ghost again, tried to stay that silent, that motionless.

Until I heard the front door open and shut.

I relaxed against the wall, and sank to a seat on the step where I hid.

I needed to get out of there.

But my eyes found the muted glow of the door above. And I was on my feet and moving again, still being careful. The double was here somewhere. He hadn't left.

I wanted a peek.

One look.

And *then* I'd leave, text SmallvilleGuy from the cab and let him know I was a-okay except for almost coming face to face with the whistling mad doctor. I'd found him, anyway, Dabney Donovan the whistler, and that meant we could confront him with Melody, make him pony up the treatment for her. Though that would be far riskier than what I was currently doing.

Plenty risky, all on its own.

I climbed up the stairs to the landing, then eased my head a fraction into the doorframe to see what could be seen.

I swallowed.

It was definitely a lab, if one that looked like I'd arrived by way of a time machine, transporting me back to the 1950s or Area 51 or something. The overhead lights were off, but there was enough illumination to reveal rows of file cabinets at one end of a room lined with gleaming black counters, some with paper files on them, others with vaguely scientific-looking equipment like test tubes and tongs and machines with cranks at their sides.

And at the lab's heart, the source of the light.

It was a large cylindrical tank, glowing softly from within, and filled with some sort of light blue liquid. Thick gray cables ran from it to the wall, and inside it, silhouetted in the blue liquid, and in the glow, was the man who looked like James's dad.

His eyes were closed, and so I risked going closer. His eyelids fluttered and I froze, but the movement stopped after a few seconds. He returned to serenity, floating there.

The doctor, Dabney Donovan, had told him to sleep, and maybe he did only and exactly what he was told.

Ugh.

My skin crawled with the creepiness of this place, the tank, the double, the experiment, and what could just as well be called Ismenios's lair as Ismenios Labs. But creeped out or not, while I was there I wanted to look for evidence.

That was the first priority. Then, no matter how much I dreaded it, I could make a more thorough inspection of the double and that tank. I'd been assuming he was some sort of fake twin, experimented on somehow to look like the ex-mayor. But he could be something else entirely.

Circling, I went to the filing cabinets, snapping a photo of the counters I passed on the way. I found a cabinet labeled *S* and flipped through folders.

Somnambulism, Sonograms, Sonic Booms, read the labels, in scrawly handwriting. And names too, Smith, Sommer, Sigler . . .

No Simpson. But what was this? Slender girl, 16, Kate.

So he didn't even bother with names, sometimes.

Some scientist.

If he described Melody, who knew what words he'd use? There were so many files. Too many to search each one.

Except . . . hold on.

I took a chance. In a few moments, I located the *P*s, pulled the drawer free, and paged through the folders.

Paleobiology, Photoelectrons, Phillips, Psychological Conditioning (that one was disturbingly thick), Porter . . .

Pretty blond girl, Melody S, 14.

"You sick jerk," I whispered, shaking my head. "She has a last name."

I lifted the file out and put it in my bag, then slid that drawer back into place. Wondering if there was anything else here I could use, I went to the *W*s on a hunch. I flicked through, faster now, looking for Worthington, James, to see if he had a file for James's dad.

Nothing there either. But if he liked to file people the way he thought of them . . .

I went to the *M*s. Bingo. Mayor Worthington. The file was thin, but I removed it, slipping it into my bag.

Now it was time to get out of this dodgy lab.

Weaving back through the counters and equipment, I clicked the button on my phone to take photos blindly, hoping I'd get useful shots to show Perry.

I paused. The only thing left was the tank. Should I risk it?

I'd come this far. One slow step and then another toward it, and I lifted the camera.

The body in the tank shifted.

I froze, every muscle at tense attention. My ears roared. I should have left as soon as I had the file.

The man in the tank had a small smile on his face, and I hadn't realized before that he had his hand in his pocket. He removed it, and gazed down at his fist. His fingers unclenched.

I squinted. He held a small plastic bag, and inside it were—I strained to see—small white shapes.

Pills. It was a small plastic bag filled with pills. He smiled down at them, then replaced the bag in his pocket. His free hand reached to circle the wrist he usually wore the tracker on, the gesture familiar. His eyes drifted shut.

Time for me to get out of there. But I hesitated at the door and turned, raising my phone. I should get one shot of the tank. Maybe someone else could explain what the double was doing in there.

I pressed the button to take the photo, and his eyes popped open. He stared straight at me from the soft glow of the blue liquid.

Whether or not he actually *saw* me was anyone's guess. Maybe he was asleep and dreaming. But his eyes stayed open and it felt like he was looking at me. I did what anyone would do if a creepy doppelgänger was staring straight at them from inside his oddity tank.

I ran, hoping he couldn't set himself free.

CHAPTER 15

I wouldn't hear if he pursued me or not, not unless he shouted—at least, I didn't think I would be able to. Not with how my feet pounded down the wood stairs, no effort made to be a quiet ghost anymore, and the way my ears kept roaring in something that might be terror.

But no shadow fell over me. I didn't see or hear anything except for myself flying down, down, down, my feet thudding on the stairs.

I reached the bottom, vaulted across the lobby to the door, and shoved. The door resisted, as immovable as if I was fighting to shove a hundred-foot-tall wall of ancient stone out of my way. I tried again, pressing hard. It still wouldn't budge. And the locking mechanism I'd picked on the way in had no visible access point on this side.

"Crap, crappity, *crap*," I said quietly, though at this point, who was I kidding? If the double in the tank was aware and not dreaming, then what he was aware of was my presence here. Whether he could follow me or not, he would have seen me, standing in front of his aquatic cage, taking his photograph.

All of which brought up another question I didn't want to deal with yet, not until I was out of here, safe and sound. But the question came anyway, looming too large to ignore: What was he? Normal men didn't climb into glowing blue tanks or wear wristband trackers or report back to their mad scientist master in respectful tones.

Not that I'd thought he was normal. I'd thought he could imitate the appearance of others.

But this was different than that. *He* was something different.

I shivered involuntarily—so yeah, what I felt beneath it all was definitely terror, terror at being trapped in here with whatever-he-was. I forced myself to take a steadying breath, sucking it into my nose slowly, and letting it out the same way.

It helped. Then I considered the door. The immovable-as-an-ancient-wall-of-stone door. It was, after all, the only way I was getting out of here. I switched on my phone's flashlight app and searched every inch, starting at the top and working my way down. I resisted the urge to rush as best I could. I didn't want to miss the magic lock-release on this side.

Nothing, nothing, nothing . . .

Not until I reached the bottom, and there, just above the floor, a small latch protruded that looked almost homemade. It was a brassy gold in color, shaped like a shell.

I bent, held my breath, and turned it. Then I pressed both hands flat against the door.

It swung free. "Turning random knobs for a thousand," I said, and stood.

The beeping began the moment my left foot crossed the threshold. As I left the building, the beep gave way to a whirring sound that was swallowed by the door closing behind me.

I didn't turn back. And Taxi Jack, bless him, didn't wait for me to run across the street. He peeled away from the curb, car rocketing over the twenty feet between us before it jerked to a halt and, out the open passenger window, he barked: "I thought you were done for! Get in!"

"I thought you'd never ask." I practically dove into the backseat.

He squealed away as soon as my door was shut.

"What happened?" he asked. "There was some weird guy who came out and I thought for sure you were—"

"Shhh—" I said, then softened it to, "just a sec."

He seemed legitimately concerned about my well-being. That was kind of sweet. I'd assumed our sometime-alliance was purely cash based on his part.

I fumbled out my phone. SmallvilleGuy would be going crazy. So crazy he might have alerted my friends, and the last thing I needed was them showing up here.

I stabbed the spot on my home screen where the chat app waited, but nothing happened. I squinted.

Nothing happened, because the icon was gone.

"What? No no no," I groaned.

All of my apps were gone.

My contact numbers were gone.

And gone too were the photos I'd taken in the lab upstairs.

Nothing remained in the image library. The only thing left was three bars of cell service.

"That noise." I punched the seat, stuffing my phone back in my bag.

"You okay, sweetheart?" the cabbie asked, and he slowed a fraction, foot off the gas.

"Don't slow down. Go. Faster than ever." I rattled off my parents' address and looked at the dashboard clock. I hadn't been in there *that* long. It just felt like I had.

I was riding the threshold of the half-hour, but surely SmallvilleGuy would grant me a grace period. I didn't have his cell number, and he didn't have mine. He'd contact Devin if he couldn't reach me, most likely. Devin wasn't prone to overreaction.

I could try to call Devin myself, let him know I was okay. But we weren't that far from our home sweet brownstone, and traffic was remarkably clear. I could contact everyone from home.

It would all be fine. Tense, but fine. Poor SmallvilleGuy.

I pressed the promised cash—plus a big tip—into Jack's hand when he pulled up at the curb in front of our apartment.

He said, "Hon, take it from me, you don't need to be going back to that kind of place again." He paused. "But if you do, make sure you call your pal. I'll look out for you."

With that, he waved me off and eased away from the curb.

"I'm touched," I told his brake lights.

Then I walked-but-didn't-run, barely, to the door and inside.

My parents were huddled around the landline phone in the living room, the receiver pressed to my dad's ear, and my mom sagged in visible relief when she saw me walk through the door. "Oh, thank god! Here she is, she's okay," she said.

Dad was in uniform, and not relieved, it seemed. He gripped the receiver tighter and said, "Can I ask again who this is and why you thought Lois was in trouble?"

Oh. My. God. He hadn't called Devin or the *Scoop*. He'd called here. My parents.

I crossed the room, knowing my face had gone bright red, and tried to snatch the receiver from my dad. "Please let me have the phone," I said. "This is my fault."

Mom gave him a significant look, and his fingers uncurled. But both of them stood there watching me closer than close as I took the receiver and held it up to my ear.

"Lois?" an almost-familiar voice asked. "Is that you? Are you really okay? I know this is against the rules, but I didn't know what to do."

I wanted to sink to the floor and hold the phone as tightly to my ear as possible. To hear his voice, drink it in, learn it so well I'd recognize it anywhere, anytime.

We talked in the game, of course, but that was different. The audio washed our voices out, made them vaguely digital. This was his real voice. I had a sudden case of envy for my parents and every generation before us that had talked on the phone instead of texting or gaming together.

"Lois?" he asked again. "Say something. You're okay, right?"

"I'm fine," I said, with a laugh more breathless than I wanted it to be. My mom exchanged a look with my dad, one of their patented "parents see all" looks. I turned away from them, pressing the phone against my cheek. "Sorry I scared you. It's just . . ." I steadied myself. "It's the way the game's played. You lose."

"The game," he said.

There was a pause, both of us breathing, my parents watching, and yet, I didn't want to hang up. I didn't want to go, and maybe he didn't either.

He said, "As long as you're all right, I win."

There was a faint click. I took a deep breath, let it out, then turned and handed my mom the receiver back.

"Sorry about that," I said carefully. I didn't know how much he'd said to them, how much they knew.

"And what was that, exactly?" my dad asked, and it wasn't a question. It was a quiet demand.

"So much for privacy," I said.

"Is that your boyfriend?" my mom put in, too eagerly.

I must have been as red as the sun. Call the fire department to come put me out.

"Mom," I said.

"Well?" she asked. "I don't like him scaring us, if it is."

"He's just a friend. What did he tell you that scared you so much?"

"That our baby girl, so gifted at getting herself in trouble, might be in danger," she said.

"He said that you *were* in danger, Lois," Dad added. "He almost gave us both a heart attack."

Poor parents. If they had any idea where I'd been and why he'd risked calling them, they probably would go straight past heart attacks and all the way into rigor mortis.

"I'm fine, as you can see," I said. Their reactions made it seem like he hadn't had a chance to say much of the incriminating variety. "It was just a prank. A game some of us play. I think I had him worried." I paused and shrugged. "You know me. Can't resist a good prank."

"Yes," my mom said thoughtfully, "we do."

"The caller ID said private," Dad said. "Who was that?"

Gulp. Think fast, Lois. "A friend—I met him at one of those schools in, uh, Ohio. He's in a game I play online with some of my friends here. We're just friends."

Neither one of them looked convinced by my explanation, but they let me pass to go upstairs. Lucy was tucked against the wall about halfway up. "It's all right," I told her. "I'm not in trouble."

"They were freaked," she said. "Don't get us both put under surveillance."

"I'll do my best," I said. She nodded, spun, and bolted up the stairs and into her room.

I needed to get to the game. Heading into my room, I locked the door behind me, unslung my bag, and put on my earpiece in moments. I pressed it on and . . .

There I was, in the fake world that felt so real. SmallvilleGuy was there, but so was Devin.

Devin sported his in-game guise, decked out in chainmail and royal threads, topped with his King Devin crown. "He was just filling me in," he said. "You shouldn't have done that alone."

"You could've stopped me," I countered.

"Yeah, right." He crossed his arms in front of his chest.

"Okay, probably not, but I'm fine." I looked at SmallvilleGuy then. He was standing there, staring at me. He was drinking me in with an intensity that was . . . intense.

I swallowed. "I found him. Them. The scientist, and the double of James's dad."

Or whatever he was.

"Really?" Devin let out a low whistle, and it reminded me of the serial killerish tune our mad scientist had made while I'd cowered on the stairs, waiting to and hoping not to get caught.

I must have shown that disconcerting flash of memory somehow—the game and its ability to capture emotion could be good *and* bad—because SmallvilleGuy took a step closer to me and put his hand on my forearm.

It helped. I felt steadier. But no, not really. I wasn't steady. Not anything like steady.

The touch stopped helping. A tremble started in my hands. I remembered the double's eyes popping open in that ghostly blue liquid. I remembered running and shoving against that immovable door, trapped inside with him. My breath grew shallower.

Devin looked from SmallvilleGuy to me and said, "You can catch me up later. I'm just glad you're all right."

He didn't sound certain that I was. And he was gone before I could protest. But I was glad that he left. I didn't like showing weakness, not to anybody. A problem, because right this second, I felt weak.

I started walking toward the turret. The closer I got, the more I hurried. Because the shakiness was still there. It wouldn't stay behind, no matter how much faster I moved.

The game wasn't the full dark of night yet, and so the torches inside the turret weren't lit. The interior was full of shadows, the only light provided by twilight coming in through the two openings far above. I *had* to stop when I got inside. There was nowhere else to go.

I stood, breathing, trying to get a grip. I didn't have to ask why I was freaking out now.

The terror had caught up to me.

That had been a close call at the lab.

The man in the tank had seen me. This hadn't been anything like visiting Advanced Research Labs, in the middle of the city and filled with people. Whatever Dabney Donovan and Ismenios Labs were, it wasn't safe to invade. No one there would raise the alarm.

But to finish this, I'd *have* to risk going back there, being seen again.

And I didn't want to. I was afraid to.

Before I knew what was happening, arms surrounded me. Light, gentle, but strong too. SmallvilleGuy pulled me into a hug. I buried my face against his character's T-shirt and closed my eyes. There were no scents in the game, not real ones.

Sometimes your mind would fill in things, like the scent of burning if smoke erupted on the horizon. But we'd never been this close to each other. My mind didn't have anything to fill in.

So I knew this wasn't really real.

But I held on to him despite that, a fist of T-shirt in my hand. His fingers traced a delicate circle on my back.

"Lois," he said after a few minutes, "no pressure, but you're scaring me. What happened to you? How bad? Can you tell me?"

I released his shirt and pulled back. I shook off what was left of my fear. For now.

Most of it, anyway.

Apparently, I'd needed a moment of weakness to process that terror I hadn't let myself feel while it was happening.

"Nothing," I said, steadier. Steadied by him. "Nothing happened to me. But it could've."

I filled him in, getting the appropriate shocked reactions and being grateful that he didn't tell me I shouldn't have done it. I had done what I had to do. Yes, I'd put myself in harm's way. But those files in my bag might be the key to everything. We knew where Donovan was now.

When I finished he said, "You're okay?"

I nodded. "About before . . ."

I broke down in front of him. So far beyond embarrassing. Weak wasn't who I was.

"We'll never speak of it again," he said. "I know you hate that I saw it, but . . . I'm glad you trusted me enough to let me be there for you."

"I shouldn't be afraid, though." I brushed hair back out of my elf eyes. "It's my job not to be. To be strong instead."

"No, it's not," he said. "It's your job to find the truth. I've been thinking about this. Courage doesn't mean never being afraid. We're all afraid sometimes. Bravery means doing the right thing anyway. That's true strength."

I blinked at him. He was earnest, not humoring me.

"That's really smart." I smiled up at him. "Like something I'd say."

"Now that's a compliment. I'm honored," he said, smiling back, hand over his heart. But then his smile slipped away. "And that's also why I have to go, since you're okay. You really are okay, right?"

"I'm okay," I said.

"Good, because it's my turn to do something stupid."

Oh no. He's still going to the sighting.

"Maybe I'm not okay after all," I said.

"Nice try. I'll let you know as soon as I get back. Stay logged in to chat."

And he was gone.

"Be careful," I said to the empty air.

CHAPTER 16

Needless to say, I wasn't going to go straight to sleep after I popped back out of the game, despite the post-adrenaline exhaustion sneaking up on me. For one thing, I was starving. And after I took care of that, I needed to tackle those files and see what goodies they might hold for us. Plus, worry worry worry about SmallvilleGuy going to that sighting until I heard from him again.

I went to the computer and logged in to chat, even though he wouldn't be back for hours. Then, I navigated to Strange Skies and skimmed through the thread. There were four or five other people going to tonight's sighting, according to their posts.

Great. I could be nervous for all of them.

On a whim, I pulled up a new private message window, plugged in TheInventor's handle, and typed him a message.

I strained for a casual tone. We'd never communicated directly, only exchanged the occasional quote-and-response on threads.

PM from **SkepticGirl1** *to* **TheInventor**: Hey, I hear you're helping SG in trying to track down the goods about this random Insider01 posting on the boards. Thanks for that. I don't like the sound of these agents either. But, you know, if you have any pull to tell SG to be careful, well, then do. I'd appreciate it.

If TheInventor told SmallvilleGuy about this message, hopefully he wouldn't take it the wrong way. Guys could be unpredictable, and I suspected sometimes they listened to each other more than to girls. Not that SmallvilleGuy seemed guilty of that—he was too smart—but it couldn't hurt to have two voices urging caution. That was my operating theory.

I waited in case TheInventor responded right away. My mental picture of him was surrounded by computers and tech equipment in some dank sub-level somewhere, rarely willing to leave and be exposed to sunlight. In which case, he'd be sitting at his monitor, as usual. When he didn't respond after a couple of minutes, I clicked the tab shut and went downstairs to forage for food.

My mom was in the kitchen, so I almost turned around and went back upstairs, but it was too late. She'd seen me.

"Lois," she said. "Hungry?"

"Pretty much always," I admitted.

"There's some leftover spaghetti." She'd already started dishing it into a bowl, and she put it in the microwave when she finished. She leaned a hip against the counter while it heated.

"Lois," she said.

With reluctance, I looked over at her.

She bit her lip against a grin, seeming highly amused. Then she said, "There's nothing wrong with liking a boy. Really. Your dad may not agree, but I think it's a good thing. I know moving has been hard on you girls."

Arghhhhh. "Mom, we're not talking about this. He's just a friend, I promise. It's just a game some of us like to play."

"Uh-huh," she said. "You'll come to me if it's something else, though? So we can talk. I know you kids know everything these days, but come to me when you need to."

The microwave dinged off and she opened the door. I reached in to get the pasta and flee this deathly embarrassing scene.

"Promise you will?" she asked. "It'll be just between us."

"I won't be able to, because I'll be dead of mortification. But my ghost will come talk to you." I twirled spaghetti around the fork and took a bite. "I, um, appreciate the offer, though, Mom. Also, this is delish."

She allowed me to leave, and I ate half the bowl before I got upstairs. The rest I inhaled back at my desk. Still nothing from TheInventor.

I dumped the files onto my bed and started on Melody's.

Subject: Pretty Blond Girl, age 14, identical twin.

Neurological profile and DNA markers most promising of samples taken to date. Age may be a factor, given that the suitability of those closer to adulthood has proved weaker. Sample one of PBG's blood showed signs of receptivity to the duplicating serum, and thus far the cell integrity is holding. However, there are also signs of a potential equivalent or cousin to quantum connection's spooky action at a distance. Einstein may have been a skeptic that such connections could exist between molecules, and would undoubtedly deny the phenomenon would be possible between two minds. However, this apparent tendency seems to bear out more recent work, as well as my own theorem about remnant spooky action and reaction in such cases. The manifestations of those effects will require further observation, but I theorize they will be limited to the empathy centers in the anterior insular cortex. They could foster a potentially unhealthy mental connection between the donor and the duplicate. A treatment to sever such ties in the donor is simple enough, but impossible to execute without the donor's knowledge. Therefore, I have begun work on a medicinal regimen that should halt the effects in the duplicate and thus suppress symptoms in the donor. This regimen I now see as a potential boon, given the client's demands. It would allow for an interesting potential behavioral corrective and help to ensure compliance in the duplicate, if I am correct, and I usually am . . .

More blah sciences punctuated with asides about "if my suspicions prove correct" and "if this theorem is as meritorious as I believe" that bugged me for a reason I couldn't identify. Finally, I reached a line that made me understand why, even if I was still struggling with the larger meaning of the notes:

Truly I am a genius. The duplication process will prove it, and once it is known, once the world is ready, all will say Einstein exists in my shadow.

Oh, *that* was it. Normal scientific notes were objective, right? They didn't include a lot of "I" and discussion about how wonderful and perfect and *genius* the scientist was.

Not surprising, given his chosen areas of interest—the ones we knew about—but off-putting. This was not any guy I wanted to meet alone on a darkened staircase. But his notes and the way he referred to Melody as PBG made me feel stabby enough that my lingering fear had begun to fade.

And what was this? There was one last note made, hastily added at the end of the file.

I have told the donor to alert me if she experiences any side effects. However, this should not be an issue. I have confirmed that I can control them at my end of the tether, with the daily dosing regimen, so the donor should detect no difference in her daily life. There is a method that would halt the connectivity permanently in the donor, which would require but a single session. But as suspected it would be impossible to administer without arousing the donor's suspicion, and while she has no authority or power to raise any alarm, that would be best avoided. After consultation with my client, we have concurred it will be more advantageous to use these "side effects" as an added mechanism of controlling the duplicate by administering the daily regimen to suppress them. Its reaction will allow greater psychological study of the duplicate ~~itself~~himself.

Hmmm. It sounded like there was some way to cure Melody of her so-called quantum connectivity—an unhealthy connection to be sure—in one swoop. The rest I didn't fully understand, but I was beginning to have a sinking feeling about the continued references to *duplication* and the *duplicate*. Especially that last part, the strikeout to change *itself* to *himself*.

Could it mean . . .

But I heard Perry's voice in my head: "A good reporter makes leaps of logic, but doesn't believe they are the same as fact without proof." I closed the folder about Melody and opened the one about James's dad.

Mayor Worthington. Male, 44 years old. Subject for duplication.

I shook my head as I read on.

Background: During the solicitation of funds to continue my research (having been unjustly deprived of the resources that used to be available to me), Mr. Mannheim agreed to become my benefactor, providing space and funds for my work. However, the deal is contingent on my assistance with an untenable problem of his. He is not interested in science for science's sake (more's the pity), but he does like its practical applications. The current mayor has proven problematic to my benefactor's agenda. He must be replaced. I saw at once how it could be done, and my benefactor was very impressed by the novelty of the idea. He brought Mayor Worthington to tour my laboratory, and the man hardly seemed impressed. I attempted to convince him to provide adequate samples by telling him I am researching the qualities of great men, but he refused. No matter, for Mister Mannheim is quite resourceful; he was able to secure the DNA sample I needed by applying adequate pressure to Mayor Worthington's personal physician. At Mister Mannheim's request, the duplication serum and sample have now been prepared to attempt my greatest work. I do not even feel nervous, so certain am I that this will succeed.

The trick, you see, is that the serum must hold the right properties. Yes, you must tell it what form the duplicate should take, but it cannot be produced by a DNA sample from the individual to be duplicated alone. You must add it to the serum first, which was created using sample 112 from subject PBG. Only then is the possibility born, along with the duplicate itself.

WHOA. And then, dated two days later . . .

My Frankenstein's monster yet lives, and he is identical to Mayor Worthington, as promised. He possesses the same mental faculties, but none of the troublesome memories. Meaning he feels no tie to the Mayor and will do as he is told. He can read the scripts provided, and the client is going to put him to the test tomorrow. I have prepared a tracker to be worn on his person, which I have assured him means he will never be lost, that I will always be able to find him.

I imagined for a moment that he looked troubled, but of course he did not. I am his creator. His god. He needs the reassurance that I will be here for him, and I shall. He is my greatest work to date. The first living clone of an existing human being.

There were a few pages more about the subject's performance on his initial assignment, which was to make a recording imitating James's dad. There was also a cross-reference tag in the notes that seemed to indicate most information about the duplicate was in a dedicated file. As it should be. It—*he*— deserved a file of his own.

Because I'd answered my own question about *what* the man in the tank was.

He was a clone.

A clone of James's dad, created with some sort of serum produced from Melody's blood in order to frame the mayor. Currently, it seemed he was being used to threaten the ex-mayor into continuing to stay silent.

I still couldn't understand why Mayor Worthington hadn't fought back at the time. That was a question I'd have to put to him directly.

But I believed the notes when they said Melody's problem *was* fixable. Awful as this scientist guy was, he clearly *was* a genius. If a far less savory one than Einstein.

Shuffling the pages back together, I noticed one last section of notes on the back sheet. I'd almost missed it.

My creature must now remain inactive, but I have vowed to Boss that I will keep him alive in case his services should be needed again. And once it is safe, I could always wake him for further study. The effect of such a period in and of itself will be a fascinating subject to explore. For now, I fear, he must sleep in peace.

And then a date two weeks ago: *Subject reactivated with minimal difficulty, per request of Boss. Conditioning underway to ensure his readiness to fulfill the purpose for which he was created. I have begun to dose him once more with the daily regimen to suppress connectivity.*

It was followed by another tag referring back to the main file on the duplicate.

Inactive? Was that what being in the tank was? Had the double been on blue-glow ice for two years, until now? It sounded that way. The question was why the side effects had emerged if he was being dosed. Perhaps it had something to do with being in the tank for so long . . . But wait. I remembered the bag the double had removed from his pocket. The round white pills inside. He wasn't taking the antidote. That was why.

Interesting too that Dr. Donovan had become more familiar about how he referred to Boss Moxie, from Mr. Mannheim to Boss in his notes in two short years.

I wanted to tell everyone what I'd learned. I wanted to show someone the proof, have them agree that however crazy the idea of a clone walking and talking and being used to frame a mayor was, all the signs pointed to that as the right conclusion.

But SmallvilleGuy wasn't back yet, TheInventor hadn't answered my PM, and I was missing every single phone number from my contacts. In fact, I wasn't even sure my phone still worked. I picked it up and dialed our landline number, heard the phone downstairs ring.

I'd just need to restore and re-enter everything from the last backup my phone had stored in the cloud. Based on what I'd read from Dabney Donovan's notes, he wouldn't be worried about stealing my data with his little gizmo. The beep and whir I'd heard was undoubtedly some kind of data-erase, devoted to preventing the theft of his vaunted ideas and research by wiping anything in the data memory of a device that visited his lab. Since he only used paper records, his own information would never be impacted.

He'd overlooked the fact that I could walk out with paper.

Cockiness led to mistakes. Pretty much always, in my experience.

There was one thing I'd have to manually restore, though. The backup wouldn't cover the secure chat app, a security measure of TheInventor's software. So I searched through my email archive until I found the private, password-protected link to download it, and started the installation process. Once I keyed in the password, I was in for an age of waiting for the installation to finish.

And that's what I did. I lay on my bed and stared up at the ceiling, thinking over what I'd learned and mulling next moves, waiting . . .

★

I woke the next morning with a start. There was no alarm, no noise to blame as the cause. I was in my clothes from the day before. My mouth tasted like old spaghetti.

I'd fallen asleep waiting—for the app to install and for SmallvilleGuy's safe return from the sighting. I jumped to my feet and scrambled to my computer. Like me, my computer had fallen asleep, so I had to rouse it to see the chat window. I also had to log back in, due to inactive time. There were a few messages waiting, but I didn't bother to read them before typing in mine.

SkepticGirl1: *Hey, I fell asleep like a stupid and just woke up and argh please tell me you're okay. Tell me you're here and everything's fine.*

Only after my message posted did I scroll up.

SmallvilleGuy: *Made it back. Must be something in the air—it was a close call for me too.*

SmallvilleGuy: *Hey, you there? Lois?*

He'd tried a couple more times, which made me feel terrible. But pure energy surged and shoved that aside when I saw a new message pop up below mine.

SmallvilleGuy: *You're not a stupid. And you probably needed the sleep.*

SmallvilleGuy: *Me, I didn't get much last night.*

SkepticGirl1: *Tell me. What happened? You had a close call? Did someone see you? Did the agents see you?*

Something occurred to me that might be worse than federal agents.

SkepticGirl1: *Did your parents know where you were going? They didn't catch you, did they?*

SmallvilleGuy: *As we expected, there was no flying man sighted. There were four people from the boards there . . . at least I assume they were from the boards. They got collared by four agents who I heard ID themselves as a "classified federal interagency task force," whatever that means. They interrogated the four, asking specifics about if they'd seen the flying man before and for details, times and dates, specific locations. Whether or not they'd been close enough to describe his facial features. No one was.*

SkepticGirl1: *How did you almost get caught?*

SkepticGirl1: *And, wait, how did you hear all that? How close were you?*

SmallvilleGuy: *Close enough. There were four agents who confronted the posters who showed up, but there were actually five agents there. One of them was sweeping the woods around the coordinates. He almost found me. I managed to move fast enough to get away.*

SkepticGirl1: *Whew. Did your parents know you went there?*

SmallvilleGuy: *They didn't. It makes me feel so guilty. They're the most honest people in the world. But . . .*

SkepticGirl1: *But?*

He was typing again, so I took a quick jaunt into my attached bathroom to brush my teeth. Yesterday's spaghetti was gross, even if he wasn't here in person to tell me my breath reeked.

I eased back into my chair to catch up.

SmallvilleGuy: *They don't know about Strange Skies. I don't think they'd approve of me hanging there if they did.*

I was nodding in sympathy.

SkepticGirl1: *Especially not with federal agents sniffing around. If my dad knew I'd shared anything about what happened to us that night, he'd flip. Like, completely. Like, I would need to dig a tunnel to leave my room probably.*

SmallvilleGuy: *Right. They mean well. They want us safe.*

SmallvilleGuy: *There's more bad news, related to that.*

My palms felt clammy.

SkepticGirl1: *What is it?*

SmallvilleGuy: *TheInventor was waiting when I got back last night and I gave him a report. He had some information to share in return.*

Uh-oh.

I hoped SmallvilleGuy wasn't mad that I'd messaged his friend.

SmallvilleGuy: *He's afraid that maybe his firewalls and security precautions aren't as impenetrable as he thought. And he's got evidence that someone—I think we know it has to be this interagency task force—is trying to break them. The only reason they could want to do that is to identify the users on the boards.*

SkepticGirl1: *Wow, that is bad news.*

SmallvilleGuy: *The worst.*

SkepticGirl1: *We can't just give this up. Not the boards.*

And not each other.

I was developing a suspicion about why SmallvilleGuy was so concerned about the fake sightings and the feds, why his parents would freak. But he wasn't ready for me to know if my suspicion was right, and so I would keep it to myself.

SmallvilleGuy: *Agreed. TheInventor wants us to meet up in the game later and discuss, after he does a little more homework.*

TheInventor had only ever helped us. But I didn't quite trust him. I couldn't explain why. So for now, if SmallvilleGuy did, that would have to be good enough for me.

SkepticGirl1: *All right. Just tell me when. I'll be there.*

SmallvilleGuy: *Good. I wasn't positive you'd say yes. But we need to come up with a way to get rid of this fake poster and his pals, and he can help us.*

SkepticGirl1: *We do. And we will. Because if my parents find out about those posts, if my dad does . . . I'll lose this.*

What I meant: *You. I'll lose you.* Dad would monitor everything I did from then on.

SmallvilleGuy: *Speaking of parents, what'd you tell yours about who I was after the call?*

I swallowed and typed out: *My mom thinks we're dating. What do you think of that? Too ridiculous? Because it might be nice if it was true.*

Then I deleted the words, backspace backspace backspace.

SkepticGirl1: *That you're from Ohio and we met when I went to school there. That we're friends who game together and I was tormenting you. They bought it.*

A subject change was what I needed at this moment, and I had the perfect one. The file folders were still spread across my bed. With the drama of SmallvilleGuy's late night adventures and TheInventor's intel, I'd nearly forgotten. Or maybe I thought I'd dreamed the answer. But I had to tell him.

SkepticGirl1: *So. Those files I took from Ismenios dude. You won't believe this, but . . .*

SkepticGirl1: *The ex-mayor was set up by that mobster Boss Moxie using a clone. The double is an actual double. An identical duplicate of Mayor Worthington made via some science whizbang using Melody's DNA and the mayor's.*

There was no response for a long moment, and I thought I'd finally sailed the boat of crazy one league too far.

SmallvilleGuy: *Good thing our lives aren't complicated.*

I snorted.

SkepticGirl1: *Isn't it though?*

SmallvilleGuy: *I have to go, but we'll talk more later, k?*

SkepticGirl1: *Later.*

I was in danger of running late for school, but I didn't rush to get ready. Instead I made sure the chat app was reinstalled on my phone (it was), then navigated to the Strange Skies site.

He must not have seen this yet.

The scourge using the handle Insider01 had already announced the next sighting. The location was just outside Wichita, Kansas—37°53'32.63"N, 97°39'14.59"W, to be precise—and the local time was given as 7 p.m. Thursday, the next night.

Why were they still doing this? They couldn't have gotten anything that helped them the night before, could they? And if they cracked the boards' security, they'd have everything they wanted.

I went to close the browser, but noticed a small number 1 on top of my PM box. I clicked, and saw that TheInventor had responded to my message.

PM from **TheInventor** *to* **SkepticGirl1**: I could tell him to be as cautious as I am, but I think we both know that it wouldn't matter. If he was going to listen to anyone, he'd listen to you. I feel we are going to make a good team to get rid of this threat that plagues us all. Best, A

CHAPTER 17

Maddy finished stashing her books inside her locker, clicked the royal blue door shut, and spun the combination lock. She turned to find Devin and me standing behind her. Her T-shirt said Nervous Takedown.

We must have been wearing "serious business" expressions, because she held out her wrists like we were police who might cuff them.

"I should've known I'd get caught, officers," she said. "Today's the day you finally take me away."

"Haha," I said. "Ha."

She lowered her wrists. "To what do I owe this dramatic interruption on the way to lunch?"

"Lois thought it was best not to give you too much warning," Devin said, not that helpfully.

I gave him a dose of side-eye before answering Maddy. "It's time to bring everyone up to speed." Devin, of course, already knew I'd been to the locations and gotten the goods—but not yet what the goods were. "I know what's going on with your sister and how it connects to James's dad."

She swallowed. "Shouldn't we wait until after school? Melody would probably rather come by the office."

I started walking in the direction of the cafeteria, joining the streaming traffic of students around us. Neither of them protested.

I waited until Maddy was on one side, and Devin was on my other. Maddy and Melody's relationship was a delicate thing to balance against the larger story, but in this case I had come to the conclusion that caution would have to be tossed into the wind. I had the other relevant party—James's dad—to brief later.

Not to mention, Perry still had no idea any of this was going on.

I told her, "Your sister's worries about being seen with the likes of us will have to wayside. I have other plans for after school. And you have a date, remember?"

"What if she ignores us?" Maddy said, only flushing a little at the mention of her date.

Devin nodded. "It could happen, Lois."

I heard what he didn't say outright. He wanted to make sure I'd thought through how Maddy would feel if Melody snubbed us in front of everyone.

"Nope," I said. She wouldn't do that to her sister, would she? I didn't think so. "I checked out her social accounts."

Melody's fixation on popularity was so strange to me, I'd figured this was the equivalent of a background check. "It's what you said the other day about popularity, Devin. Melody's is the second kind. She carefully curates everything she does. Every outfit, every selfie she snaps, every status update. They're all so . . . crafted. She's not a mean girl, even if she can turn on the snob factor. She doesn't joke around. She wants to be perfect, unattainable, untouchable."

"Tell me about it," Maddy muttered.

"But no one is all that, not really. So it's an act," I said. "She's just afraid someone will notice if she's hanging out with us. That they might discover something she doesn't want them to see, something she didn't choose to show. She won't risk making a scene once it's clear that's going to happen no matter what. I already gave James the heads-up that we're coming to get her. He'll play along."

We were near the point of no return, aka the cafeteria doors, when Maddy grabbed my arm. "Even if you're right, she'll never forgive me," she said. "Not for messing up the act."

"She will." I sounded more confident than I felt. But I wanted to figure out what had distanced the sisters from each other. I wanted to help them bridge that distance. They clearly cared for each other—at least, Maddy clearly cared for Melody. That was enough for me to want them to be friends as well as sisters. Even if they'd never be best friends. "Were you guys close when you were little?" I asked.

"What does that have to do with anything?" she asked.

I waited.

She smoothed her streaked hair behind her ear. "Yes."

"How old were you when that stopped?"

"I don't know, twelve and a half." Maddy shrugged, but her specificity gave her away. She must know the precise instant. "Or sometime around then. I think."

So, seventh grade. A crucible that many relationships did not survive. Hadn't Melody said Maddy ditched piano lessons around then too?

"Good to know. Let's do this."

"Enter, miladies," Devin said, stepping out front and pushing open the cafeteria doors for us. We'd managed to wait until the rest of the students in our period were inside, many of them already ensconced at their usual tables. That included Melody and her cluster of popular perfection, which included James, and another similarly glossy-toothed guy I didn't know, and three smiling, chatting girls.

I took a handful of Maddy's shirt in my fist to prevent her from bolting as we approached. "I'm not going to run *now*," she said under her breath.

"I know," I countered. "Because I'm not letting go of your shirt."

James had been watching for us, because he lifted a hand in greeting when we reached the table. A redhead in glasses aimed a coy smile at one member of our party. "Hi, Devin, what's up?"

I recognized her from Melody's social media as a girl who juggled cheerleading squad with Latin Club *and* a handful of charities. She'd posted a photo of herself and Melody volunteer bathing extremely cute, extremely shaggy dogs. The photo had made me like Melody more. An act that included helping out at a dog shelter hopefully wasn't *entirely* an act.

"Hey, Clara," Devin said. "We need to borrow James."

"And Melody," I added. "Impromptu staff meeting."

Melody hadn't said a word.

Clara blinked at her. "You didn't tell me you were joining the *Scoop*."

"She's not," Maddy put in.

I moved to the left, so I was closer to James. "Operation exit strategy."

James chimed in. "I asked Melody for some input on what types of stories we should cover, what students really want to read. I take it we're focus grouping now?"

"Oh," Clara said, "I'd love to do that too. No one covers the school's charity efforts. I can come now, if you want."

"No!" Melody blurted. And when silence descended on everyone, she seemed to realize she'd practically shrieked it. She patted Clara's shoulder, then stood up. "That's an excellent idea. I'll bring it up. But I wouldn't dream of volunteering your lunch hour." When Clara still looked offended, she added, "Not when Seth's here."

That effectively shut up Clara, but she didn't blush. She smiled at Seth, who returned it. So much for her interest in Devin. Nicely played, Melody Simpson.

But it made sense. Melody's act was carefully calibrated, which meant taking in everything around her at all times.

I could not understand why she'd ever gotten mixed up with the very shady Ismenios Labs in the first place.

Melody pushed her chair in and attached herself to James's side as we left in a group. "Were the theatrics necessary?" she asked me.

"I didn't know any other way to get you to come peacefully," I said.

"I told her you wouldn't like it." Maddy didn't look over at us, but clearly she was listening to each and every syllable.

We headed toward the corner table where Maddy and I usually sat, sometimes joined by Devin. Or, other times, by Anavi, the girl we'd helped with a bullying problem, who I considered a friend now too. These days, though, Anavi was usually hanging out with her next-door neighbor friend Will. They'd buried the gaming hatchet, and from how much Anavi was talking soccer, I wouldn't be surprised if they were hooking up soon. I scanned the crowd for her, and saw the two of them laughing together.

With Queen Melody in our midst, we earned some curious looks, but Melody didn't turn back or protest again. Devin broke off to go retrieve a pizza for us since it was Wednesday, aka the only day you could put in delivery orders to come into the cafeteria. At our table, I steered Melody to the head, and sat down at her right side. James and Maddy took seats opposite me. Surprising me again, James didn't claim the one beside Melody, but left it to Maddy. In fact, he pulled it out for her. What was going on there?

But my train of thought was interrupted by Melody.

"What is this?" she asked, steelier now.

"You're not worried about being seen with us?" Maddy asked.

"James is here," Melody said with a half-shrug.

But James didn't look thrilled with that response. "Lois," he said, "let's get this over with. Come on, tell us. What did you find out?"

"Okay," I said, "well." I waved Devin toward us when I spotted him, waiting so I wouldn't have to tell them twice. He slid a pizza box into the center of the table and then himself into a seat. None of us moved to eat. If this was a focus group, it was a deadly serious one.

"This is all going to sound crazy, so just be aware. But I have actual documents from Dabney Donovan's relocated lab that confirms it all. Plus, I saw . . . things." I managed to suppress a visible shudder, barely, remembering the double in the tank.

"Things, got it," James said. He leaned farther across the table. "Tell us what they were."

"Here's the bottom-line all around: Melody's blood and DNA sample were used to make some sort of serum. And the serum was used to, well, clone James's dad, in order to solve a problem for Boss Moxie. Apparently Mayor Worthington was proving troublesome for the Boss. So Dabney Donovan creates the clone, and then the clone is used to set up James's dad. Donovan needed a bankroll for his shady research, and Moxie was it." I paused. That about covered it, in truth. "Who's got questions?"

They were quiet for a moment, and I thought maybe I was

going to get off easy. But then they started asking questions in a staccato, overlapping fashion. This must be what the mayor felt like at press conferences.

"A clone? But why?" James asked.

"My mom would kill to see Boss Moxie nailed to the wall. Evidence?" asked Devin.

Maddy said, "But why does Melody have side effects?"

And Melody, getting to the heart of it: "Is there a cure or am I stuck this way?"

At least no one questioned the basic facts. That was trust. I'd been prepared to lay out my case, divulge every detail in the files. I was touched.

So I took their questions in order, starting with James. "Okay. Why. From what I can tell, maybe just because Donovan showed up with a request for an investor. Moxie had a need and the solution Donovan came up with, to get his money and lab space, was a clone. It was just perverse enough for Moxie to love it. And it makes sense. The prints, the voice recordings, photos. All the physical evidence that could possibly be needed to make the case against your dad ironclad. Who would jump to this conclusion? It's the perfect frame job set-up."

"But still, I don't get why," James said. He sounded quiet, upset. "What kind of trouble was Dad being that Boss Moxie would go to all this effort?"

"That's something I plan to ask your dad after school today. Don't let him know to expect it. I want his real reaction. Sound good?"

"Fine by me."

I shifted to face Devin. "Evidence. Well, not enough yet, but your mom would make a great ally. We should keep her in mind as we try to get more proof. It would be nice if Boss Moxie went down for this, and also safer for us."

I hoped. Because what would the mob boss do if he was free and found out what we were up to?

"Deal," Devin said.

I was in over my head. I knew it. I couldn't let it stop me. But I had to be honest with these guys. Make sure they understood.

Next up was Maddy. "The side effects have to do with some sort of quantum connection between a part of the double's brain and Melody's. I don't really understand it, something about empathy centers and spooky action at a vantage point, or that's not it exactly—"

"Spooky action at a distance?" Melody cut in. "Quantum connection and spooky action at a distance are usually talked about at the atomic level, sometimes computers. You're saying that's what this is?" She paused and bit her lip. Then she went on, "It makes sense now. The spells, that's only the times it's worse. But the past couple of days, I feel those odd feelings, like part of me is here, experiencing my surroundings, but part of me is somewhere else, experiencing other things. I feel it . . . always. The connection. I try to wall it off, not feel it. But it's there. It's been there for the last two weeks. I only feel normal at night. Why?"

"To answer your first question," I began carefully. Maddy's

mouth had dropped open. I guessed she wasn't aware Melody was some kind of science whiz. "There is a cure, I think. The double is supposed to be taking meds every day—"

Melody interrupted again. "To control them. But he hasn't been. Not for the last two weeks. But why wouldn't I have felt something before now? And why am I okay at night?"

I'd been wondering about that too. And about how a man who looked just like the confined ex-mayor would be able to waltz around town with no one ever noticing, even to remark on the resemblance, except for the other day. Mayor Worthington wasn't supposed to have a twin, after all.

"At night, he's in this tank," I said. "And he was 'inactive'— whatever that means—for most of the last two years. Maybe it means he was in the tank the whole time? I think that they only brought him back to wakefulness so he could be used to impress upon James's dad that if he had any plans of trying to reverse the charges, he'd better not try. James, your dad is a threat. Which brings me to the two problems we have."

"Only two?" Devin scoffed.

"Two biggest. One, the nature of the cure isn't entirely clear—" Melody's alarm was plain, so I went on, "—but it is clear there *is* one, and we'll figure that out. Two, we'll have to be cautious, really cautious. Which isn't my strong suit. But . . ." I swallowed, and the double's eyelids popped open in my memory. "There's a chance he knows I was there."

Melody sat back. "He? He who?"

"The double." I flinched when I remembered crouching on the stairs. "And his master. There was a trigger that went off when I left, wiped my phone of everything—including all the photos I took in the lab."

"Huh," Devin said. "That's an interesting idea. It would have to be pretty high-tech to be so specific."

"Stop talking around the real issue." Maddy banged her hand on the table. "I can't believe you did this."

I recoiled. "Maddy, I'm sorry, I—"

"Not you," she said. "My sister. Melody, how could you have been so stupid? Gotten yourself mixed up in this? For what? A few hundred bucks? Why did you do this?"

Melody's face went an interesting shade of red, blood flooding it. If I knew the sensation, and I did, she was consumed with anger. No one could push your buttons like a sibling.

"I needed the money for concert tickets," Melody said finally. "For the Zombies Away, okay? Are you happy now? I know it was dumb."

Maddy's mouth opened and closed and then she said, "But you don't even like them!"

Melody shoved her chair away from the table and jumped to her feet. Her hand trembled on the back of the chair, and I wondered if the double's hand was trembling somewhere else. If he was tempted to push away a chair too. If his heart beat fast, his face flushed with anger.

"They're my favorite band," Melody said, "actually. But I knew how you'd react if I just asked to borrow the money. Just like you're doing now. Like I was trying to take something of yours. I know you'd just quit liking them, for all I know change your entire personality again, and so I got the money another way. I didn't want to risk making you lose something you loved, because of me. Not again."

Then Melody stalked out of the cafeteria. For once, she gave no indication of caring what anyone thought. Which was good, because the tables around us were gleefully discussing and gaping at the scene.

We all just sat there, Maddy breathing hard. When I started to say something, to ask how she was, she held up her hand. "Don't," she said.

To lighten the mood, I said, "But that went so well. Don't you think?"

The mood did not lighten.

CHAPTER 18

Lunch ended on such a disastrous note that I was almost looking forward to biology class afterward. Maybe I could uncover a little more science to understand this whole clone business. Or Melody could teach me later, since she would probably research—whatever she didn't understand about spooky action at a distance already, she would soon enough, if I had my guess.

Turned out there was a *lot* going on beneath her perfect act. That was no surprise at all, actually.

I slipped into my seat at the back of the classroom, and my phone buzzed. Given everything going on, I'd logged in to chat after lunch. I wanted to share how things had gone and see what SmallvilleGuy thought of how I'd handled it.

SmallvilleGuy: *How'd Melody take it?*

Ms. Smits, our teacher, a career East Metropolis High employee who'd been at this for at least twenty years and thus knew every trick in every book, wasn't paying attention yet. She was digging around in her desk. So I chanced tapping out a response.

SkepticGirl1: *Not great. I made her come to our lunch table.*

SmallvilleGuy: *You had to do it somewhere.*

True. And, as usual during our chats, I felt better already. A little.

SkepticGirl1: *Any bright ideas about our boards problem yet?*

SmallvilleGuy: *Nope, but TI wants us to meet him in the game @ 10 tonight.*

I frowned before I even knew why. But once I considered it, the diagnosis came fast.

SkepticGirl1: *How much do you trust him?*

There was no actual indication that TheInventor was a guy. The handle could just as easily belong to a girl. But there was something about the slight defensiveness in the private message he'd sent that read guy to me—and the odd presumptiveness in saying we would be a team. I couldn't put my finger on what it was exactly. A gut feeling.

The truth was we knew *nothing* about TheInventor. I didn't, anyway. That bothered me.

SmallvilleGuy hadn't responded yet.

SkepticGirl1: *I trust you. I'm careful with anybody else. That's all I'm saying.*

I didn't add: *All I'm saying for now.* But I thought it.

"Ahem," Ms. Smits said, and I glanced up to confirm that . . . yep, I was busted.

Phones were allowed in school, but we weren't supposed to use them except between classes and during lunch. Sheepishly, I stowed mine in my messenger bag, on the floor beside the desk.

I heard a buzz of reply from SmallvilleGuy and forced myself to keep staring straight at Ms. Smits. She was in a pale blue pantsuit, from a closet that had to be filled with so many variations on the theme that it would be the envy of any pantsuit fan.

"I know you're all very excited about this momentous, long-awaited occasion," she said.

When no one reacted, she added, "Time for our test on chapter five."

The test was today?

I sighed. Out loud. *Oops.*

Today needed to get its act together and shape up. So did I.

"Everything all right, Ms. Lane?" she asked. "This has been on the schedule since last week. Bad timing for you?"

You could say that. I had completely forgotten about it—including the ever-important studying-for-it part. I had no illusions that this was the response to give her, however.

"Nope," I said. "You're such a good teacher, it's in my DNA by now. Bring on the test."

"Nice flattery. Let's see you back it up," was her response. She placed a test sheet on my desk.

We'd had a Hawthorne quiz in English, and I'd maybe managed a B at best. Being in over my head elsewhere meant that keeping the old GPA up was proving harder than normal this week. The last thing I wanted was something—like dipping grades—that Butler could bring up in our next tête-à-tête or that might give him justification for a meeting with my parents.

I handed in the test at the end of the period with a feeling that I might have passed, if not with flying colors. Ms. Smits was a great teacher, and the building blocks of the natural world weren't dull. As soon as I hit the hallway, I whipped out my phone to read SmallvilleGuy's response.

SmallvilleGuy: *I would never put you at risk. We need his help. See you @ 10.*

I sent back a quick reply.

SkepticGirl1: *I'll get there a few minutes early, so maybe we can talk first.*

The rest of the afternoon proved quiet by comparison, and during last period study hall, I took the opportunity to stay off my phone, not stress about everything stressful, and catch up on homework instead of researching for my story. By near the end of the hour, my ability to sit tight and be good wore off.

And so I unearthed one of five pink authorized hall passes I'd borrowed from Ronda's desk the second week I'd met with Principal Butler. She'd had to go back and see if he was ready for me, and they'd been sitting right on the corner, as tempting as a powdered sugar donut.

I threaded my way through the desks to the teacher's, and waved the pass in front of the thin and pasty Mr. Fowler.

"I need to take off a couple of minutes early today," I said. "An appointment after school." That much was true.

He did not examine or collect the vaunted hall pass. Given his usual lack of commitment to a rigorous study hall (naps were not just okay by him, but almost encouraged), I'd assumed he wouldn't and hadn't bothered to fill it out. I only had a few of these, and needed to make them last.

Out in the hall, I hurried toward the last period class James and Maddy shared. This would allow me to check in with Maddy after the scene at lunch and pick up James for our trip to his house in one fell swoop.

"Ms. Lane, where are you off to in such a hurry?" came a familiarly smarmy voice.

My luck. Rotten, as usual.

"Principal Butler, hi—I have to meet my *Scoop* colleagues. We're having an, um, extra-important staff meeting after school. I was done with my homework, so I asked for permission to leave study hall a little early."

He was shark-like as ever, and he didn't give any indication whether he was about to bust me or not. I shuddered at the thought of another date with detention. And Ronda would get blamed if he was the one who discovered my ill-gotten passes. I had no doubt of that.

"We've got, uh, good rapport now, don't we?" I gritted out the words, but tried not to make them sound gritty. I forced a smile at him. "I was thinking of pitching Perry a piece about all the charity work the school does. What do you think?"

Pearly teeth emerged in a self-satisfied grin. "I'm glad

you're coming around to my way of thinking, Lois. I'd be happy to give you an interview on that. Better hurry if you're going to be there when the class lets out. Tell James I hope his family liked the flowers."

James can take the charity story. No way I'm interviewing Butler.

But I seized the opportunity to vamoose. The bell rang as I reached the end of the hall and the classroom door I was looking for. James was visible through the narrow window, seated near the front of the room. Maddy's desk was beside his. Even though everyone else was starting to file out, he got up slowly and lingered by hers. He was waiting for her.

What is up with him? He'd barely paid any attention to Maddy before the last day or so.

"Oh, hey, Lois," Dante said as he walked up next to me. "You're not here for Maddy, are you? We were going to grab a coffee."

"I remember," I said. "Taking time off from the mural?"

But there was a splotch of red paint on his arm and on his jeans, so maybe not. He saw me looking, and said, "I finally have the right concept. I worked on it before school today."

Unsaid was, "So I could meet Maddy for coffee after school." I was officially on board this ship.

"She's all yours after just a sec," I said. "I'm meeting James."

"What's the deal with that guy?" he asked. "I must have done something to offend him."

But I didn't have time to answer, even if I could've. James and Maddy were the last ones out of the classroom, and greeted the sight of us with varying degrees of excitement.

By which I mean Maddy beamed at Dante and then dimmed her smile for me. James scowled at us both.

"What are you doing here?" he asked, the question directed at Dante.

"Where are those golden boy manners that were bred into you since birth?" I asked, teasing. Mostly.

"Sorry," he said. "Hi, uh . . ."

C'mon, James. You know his name by now.

"Dante," Dante said, barely glancing at James. He had eyes only for Maddy. "You ready to go?"

"Still need that one sec," I said, and gave Dante an apologetic grimace for leaving him with James. To James I said, "Behave," while I towed Maddy away by her arm. She looked amused, and so here was hoping our friendship wasn't dead to her after lunch.

"What's the deal with James?" I asked when we were well out of the boys' earshot.

She frowned, puzzled. "What do you mean?"

She hadn't noticed his attention? Maybe I was imagining it. I didn't think so, but I dropped it for the time being.

"Never mind," I said. "I just wanted to make sure you were okay and not mad. You know . . . at me."

"I'm not mad at anyone, not about lunch. Melody used to have a flair for the dramatic and I see she's still got it."

Now it was my turn to frown.

"That doesn't really seem fair. She was upset—she's going through a lot."

"And yet still she managed to turn it around on me." Maddy

heaved a breath and continued. Just like the other day, once the words started, they kept on coming. "It was my fault she got herself into this mess, because I like the same band as her? And she felt like she had to keep going to their concert a secret for that reason alone? That it's somehow my fault, instead of asking our parents for the money she went and sold her DNA to some creepy doctor? How is putting that on me fair?"

I thought about Lucy saying there was nothing that could drive us apart forever. "But she's your sister."

"Yeah, and ever since we were kids, she was the prettier one, the more perfect one. When we were close, I didn't see it, that people looked at us that way. That our parents did. But when we got older, when I . . . fell out of step with her, tried to get out of her shadow . . . She never forgave me. What's funny is, I never minded being in her shadow, really. Until I did. I just felt like I had to have some things of my own, or I'd end up with nothing." She'd said all that barely taking a breath, and she sucked in a gulp of air.

James and Dante watched us intently from a dozen feet away. They were definitely not making polite chitchat with each other.

"Until you did mind—when you were twelve?" She'd given that much away before lunch when I'd asked about their relationship. "What happened?"

She shook her head, lips tight.

I could tell she wanted me to stop pushing, to leave this alone. And I didn't know whether it was smart not to—whether pushing was what a good friend would do or if it would simply drive her away. But I *was* her friend, and so I couldn't make this decision based on not stepping on her toes. That wasn't the kind of friend I could be.

"Maddy, tell me."

She hesitated. "We took piano lessons together. I loved this piece by Gershwin and I tried out to do it for this big recital. She knew how much I wanted it."

Oh no. I could see where this was going. "What happened?"

"She auditioned the same piece, and she was better than me. Way better. You heard her the other day. So she got to do my piece. I know it's stupid, but I just wanted to play music I loved. She wanted to show me up and she did. I quit lessons after that. And, after that happened, I saw her doing it all the time. Taking the last of my favorite ice cream, even though there was plenty left of hers. Getting Mom to buy her a dress I'd picked out, while I was in the dressing room trying it on. It was endless. And when you're a twin, there's so much pressure to be the same—but I could never measure up. So I decided it was time to get things of my own, things that she couldn't steal. Things she wouldn't even like."

Things of my own, things that she couldn't steal.

Based on what Melody had said at lunch, she deeply regretted how she'd acted back then, that it had changed Maddy— and that she'd lost her relationship with Maddy because of it. So much that she wasn't willing to risk taking something from her again, even something as small as a band she liked. Given how much Maddy's identity was tied up in the music she listened to (and the imaginary bands she made up names for), it made me think that Melody understood her sister far better than I'd assumed.

Our friendship was new, but we *were* friends. My kind of friends told each other the truth.

"Don't hate me for saying this, but I think you need to cut Melody some slack. That was years ago. Think of it from her POV. She had this awesome twin sister, who all of a sudden seemed not to want to be with her anymore. It had to hurt." When Maddy started to protest, I added, "Even and maybe especially if she did a bunch of things to cause it. From what she said today, it's clear she regrets that."

I hoped friends told each other the truth, anyway. I expected her to argue, direct some bristle my way, and I braced for it.

She was quiet. So I asked, "Has she done anything like those bratty things she did back then to you lately?"

"No," she said, and sighed. "Not for years. She mostly avoids me and . . . I avoid her back. And I never thought about her wishing she hadn't done those things." Before I could be relieved, she added, "Fine, I'll *consider* cutting her some slack. But I have to go. I have a . . ." She smiled, making fun of herself. "A date."

Well, the two of us must be okay, at least.

"With a very cute boy," I returned.

She smiled wider.

We walked back to the waiting, silent boys, and the very cute Dante offered her his hand.

After a moment's hesitation, she put hers in his, and they left us standing there.

"You ready to take me to the ex-leader?" I asked James. I was ready to move on to the next stage. We needed a plan. Which meant I needed to know the former mayor's secrets, the ones he thought I couldn't handle because they were too dangerous.

"James?" I asked when he still hadn't responded.

"Oh, of course," he said. "This should be interesting. Pretty sure Dad thought he was *sui generis*." He raised an eyebrow and added, "That means one of a kind."

Just when I was feeling sorry for James, he assumed I didn't know something. "Actually, the literal translation is just 'of its own kind.' But, yeah, let's hit it."

The sooner we got done with this, the sooner I could be nervous about that night's meeting with TheInventor.

CHAPTER 19

A gargoyle grimaced down at me as James unlocked the door to the Worthington manse and admitted us both into its dark, cool interior. It occurred to me this was what real money smelled like, old wood that barely creaked when you stepped on it and a hint of cleaning supplies. No dust, no must, and no messiness in sight either.

The contrast to my own home, which almost always smelled of delicious food when I came home and was always tidy but not immaculate, was striking.

"Who cooks for you?" I asked. "Your mom?"

James snorted. "Mom's not what I'd call domestic. We used to have a full-time housekeeper. Mom had to go back to her accounting firm after . . . after. So me, mostly. I've gotten a lot better. Or we order Chinese."

Everyone was bringing out the hidden depths today.

I knew we couldn't speak freely, in case of the likely bug-planters listening in, but I extracted my notepad and pen and scrawled: *We're going to make it right.*

I tried to believe it.

James nodded, but I could tell he was more uncertain than me. That probably went along with your dad being away in prison for a year. He'd never said so, but I suspected that James had idolized his father growing up. Couldn't have been easy to watch him tumble off his pedestal.

Especially since it turned out he never deserved the fall.

"And, hey," I said, out loud. "I guess one good thing about house arrest is we know your dad will be here. If only all interview subjects were so easy to track down."

"What a silver lining," James countered dryly. "Don't tell him it's an interview, or he'll refuse to talk."

"Oh, no way. Politicians always love to chat about their glory days." I was writing as I said it, and I held up the note to show James: *More like a police interview. An interrogation of sorts.*

James's eyebrows lifted, but he continued up the hall. Music crescendoed from the room we'd used the other day, stormy classical rather than mellow pop. This must not have raised any red flags or been unusual, given James's lack of reaction to it.

Inside the dimly lit room, James's dad sat on the leather sofa, his head tipped back and eyes closed. I wasn't sure if he was napping or soaking in the tempestuous tunes. I spotted a dimmer switch on the wall and twisted it to full brightness.

His head popped up. Awake, then.

"You can turn down the music," I said to James.

"I was going to," he answered.

His dad was frowning at me in a spooky mirror of what it looked like when James frowned at me, only a few decades older. James had been sleeping well enough the last two days that the dark circles had left his eyes, but they'd apparently taken up permanent residence under his dad's. Of course he'd be troubled, with the visit from the police and my questions about Boss Moxie and Ismenios Labs. I owed him for giving us Dabney Donovan's name, even if the man was a ghost as far as Google was concerned.

But off balance wasn't an unwelcome state to find Mayor Worthington in. I expected resistance.

It was too bad for him that he'd never met my dad. The former mayor was bound to underestimate my ability to stand up to him.

"Hello again, Mr. Mayor," I said, not too sweet and not too angry. My voice was neutral. "I thought I'd do that post-jail interview, let everyone know how you're doing now. An exclusive for the *Scoop* that will be worthy of the *Planet* too."

And if he went along with me, it might even convince those listening in that he was no threat. While we transformed him into a much bigger one.

"I have a headache, Miss—" he paused. "What was your name again? I've always had trouble keeping track of James's little friends."

He was trying to insult me. My eyes narrowed.

"This is Lois," James said, playing at peacemaker. "You should talk to her. It's good for us to get you on the record."

His dad wasn't going to be cooperative, I could tell from the sour lemon face he pulled next. But he scooted forward on the sofa, no longer in napping posture.

"Now," I said, my boots sinking into the thick carpet as I made my way over and onto the buttery leather couch next to him. I placed my bag between us and poised my notebook and pen on top, so he could feel free to grab it when he wanted to communicate. "Where should we start? How about when you knew you were going away? Was there anything you did to prepare? Matters to put in order?"

I wrote my corollary question down: *We know you refused to cooperate w/ Boss Moxie's agenda. Did you have anything on him? Why were you such a threat?*

It didn't make sense to me that Moxie would have gone to such extremes over a simple refusal to play dirty pool. My instincts told me there was more. More that would be useful to us.

Mayor Worthington read the notepad and shook his head slightly.

"Let me think back for a minute. I try not to rehash painful memories," he said.

"I understand," I said. "But this is important."

James cleared his throat.

"So the readers can understand your state of mind. Take your time." I extended the pen to him, turned the pad around to face him.

He shook his head again. Then he accepted the pen and in sharp strokes wrote: *NO.*

"You must remember something," I said, undeterred. "What did you do with all your paperwork? Did you have to archive anything?"

His eyes went wide. Only for a few seconds, but I saw it.

"The mayor doesn't archive his own papers. I wasn't around when they were taken care of. I don't know what happened to them," he said. "I'm feeling that headache coming on again."

Fine. Time to shock him. Because with that weak denial he'd as much as admitted he had some documentation and it remained somewhere—not destroyed. He was likely the only person who knew its precise location.

Proof was what we needed. I wasn't about to give up.

"Just breathe. There's a pressure point right here." I tapped a spot above the thumb. It was actually true. My mom used it to get rid of tension headaches. "Then we'll start."

He ignored my pressure point advice.

"You don't give up easy," he said, almost admiring. Almost.

"True." I busied myself writing on the pad, and then I flipped the sheet and wrote a little more, pen scratching on the paper. Hopefully, the sound of my writing was too quiet for the bug to pick up. I doubted the tech the mobsters had was as good as Dad's and the military's, but you never knew. After all, they'd found a mad scientist capable of producing a duplicate mayor.

Flipping back, I showed James and Mayor Worthington the first page I'd written on.

You remember the guy I showed you the picture of—the one the cops thought was you? You want to know what he is?

The ex-mayor nodded.

I flipped the page to show him more: *He's an exact clone of you, made by that scientist Dabney Donovan to set you up. You had to have something on Boss Moxie for him to go that far.*

His mouth opened and shut. I waited, with no way to estimate how long it would take to absorb that kind of news. But I respected how fast he grew calm enough to engage with it. Being mayor probably presented its share of surprises too, not least landing in the sights of a mobster.

He grabbed the pad and scribbled: *What is this?*

"Just the truth of the matter is all I want, Mayor," I said. "It's what the people of this city deserve."

He wrote again. *A clone? You expect me to believe that.*

I nodded. "Maybe I should give you a short time to think. But not too long. You don't want news getting stale—I think it will really put people's minds at ease, make them feel safe to have your side," I said.

He looked from the pad to me and back again.

"People believe what they want to believe," he said. "Thinking you can change their minds is crazy."

"Call me crazy, then." I took my notebook back from him. "Because I think I'm up to the task. I can help you . . . get your side across to them. Trust me. Look past seeing me as James's 'little friend.' You know James has been working at the *Scoop*, helping around the house, and getting good grades while you've been gone? You should give him more credit too."

"Lois," James protested, though more in surprise than anything else, I thought. He never revealed much. I recognized these defense mechanisms, because I sometimes employed them myself.

"It's okay, you can thank me later. You too, Mayor Worthington. We'll try this again. Soon."

He waved for me to give him back the paper and pen. He wrote: *I'm sorry, but no we won't. You and James are just kids. Too dangerous.*

"You'll find out I'm a lot harder to get rid of than a headache," I told him. "See you soon."

He shook his head, annoyed, and James escorted me to the door. "That went terribly," James said.

"You keep an eye on him. Let me know if he . . . changes his mind about anything." I paused, then spoke louder, for the benefit of any eavesdroppers. "I want this interview."

"And what Lois Lane wants, she gets," James said.

"From your lips to the front page of the *Scoop*. I'll show myself the rest of the way out."

As soon as I was outside, safe from prying ears on the stoop, I texted James: *In case it wasn't clear, I want to know any calls he makes, anything strange. Watch him. Don't let him know, but make sure you keep an eye on him.*

James texted back immediately: *What if he's right?*

I didn't dignify that with an answer. Instead: *Keep working on him. And let me know right away if he does something risky.*

★

When I got home, there were takeout containers on the kitchen table. Thai food.

I thought of James learning how to cook, and wondered whether he was even telling the truth about delivery being a heavy part of the rotation. Maintaining that address and a once-a-week cleaning lady couldn't be cheap, not if they'd taken such a financial hit that his mom had needed to go back to work.

My culinary skills extended to excellent ordering, beyond-excellent eating, and the ability to heat up pizza and boil water to make pasta. When I was on my own, I'd live near good restaurants, that was a given. No sketchy takeout like many of the places we'd lived before we came here.

As I paused in the kitchen threshold, it was clear.

My future was here. Metropolis. Someday I'd graduate from the *Scoop* to the *Daily Planet*, working alongside Perry. I'd look out over that killer view of the city from upstairs in the Daily Planet Building every day.

My heart soared. This vision might be a reality someday.

If Perry didn't fire me when he found out my efforts on behalf of James's dad, that was.

Speaking of dads, mine loathed Thai food, for unfathomable reasons since it was delicious. But it was unassailable fact. We only had Thai when he wasn't going to partake. Which meant this was the perfect chance to return the lock pick set I'd borrowed.

I did my best not to keep things more than a couple of days. No need to arouse suspicion or run the risk of him catching me.

I hurried up the hall and into his study, removed the key from its hiding spot behind the photograph frame, and scurried over to the cabinet. There, I replaced the handy tools that had gained me access first to Boss Moxie's abandoned building, then Donovan's creepy lab.

Hesitating, I wondered if there was anything I'd need for the days ahead that I should grab while I was here.

But then Mom called out, "Lois? That you?"

She was upstairs. But she was looking for me. If I needed the lock picks again, I'd come back for them. Better safe than sorry. Hastily, I secured the cabinet door, darted across the room to re-stick the key to its hiding spot, and continued out into the hall.

"Here! Just got home!" I called back and made a beeline for the kitchen.

Mom bounded down the steps just as I reached the threshold. She wore her fuzzy gray bathrobe over pajamas. "Hi," she said, "big date tonight?"

"Um, no," I said, embarrassed despite how ridiculous the question was. "It's Wednesday night. So, homework, research for a story I'm working on, the usual. Sorry to disappoint."

"Have your secrets," Mom said.

I stopped myself from protesting that I didn't. Because I did, as evidenced by my mad dash to keep from getting busted in Dad's study. And there was the game meet-up with SmallvilleGuy and the even more mysterious TheInventor later. Lying would only make her suspicious. She might be the less uptight of my parents, but that didn't mean Mom was a pushover. Her lie detection skills were finely honed. I must have inherited mine from her.

"Where's Dad?" I asked. The soaring feeling I'd had before evaporated completely, as I had a terrible thought. "We're not moving again, are we? You guys promised. I thought he was going to travel less."

"He has a quick business trip," Mom said. "Out and back for a couple of days to . . ." She paused on the way to the fridge.

This was the first travel he'd done since we arrived in Metropolis, but before we'd come here Dad was always going somewhere or another, even when it *didn't* involve a move.

Still, it made me nervous. The pattern of my life to date had been move, move, and then move again. This was my home. Already, I felt it. I wouldn't leave.

"Somewhere," she said, opening the fridge and pouring herself a glass of white wine. "I know this is horrible, but I'm blanking on the place's name. He'll be back either late tomorrow night or the next night. A quick trip, like I said." She faced me. "We're not moving again. We promised."

Dad had promised all of us. I hadn't known Mom was sick of rootless existence too, until the moment he'd said that at our family meeting a month and a half ago. We'd been gathered around the kitchen table, expecting simply the latest itinerary, when he'd told us the move to Metropolis would be permanent and acknowledged we deserved to be able to stay in one place. Especially if it "helped Lois behave herself."

Oh well, couldn't have everything.

"Good," I said.

"I just took a bath, and figured I'd take dinner upstairs. Hot date with a cheesy TV marathon, since your dad isn't here." She lowered her voice conspiratorially and took a step toward me. "That is the one thing I miss from all the travel and moving. He has no idea some of the awful shows I like."

"I'll never tell," I said, smiling. "Our secret."

"You want to join me? We can watch whatever you want."

I didn't have anywhere to be for a few hours. "Tempting. Maybe I will."

I loved endless movie and TV marathons with Mom and usually Lucy. It had been a while. We liked to watch everything from cerebral dramas to fashion reality shows together, taking turns picking. Occasionally I was even able to convince them to watch my favorite mystery series, which starred an awesome woman detective in the 1930s who prevailed in the face of impossible odds and people underestimating her. Lucy semi-liked it too, but Mom always fell asleep.

Tonight, maybe we could watch that old movie Lucy had referenced in her piece on journalism: *His Girl Friday.* "Is Luce home?" I asked.

Mom nodded, and started to load up a plate. "I'll knock on her door on my way up and alert her. Although, I interrupted her unicorn game earlier and she wasn't happy about it."

"I'm in," I said. "And I'll get Lucy."

Seeing how Maddy and Melody related to each other—it made me realize I never wanted that to happen to my sister and me. I could afford this time to help make sure it never did.

CHAPTER 20

I slowed at the top of the stairs and paused in front of Lucy's door. Taped to it, a hand-lettered sign drawn in black marker said *Keep Out*. The sign was new. So new if I touched it, marker might have come away on my fingertip.

It made me smile. I remembered creating a similar sign of my own at her age.

Besides being somewhat tricky with our parents when it suited our purposes, Lucy and I shared other traits. Stubbornness was among them.

I knocked softly, preparing to gently coax her if she was truly mad at Mom. Even if *that* didn't come easily to me.

"Lucy, can I come in? Even though there's this sign that says not to?"

"Very funny," she said, stepping aside to admit me. "That's

for Mom and Dad. They think they can just barge in whenever they want."

I tapped the knob as I entered. "Use the lock when you need privacy."

"Oh!" As if it had never occurred to her.

Lucy's room was a mass of contradictions, a perfect reflection of its inhabitant. She was on the cusp of moving from childhood to teendom, and her room was too. There was the pastel color scheme she might never have been into, but had agreed to, and several unicorn posters I was positive were ironic after my discovery about her renegade band of friends in the holoset game she played, *Unicorn University*. In support of my theory, the pinkest, prettiest unicorn of them all had a pirate eye patch drawn on in marker.

"So . . . what's up?" she asked.

"Did you get a good grade on your paper?" I went over and eased down onto the side of her bed.

"An A," she said, with a small smile. "And the teacher made this whole big deal about not having realized I was related to *the* Lois Lane who wrote that story about Principal Butler."

Teachers would love that story, wouldn't they? Even the ones who taught elsewhere could probably read between the lines and guess what he would be like as a boss.

"Will you sit too?" I asked.

She shrugged, but with a suspicious squint.

I patted the bed beside me. "I know sometimes I make assumptions. But you're too important for me not to check mine about you. About us."

One bare foot padded in front of another, bringing her closer. She sat down, a little farther away than I'd patted. "What is this about?"

"When I expert consulted you the other night, it was because a friend of mine and her sister don't get along at all. I was talking to her about why today, and I wanted to make sure I don't ever do the same thing. So . . . I wanted to check and make sure that I haven't already." I paused. "Do you ever feel like I'm sucking up all the attention?"

"I told you I wrote that article because I was proud," she said. Before I could begin to respond, she blurted, "It wasn't because I want to be you."

I was making a mess of this. Lucy had been happy with me when I'd knocked on her door.

"Little sister, believe me. I'd be way more worried about you if you did." I wrinkled my nose, the way she usually did when she disapproved of something. She softened a fraction. "I have a habit of doing things the hard way. And for you, I want things to be easy."

"I don't need things to be easy," she said.

"I know that. We've never had things easy. Not really."

She nodded.

"So," I said, encouraged, "I just wanted to talk to you and tell you that we're not going to grow apart here. Now that we have a permanent place, to grow roots and all that stuff Dad and Mom talked about. I know I've been really busy since we got here. But you are important to me."

"What have you done with my sister?" she asked.

"Funny," I said. "I'm being sincere."

"I know, and it's weird."

"Tell me about it," I said. "But Luce? I want you to know two things. Even though I'm kind of a monster for not saying this stuff before now."

"Monster is a *little* strong."

A little? I stifled a grin at the qualifier. "You don't even know what I'm going to say. Anyway, number one, I will always be your sister. I am always here for you, even if you're mad at me. No matter if we live far apart from each other someday. We're sisters. Forever. Got that?"

"What's the second thing?"

"I know you don't want to be me. But I'd hate for you to ever feel like you're in my shadow. You're not and you never will be. You are awesome, and there is some kind of amazing future waiting for you. You know how I know?"

She shook her head no, her small chin swiping through the air back and forth. "What if there's not?"

"There is. How could there not be? I know because you're pretty amazing already. I don't think you're going to get *less* amazing when you grow up. In fact, let's make a pact. You think?"

This interested her. Lucy liked bargains and deals and bets. Another thing we had in common.

"What pact?"

I stuck out my hand, and after a second's hesitation, she placed hers on top of it. I repeated the gesture with mine, and she laid her second hand on top of the pile.

"We do so solemnly swear by this very important pact that the Lane sisters will always be sisters and friends and only get more amazing, the older we get. We will . . ." I tried to think of something appropriate . . . "We will show the future who's boss. I swear it as your sister."

"I swear it as your sister," she repeated.

And the room went quiet, as if we'd sealed the pact in blood.

We dropped our hands, both embarrassed by the sincerity of the moment. But I was learning. Sometimes you had to put it all out there, no matter how hard it felt to do so. When the people in your life were worth it, so was the risk.

I said, "There's Thai food, because Dad's on some trip."

"I know," Lucy said.

"And Mom is in for a TV marathon night. You too? I thought we could watch that old movie you mentioned in your essay."

She didn't hesitate. "Yes!" She paused. "As long as I get to drive the remote?"

"We wouldn't dream of anything else."

I had a pang—I should probably go check in with SmallvilleGuy, let him know I would be MIA for a bit in case he needed me. But . . .

I'd told him I would show up a little early tonight, and I'd have plenty of time to. The next sighting wasn't until tomorrow night. And I had to wait for James to catch his dad trying to do something dumb, like attempt to leave their house or send James's mom wherever the evidence was. Then I could make a renewed effort at convincing him to cooperate with us.

But I fully expected him to make me wait a few more days. My fingers were crossed Melody could survive the waiting too.

"Lois? You coming?" Lucy said in the doorway.

With everything else in a state of delay anyway, it was a no-brainer that Mom-and-sister bonding night should take precedence over plotting and planning for now. "One sec," I said, and I pulled out my phone and tapped a quick message into the app.

SkepticGirl1: *Having movie night with Mom and Luce if you need me before game time.*

I joined Lucy and nudged her to the top of the stairs. "Last one down is a rotten sister!" I said.

We pounded down them together, laughing, and reached the bottom at the same time.

For my part, that was on purpose.

★

Two hours later, Mom was doing her drowsy, about-to-fall-asleep thing, while Lucy showed no signs of flagging. We were upstairs in Mom and Dad's room in full slumber party formation, propped on a mixture of pillows from their room and our own.

We hadn't done this in so long. It had been fun. Part of me didn't want it to end, but the rest of me had been quietly obsessing the entire time about inviting TheInventor into our secret place in *Worlds* and how to deal with the boards drama over the flying man and clones and my friends' sibling rivalry and how we were going to get the info we needed to *fix*

Melody's problem and how quickly James's dad would come around . . .

"We do have school tomorrow," I said as the music swooped up and the credits for the black-and-white movie rolled.

Mom's head snapped up, and she consulted the clock. "It's only nine forty." She blinked to full awakeness. "The movie's over, but we can watch an episode of something if Lucy wants to."

"Lucy wants to," Lucy said, and hefted the remote to click over to the instant watch menu. She scrolled through the menu and settled on a cop show she and Mom liked and I didn't mind. It was slightly gruesome but lightened by fun banter among the characters.

"All right, then," I said, giving an exaggerated yawn. That should set the stage for me to make my exit soon.

His Girl Friday had instantly joined my favorite movies of all time—and had me wishing people still wore hats every day. The reporter heroine, Hildy Johnson, sported classy ensembles while talking as fast as I usually did and pressing for the truth without cease. She'd wanted to quit reporting to get married, but she couldn't leave her real love: journalism. Not to mention, she re-fell in love with a newspaperman, a dreamy, suit-wearing newspaperman. Men should still wear suits like his too.

The cop show episode began, and my phone buzzed in my robe pocket. I scooted back against the headboard where my every move wouldn't be quite so visible to Mom and Lucy.

I pulled out my phone as discreetly as possible and casually checked the screen. I had a new message in the app.

SmallvilleGuy: *Movie night still going? How much longer?*

I tapped out a response, as on the down low as I could manage.

SkepticGirl1: *I shall attempt Mission Self-Extraction in five mins. Wish me luck.*

SmallvilleGuy: *Break a leg.*

SkepticGirl1: *I'm not an actor.*

SmallvilleGuy: *Coulda fooled me, drama queen.*

SmallvilleGuy: *Kidding! ;-P*

When I looked up, Mom was watching me with a barely concealed grin. "Still no boyfriend?" she asked.

Lucy whipped around, instantly distracted from her show's latest body discovery. "Really? *You* have a *boyfriend*?!"

I couldn't tell whether her tone was more excitement or accusation. "I do not." He wasn't my boyfriend, and we'd never even met. No matter how much I might wish for both of those things.

"Then who are you texting with?" Lucy asked.

"Um, James, about a story," I lied.

Mom seemed surprised. "I thought he was the one you semi-couldn't stand."

"He is," I said, regretting that I hadn't said I was texting with Maddy. "He was, I mean. We're friends now. *Just* friends."

"If you say so," Mom said, with a shrug to Lucy. They exchanged conspiratorial grins.

I leaned forward, picked up two potato chips from our feast of snacks, and tossed one at each of them. They just laughed.

Lucy restarted the show. On second thought, it might not be a bad idea to check in with James, make sure he was watching his father as closely as I wanted him to be. So I texted him:

Anything risky yet? You are tailing your dad, right?

The response came about half a minute later.

I am, and it's a little weird following him around the house. He's almost caught me twice. Nothing unusual.

"I think I might go to bed," I said in a vaguely irritated tone. *Hurry it up, ex-mayor.*

"We didn't mean to offend you, Lois," Mom said.

I suppressed a sigh. Lying to the people I cared about was not my favorite. "You didn't. I promise. Tough story to crack, and it's majorly resisting. I should probably get some sleep."

"Then good night," she said.

I ruffled Lucy's hair as I left. "Night, brat."

"Night, monster," she returned.

"My sweet, sweet girls," Mom said, thick with irony. Lucy threw a chip at her.

The part of me that had enjoyed tonight—so much—wished I could stay with them, here in this uncomplicated space, watching TV and eating too much food and simply hanging out with my mom and sister. But I'd probably overindulged the length of this hiatus as it was.

What would it be like to be normal? To not always be worrying about what needed to happen next?

"Deathly dull," I said, answering my question aloud as I entered my room and locked the door behind me.

CHAPTER 21

I ran my hands nervously through my hair, smoothing it down even though no one was going to see it, and deposited my phone on the desk. Then I fished the holoset out of the desk drawer where I kept it tucked away, and hooked it over my ear. Once I was on the bed, I took a tiny pause to draw in and release a deep breath, then pressed it on.

Night rose up in front of me, the brightly colored kind in the game. Tonight's theme seemed to be a variation on the northern lights by way of neon, painting the sky like unnatural fireworks. A distant spaceship cruised across it, and the bat with red lasers on its wings flew overhead—no, wait, there were several bats of the type and they winged past displaying zero interest in me.

"Hey," said a familiar voice.

"Hey yourself," I said, turning to find my favorite friendly alien. "Sorry if I'm late."

He smiled. "Not at all. What'd you guys watch?"

"*His Girl Friday*, aka the best movie ever."

He hooked his arm through mine, and began to walk us away from Devin's castle. We were going in the opposite direction we would usually, down a slope toward a thick stand of trees. There was a vaguely menacing green glow within them. I'd never noticed a forest so close before.

"Where are we going?" I asked.

"TheInventor gave me coordinates—I asked for them, giving him a general area. I know you have your doubts, and so I didn't necessarily want to give him a tour of our turret. They're this way, in the forest."

Our turret. "You are too thoughtful to hang out with the likes of me."

"Take it back," he said.

I was more relieved than I probably should have been that TheInventor wasn't going to be privy to all our secrets—maybe. I'd wanted to get here early to talk strategy, but SmallvilleGuy seemed to be on my "let's be careful here" page.

"Never," I quipped.

"Fine." His hand was warm on my arm as he guided me down the hill. "And what did you talk about with Lucy and your mom?"

I considered telling him that they'd teased me about possibly having a boyfriend. But this wasn't the time or place, heading into the sketchy glowing woods.

"We discussed which boys are as hot as Cary Grant, the guy in the movie. Also our nails. Our hair. Makeup. Girl stuff." I paused. "I'm kidding, obviously. We talked about our feelings."

He burst out laughing. Good laugh, as usual. I suspected the grin I wore was entirely goofy, and I didn't care.

"Yep, still kidding," I confirmed.

We reached the edge of the trees. The glow made it possible to see where a normal forest would have been pitch dark, casting light enough to reveal that the bark wasn't designed to look like normal tree bark. It had small oval gray-skinned faces with big black eyes traced over it instead. Like some of the other alien character designs in the game.

"Sounds like you had a good time," he said.

"I did. But it was weird to have a night off. Sorta off, I mean. Speaking of . . . do we need to make any plans before we meet this guy?"

"What made you ask about him earlier, by the way?" he asked, tone curious.

"I'm not as trusting as you. Except with you."

His hand tightened a fraction on my arm, a pleasant distraction from the topic of our conversation.

It was true—he might not be willing to tell me who he was, but it wasn't for lack of trust in me. He was protecting someone else. His parents were likeliest, I'd decided. And he clearly thought he was protecting me too by keeping his secret, even though I didn't need his protection.

But I understood wanting to look out for the people you cared about.

"Why shouldn't we trust him, though?" he said, finally. "I think he'll help us. He helped us before and just because I asked. He didn't even pry for details about why."

"True," I said, "and again, I trust you. And he's the only one who has the access we need to track what's going on at the boards. The only way we'd know if our IP addresses—or who we are—had been compromised."

"This is our best option," he agreed. But more grimly now that I brought up the threat of us being found and found out.

His words put me in mind of Melody's description of me when I'd vowed to help her. Maybe I wasn't being entirely fair to this strange computer expert. He *had* built the platforms that brought SmallvilleGuy and me together, after all.

"Wow," SmallvilleGuy said, releasing my arm and taking a step in front of me. "This wasn't here before."

I had been so focused on him, and he'd been guiding us so easily through the woods, that I hadn't been keeping my eyes on where we were going.

In front of us was a clearing and smack in the middle of it sat a spaceship. It was a tall, deep silver disk about thirty feet across, ringed with multi-hued lights that cycled in an almost soothing pattern over and over again. As we watched, part of the side detached and unfurled like a silvery tongue.

The silvery tongue was a walkway that led to an opening. An entrance.

Hopefully we weren't about to be attacked by random aliens.

I looked back to SmallvilleGuy and he was squinting off to

the side of the ship. Sometimes that brought up more information and stats in the game. "Nothing comes up," he said.

I tried and confirmed the same result.

"But these *are* the coordinates," he said after a moment. "I scoped them out earlier."

I jumped when a deep voice greeted us, emanating from inside the ship: "Good evening. Please come inside."

SmallvilleGuy steadied me with a hand on my arm. "Not until you tell us who you are," he said.

"I would think it is quite obvious, SmallvilleGuy and SkepticGirl1. I'm your friend, TheInventor."

My heart thudded.

"I'd say he likes to make an entrance, but this is more of a statement piece," I said, low.

"SkepticGirl1, I suspected you'd be funny." The voice paused. "I did not, however, foresee that you would be an elf princess."

"I didn't pick it," I muttered. Self-conscious as always when I remembered my short dress and bare feet. Not to mention the pointy ears. *Thanks again, Devin.*

A laugh rolled outward. "I pity the person who did. It wasn't you, was it, SmallvilleGuy?"

SmallvilleGuy was smiling, though there was a tense set to the line of his shoulders that told me he was only slightly more comfortable with this than me. "I'm not that foolish," he said.

"Enough," I said, embarrassed that they were talking about me so familiarly. I didn't even *know* TheInventor, not really. "Are we going on board or not?"

I'd always wondered what it looked like inside the ships that to and froed in the skies of *Worlds*. They were usually busy warring with each other or starting fights with mercenaries or high fantasy kingdoms.

"I hope so, or I've gone to all this trouble for nothing," TheInventor's voice said.

"Looks slippery," I said as we each took a step closer to the metal walkway. SmallvilleGuy offered me his hand, and I took it gratefully, even if we were being watched.

The moment we stepped onto it, the metal began to shift—

I grabbed onto SmallvilleGuy as the walkway retracted into the ship, taking us with it. And then we were inside, the door sealed behind us like it hadn't existed.

"We're safe here, from overhearing ears or prying eyes," the voice said.

I'd expected to see its owner, but the voice seemed to come from, well, the ship itself. Holographic screens ringed the circular interior, offering a 360-degree view of the forest outside and a glimpse of the slope past it. Above them were other screens, which revealed different exteriors entirely—other parts of the game—both on the ground and in the sky. There was a console with buttons and a joystick, and the floor was more of the seamless metal that had ferried us inside.

"Nice place," I said, letting go of SmallvilleGuy even though I didn't want to. "But you can come out now if we're all safe."

"Oh," TheInventor said. "I didn't bother to create a character. I commandeered a ship instead and made a few customizations, designed a secure location. Games bore me, typically."

"It's not like we're playing," SmallvilleGuy said. Which confirmed he thought that the choice was odd too.

"Au contraire, we are locked in a dangerous game, as you know. People who are not our friends are hunting a man."

There was something shivery about the phrasing, saying it outright like that. But talk about overkill on the drama. "You sound like that short story everyone reads in school, the one on the island where 'man is the most dangerous game,'" I said.

"You *are* a surprise, SkepticGirl1," TheInventor said.

"Should I feel insulted by that? What were you expecting?" I asked before I could stop myself. I quickly added, "Don't answer."

"Please don't," SmallvilleGuy said lightly. "If she feels insulted, we have to leave. And you're right, we've been forced into playing a game and it's a dangerous one. We should get down to business."

There was nowhere to sit besides the flight console, so I stayed near SmallvilleGuy. The screens around us dimmed, leaving one lit. It showed the Strange Skies boards.

TheInventor started talking. "I've gotten private messages now from several people interviewed after these fake 'sightings' and they are all frightened to come back to Strange Skies. I can hardly tell them not to worry, when I know that federal agencies are attempting to hack into my servers and discover their real identities. And ours. I am at a loss as to how we combat this in time to keep that from happening."

"I thought the site was over-the-top secure. Are they that good?" I asked.

"They must be," SmallvilleGuy said.

"No, she is right. I may have been a bit . . . cocky about the impenetrability of my defenses, and perhaps also underestimated their capabilities."

Like he'd apparently underestimated me. Saying that wouldn't get us anywhere, though.

Instead, I said, "But maybe they've underestimated yours."

"I would like to think so."

I started to pace back and forth. "Doesn't it seem weird to you both that they targeted Skies at all?"

SmallvilleGuy nodded. "To come to the boards looking for . . . the flying man . . . makes me think that they are striking in the dark. One element in a larger search."

"Intelligence gathering is the term you're looking for," TheInventor's voice responded.

My bare feet felt cold against the metal of the ship, and so I walked a little faster. "They want the flying man," I said. "We know that much. But do we have any clue who these people are, besides an interagency task force? What agencies?"

TheInventor heaved a sigh. "No one has been able to get them to show an ID at the scenes so far."

"No," I said, "do *you* have any idea?"

The ship went quiet briefly, then he responded.

"I haven't focused my attention too closely on the matter." He sounded defensive.

Hmmm.

SmallvilleGuy leaned against one of the darkened screens, essentially the wall. "What are you thinking?" he asked me.

"I'm thinking that our main concern is being found out, right? Our identities being compromised, and them tracking us down—our parents finding out about the site. For you, TheInventor, I assume it's the privacy of users of your site."

"And my own privacy. I value that too," the voice said quickly.

"What if we made it so they had the same concern as us?"

The lights inside the ship blinked, like a reaction almost, and I noticed my feet weren't cold anymore. The floor had warmed.

I didn't like that. It kind of made me want to walk over and put my feet on top of SmallvilleGuy's sneakers or something so I could stop touching it. It was probably some automatic function of the ship, though, so that would be ridiculous.

"I don't understand. What are you suggesting?" TheInventor asked.

"If you were some top-secret interagency government task force, would you want the everyday person out in the world to know you're looking for someone who can fly? At best, you become a laughingstock. At worst, you've confirmed for your enemies that such a person exists and started a race to find them."

SmallvilleGuy's blue eyes were locked on me. "You're right. But how does that not just make them more dangerous?"

"First things first," I said. "Mr. TheInventor, do you think you could get us some information about what agency Insider01 is affiliated with and anything else on this interagency task force?"

"To publish on the site?" he asked.

"Hopefully it won't come to that. Something tells me that if we're able to send them a message telling them that not only do they have nothing to learn from Strange Skies or its members, but that the owner of the site knows who they are and will tell the entire world, then they might back off. The threat of exposure is a powerful motivator."

"But how would we know if they did back off?" SmallvilleGuy asked.

"I could monitor that," TheInventor said. "Their activity. In fact, it could be part of the message itself, the caution that I will be watching for them to return."

His voice made him sound pleased with that idea. Good.

"Could we ask them to delete the account if they agree to the terms? Set a deadline?" I asked.

"It should be before the next scheduled sighting, which gives me less than twenty-four hours," TheInventor said. "But if I can manage to crack the firewall, it could work." He paused. "You two are as interesting as I'd hoped."

I didn't want to hear how interesting we were. Not that I didn't trust him—I thought he was on our team and would do as he said. But my relationship with SmallvilleGuy had always been ours, between us, no one else invited to participate.

It was small, probably, to have only realized I'd miss that after it was gone.

SmallvilleGuy said, "I don't know about this. Are we crossing a line here?"

I shook my head and walked closer to him. "The flying

man needs our help. I assume he's been alerted to their searching, but he can't risk showing himself. We have to scare them off."

"For our own benefit."

"And for his. I owe him, and he's never done any harm that we know of. For all we know this is some kind of rogue task force. There's no good reason to be searching for him in this way, scaring innocent people."

He was quiet for a long moment, considering. TheInventor could go on and do this without him. But I wouldn't be a part of it unless he was on board, no matter the risk.

"I really do think it's the right thing to do," I said. "And if they don't leave the boards, we can talk about whether it makes sense for me to write the story. Not exposing the flying man, but that there's an interagency task force messing around with people who frequent message boards about weird stuff. I'd do whatever I had to in order to get it on the front page."

"You couldn't," he said. Meaning if I did, Dad would want to know how I'd found out. I'd have to tell him.

"I could. All we'd be doing is bringing something underhanded out into the light. And all we're trying to do is stop it before that becomes necessary. That it protects us too is just an extra benefit."

Finally, he gave a short nod. "We're the good guys," he said.

I smiled at him. "We're the good guys. Always."

TheInventor spoke up, and I nearly jumped again. I'd almost forgotten he was with us. "I had no idea you were a journalist, SkepticGirl1."

"Oh. Yeah," I said.

SmallvilleGuy was at my side. He said, "You'd better go get to work, friend."

"Yes. And I will be in touch soon," TheInventor said.

I was looking for the exit when TheInventor added: "Hold on." I grabbed for SmallvilleGuy's arm once again, but this time he was ready and took both my hands in his, steadying me as the floor moved under our feet. The silver ribbon of metal unfurled once more, lowering us back to the forest floor.

As soon as we stepped off, before we could so much as wave, it returned to its spot and the spaceship lifted off and zoomed away into the neon northern lights sky. Leaving us in the faint glow of the forest.

"Do you think it'll work?" SmallvilleGuy asked.

I echoed his words from earlier. "The best option we have."

A noise startled me, and it took me a moment to identify it. It was my phone, ringing back in the real world.

CHAPTER 22

This was not good.

"My phone is ringing. No one ever calls me except my parents," I said. "So either my mom figured out I'm gone, or—"

"You'd better go," he said.

He was right. "It'll work," I said. "I bet you."

"You already did," I heard, as I depressed the button on the earpiece and came out of the game and back to reality. I blinked, adjusting to having left virtual reality more quickly than I should've.

The phone had already stopped ringing, but now it was buzzing with a text. I hurried across to the desk and grabbed it.

There was one missed call and a series of messages from the last ten minutes: *We have a problem. Where are you? Lois, answer your messages. Answer your phone. Please.*

They were from James. And the last one: *I was calling to tell you Dad just summoned Boss Moxie and Mayor Ellis to my house and told them to bring the clone. Right now.*

For a second I was frozen, an icy chill fixing me in place. I hadn't expected James's dad to do something *this* risky. Or this soon. *Way to surprise a girl, Mayor Worthington.*

Then I was in motion, texting back: *Be right there.*

I typed a quick message to SmallvilleGuy, to excuse the abrupt ending to our evening. A quick, surreal message.

SkepticGirl1: *Mobster and company heading to James's. Going there now.*

He didn't even question me.

SmallvilleGuy: *Keep the app open. And be careful.*

At least he hadn't told me not to go.

Although, the going—aka getting out of the house—was going to be complicated enough. Mom and Lucy were still awake.

It was well after ten p.m. So I couldn't ask permission to leave, not even with Mom the sole parent in residence. Not even with a truthful-ish cover explanation about it being related to the tough story I'd mentioned before. (Related to the story, yes. Something safe enough that she'd let me leave this late, not so much.)

Think, Lois, think.

I scrolled through my recent texts to the name Taxi Jack and tapped a quick message to him. *I need a ride fast. Big story.*

I gave him the cross street address at the end of the block. While I traded my pajama bottoms for jeans and threw a leather jacket on over the top, I worried that he wasn't working. When I was adding my boots, and making a plan B to walk up the block and hail a random taxi, two texts came in quick succession.

Taxi Jack's said, *Confirmed.*

James's text gave a different address than the one Devin and I had used. *This is our garden's back gate. Meet you there.*

No surprise James's family home was fancy enough to have a garden with its own back gate, probably one of the few non-public gardens in Metropolis that wasn't on a rooftop or off the island of New Troy.

Creeping from my room, placing one shoe softly in front of another, I heard the shuffle of Lucy coming out of Mom's room and I went faster, motivated by the knowledge I might get caught. I made it down the stairs and to the door, where I forced myself to slow down and shut it as quietly as I could to avoid a telltale slam or click.

In the still-warm night air, I did not linger to see if anyone had detected my exit. I could deal with that fallout later, if it existed. No one was chasing me yet, which could mean I'd made a clean getaway. I jogged the rest of the way up the block, and I ducked into the taxi the moment it showed.

"A little late for you, isn't it, chickadee?" Jack asked.

"Thanks for coming," I told him, then read off the address James had given.

"Fancy neighborhood," he said, but that was all. Not so chatty this late, and I didn't blame him. This felt dangerous, even to me.

He'd been there when I'd raced from the Ismenios building. I wondered if Dabney Donovan, creepy mad scientist, would be at James's. I didn't know whether to approach him directly or not, even if he was. We needed more information about how to cure Melody, but I wasn't convinced it was possible to make Donovan help us out.

More danger was unavoidable. All this was necessary to play the situation out and reach an endgame where I had a story to tell.

A story where James had his father back, for real. Where Maddy had her sister back, fear-free. Where we helped scrub the city clean of the kind of corruption that allowed a neighborhood to become both hideout and real estate pawn for the likes of Boss Moxie.

I steeled myself for whatever the night held, and made sure my pajamas didn't show around the edges of my coat. It had already been a night of surprises. TheInventor hadn't been what I expected him to be either—and I hadn't figured out if I meant that in a good or bad way. At least we had a plan, assuming he delivered.

"This is the place, but is this a good idea?" Jack asked a few minutes later, braking as we neared the back of James's building via a small alley.

"Positive," I said, climbing out of the car. "Can you wait?"

He killed both the growling engine and bright headlights. "I'll be here."

A stone fence bordered the sidewalk. It reminded me of our tower at Devin's castle in the game. As promised, in the center of this looming castle-like protective wall was a tall iron gate, twisted into shapes that resisted interpretation under moonlight and sans streetlights.

"Lois?" James whispered. I couldn't see him yet.

I pushed down the instinct to jump and walked closer. I spoke low, "Scare a girl, why don't you, James? Am I climbing this, or . . ."

The wrought iron swung open a fraction, then wide enough to admit me. "Come on," he said. "They got here five minutes before you."

I quickened my step. He pulled the iron gate nearly shut behind me, leaving a crack for my escape. The no-longer-so-manicured shapes of shrubs and flowers were recognizable along the narrow garden in front of us, and off to one side, a narrow walkway that seemed to lead to the front of the building. James put a light hand on my elbow to guide us, and we moved onto a smooth stone path that went directly toward the back of the manse.

Metropolis air wasn't that smoggy, but it smelled like a city. James's back garden, in contrast, carried the sweetly pungent bouquet of night-blooming flowers.

"There's a place we can listen unobserved?" I asked.

"That's why I had you come in this way."

We stopped a few feet away from the looming shape of the house. The door in front of us could have been made of gingerbread, crossed with pale, pretty panes. It felt like it belonged in a midnight fairy tale. "Through here," he said, and pressed the door. He'd left it open.

A small kitchen waited inside—not big enough to be the main one, so maybe it was some sort of garden kitchen? Hard to say. We didn't have a room like this in Chez Lane. Just past the kitchen, a small fountain burbled quietly in the center of a high-ceilinged alcove, a watering can beside it. Beyond the water, though, I heard voices, not so far away. Men were talking. They weren't shouting, but their voices were raised.

"Nice," I whispered to James, and went toward the voices, like a moth who loved to play with fire too much to stay away from it. No matter how it might burn to the touch.

There was an arched opening with nothing to block our access to the sounds in the room beyond. A short passage hid the people inside it from view. But we'd still have to be careful not to be seen or heard.

James took my elbow again and guided me along the wall, past the fountain. When we reached the side of the arch, he slid down to sit on the floor. I did the same.

The sound was better down here. I pictured a younger James, eavesdropping on family conversations or his dad's business meetings. I listened.

"You seem to be under the impression you have leverage," said a man's rough voice. It didn't belong to either mayor, current or former, so I thought he must be Boss Moxie. "I might have let you get away with not playing ball on the waterfront, but then you decided to try to bring me down. I hope you've learned that lesson. I own you. I own this man here, who looks just like you. I own this city. Forgetting that is what got you in trouble in the first place."

Oh no, Boss Moxie, that's where you're wrong. This city doesn't belong to you. It belongs to all of us. And that means it's my city too.

You won't take it without a fight.

After a loaded silence, James's dad countered him, silky smooth. "You may have that . . . imposter. But I do have leverage. I kept the evidence."

Boss Moxie laughed. "I'll find it," he said.

But James's dad responded, "It's not on a computer, where you could easily hack into it. It's somewhere you'll never think to look, never find it. Your threats against my family worked back then. I need you to know that their safety is paramount, and I will not go back to jail. You control my peace of mind, but I could take yours too."

So he does have evidence. Just as I'd suspected.

He'd better not offer it to them.

Mayor Ellis spoke next. "It'd be a shame for something else to happen to your precious family. They've been through so much. But we can always force you to tell us where it is." He was as slick as he had been in front of the courthouse, but way more menacing.

"No, you can't," James's dad returned, but there was a hint of weakness in it. "Get rid of this . . . person, and leave us alone. In return, I promise any evidence in my possession will stay buried."

No, no, no. That wasn't going to work for me. No way they were getting away with this.

I subtly checked out James's reaction and saw him shaking his head *no*, in the same reflexive disagreement.

"I don't like loose ends," said Boss Moxie's rough voice. Then, "Can you excuse us for a moment?"

"Of course," said a voice with a flatness of tone, but otherwise identical to that of James's father. That must be the clone.

A few moments later, we heard the faint sound of the front door opening and closing. Only when the double was outside did the men begin to speak again.

"You drive a hard bargain, Jimmy," said Boss Moxie. "I don't like leaving things out there that could hurt me."

"I don't like sitting here, pretending we have to listen to him," said Mayor Ellis.

"Take it or leave it," James's dad said. "But that . . . thing . . . whoever, whatever it is, *is* a threat to my family. To me. Do we have a deal?"

"Not as such," Boss Moxie said. "Here's the thing about our friend . . ."

There was a soft click from the direction of the back door we'd come through, and I looked at the doorway—and straight into the face of the clone. Immediately, I lost track of what was happening in the next room.

He gave every appearance of being James's father, of course. Tonight, he wore a plain suit and one hand touched his bracelet tracking device, just as Melody had described. He released the device to raise his hand, beckoning me.

James had stilled beside me. "Stay here," I whispered. "Keep listening. I'll be fine."

I rose before James could protest. And I truly didn't think the clone would hurt me, not here and now. He'd snuck around the back of the house. I had no idea how he knew we were here and eavesdropping, and yet he must have. That also meant he hadn't raised an alarm and given us away.

I wanted to know why.

The clone retreated into the darkness as soon as he saw I was walking toward him. I met him on the stone porch, and we walked into the garden together. We went far enough to talk without danger of alerting the men inside. But not so far that James would freak out because he couldn't see where we were. The glow from the door was a beacon in the dark.

"What's your name?" I asked. He'd been referred to mostly as the duplicate or a creation in the documents I'd stolen.

"I'm nobody," he said, blithe, like it didn't matter. "Who are you? You were at the courthouse, and the lab, and you know *her*."

Her. Melody. I wasn't ready to ask him about her. I needed to circle, make him feel comfortable first. Even though I felt the furthest thing from it.

"Why did they send you out of the room?" I asked.

His eyes glittered black in the darkness of the yard. "They are talking about me, about deactivating me. Permanently. That will be the offer they make the man whose face I was given."

"What does that mean?" I asked. "Deactivation?"

"You know what it means. You have seen a lesser form of it." He shuddered, shoulders and face shaking. "It means the tank, indefinitely. It is what they did last time, when they were done with me."

He gazed out into the night.

"They put you to sleep," I said.

"Being in stasis is not like sleeping. There are no dreams. I am awake but not exactly alive. Not exactly dead, either. For two years, I had no promise that I would ever be allowed to walk freely again. I was like a small child, trusting. But I am not free. I see that now."

He said it almost philosophically. Which threw me. I wasn't even convinced he was precisely human.

"Is that why you stopped taking the medication?" I asked carefully. "You feel it too? The connection to Melody, I mean. It's because you stopped taking the pills."

"I can speak to you because you saw me at the laboratory. You know the truth."

Well, some of it. "Yes. But answer the question. Do you feel the connection?"

"Why do you think I refuse the treatment?" His eyes closed. "I feel her out there right now, sleeping peacefully." His eyelids fluttered, then finally opened. Reluctantly. "The only time I feel anything much at all is through her. I am not alone."

"I'm sorry," I said, deciding to be blunt. "It must suck to feel that way. But she has a life of her own. And this . . . connection between you is siphoning that away. She needs her life back. It's not enough to just accept the treatment. Do you know how to break the bond? For good."

"Why would I tell you? Why would I let go of her willingly?"

I hadn't prepared for the possibility he *liked* their connection. Oh, this was bad.

While I was still searching for a response, his head dropped to one side. He straightened it and walked away, back toward the path to the front of the house. "They're leaving now. I have to go."

So he heard them. I strained to pick up whatever he had heard, but my own ears detected nothing. He had heightened senses.

"But you know how to break it." I followed him. "There's a way. Why would you want to put someone else in a metaphorical tank? Why would you take Melody's freedom away?" I fired the questions off quick, before he was too far away to pretend he didn't hear. I added, "You have to let her go."

His step faltered, but then he hurried on into the night without answering. I stood, trying to decide whether to keep tailing him and force the issue or let him go. For the moment.

James made the choice for me, bursting out of the back door to find me. "They just left. My dad is trying to make a deal," he said, like he couldn't believe it.

"I gathered," I said and hefted my messenger bag. "Take me to the idiot. The only deal he's making is with us."

CHAPTER 23

I removed my notepad and pen from my bag on the way through the garden kitchen and into the living room. The room was all leather and wood, with one wall dominated by a fully stocked bar. James's dad stood at it, pouring himself a drink. As I rushed toward him, I was busy scrawling my first question.

I held it up a foot from James's dad, right in his face: *ARE YOU STUPID?*

He scowled and set down his drink. "What are you doing?" But he caught himself, in case anyone was listening. "... awake, James? Don't you have school tomorrow?"

"I just wanted to see what in the world you thought you were ... doing down here," James said, catching himself too. "If you, um, needed anything."

I was writing again. I hefted the pad: *What did you agree to?*

"Nothing that's your business," James's dad said. He crossed his arms in front of his chest.

The gesture only irritated me more. What was wrong with him?

Stop being stupid, I wrote. *You need to work with us. We can fix this. All of it. We can get your life back.*

I put the pad down next to his drink and tossed the pen at him. He unfolded his arms to catch it and leaned over to read the message on the notebook. He shook his head disdainfully. But I saw a flicker of something else.

Longing.

He wanted it to be true. He wanted to be able to have his life back. He hid it, but too late.

I grabbed the pad back again, and held out a hand for him to give me the pen.

I'm serious, I wrote. *I know you think we're just kids, but we can do this. We can make it right. Send those jerks to jail. Why didn't you reveal what you had on them in the first place?*

I passed it back.

He looked at it for a long time, thoughtfully, while James and I exchanged semi-hopeful glances. Staying quiet and not convincing him out loud was beyond hard. The silent waiting made me want to jump out of my skin.

Finally, ex-Mayor Worthington started to write a response. He shielded it with his forearm, so I had to wait until he was done to see the words. *I have to be realistic. I'm not ever going to be that man again.*

I couldn't stay quiet any longer. Hopefully, the fact Boss Moxie was on the way home from here meant he or his goons weren't paying attention. I whispered, "What's *realistic* is you need help. From us. The city deserves to know the truth about you. Your family deserves more. Don't be a coward."

The word—coward—hit its mark like an arrow. His face pinched in, angry.

He reached down to write a note, but James blocked him and took the notebook himself. He wrote his own message. His handwriting was blockier than mine.

Dad, please. You can't give it to them like you said. She's right. Be brave.

My jaw dropped open. He'd promised the evidence to them. I whispered, "You did what?"

James's dad lifted his finger to his lips, shushing me. He waved for the notepad and started to write again.

But my mind was racing, and I grabbed it, flipped the page, not even bothering to look at what he'd written.

Why give it up now?

Stone-faced, he refused to answer. But his eyes flicked to James.

I pointed to a stereo in the corner, and James took my meaning. He turned on a suite of classical music. I kept my voice low. "You think you're protecting your family, but you're not. How will they feel knowing you changed who you are into something worse, for them?"

"You have no right," the ex-mayor said, choking out the words. "I'm not that man anymore. The idealist."

"You are," I said. "You're pretending not to be."

"Dad?" James said. "That's the man I believed in, growing up."

The ex-mayor lifted his fingers to his lips, shushing us again. But he was bending our way. I didn't want to break him—I wanted to push him, make him bend far enough, like a tree in the wind that then snapped back. I wanted him to stand tall.

I thought he wanted the same thing, underneath his denials. Otherwise, why not destroy whatever evidence he'd amassed in the first place? He might have convinced himself it was an insurance policy only, something to give him leverage should he need it, one final card to play. It was, but not the way he thought.

A man like James's dad—a former reporter for the Harvard *Crimson,* no matter how long ago that was—didn't keep evidence like that unless someday, somehow, he thought he might finally use it. Finding out about the clone and the threat of returning to jail had scared him, made him almost toss away that last chance. I agreed to his request to be quiet, taking the pen again and writing another question for him. *The* question.

Did you tell them where it is?

He stared at me for a long moment, then he shook his head. He mouthed an answer to me and James. *Not yet.*

I released a long breath. I could work with that. He was weakening. I could feel it. He wanted James to be proud of him, but also to protect his family. We had to make him see that rolling over and exposing his soft belly to the bad guys meant he'd never be able to.

Not ever. But this is perfect, I wrote. *Now you just need to tell us where it is. Where did you hide it?*

James stepped in front of his dad, forcing the older man to look at him. He whispered, "Dad, put your faith in me. We can do this." He paused, and then said, "You deserve this. You deserve for people to know the truth. For us, and for you."

The ex-mayor was still torn, and he didn't want to put his family in danger. That much was plain. But I saw the moment he decided to give in, that he bent far enough to snap back. To hope. To believe in the possibility of who he was, underneath the lies that had been attached to his name.

James meant that his father deserved for people to know the truth about him, that he was a good man.

The ex-mayor's spine straightened. He stood tall.

I underlined my question about where the evidence was and held up the pad again. He started to reach out for the pad and pen, but then dropped his hands, hesitation returning.

James had a bit of a temper, could be pushed into a rash response. Maybe his dad did too. So I flipped the page and scribbled ridiculous options for where the evidence might be: *What, did you bury it in the back garden? In the mayor's office?*

He shook his head at first, but flinched.

Flinched as if I'd hit home. "Are you kidding?" I whispered.

But I could tell by the stricken look on his face: He obviously wasn't.

He reached out and took the notepad from me, and he wrote something. He held it against his chest, hesitating one final time. Then he showed us what he'd written.

In the ceiling above my desk. It was the safest place.

Triumph flooded me . . . for a few seconds, before the urge to strangle him returned. I laughed quietly. Nothing was ever easy.

I held my hands out and took the pad. I wrote: *Great! Why couldn't you have put it somewhere harder to get to?* I paused and added: *Yes, I'm being sarcastic.*

He hadn't told *them* it was there. And he was right. They'd never guess.

I wrote one more sentence: *We'll talk tomorrow. We're going to make this right.*

James's dad picked up his drink, and it was a clear sign we were dismissed.

Which was fine with me. I had somewhere else to go, someone else to see. We were finally making progress, and we'd have to move fast from here on out. The story train was leaving the station.

Ticking my head to the side, I waved for James to walk me out. In the garden, he said, "There's no way we'll be able to get into Ellis's office."

"We will," I said. "I'm not worried about that."

Not as my first-tier worry, anyway.

"What's your plan?" he asked. "Pretend you're doing an article on Mayor Ellis? It won't work. Trust me, he'll be a lot harder to get access to than my dad."

"I'll get Devin to look over the City Hall plans. That part should be relatively easy. Maybe."

James huffed. "Which part won't? Dad told them he would

provide the location of the evidence in exchange for them permanently deactivating—that's the word Moxie used—the clone thing. They didn't like having to give anything up, and there were some definite veiled threats exchanged. They were only willing to discuss that *if* Dad gives them the evidence. I'm not sure what their next move will be."

"They'll show your dad they mean business. We're going to have to double down after his stunt tonight. We need to make them believe he's changed his mind and is willing to give it to them. But on our timetable."

The clone's suspicions had been correct. The fact that he liked being connected to Melody made things complicated. But the connection had to end regardless, for Melody's sanity and so I could keep my promise to Maddy. In addition to retrieving the evidence tomorrow, we'd have to figure out *how* to separate the double and Melody permanently and then manage to do it before we exposed Boss Moxie.

I suspected the double himself—despite his protests—was our best hope. He understood what a lack of freedom was like, obviously knew what the cure was, *and* he seemed to care about Melody. But was I giving him too human a psychology? Probably. It was a gamble as an approach to the problem.

Still, none of that was the biggest obstacle in front of me at the moment.

"And you're not worried about that?" James asked. "Doubling down?"

"No, I'm worried about the worst thing this means. It's time for me to talk to Perry," I said. "We'll need his help."

James was quiet. We'd reached the heavy back gate, and he pulled it open for me. There was a face in the iron visible from this direction. It was solemn, with leaves and branches growing up and out, forming the rest of the gate itself.

James latched the gate behind me, but I could see his face between the shapes illuminated by a streetlight.

"You're right," he said, grim. "That is worse. Good luck."

"Text Devin for me, if you don't mind, get him started on the building plans?" I asked.

"Will do."

I crossed the sidewalk and climbed into the cab's backseat. The cabbie said, "Home?"

"Give me a second."

After digging out my phone, I sent SmallvilleGuy a message. He'd be waiting for word from me.

SkepticGirl1: *All is . . . not well. But the mobster is gone. Time to talk to my boss, tho. Perry.*

SmallvilleGuy: *I'm on Bess and Nellie duty overnight, but I want to hear how it goes ASAP.*

SkepticGirl1: *First thing in the a.m.?*

SmallvilleGuy: *Definitely. But message if there's an emergency.*

SkepticGirl1: *You too. Anything from TheInventor?*

SmallvilleGuy: *Not yet—imagine he's hard at work.*

SkepticGirl1: *K. Hug Nellie for me.*

"Ready?" the cabbie prompted.

"One more second." I scrolled through my contacts to Perry's cell phone number. We were only supposed to use it in case of emergency. Like, "if you need to be bailed out of jail," he'd said when he gave it to me.

I hit it and called him. He answered on the second ring.

"Lane?" he said. "It's late. Shouldn't you be asleep?" A pause. "Do you need to be bailed out of jail?"

"Funny," I said. "Not exactly. I need to tell you about the story I've really been working on."

Another pause stretched between us. "This can't wait until tomorrow?"

"I'm afraid not."

"I'm still at the office anyway," he said. "Shoot."

This wasn't a conversation to have over the phone. I'd already snuck out, so I might as well do all the business I needed to while I was on the lam. Lucky for me, all that quality time with Mom and Lucy meant less chance either would look in on me in my room, and Dad was gone. As far as I could tell, I was home free.

"I'll meet you at the *Scoop* in twenty minutes," I said.

CHAPTER 24

I'd never been to the Daily Planet Building this late at night. But neither news nor the city slept. So while the building was less busy than during the bustling day and early evening hours, that didn't mean it was deserted.

The freckled desk guy was signing to accept an after-hours messenger delivery, probably headed up to the newsroom. He glanced up at the clock above the elevators when he saw me, but he waved me on by.

The lower level where our office was housed was dead. It was dark enough that I had to hold my phone out in front of me and use the screen to light the way. Somehow it seemed fitting that I had to travel in darkness toward this certain doom.

Perry would not be happy about what I had to tell him. To say the very, very least.

Each step made me want to turn around, leave, chicken out, talk to him over the phone. Or send a nice, long email. So when the light in the *Scoop* office popped on as I approached, I made an embarrassingly high-pitched squeak of surprise.

"Lane? You almost gave me a heart attack. You sound like a giant, dying mouse," Perry said, appearing in the doorway. "I barely beat you here. You're on time, though. Twenty minutes on the dot."

My phone vibrated in my hand, and I looked down at it, half-hoping it would show MOM on the screen and give me an excuse to run. Instead, it showed a new text from Maddy. It said: *DO NOT TELL PERRY ABOUT MELODY.*

All caps. I frowned, and in the next second the phone rang, blaring the song Maddy had made her ringtone on my phone.

"Lois?" Perry wasn't the most patient man in the world.

"I have to take this," I said, with a sick feeling in my stomach. I *had* to tell Perry about Melody, didn't I?

I answered the phone and said, "Hang on," then held it against my chest. "Can you give me a few minutes?" I asked Perry.

"Don't keep me waiting forever," Perry said. "And whatever you have to tell me better be good. I'll be in my office."

He meant the dank office cave in the back of the *Scoop* offices, where he occasionally came to work in quiet.

I stepped back into the darkness of the hallway, out of earshot, in case he was motivated to eavesdrop.

"Maddy?" I asked, lifting the receiver to my ear. "Why? What's the big deal?"

"Lois, you haven't told him yet, right? I heard Perry's voice. Is it too late?"

"I'm just getting ready to talk to him." I leaned against the wall, holding the receiver close. "How do you even know . . . Oh. James."

"He called me," she confirmed. "You could have too, you know."

She was right. I could have, and I should have. It hadn't even occurred to me, in the midst of my dread. I couldn't even swear to her I would have before morning.

"You're right. I suck," I said. "But don't you think we have to tell him?"

"No!" she said. "You told us that Melody's DNA sample was the only one that had worked for this so far. If the world finds out about this, don't you think her life will be—maybe not ruined, but it'll be forever changed. Anyone who Googles her will find out about this. This stupid mistake she made. That she's linked to this *thing*. They'll study her." Maddy paused. "She had another spell tonight. She woke up, thirty minutes ago, crying in her sleep."

When I'd been talking to the clone. When he reached out to her.

"But how can I not tell him?" I asked.

"Put me on video."

I switched over, holding the phone out so I could see her. Maddy's face appeared in the narrow window. She'd been crying too, I saw. Her eyes were so red.

"She's my sister," she said. "I can't stand by and let you mess up her life. Perry probably won't even believe the cloning part. Think about it. There's another way."

Her face convinced me. I might not have seen the other way yet, but I wouldn't betray my friend. And she was likely right about Perry not buying the cloning stuff, not easily.

More than that, I understood. We protect the people we care about when we can, especially when they've done nothing wrong. It was like keeping SmallvilleGuy a secret. I did it because it was right to.

I was the one who'd prodded Maddy to begin the process of forgiving Melody in the first place.

I nodded, so she'd see I meant it. "Okay. But I need something to explain . . . him. You have an idea?"

She released a sigh of relief. "A twin is a clone—but a natural one," Maddy said, rushing through the explanation. "The double could just be a twin James's dad didn't know he had, as far as the rest of the world is concerned. The fingerprints, you said those could have been planted."

"That's a lot more feasible," I agreed. "We can come up with some story about how Moxie located this unknown twin brother and hired him."

"See, it might work," she said.

"It will work," I said. "I'll loop in James. We'll have to come up with another way to deal with the scientist, though. Because he has to be stopped."

My mind rushed ahead. I could retrieve the lock picks when I got home. We'd have to go to the Ismenios building first thing in the morning, try to beat Donovan there, and convince the clone to help us disconnect Melody from him. Once her tie to the clone was broken, we'd have more leeway to handle the mad doctor.

"You two be ready to meet me early in the morning. We'll have to take a field trip to Suicide Slum before school. I know it's quick, but it can't wait. Everything's moving now. Assuming I survive the next half hour."

"You will. And you promise, about Mel?" Maddy asked one last time.

"I do so solemnly swear. If Perry kills me, it was nice knowing you. Make sure the *Planet* gives me a full obit."

"Thank you, Lois. For everything. You don't suck. You're . . . you're my best friend."

There was a wet sting in my eyes suddenly. I was important to Maddy too. I was her *best friend*. "Back at you. Now stop with the mush. I'll text you if I survive."

I hung up, sniffed to banish the threatening tears, and walked into the office. Passing my own desk and everyone else's, computers dark, I went straight to the corner and into the hot seat across from Perry's sometime-desk.

"This must be good," he said. "If it's not, I'm going to be really disappointed."

No pressure or anything. "Good may not be the right word."

How could I tell the best reporter I knew, my own hero, that he'd been fooled? That the stories he was proudest of were phony?

"It's late and I'm waiting," Perry said. "Give me the bad news, then."

"It's not exactly bad news either." The answer was clear. I had to say it straight out. I thought of what James had told his dad.

It was time to be brave.

We needed Perry. He was a key component of my plan to throw off the mobster and his henchmen, and then take them down. I was too much of a realist to see this unspooling in our favor otherwise.

"I'm ready, Lane," he said.

No more shying away. The clock was ticking. "I've found evidence that suggests Mayor Worthington was set up by Boss Moxie. That he used—" I phrased it with care, per my promise to Maddy, "—an unknown twin brother of the mayor's to fake most of the evidence that convinced you and the rest of the world he was corrupt, because Mayor Worthington was planning to take Moxie down. And so Boss Moxie could get a more amenable politician—Mayor Ellis, who was in on the whole thing—into office and get richer and more powerful off this waterfront project. Among, no doubt, countless other unsavory things." Like clones. But that had to go unsaid.

Perry blinked twice, in rapid succession, but the rest of him was still. "What kind of evidence do you have?" he asked.

I couldn't interpret his tone. I'd never heard him use it before. It was . . . neutral.

Giving me no hint how he was taking this.

"The twin is here in town. I've seen him, and so have plenty of other people. You just missed him the other day—that was him at City Hall. That's why people were whispering about seeing Mayor Worthington. But I—not to mention the police—confirmed that Mayor Worthington was at home at the time, and James was there with him. Moxie knows that James's dad still has the evidence and wants *him* to know he can be sent away again if he becomes inconvenient. So they arranged for the twin to be spotted. A threat."

"Why not just take him out?" Perry asked. "Moxie's done it before."

I'd wondered the same thing. "I don't know. I think maybe Moxie has a love for the dramatic? And a mayor is different than another mobster. Even an ex-mayor."

Perry inhaled deeply, and then nodded. "And maybe they worried the wife would come forward with the evidence if they did that. He does still have it? I'm assuming he kept quiet about this fact because Moxie convinced him James and Leah were toast if he revealed it at the time."

This sounded an awful lot like he *believed* me.

"Mr. White," I said, and when he frowned at me, "Perry. Are you saying that you think I'm right? That this is the truth?"

"Lane, you're a good reporter. I'm assuming James has been helping you, giving you unprecedented access." He paused. "But I'll admit it's that I had a feeling back then. You know the one, that some piece is missing. It was all too neat. The story, the tapes, everything, it fell into my lap. James's dad never defended himself against the charges, even though I've never seen a politician more in love with his job or the city. And he was the *only* one who went down for it. In my experience, corruption hardly ever stops at one person. But that time it did. A twin would explain the tapes, eye witnesses who said he asked them to transfer funds, all of it."

I shouldn't be arguing against my own case. But . . . "You were nominated for a Pulitzer."

"We don't do *this* for awards." He waved his hand to indicate the walls around us. "They're nice, and I was proud of my stories. I put everything I had into them. But if awards are more important to us than the truth, we have no business being here. So, you called me here for a reason. What's our next step?"

Of all the ways I'd imagined this conversation going, this was not one of them. He was on board. He was going to help us.

Our next step.

I hadn't even been forced to beg.

"James's dad called Moxie and Ellis tonight. He has them motivated to threaten his freedom again. But I know now where the evidence is, the stuff he had on Moxie. We need to get it, and get someone on our side who can arrest them. Maybe—" I'd been putting this together in my head on the way over. Maddy's request changed things a little, but my general idea might work. "If James's dad tells Moxie and Ellis he's changed his mind and is willing to hand it over, we can keep them occupied tomorrow while we work out the arrest part. But we need somebody who can handle the court side too, who'll defend James's dad and go after Moxie and Ellis." That's when it occurred to me. "Devin said his mom isn't a fan of Moxie."

"Angela Harris? Runs the public defender's office, well respected. We could go to the DA's office, but—" He shook his head. "They have to have someone on Moxie's payroll. They've tried to bring him down, but the cases always fall apart early on. I think Harris would listen to what we have to say. She believes in justice, and she'll take up Worthington's cause if she thinks he's innocent. We'll need the arrests to happen in public, so we can make all this known if we're going to clear his name. Before they have time to try to clean up the mess. You're sure Worthington's innocent?"

"The evidence should show it."

"And we can get to the evidence?"

I'd bluffed a little with James about how easy that would be. Here was hoping that Devin was out there scouring the plans for City Hall and discovering some magical way for me to access the ceiling in the mayor's office without getting caught in the process.

"We don't have a choice. But it'll be complicated, and probably a good thing you have someone under eighteen to do it."

"Why?" he asked.

I shrugged. "Well, how much trouble can a minor get into for B and E into the mayor's office? In broad daylight."

He blinked at me again.

"Forget I said anything. It was a joke. You'll be busy getting Devin's mom on board. We'll set a rendezvous point around City Hall, and leave the rest to me and James."

I waited, and it occurred to me I may have said too much about the location of the goods.

Finally, he nodded. "You are not, under any circumstances, to get arrested, Lane."

We talked for a while longer, coming to an agreement about how we'd proceed the next day. Perry was on board with acting fast, before Moxie had a chance to get wind of our plot or to do something to James and his family. I had to buy the morning free to try to get Melody clear, because when the rest of these dominoes started to fall—well, we couldn't have her still standing in the way of them.

CHAPTER 25

Perry insisted on seeing me home. So I texted Taxi Jack: *I have an escort, so go home and I'll add an extra tip next time. Which will probably be tomorrow.* Part of me expected a fight, and that the car would be waiting when we left the *Planet,* but he was nowhere to be seen as we walked a block and then navigated across town by subway. We were quiet, possibly paranoid that Boss Moxie's spies were everywhere.

They probably were.

"I'll go on from here alone," I told Perry when we reached my stop. I hopped off the train. "It's less than a block. Well, a block and a half. But close."

It was also well after midnight.

"Your parents don't know you're out, I'm assuming? I'm walking you." Perry stepped off the train seconds before the doors closed, and held up a hand when I started to protest. He kept talking as we hit the stairs up to the street. It wasn't crowded, but there were a few other people on the sidewalk. "I'm not going to tell them what happened. Not tonight. *But* no more sneaking out for the job. You're too good a reporter and I don't want to have to fire you. You need to recognize some rules are rules for a reason, there to protect you."

I ignored the ridiculous part about rules and protection. Affronted, I asked, *"Fire* me?"

Like I hadn't just brought him the story of the year. I sniffed in the cooler night air, pulled my jacket tighter around myself.

"I said I don't want to have to." He paused on the sidewalk until I pointed ahead. We turned onto the block where our brownstone was.

He went on. "And, yes, I know you're thinking you can't believe I called you out on this after you brought me this story. I am impressed that you put all this together. But you're only sixteen. You're still in high school. Not an adult."

"Fine," I grumbled, feeling a keen sense of betrayal.

"You might not even want to do this with the rest of your life," he added.

"I will punch you," I said.

"No, you won't," Perry said. "I was kidding about that anyway. I know another lifer when I see one."

My disgruntlement faded.

We made quick work of the rest of the walk, and when we reached the brownstone—dark, thankfully—I waved and he headed back the way we'd come.

I twisted the doorknob oh-so-quietly, praying my mom was sound asleep. And . . . I made it inside. So far, so good. The living room was dark, and my knee banged a coffee table. I swallowed my ouch, and soft-shoed toward the hall and Dad's study. I'd grab the lock picks so I was ready for morning, then try for a few hours of fitful sleep, wake to check in with SmallvilleGuy.

That was my plan.

Until I realized something was wrong. The light in Dad's study was on.

I was almost positive it hadn't been when I left. He confirmed it by appearing in the doorway a heartbeat later, a dark silhouette.

"Where have you been?" he asked, his voice a hush.

The house around us was silent except for the hum of the heating system. Lucy and Mom must have been sound asleep upstairs.

I was busted. There was no point pretending otherwise.

I continued toward him. When I was a foot away, I said, softly, "Working. I thought you were too."

"I have an interagency meeting in Wichita tomorrow," Dad said, keeping his voice low, controlled. "But my flight got canceled. I'll go out in the morning."

This was a deceptively civil exchange.

He retreated into the study. But I knew our conversation wasn't over. So I followed without him having to ask, and then took the chair in front of his imposing wooden desk.

Dad had a slower gait when he was tired, and he employed

it to go over and pick up the framed photograph of our family. The one where I was the lone scowler. The one where he hid the key to his goodie stash.

My heart picked up its pace. This wasn't good. I had put back the key, right? I'd been in such a rush to get back to the kitchen. And he wasn't supposed to be home.

Tiredness wasn't just in the way he moved as he walked back toward me with the photograph. His expression was weary, his face pale. I pictured him sitting in the terminal at the airport for hours, waiting for a flight before he gave up and decided to come back and try again tomorrow. He was still in his uniform.

He reached me and extended the photograph toward me. "Take it," he said.

I did so, and felt along the back instinctively. There was nothing there.

"Dad," I started, searching for some explanation to rattle off. Some cover story.

"No. No excuses," he said and lumbered around the desk to take his own seat. He considered me, folding his hands in front of him. For the third time in one night, I sat across from a powerful authority figure. Somehow I didn't think this would go as well as my confabs with the ex-mayor or Perry had.

But I marshaled my arguments to make the attempt. "Dad—"

"No. Keep it down. Your mother told me about your girls' night. I don't want her to know about this. It would ruin it for her, make her feel tricked."

My eyes narrowed. "I wasn't fooling her. We were having fun. And you can't just decide what people know and don't know. She should make her own call."

His lips quirked up on one side. "That's my daughter, so contrary she's now arguing that I should probably inform her mother I caught her sneaking in forty-five minutes after midnight." He lifted one of his hands and pointed to the photograph currently in a death grip in my hands. "Look at it."

It hardly seemed possible the key could be missing and he *didn't know* I'd been "borrowing" it and items from his stash, but maybe. I stared down at our faces, frozen on that day. Here I was again, facing off against Dad, like I had right before it was taken.

"I think more people should get realistic portraits like this." I held it up for his inspection. "It might catch on."

"This is no time for jokes."

"Gallows humor." I placed the photograph on his desk.

"You've been stealing things from me," he said.

"Borrowing," I clarified.

"Some of those things are dangerous."

No kidding. Like the prism flares. Even a lock pick was dangerous in the right hands.

Hands like mine.

"I've only borrowed a couple of little things. Nothing big," I said. It wasn't an outright lie. "And I returned them."

"Well, it stops now."

"No kidding. You put the key somewhere new. I'm guessing someplace harder to get to."

He smiled at that. "You're right."

Crap. That meant no lock picks in time for the morning. There went my plan for getting into Ismenios.

"Fun talk," I said, and rose, fighting down a surge of panic. We'd have to regroup on the fly in the morning. Dabney Donovan's whistling still gave me the shivery creeps, and my original idea was to avoid confronting him directly. But there might not be another way . . . "I've had a long night. If we're not telling Mom, can I get some sleep?"

"Sit. Down."

It was the General's command voice. Even I didn't disobey that. Not unless it was absolutely unavoidable. I sat, my palms damp.

"Yes, Dad?"

"We're going to try an experiment. I have to go out of town tomorrow, for my interagency meeting. I'll be back Friday night. You are grounded for the next twenty-four hours, but it's going to be up to you to police yourself. You'll go to school, then come straight home. If you abide by this, I might actually not tell your mother once I'm back. As long as you know you will never leave this house so late without asking permission again." He paused. "If you can't manage to police yourself, then we're going to have a more serious chat."

My head was shaking no in reflex. Tomorrow wasn't a good day for this.

I swallowed the truth. "Got it."

Which, again, wasn't a lie. I did understand the agreement I'd be violating.

"Go get some sleep," he said. "I know you think you've found your calling, and maybe you have. But you can't worry your mother."

Or you. You're really the one who's worried.

"Got it twice," I said. "Have fun in Kansas City."

"Wichita," he said. "Goodnight."

I left and climbed the stairs to my room. What tomorrow held was a mystery, but I couldn't see any way to observe the terms of the agreement. I pushed aside my concern about what Dad would do when he found out I hadn't come straight home after school.

Because I was thinking about something else.

Wichita.

Crossing to my computer, I keyed in the passwords and pulled up Strange Skies.

The next night's sighting was scheduled to take place at coordinates not far outside Wichita, Kansas. Not far from where Dad and I had seen the teetering rock tower and encountered the flying man two years ago, something we'd never mentioned to each other since that night.

"This is an unwelcome coincidence," I said.

But my gut told me it was no coincidence at all.

*

My fingers were back on the keyboard pre-dawn the next morning. SmallvilleGuy's name showed as logged in to chat, but he might have left it that way.

SkepticGirl1: *You there?*

Sleep had been a dreamless miracle, like I was in that glowing blue tank across town instead of my bed. I hadn't expected to grab so much as a wink, but I had a feeling my body sensed I'd need it for the day ahead.

Mob bosses and mad scientists and spooky mental links to somehow sever, oh my. Plus, my dad in Kansas, probably up to no good. And TheInventor was out there hacking to figure out who was on the task force.

Worlds that weren't meant to collide were about to.

SmallvilleGuy: *I'm here. Came in a little while ago. Bess is finally almost well. Nellie Bly made me give her an extra bottle. She wouldn't stop looking at me with those big eyes.*

SmallvilleGuy: *How did things go with Perry?*

I sucked in a breath, the many events of the night before flooding back. Deciding where to start wasn't easy . . .

SkepticGirl1: *Before I tell you about that: I think my dad might be part of the interagency task force.*

I waited for the shocked response and waited and, finally, after half a minute, it came.

SmallvilleGuy: *How do you know?*

SkepticGirl1: *He caught me last night, coming home after talking to Perry. And he said his flight had gotten bumped but he was going to an interagency meeting in Wichita.*

SmallvilleGuy: *So he didn't outright say it?*

SkepticGirl1: *No, but I think we can assume. The coordinates for tonight? I looked them up. They're exactly where my own sighting happened.*

SmallvilleGuy: *I know.*

I frowned at the screen and made an entry in my mental ledger of information that didn't quite add up.

SkepticGirl1: *How? I never got that specific about the location.*

SmallvilleGuy: *I haven't checked the coordinates myself, but seems like you must be right if your dad's involved.*

He hadn't exactly answered my question, but I backed off. We had something bigger to discuss.

SkepticGirl1: *Okay. So, I don't have much time—do you think we should tell TheInventor about this? We can if you think we should. But, you know, if my dad finds out that I've been on the boards, bad things will happen. He's already about to lower the ax. Off with her head, etc.*

SmallvilleGuy: *Can't let that happen. I like your head on your shoulders. It's good there.*

He was always able to do that. But his joke had made me feel better.

Much.

How did he know to do that when we'd never met for real?

SkepticGirl1: *I was serious last night. If it comes to a big reveal, it comes to that. But I'd rather it not.*

SmallvilleGuy: *Agreed. I don't think we should tell TheInventor. He doesn't know who you are.*

Now this was an interesting twist.

SkepticGirl1: *You trust him still?*

SmallvilleGuy: *I do, but not with your secrets. Not even with all of mine. He as much as said he has his own reasons and he's not necessarily sharing them with us.*

SmallvilleGuy: *I trust him to help us and to do what we discussed if he can. But . . . that's far enough. When in doubt, I ask What Would Lois Do?*

SmallvilleGuy: *I trust you and your gut more.*

I found my fingers rising to touch the screen. I was smiling.

SkepticGirl1: *So we'll keep that to ourselves then. It shouldn't matter. Either he gets the info and scares off Insider01 with his message . . . or not, and we deal with it.*

But I was feeling more optimistic about the plan. If my dad was part of this task force, I could imagine his reaction all too easily. He'd urge retreat, find a different method to attack their problem. They hadn't turned up anything that resembled a lead that we knew about, and if they had, they wouldn't be continuing to post fake sightings.

My phone buzzed beside me and I saw Devin's name pop up in a text message. Followed by Maddy's. And then James's.

They'd restarted our group confab from the other night. I was beyond fully awake now, and all the way into wired territory.

SkepticGirl1: *I'm going to have to take off. Today's the day. James's dad pushed things. We have to act fast. Perry's recruiting help from Devin's mom. She's a lawyer.*

SmallvilleGuy: *What does that mean? What are you going to do?*

SkepticGirl1: *A game of misdirection not unlike our own. But the first thing we have to do is get Melody safely separated from the clone. Which probably isn't going to be easy. After that, it's a matter of tricking Boss Moxie and his mayor friend to the Worthington manor at the right time for me to rifle through the mayor's office, us to get a warrant for their arrest, and arrange for James's dad to be seen in public at just the right moment and them to do likewise and get handcuffs. Easy, right?*

SmallvilleGuy: *I could barely follow that. Lois, I want to know everything, when you have time. And you can only tell me if you aren't hurt. Or in jail.*

SkepticGirl1: *Relax, the most dangerous thing I'm doing is crawling around in the ceiling at City Hall.*

SmallvilleGuy: *I hope that's a joke.*

SkepticGirl1: *Not as such. Technically I'm crawling around in the mayor's office ceiling at City Hall. Let me know if you hear news from TI.*

And there was also the impending visit to the lab. But he knew how scared I'd been after the last one. Best to keep that to myself, and not worry him unnecessarily. I'd have my friends with me this time around.

SmallvilleGuy: *Look, I know you're going back to that lab too. Please be careful—I don't know what I'd do if something happened to you.*

I wanted to tell him how I felt, right away, in case of the worst. But I didn't.

SkepticGirl1: *Something happens to me every day. You be careful too.*

I paused, then added one final note.

SkepticGirl1: *<3*

I closed my laptop lid, too embarrassed to wait for a response.

Picking up my phone, I read through the texts from my friends.

Devin was still working through the City Hall schematics to find my angle of attack. I told him to stay on it and we'd see him at school. We didn't need everyone on this morning's field trip.

Maddy's last message was: *I asked Dante if he'd meet us. He knows the neighborhood.*

If she was willing to vouch for him after one coffee date, it wasn't a terrible argument. I pasted in the address of the building across the street and texted back: *See you there in half an hour. Keep a low profile if you get there first.*

James sent back a response: *I'm coming too.*

I returned: *Stay with your dad. We'll see you at school.*

Maddy said: *Thanks. See u guys soon.*

My first step was to type and print off a note to Dabney Donovan. Given his avoidance of all things electronic, it seemed likely he'd want his communiqués to come old school. Soon, we'd see if I was right. Next, I wrote the note I expected Principal Butler to deliver to Boss Moxie and Mayor Ellis later in the afternoon, summoning them back to City Hall. That was as big a gamble as anything else.

Good thing I loved to live dangerously.

CHAPTER 26

Mom was in the kitchen when I came downstairs—early, even for early-bird her. And I was up way early for me. That did not escape her.

"Lois?" she asked. "Where are you off to at this hour?"

So far, it seemed like Dad hadn't filled her in. He was sticking to our deal.

"That story I mentioned. I think I found a crack, and now I need to pry it open."

"Colorful metaphor," she said, pulling her robe belt tighter. "Here, take my toast so you have something to eat. I'll make more."

He *definitely* hadn't told her. Toast was for daughters on good terms with their parents.

"Why are you up so early?" I asked, accepting the buttery

bread. It was slightly blackened around the edges, the way we both liked it.

She yawned. "I might go back to bed after I get Lucy to school. I stayed up awhile after our junk food bonanza, and then your dad didn't manage to leave after all. He came home late and had to go out early this morning. He told me not to get up, but I did anyway." She stopped for a second. "He asked how you seemed last night. I told him fine. Are you fine?"

Part of me wanted to tell her everything. The rest of me knew there wasn't time. And that no mother would be thrilled her daughter was doing what I was with her day. Dad had made clear there would be consequences for my straying from the path and not coming home straight after school. I didn't approve of him keeping this from her.

However, I'd come up with a thin possibility of making everything happen *during* school that might allow me to fill Dad's terms while still getting my job done. It was a long shot, but there was a chance.

"Better than fine," I said. "Looking forward to getting this scoop."

"Then go get it. Take some extra money from my purse in case you need cab fare."

Something in her voice made me wonder if she was in the loop on everything, after all.

But I wasn't going to question her generosity. "Thanks, Mom," I said.

Her purse was on the table next to the front door, and she watched, lingering in the kitchen, as I removed a twenty.

Out the door I went, and hailed the first random cab I saw. The driver was an older woman with a faint Russian accent, who didn't so much as blink at the address when I gave it. Safer place to visit during the early a.m., I supposed. No text messages from my friends, no nothing, all the way there.

I reread the note I'd prepared to get rid of Donovan, typed and printed so the handwriting wouldn't give anything away:

Doc, your angel investor needs a word. Not later, now. Come alone.

Then I'd provided an address: the one from Devin's list with all the flashy cars and suited men outside it when I'd driven by. Moxie himself likely wouldn't be there, and it wouldn't take Donovan away for long. But I was hoping it'd be long enough for us to get in and do what needed to be done. If only I knew more about what that was.

On the brighter side, Dante would make a handy fake courier to deliver the note. I didn't think there'd been any security cameras at the lab to get a shot of me last time, just the evil phone-wiping thing. I couldn't be sure though. And Doc D might recognize Maddy, but especially Melody, even if he wouldn't remember her name.

The cab pulled up at the curb of my destination, the back end of an alley that spilled out onto the street across from Ismenios's offices. I pressed the twenty into the driver's hand, adding a fiver for a tip. The only words we'd exchanged were the address, and now her bland "Thank you." The car rolled away, and I'd have bet the same twenty-five bucks she'd never think of me again. There was a comfort in that.

Metropolis was small enough to go most anywhere inside the city in half an hour and yet large enough to be anonymous about it. The ability to get from place to place with no one the wiser was the exact opposite of the bases I'd grown up on and most of the towns where we'd lived, small enough someone was always watching. Here, there were people heading toward the subway and their work days, but they paid no attention to a strange girl on the sidewalk.

The sky above was filled with heavy gray clouds. I hoped they weren't a bad omen. The weather report had called for a perfectly sunny day, and if this unfolded like I wanted, we'd be enjoying it at the end, out in the light on the steps of City Hall, basking in the glow of justice having been served.

As I breached the lip of the alley, I saw Melody, Maddy, and Dante were already there, waiting close to the far end. Melody leaned against a wall, but Maddy and Dante were facing each other and huddled together. Their date must have gone very well.

I was happy for my friend. But I couldn't help thinking— what about me? That stupid heart symbol I'd typed—I wondered what SmallvilleGuy had made of it, if anything.

I paused and sent Taxi Jack a message with my current location: *Pick us up here in half an hour? Last night's tip is waiting.*

"Lois?" The voice came from behind me.

I turned on my heel. "James? What are you doing here? I told you to stay home and just come to school."

James sported jeans and a crisp white button-down. He

peered past me into the shadowy alley to where Maddy and Dante were—reluctantly, based on the speed—stepping apart.

"We don't know him very well," he said.

"What are you, pulling some sort of big brother routine?" I asked, genuinely confused by his reactions, like I had been for the past couple of days.

"No," he said, but he didn't elaborate.

"Be a secret-keeping weirdo," I countered, and started walking again. "I trust you can make yourself useful—but you can't be seen by the mad doctor. How's your dad? Not going to do anything to mess this up, is he?"

"He's so hard to read these days," James said. "But I don't think so."

The dank alley was wide enough for us to walk next to each other, and he hurried to my side. The graffiti we passed consisted of random tagging, nothing that shouted "Bossland" to me or that was fancy enough to merit Dante's approval.

James continued. "I heard him . . . whistling this morning."

I suppressed a shudder at the memory of Doctor Donovan on the stairs.

"Not like a serial killer," James clarified. "Like he was happy. And he gave me a big hug before I left. Said thanks and be careful."

Those words could foreshadow some sort of kamikaze last ditch on his part, but I didn't think so. "We gave him hope. You believing in him, it's what made the difference."

James didn't respond, but when I glanced over, he seemed to be walking taller, prouder.

The others met us halfway, but I waved us back in the direction they'd come. "Have you seen him yet?"

Melody spoke up. "No one's gone in or out yet." She hesitated. "I can feel him in there though. He's awake."

"I need you to prepare yourself, mentally. We're going to have to convince him to help us."

"Him? The . . ." James lifted his hand and waved it at his face to indicate the clone.

"Yes," I said, "we're sending away the doctor. Which, Dante, you're here to help?"

I had no idea how much Dante knew, but what Melody had said made me think it was more than a little. Maddy must trust him already, to give up her sister's secrets.

"I'm here to help," he said, smiling at Maddy. Who smiled back.

"Stop or I'm going to have to call the adorable police," I said.

They grinned wider. Interestingly enough, Maddy was wearing a repeat band shirt, something she hardly ever did. I'd seen the one she had on, Dangerous Ladies, before.

James's scowl was back, and I could tell from Melody's thoughtful glance between him and the cute couple that she noticed too.

"James, stop being weird," I said, low.

"Well, his dad is having a pretty big day," Maddy said.

James beamed at her.

"I can't deal with another mystery right now." I fished out the note and handed it to Dante. "This is for Donovan. We know he goes home at night, and the clone stays here in his tank. You'll be waiting so you can give this to him when he gets here. Let him unlock the door first. I'm hoping we won't have to break in, but we might and I wasn't able to bring my picks. If he asks you anything, you just say, 'I was just given twenty bucks to make sure you got this,' and then you leave. Come back over here. Fast. Questions?"

"Seems simple enough," he said.

"We'll stay over here until he's on the move again." I spoke to the girls next. "Ladies, give your phones to James."

I handed over mine too.

"What's this for?" he asked.

"Dante will come back to join you. You guys will stay over here, being lookouts. If you need to get our attention, well, I don't know. Break down the front door or something. But do *not* bring the phones in with you."

"I don't want you guys going in alone," James said. "Especially without your phones. And I don't want to be rude, but should someone we just met be part of this at all?"

Dante hooked a thumb in his pocket, as casual as if we weren't on post-dawn maneuvers. "Don't worry about me. Maddy told me everything. I've seen some things . . . It's not so hard to believe. She also told me this is about taking down the Boss—" he lowered his voice on the word, even though we were the only ones around. "That needs to happen."

I wanted to know what kind of things Dante had seen, but I decided to interrupt before James could. It was a question for later. For after.

"We can't take our phones in," I said. "But more than that,

it's just a feeling I have. You two can distract Donovan if he comes back early. I think the three of us will have better luck with the clone. Seeing you . . . You look too much like your dad. It'll be painful. It'll remind him too much of the life his twin has that he doesn't. I need him focused on Melody."

"What? Why?" Maddy had her hand at her throat, like it was the most alarming thing she'd ever heard.

"He cares about her. That's why."

Maddy got ready to ask another question, but Dante peeled away toward the end of the alley. "Where are you going?" Maddy asked.

"The weird dude in the suit just walked past," Dante said over his shoulder. "I'm going to deliver my message."

And he was out of the alley like he'd been ejected from a slingshot.

CHAPTER 27

We crowded around the leftmost edge of the alley's wall.
Dante raced across the street and up the sidewalk.

Maddy jostled against me, causing my arm to brush the wall. It came away damp with what I hoped was the alley version of morning condensation. "Ew," I said.

"Sorry." Maddy wiped at my arm.

"We have bigger problems than alley slime," I said. "Um, luckily?"

The weird man in a suit was still well in front of Dante, nearing the door, with its monster. Most people would turn if they heard sneakers slapping the pavement behind them—particularly in this neighborhood—but our mad scientist gave no indication he even noticed.

His suit was dove gray, and he was otherwise as Melody

had described. Unassuming, contained. Like he traveled with a bubble around him, separating him from the outside world—the likely reasons being his intellect and the vast genius superiority complex that accompanied it. He gave every impression of being the definition of self-involved.

At the door, he stopped and did something unexpected. He lifted his hand and raised one fingertip to touch the image of the hero fighting the dragon-monster. The act was done almost lovingly. But then, for him to have taken the time to fix up a logo and apply it, it must be meaningful to him.

He'd named himself after the dragon Ismenios. Its teeth turned to warriors, still fighting even after Cadmus defeated it to found a new city. No way this guy was founding any kind of new anything, if I could stop it.

Some sort of flat card dangled from his hand. A key card?

Dante slowed, then stopped six feet away. He appeared to be waiting for something.

Now, Dante. Now. Once he's inside, things get a lot more complicated.

Donovan confirmed my suspicion about the card when he waved his hand in front of door, and then reached out for the handle, pulling it open—

He's going to get away.

I shifted my weight to my back foot, preparing to jump out of the alley and intervene. But Dante called out to him then, before he could step over the threshold.

"Hey, mister!" Dante sprang into motion. "Doctor, I have a message for you!"

Dante stopped an arm's length away and extended my phony note toward Donovan. The paper flapped in the breeze.

The man turned his head to the side and regarded the piece of paper, not releasing the door handle. Not yet.

I felt Maddy's sharp intake of breath beside me. "He wouldn't hurt Dante, would he?" she asked.

"After what he did to me?" Melody said from her other side. "Yes."

"We all saw how fast Dante can run," I murmured, afraid to reassure either of them too much.

I thought hard at Dante: *Be ready to get away, like I told you.*

Donovan apparently decided Dante wasn't worth his notice, because he pulled the door the rest of the way open, intent on getting inside.

Dante was talking louder than normal, probably so we'd be able to hear what he was saying. None of this had been included in my directions.

"Doctor, didn't you hear?" Dante said, infusing it with a cocky swagger. "I have a message. From *the Boss.*"

That got Donovan's full attention. Still with the door half-open, he extended his other hand and accepted the piece of paper. Given how Dante usually said the mobster's name in a hush, he really was committed to helping us.

Maybe too committed.

Dante should have left, but he lingered.

Donovan unfolded and examined the paper for much longer than reading my brief message could've taken, then— finally—he released the door and started up the street in the opposite direction. It was the direction of the address I'd given, and he went without missing a beat, without even looking back at Dante.

Unsurprising. He assumed most life forms were beneath his notice. All except his creation.

"Nice tip!" Dante called after him, which I wouldn't have, on the odds he looked back.

He would see that Dante had caught the handle before the door could close completely. But Donovan paid his complaint no attention, and his wide strides took him farther and farther away. I wouldn't know until we got over there, but Dante might have saved us from having to break in.

"Good choice of boyfriend," I said to Maddy.

I figured she'd be blushing when I looked over, but instead she said, "I know."

James said something under his breath. Donovan turned the corner, officially out of our sight.

"We're on," I said.

I stepped out of the alley, and Maddy and Melody did likewise.

"Guys," James said, and we paused. "Be safe. I'm a little attached to you three being alive."

His eyes rested on Maddy for a second before meeting mine. "Touching," I said, not entirely sarcastically. Was it my imagination, or was he suddenly really interested in Maddy? Too interested, given that she was in a promising place with a great new guy. "We'll do our best. We still have your dad to save, after all."

There was nothing more to say. Our time wasn't limitless. Already, while we'd been standing out here, waiting and watching, the day was brightening. The gray sky had grown a shade lighter.

As we crossed the street, dodging through traffic, Maddy asked, "You don't really think we might not make it out of here?"

"I'm attached to the idea of being alive *and* seeing Moxie go down, so here's hoping," I said, hurrying us onto the sidewalk.

"Not a time for morgue humor," Melody said. In a more measured tone, she added, "Though I've read it's part of newsroom culture."

"Everyone's an expert on journalism," I said.

But it was noteworthy that Melody had been reading up. Was it a gesture to her sister? And had my conversation with Maddy softened her up any toward Melody?

Time would tell. Assuming we made it out of Ismenios intact.

We reached Dante, who pulled the front door the rest of the way open to admit us. I got a good look at the dragon battling the man with the sword. Since in the myth the man won, I decided we'd be him in this fight. Donovan and his clone were playing the part of the monster.

"Good luck," Dante said.

Maddy leaned over and kissed his cheek, quickly, as she passed.

"Take it easy on James until we get back," I said to him. "And thanks."

"My pleasure," he said. Then he jogged away, toward James.

I bent down and put a piece of paper torn from my notepad in place to block the lock's engagement, in case the boys did need to get in here and come to our rescue. I let the door close.

The interior of the lobby was dark; the light that came in from outside was weak. I unearthed my flashlight and traced its circle of light up the stairs.

"This is totally different than the other place," Melody said. "I don't think I'd have gone through with it if the building had been this old and clearly abandoned."

I'd had that question in the back of my mind. "He probably chose a nicer place then, because he knew he needed to lure in subjects."

"The verb lure," Maddy said, "is seriously creepy."

"No argument with that or its appropriateness applied to that creep," I said.

We started up the first set of steps, which were wide enough that we could have stayed next to each other. But the twins let me lead. It was logical because I had the flashlight, but I sensed they were as afraid as I was. Logic wasn't much a part of it.

My heart pounded annoyingly in my ears, and it was getting harder to stay focused. I'd almost gotten trapped in here, and now I'd come back. Sometimes I did have truly terrible ideas.

"He's up there," Melody said.

"We better hope so."

"No," she said, "he's waiting for us. For me."

I looked back at her. She needed me to get her through this. So did Maddy. I ordered my pounding heart to calm down.

I had to be the strong one. I had to get us out of here in one piece.

"Good," I said, infusing it with confidence. "I wasn't sure how to wake him. Something tells me he'll be eager to say hi."

My steps were steadier as we climbed. Maddy and Melody must have taken some comfort from that, because we didn't stop again. We kept on, climbing up and up the stairs that twined like the DNA Donovan had harvested from Melody two years before. Until we reached the top landing.

The door was open. The light in the lab beckoned, already on. I flicked off my flashlight. "Here we go." I paused, and then added, "If I tell you to run, do it. Leave if you have to."

"No way—" Maddy started to protest, but we were interrupted.

"So brave and valiant," the clone said, in its stolen dulcet tones, an exact echo of Mayor Worthington's. "And dramatic. Please, come in."

"I forgot to mention, he has crazy good hearing," I said, not bothering to lower my voice.

That got a chuckle in response. "One of the few perks of being me. You have nothing to fear here. Come in."

I nodded to Maddy, and then Melody. We were ready, though I bought no part of his "nothing to fear" reassurance.

I entered the door to the lab first, but Maddy and Melody— more alike than they realized—stayed close behind me. I had no fear now that either of them would chicken out.

And, in fact, Maddy stepped in front of me once we were inside, taking in the strange surroundings. The long file cabinets; the tidy but covered work counters; the glowing, human-sized tube filled with liquid but otherwise empty. Empty, because its occupant awaited us.

He sat on a stool at one of the counters, in his usual suit. Slowly, his feet dropped to the floor and he stood, gazing at Melody. His eyes were creepily wide, as if she was some sort of miracle happening in front of his eyes and he was afraid she'd vanish with so much as a blink. Like she was a figment of his imagination turned reality.

She was gazing back at him in much the same way, only with a touch of horror.

"You do not have to fear me," he said soothingly. "You are real."

Maddy took another step toward him, and I couldn't grab her fast enough to prevent it.

"Oh, really?" she said angrily. "That's some story, given how she's been suffering because of you. And how you told Lois you intend for her to keep on suffering."

"Maddy, stop," Melody said.

Maddy did not stop. "Yeah, she's a real girl, and you're taking her life away, piece by piece. She cries. She trembles. She screams. It's *your* fault."

The clone shook his head slightly, back and forth, like he didn't want to hear. "Is it true?" he asked Melody.

She walked forward then, past Maddy—evading her sister when she tried to stop her.

"Melody?" I asked.

"I'm all right," she said. She didn't look back. She stopped a foot away from him, a funny sort of smile on her face. He echoed it.

She lifted a hand. He did the same.

Then the other hand. They didn't touch, but they stood facing each other, movements identical. In sync.

I had the same shivery sense of wrongness that I'd had with the Warheads and Anavi. Feeling connected to people was one thing, but being forcibly connected to them was something entirely different.

Maddy turned to me and whispered, "What is she doing?"

I didn't know what to say. I moved, going wide around a counter so I could stand to the side of Melody and the clone. They gave every impression of being either side of a mirror. But the gap between them was important, and I intended to widen it.

"Do you have any desire to hurt Melody?" I asked.

"Melody." The name rolled off his lips. "It fits you, you know."

Melody said nothing, but her half-smile had been replaced by a grimly serious expression.

"Answer my question," I said.

"The girl reporter demands," the clone said, but not harshly. "What was it you asked again?"

"Do you want to hurt Melody?"

His eyes went wide. His hands dropped, and Melody's fell too. The spell they'd put each other under was broken.

"Never," he said. "I have few desires, but one of them is to never see her injured."

That is definitely better than if he'd said, "Yes, I dream of murder."

"I've noticed you mess with your tracker." I nodded to his arm, where it firmly circled his wrist. "Melody used to mirror that gesture, like it stuck with her. You said you stopped taking the meds for a reason. Tell her why."

"I didn't trust my maker anymore," he said, "after he put me to sleep and left me there, inactive, for long years. The first day I was awake, I declined to take the medication and hid it from him. The action was petty, the whim of an angry child, even though I am not a child. I have never been a child." His entire focus shifted back to Melody. "But you were. I bet you were a lovely child, young Melody. That day, the day I woke up, and discovered our bond, it was the first time I ever felt what it must mean to be truly alive. To be a real person. Your sister is right. You are real, and I am nothing."

"You're breathing, you're talking, and you can do something." I'd seen an opening in his monologue. We could convince him to do the right thing. We had to. "Why would you let Dabney Donovan, who has mistreated you so badly, mistreat Melody?"

He shook his head side to side. "Weak argument. Donovan does not even think of her anymore."

Wrong approach. Melody was simply listening, giving me no help. She might not be capable of it. I couldn't know what it would feel like to be linked to someone like this, some stranger who wasn't truly human.

"Do you think of running away?" I asked. "Is that why you mess with the tracker? Maybe we can help each other out.

I want to send your maker away, along with the men you accompanied last night. For a very long time."

"You will not catch him," he said. "I constantly think of leaving. But where would I go? I never had a life of my own. I have nothing to run *to*. My purpose was to be a mimic, to imitate a man I had never met until last night. I was programmed with knowledge, but none of it is more than skin deep. I *know* so little. Now, you, girl reporter, tell me that my lone purpose of existence is almost at an end. I will not go back to sleep. But he will never let me be free, not of him. I will always wear his tracker."

Finally, a way out. I moved closer.

"Free, like Melody is free?" I asked. "That's what you want?"

"Yes," he said.

"But Melody isn't free, not since you woke up and stopped taking the treatments. Even if you went back to sleep, she'd have to go through every day wondering, always wondering, if today would be the last day she got to live without suddenly losing track of herself, without you butting in and taking over her ability to function. What kind of life is that? I think you do have a life, and I think you know how terrible it is to be confined, shut in, limited, always under surveillance. There are worse things than being alone."

I waved my hand to indicate Melody. "But you, you hold the power to set her free again. You know the cure for her, the way to end this. If you are better than your maker, this is how you prove it. Once she's free, I will help you. We can find you a place to go. Mayor Worthington would help."

The room became like the inside of a clock, and instead of the seconds ticking away to count off the time, it was our breathing amid the silent weight of the moment, of our surroundings, of what things Dabney Donovan might have done in this lab. Doctor Donovan, who could come back any time now. Our diversion wouldn't keep him long. We were running out of time, with no other choice but to wait.

"You did not hear what I said," the clone said at last. "I am nobody. There is nothing I can do with your help."

"Then free her anyway," I said. "Because you care for her. Be a good person."

"I am not a good person. I do not even truly understand what the term means, but I know that she is one." He turned away from us, looking blankly toward the window. He spun back to us, then reached out, touching Melody's cheek. "I do know the cure for her. I am here sometimes when he is not, and I did read her file. The pretty blond girl who gave me a taste of life. I've read all the files. Mine included. The details were in it."

Melody did not shrink from his touch. She waited.

"Please," she said.

I wanted to push him away from her. "His notes said it was a one-time thing for her, but that it wasn't like the pills he used to manage your symptoms and keep her in the dark. That she couldn't be cured without figuring out he was Doctor Shady Shadiest of All Time. So what is it? How do we do it?"

The ticking clock resumed, all of us waiting to see if he'd give us the answer.

"She has to go in the tank," he said, at last. "Once only, not even to sleep, simply to receive the chemical neuroshock that will terminate her role in the experiment, erase our mental bond."

"No more cousin to spooky action at a distance?" I asked.

"No more connection between us, quantum or otherwise," the clone said. "No more action and reaction. She must go into the tank."

"Thank you," Melody said, shaky.

He dropped his hand. "I did not mean to frighten you."

"Too late," Maddy said. She went over to the tank, eyeing it with skepticism. "Won't she drown? Lois, is he telling the truth?"

Considering Donovan's certainty in his notes that the treatment wasn't possible to administer without Melody's knowledge and consent—unlike what he'd planned to do with her DNA—I supposed I should have guessed the tank would be the answer. I didn't trust the clone, either.

"I could check the file, but Donovan will be back any second," I said.

"He's telling the truth." Melody pulled herself straighter and walked over to join her sister. The blue glow of the liquid inside illuminated their faces. "The fluid will not hurt me."

"Okay, then," I said. "I don't mean to rush anyone, but Donovan really will be back soon enough. He's bound to have figured out the note was a trick by now."

The double went to Melody, the cloth of his anonymous suit whispering with the movement. He offered her his hand, almost like he planned to dance with her. She took it.

With his other fingers, he pressed a button on the side of the tank, and it slid open, the door mechanism pressing back the liquid to make a dry area for the person to climb into. Without a word, Melody stepped in.

He pressed the button and the opening closed again. She was sealed inside, eyes open and scared, the glowing blue liquid surrounding her completely.

"I told you," he said. "I am not a good man."

CHAPTER 28

Maddy pressed a hand to the glass, and her sister's raised through the blue liquid to meet it. *Look at me*, Maddy mouthed to her. Melody did.

"Are you hurting her?" I asked, because I knew Maddy needed to know the answer.

"Do you always ask the same questions over and over again, girl reporter?" the clone said. "No, I am hurting only myself. I do not understand why I am doing this."

"You're doing it for her," I said. "You might not be a good person, but I don't think you're a bad one either."

"I am hardly a person at all," he said.

Melody's hair spread out around her head. Her movements were deliberate, controlled. She wasn't thrashing around or giving any sign of alarm.

"What is the liquid?" I asked.

"His special creation. Think of it as a type of amniotic fluid. He says I am reborn each time I enter it."

"Um, so . . . will she be the same person when she comes out?" Maddy asked, eyes remaining on her sister.

"Its effect here will be more immediate and less dramatic for her. She will be the same. And I will be alone." The button the clone had pressed to open the tank's door was part of a small keypad, and he concentrated on it. "The shock may sting, however, it cannot be avoided."

He pressed another button.

Melody jerked once in the tank, then a second time.

Maddy gasped, pressing her other hand to the glass. "What's happening?" she demanded.

"It will not last long," he said. "This is what you asked for. Quantum disentanglement."

Melody's limbs froze, seizing up, and then she flew into motion. She shook her head. Her hands hit the glass, roughly opposite Maddy's. My heart began to pound again. What if I'd risked my friend's sister by listening to this guy, and we lost her?

But her hands moved back to push her hair out of her face. Her eyes closed, and then opened. She looked right at me and smiled.

Melody was still Melody.

She angled her face to nod—not to Maddy or to me, but to him.

"It is done," he said.

He pressed another button, and Maddy retracted her arms as the door whisked open again. Her clothes were damp, but the liquid must not have been water. Nothing dripped to the floor as she stepped from the chamber, free, and he sealed it once more. Maddy instantly folded her into a hug, and Melody returned it.

When they parted, the clone was messing with the keypad again. She waited until he'd finished and snapped her fingers to get his attention.

In case he didn't get the message, she added, "Look at me," in the same imperious tone she'd used on me when we first met.

He did as ordered.

"You're not so bad as all that," she said to him.

"Someone who affects other people, who takes action, sounds like a real person to me," I added. "You are one, whether you believe it or not. Do you need that tank to live?"

"I do not need anything," the clone said. "Not now that she is free. Confining me is simply part of his protocols, more convenient to keep me close." He paused, and spoke to Melody directly. "Look at Donovan, my creator, spurned by his former employers at Cadmus . . . Now he fancies himself the enemy of Cadmus, and who knows what he is capable of? I know you think I am not bad, but I do not know what I would do if I had no leash."

The clone couldn't want to exist that way. Could he? I didn't trust him, but we needed him and I'd made him a promise before. He helped Melody. We owed him.

But first, we had to finish this. "We need the public to see you," I said, "believe you are Mayor Worthington's twin—in order to protect Melody's part in this—but you can say Moxie forced your hand. They'll believe it. We can get Worthington to help, get you away from Donovan. You could be free too."

"I will give it due consideration," he said. His head shifted toward the door. "You should not have delayed to talk with me. He has returned. I can hear him. The door just opened, a slip of paper fluttered to the ground. He is hurrying up the stairs."

We had what we'd come for—Melody was no longer in danger. The connection was broken.

I *would* remain calm. I *would* get us out of here.

But I hesitated, one last loose end to tie. "You won't tell him our plans?" The clone could wreck everything by mentioning jail and Boss Moxie and Mayor Ellis.

"You have to go." He sat back down on the stool. "He won't hear anything from me. I am nobody. I have no reason to tell."

"Well, thanks, nobody," I said. "You were very helpful for a nonexistent being. Think about what I said. We'll see you later."

Maddy and Melody were already at the door, and I grabbed their arms. "We are going to wait until he's almost up his side of the stairs and then we are going to *run*—as fast as we can—down on the other side. Got it?"

"I hate running," Maddy said.

I laughed. "But you'd probably hate getting caught by whistling science creeps more."

We stepped out onto the landing. The sisters followed my lead and we went slow and quiet over to the stairs we'd come up. The doctor's feet landed hard with every step on his way up the other side.

I wanted to run now, this second, like we were in a race. And we were, but we had to wait for our moment if we were going to win. If we went too soon, he'd change course and beat us down, intercept us at the door.

Donovan lived like a ghost, leaving no tracks in the world outside this building. As the clone had said, I couldn't predict what this ghost was capable of.

We would leave here, and then I'd provide a tip about this building later. Have it raided as an illegal laboratory. I had Mayor Worthington's file, so there was nothing to tie him back to it except the twin. No one would admit he was a clone, and I had my hopes that he'd come to see the opportunity I offered was real. We could help him, while the others went away.

Donovan reached the top landing, face tight with anger and trained on the door.

"Now!" I said, and pressed Maddy and Melody ahead. Their feet made a terrible racket, but they were moving fast, like they were supposed to.

I should have been moving too.

But the mad scientist and I looked at each other. I needed to start running, follow Maddy and Melody, but I seemed as frozen as Melody had been in the tank.

The anger disappeared from Dabney Donovan's face, replaced by a weird calm. "You will not see me again," he said.

I don't know what made me move—the creepy certainty in his words, or Maddy shouting, "Lois! Come on!"

Donovan continued across the landing and into the laboratory, no longer rushing. And with not so much as another glance in my direction.

I didn't think running was strictly necessary anymore, after his odd reaction, but I ran anyway. Flying down the steps, I didn't slow until I hit the bottom, praying the doors would open, that Donovan hadn't locked himself in.

They did, and I burst outside onto the sidewalk, where Melody and Maddy were waiting. James and Dante were headed toward us.

"When you tell other people to run, they expect you to run too," Maddy said. "Let's go!"

James dashed up to us, and then pivoted to head back the way he'd come as we all went to the alley. "Cabbie's waiting at the other end," he said. My friend had come through again.

"What happened? Mel, did you get cured?" James asked as we reached the alley and its welcome shadows.

"Yes," Melody said. "I think I did. I don't feel him anymore."

"Phase one, down," I said. "It went as well as we could've expected, except . . . Donovan saw me."

"What?" James said. "Do you think the rest of the plan is blown?"

"I don't think so. The double won't tell him anything, except that we were there for Melody." I wondered what kind of conversation Donovan and the clone were having. If Donovan deactivated him, we'd be missing a key piece of evidence. But I didn't think he would. Not yet. Moxie was too important to tick off.

But an insurance policy on that would be nice.

"James, you mind going back home and making sure your dad makes the call, now?" I asked. "Tell them to be at your house at 2:45, and make sure he specifies that he wants to see the clone there too."

James blinked. "I thought we were shooting for after school."

We'd reached the opposite end of the alley. My cabbie pal stuck his meaty hand out the window and waggled his ringed fingers in a wave. I held my finger up: one sec.

"We were, but my dad busted me last night. If I can make it home at the normal time, like I was at school all day, that'd be a good thing." As long as Dad decided to enforce the rules exactly, and not in spirit. It was my only shot. "I'll deal with our compatriot at school so we can take off the rest of the day to get the plan done. Perry's working the lawyer angle this morning."

"Who's our compatriot at school?" Maddy asked.

"Butler," I said. "He loves James's dad, so even if he hates me . . ."

Melody shook her head. "I don't know how you guys keep up with each other," she said, "and I'm a science nerd."

I faced Melody. The fluid from the tank must have evaporated, because there was no sign she'd been soaking wet a few minutes before. She wore a long shirt over leggings with tall boots, bone dry.

Onto the second matter . . . "Speaking of keeping up with each other. You guys going to be good now? With each other? Sisters simpatico?"

Maddy said, "I think we—"

"Wait!" Melody sucked in a deep breath and huffed it out. "Maddy, I'm sorry. About stealing your piece when we were twelve and everything else. I'll prove it to you, however I need to." She paused sheepishly. "James, did you bring what I asked?"

He nodded and removed several sheets of paper from his pocket, folded in half lengthways. He handed them to her. Maddy was riveted, like the rest of us, and Dante took her hand in his. We didn't have time for this, but I wasn't about to stop it.

Melody took another breath, then unfolded the papers. I saw *PRELUDE No. 2* and *Gershwin* at the top. It was sheet music. She raised it high and ripped it in half, discarding the pieces. "I'll give up playing music myself, if that's what it takes. I want us to be like sisters again."

"That's not necessary." Maddy bent to pick up the pages. "Mel, you're forgiven. After all this . . . Lois made me see I've been kind of judgy too." Melody smiled at her, a real smile. Then Maddy looked over at James. "Why did you bring the music?"

Melody was sheepish again. "I didn't really have anywhere to put it, but I thought this deserved a grand gesture."

"Which you saved until *after* we saved you," I said lightly.

"Hey, no one said I'm a saint," she said, and Maddy laughed.

I believed the rift between these two had officially been closed. "This makes me so happy, but . . ."

"We need to get going," Maddy said. "Got it."

Dante turned toward me. "You need me for anything else?"

"You were a big help," I said, "but I believe we've got it from here."

"I'm spending the day on the mural, then," he said, now speaking to Maddy. "I have a pass and need to get it done for tomorrow. I'll alert you if there are any strange movements going on in the neighborhood. One of Moxie's residences is nearby, and his lieutenants are around a lot."

He squeezed her hand and pecked Maddy on the cheek before he took off up the sidewalk.

We watched him go. "You really did luck out with that one," I said.

"Speaking of which, I want to know about this boyfriend Devin says you have in the game," she said.

I was not prepared for that. So I ignored it. "And on that note, those who are going to school, get in the cab. Those who aren't . . . make your way to your next destination." James had gone quiet again. He fished our phones out of his other pocket. "You want us to drop you at home?" I asked.

"Nah, I'll grab another taxi," he said, passing back my phone, then Melody's and Maddy's. He took a second longer than he had to with Maddy's. Semi-awkwardly, he said, "Better get going or you'll be late for school."

"We wouldn't want that," I said. "Butler awaits."

And so did Devin, hopefully with a plan of attack for infiltrating the mayor's office.

CHAPTER 29

Maddy, Melody, and I climbed into the cab's backseat, me next to the driver's-side window. Jack waited until we were settled. "Where to? You girls robbing a bank today?"

"As if we're criminals," I said. "Villains fear us."

"I'm sure they do," he said. "Where we going, though? I was afraid something bad happened when you called me off after your midnight ride."

"You'll get your money," I said, to answer the concern embedded in the question. "We're going to school."

"Good call. Tangling with villains still requires an education." He levered the car into gear and pulled into traffic.

SmallvilleGuy would want to know we made it out of Ismenios unscathed. Something I barely believed myself—even if Donovan had gotten an eyeful of my face.

I keyed in the password on my phone to log in to the messaging app, sighing when the screen took longer than usual to load.

Part of me worried the radius of Donovan's gadget had expanded and zapped it, and another part kept mulling over what the mad scientist had said about never seeing him again. The words lingered like disquieting music to my ears. I wanted him to go away for what he'd done.

That didn't mean *I* needed to see him again. He couldn't know that, though. Could he? And what had the double meant about Donovan fancying himself the enemy of his former employer, Cadmus?

Finally, the message screen came up.

SkepticGirl1: *Success is ours. Melody is by all appearances peachy. No longer spooky reacting or whatever else fancy science terms.*

SmallvilleGuy: *I was beginning to get a little nervous. What if you decided to take over the lab? Embrace your inner mad scientist.*

I grinned down at the phone.

SkepticGirl1: *You're not getting rid of me that easy.*

SmallvilleGuy: *Glad to hear it. TheInventor says he's getting closer.*

SkepticGirl1: *Great news.*

Maddy nudged me with her elbow. "Is that him? The boyfriend?" She wasn't reading the screen on my phone, because I was holding it cupped so no one could but me.

SkepticGirl1: *Gotta dash. I just wanted to check in.*

SmallvilleGuy: *Go get the bad guys. We'll talk later.*

I was keenly aware that Maddy and Melody were watching me. I closed my eyes, took a breath, and then faced them. "What?" I said, pretending I hadn't heard Maddy's question.

"Lois," Maddy said, "it's really nothing to act so hush-hush about. A boyfriend, even a long-distance one, isn't exactly top-secret material."

If only you knew.

"It's complicated."

"How so?" Melody asked.

"We're not . . . He's not . . . We're just friends. Good friends, who've been . . . talking online for a couple of years. And who started meeting in *Worlds* recently."

"Wait," Melody said. "You've been talking online and in *Worlds*. Hold up. You've never met him?"

"Like I said, complicated. Speaking of, shouldn't we be talking about the rest of the day?"

"Nope," Maddy said. "We are talking about you. There's nothing else we can do until we get to school."

"But we don't want to turn into those girls, you know, who only talk about boys."

"Yes, because we're really in danger of that, given where we just came from and what's on the itinerary for today." Maddy stared at me. "Give me a real reason not to, or start talking."

I'd wanted to talk to her about this since we met. I didn't know how, though. Having someone I could talk to about anything—besides SmallvilleGuy—was so new. And it wasn't like I could talk about him *to* him.

"You and Dante," I said, and when she held up a hand, added, "I'm not trying to change the subject. I promise. But you're starting to be together, and you met a couple of days ago. The boy in question on my side, we've known each other for two years. I think maybe if it was meant to happen . . ."

"But you also said you've never met. Dante and I had the benefit of being in the same place. Do you know this guy isn't some middle-aged creep?"

Please, give me a little credit. "Do you know me? What do you think? He's our age."

"So he's not a creep," she said. "But he must be something more than a friend if he makes Lois Lane turn three shades of red and get too flustered to talk to me about him."

I pursed my lips, then blew out a breath. "You should be an interrogator, not a reporter."

"Back at you," Maddy said. "It's comforting, to be honest, to know you get crushes like the rest of us. You always seem so . . . *together.*"

"It's only with him that I get this way. I hate it." Which wasn't precisely true. I liked what we were to each other. Too much. If he didn't feel the same way . . .

Melody hadn't butted in. It seemed like she was letting us have friendly girl talk and didn't want to intrude. She'd extracted lipstick and a compact from inside one of her tall boots, and she finished smoothing a rosy pink over her lips, then examined them in the small mirror. She lowered the lipstick tube. "This guy, Mr. Internet, you must know each other pretty well if you've been talking for two years."

"We do." *Except for me not knowing who he is in real life.*

"And you haven't dated anyone else?" she asked.

"Not really. A couple of guys before I moved here, but not in a year."

Melody nodded. "Does he know how you feel?"

I didn't answer.

"You should tell him," Maddy said. "That's why Dante and I got together so fast. Because he told me. I've never been able to make the first move, but . . . It gets lonely being alone. I like him, though. A lot."

"We know," Melody said. "The perfect artsy couple."

"Sorry to break up the slumber party," Jack said, "but here we are."

"Oh," I said, surprised. "Thanks."

I looked outside. Even though we'd started our day early, we must have been a little late for school, as evidenced by the no one still lingering out front.

I got out and paid the man his money. "You need me later, just text," he said. "It's always an adventure. And I agree with your friends—if you like that boy, you should tell him. My daughter's just like you. Afraid to say anything."

"I am not afraid." But it sounded weak, even to me.

"Sure, sweetheart," he said, rolling up the window and pulling away.

Maddy tugged on my sleeve. "It's weird to say this, but: the cab driver is right. If you feel this way about your mystery man, I can't imagine he doesn't feel the same. You're pretty amazing, Lois Lane."

So this was what having a friend was like. It had wildly exceeded any expectations I had when I made up the plan for Metropolis.

"You too, Maddy Simpson."

"Wow, you two are enormous nerds," Melody said, but not unkindly. "You should found a mutual admiration society already."

"Look who's talking about nerds," I said. "Ms. Quantum Connectivity herself."

"Mel, I'm glad you're okay," Maddy said. "Which you must be, if you're back to saying stuff like that."

"See you later," Melody said. "I'm guessing you have more stuff to do. You know how to find me if you need me." She paused on the sidewalk. "I just didn't want you to think I didn't want to be seen with you two. I don't care about that anymore."

"Devin said he'd grab the study room, so I'll go meet him," Maddy said. "You'll join us after your date with Principal Butler?"

"That," I said, wrinkling my nose at the odiousness of having to ask Butler for anything, "is definitely *not* a date."

*

Ronda was typing away at something when I came into the outer office. She glanced over to see who was darkening her door and her face fell.

"Sorry," I said, "I know I do not come bearing donuts. Next time. He in?"

She regarded me through mascaraed lashes. "But it's not Monday. You don't have to see him today."

"I know, I can't believe I'm here either. Voluntarily. I need to talk to him."

She swiveled in her chair. "You're not going to put him in a mood, are you? Be honest."

I lifted my hand in a scout pledge position. "I swear."

"Something tells me you were never a Girl Scout," she said. "But fine. He's here. Go on back. I'll let you surprise him."

Ronda couldn't know I'd been kicked out of the Girl Scout troop I'd briefly been a part of in Nebraska. The parent adviser had been skimming money off the top of our cookie sales, and I'd turned her into the national organization. Apparently I couldn't earn any badges that way. It had been kept quiet though, so I didn't *think* it was in my giant permanent record.

Although Ronda's Mona Lisa smile made me wonder as I headed back to the hallway to storm Principal Butler's office. Perhaps the principal there had made a note. The troop leader had been his wife, after all.

When I reached Butler's office, the door was open and he was outfitted in one of his usual fashion week suits, squinting at his computer screen. Could he be . . . working?

Today truly was one for the books. I knocked on the doorframe.

He gave me the same confused and slightly dismayed reaction I'd gotten from Ronda. "Miss Lane?"

"Do you have a second? It's an urgent matter. Confidential," I said.

I suspected that word would get him. I was right.

"Come in," he said. "I always have time for students, as you know. Particularly with urgent troubles."

I shut the door with a click.

His silver eyebrows rose.

"Confidential, like I said." I took my usual seat. And I spotted my massive permanent file still on the corner of his desk—even though it wasn't Monday. Someday I *would* get a look at that thing.

Not today, however.

"I need a favor," I said.

His tie tack had little faux diamonds on it that caught the light when he leaned back in his chair. "I know we've developed a rapport over these few weeks, but principals don't normally do favors for students."

James owed me for this. Big.

"I agree, but I'm convinced you mean it when you say the Warheads thing was out of character—that you *care about your students*." I tried to tell myself to soften it, but I was only capable of so much.

"I do care," he said, eyes narrowing. "Which is why I was so concerned to hear your performance on your biology test this week wasn't up to par. That's a golf term, by the way. I was thinking I might call up your father for a round or two. I never have managed to meet him."

Right, he just reminded you he's a climber. Use that.

"I promise I'll get on my grades ASAP," I said. "Well, after today. I know you'll understand why once I tell you what I'm about to, but first I need to secure your promise you'll keep quiet." I paused, waited to make sure he was listening closely, then reeled him in. "You see, the favor isn't really for me. Or not just for me. It's for James. More specifically, it's for James's father, Mayor Worthington. What would you say if I told you that he was innocent and you could help clear his name? Get him back into office?"

He was speechless.

That was a welcome development.

"I can only imagine how *thankful* he'd be," I said.

"Explain," he said.

Yesssss. One more piece, falling into place. "Let me send one quick note," I said, and pulled out my phone before he could tell me not to. I sent a text to Maddy, Devin, and James: *I've got him. I'll meet you all in the study room. Don't bother going to class.*

I hit send, then directed my attention back to the curiously, peevishly waiting principal.

"The main thing I'll need you to do is go to Worthington Manor and give a letter of invitation to some . . . guests . . . of the ex-mayor at precisely two thirty."

"He's on house arrest. Won't he be there?" he asked.

I smiled. "Not if everything goes as planned."

CHAPTER 30

The library was filled with students either working studiously away with reference books or goofing off and ignoring the same. I hurried to our usual private study room, and found Devin and Maddy tucked away inside.

"Finally," Devin said. "Maddy was getting antsy."

Devin had a set of plans spread across the work table, with a few annotations made in marker in his incredibly neat handwriting. From the look of it, he'd printed a dozen sheets of letter-size paper with various parts of the schematic, and then taped them together to build the plans for City Hall.

"How very crafty of you," I said, peering at the lines and shapes. Architecture was practically art. I asked Maddy, "Why so antsy?"

"Because I had to get the librarian to bump the study group

who had the room reserved," Maddy said. "And I couldn't come up with a decent excuse, so I told her *Scoop* business."

"The truth is always a decent excuse." I dropped my bag on the table beside the printouts. "But I can tell you're off your game—you didn't even make me use a password."

"True," Maddy said. "I'm just glad Melody's safe. That guy . . . well, both of them, but especially the scientist. Yikes to the nth degree."

Donovan, she meant. Yikes was right. "I join you in a mental shudder. Dev, what options do we have? And by we, I mean me." I pulled out the chair beside him and slid into it. My experience with architectural plans was extremely limited. As in zero.

"How'd it go with Butler? Are we in trouble for skipping class?" Devin asked.

"I told you he was handled, and he is."

To prove it, I reached over and dug in my bag to produce the pink excused absence slips. They weren't even stolen ones. He'd filled them out.

"One for each of us." I handed Maddy and Devin theirs, and left James's out for when he joined the prep party.

"Nicely done, and a little scary," Devin said. "I hope you didn't have to promise to meet with him daily instead of weekly."

"Even my sense of duty has limits," I said. "I forgot to ask about your mom—anything from her yet?"

"She left early to go to a breakfast meeting with Perry. If she thinks there's any way it's true and proving Mayor

Worthington's innocence will take down Moxie or Ellis, she'll go for it."

I held up crossed fingers.

So far, so good. Everything was coming into alignment. James had instructions to call his grandparents and make sure they would fall in line with the cover story about the secret twin if asked. As long as he convinced them, it was just a matter of . . . everything else working out exactly according to our plan. The plan to clear James's dad and send away a certain mobster and mayor, ending with a press conference and a front-page scoop.

We had a big, complicated day ahead. Which meant it was time to discuss breaking and entering City Hall—or, more precisely, my uninvited visit to the mayor's office and taking James's dad's stockpile of proof—upon which the rest depended. Without that evidence, our efforts would be worth precisely nada.

"Tell me you've got me a way into the mayor's office, and his ceiling," I said. "We'll have a limited window—as soon as he's summoned by Boss Moxie, I'll need to get in there."

There was a tap on the skinny rectangular window. James. He opened the door and joined us. He was more mussed than usual, his hair messy and button-down untucked, probably from racing across town all morning.

"All good?" I asked.

"All good as far as Dad, Mom, and grandparents are concerned," he confirmed. "The calls have been made. Dad wrote a letter for me to read them once I was out of the house, so they'd buy the clone part but not *talk* about it. My granddad is more skeptical, but he said as long as it played out like I described then he'd believe it and go along. My grandmother, on the other hand, was a little too enthusiastic about helping come up with a whole story about how my dad's twin left the family as a teenager for a life of crime and so they destroyed all records of his existence to protect their squeaky-clean son's future. She seems to think this is the kind of thing rich people do every day."

"She's probably right," I said.

The Worthington family money was probably how they'd kept the house, when Moxie hit the mayor's own finances.

"Do we think that's going to be enough?" Devin asked.

"Easier for the public to swallow than the existence of a clone, don't you think?" I shrugged, and no one challenged the point.

James asked, "Where are we on everything else?"

"Devin's just getting ready to tell me it turns out there's a simple, easy way for me to get to the hidden evidence. Aren't you, Devin?"

"Not exactly." He laid a finger on a square in the center of the plans he'd assembled. "This is Ellis's office."

"Not for much longer," James said.

I smiled. "I like the enthusiasm. Go on, Dev."

"As you'll see, there's a reason they put it there. The security people did a good job of situating it for maximum protection. Second floor. And there's only one door in and out. I'm guessing his assistant isn't going to let you waltz in through it."

Argh. Neither would the security guys who'd been posted outside the other day. "What politician doesn't have a secret exit?"

"I could've told you there isn't one of those," James said. "But if Dad hid the evidence in the ceiling, doesn't that mean the ceiling has room in it? What about going in that way?"

"Yes, it does have room." Devin leaned over the plans, feverishly tracing a line with his finger. "There are offices on either side, occupied, but here. There's this larger room in the mayor's office suite, maybe a conference room. If it was unoccupied and you could get in the ceiling there, it looks like you wouldn't have to go *that* far. And it has an entrance from the hallway."

"That door is always locked," James said, examining the plans. "It's not a conference room, it's the break room for the mayor's key staff. And because the break room door is always locked, in order to get to it you have to go through an internal hallway that passes by about five offices inside the mayoral suite."

Maddy and Devin, in unison, asked, "Can you pick the lock?"

Thanks again, Dad. I should've known this wouldn't go so easily.

"A rule-follower like James wouldn't want me to do that. Not again. Not in City Hall."

"That's . . . true," James said. "But what's the real reason?"

"I lost my tools in the Great Dad Showdown of last night."

"Oh." James was examining the plans too now. "I have an idea. I do know Ellis's assistant—he's a holdover from Dad's time there. His desk is right here." He tapped an area inside the main entrance to the mayor's office, directly in front of where

I needed to get. I could see the inside, non-public hallway and offices James mentioned, leading up to the break room. "I could go in and say hi to him, ask if I can snag a candy bar from the machine in the break room—"

"And open the door to admit me. Are there tables and stuff in there?"

James smiled. "It's a break room, so yes."

"Ones that I could use to climb up into the ceiling?"

"Oh, yes, and I can give you a boost." He shook his head. "We're just bending the rules."

"Lois crawling through the ceiling is bending rules?" Maddy asked, grinning. She added, singsong, "Someone's rationalizing."

She wasn't wrong. James didn't like even bending the rules, not if we didn't have to.

I tried to think of any other plan we could use that wouldn't depend so much on James's rule bending. But this was it, as far as my brain was concerned. "This is the best way we have. We'll have to go with it. And hope I don't fall through the ceiling."

"But—but—" James said, struggling to find words, "did you think about what if someone's there? What if it doesn't work? That's a really high ceiling."

"It was your idea," I said. "And you're the one who was so confident we're getting rid of shady mayor. If we run into trouble, we'll wing it."

"Wing it? Our plan is to wing it?" James was definitely getting worried.

I patted his arm. "This is going to be good for you. A growth experience."

"I almost wish we could go just to watch," Maddy said.

I could sense an invite in the offing from James to Maddy to join us, a reflection of his shifting feelings for her.

He opened his mouth, but I spoke before he could. "Too many of us might make it harder to stay under the radar. Especially since I have the tendency to show up like a heat-seeking missile on the radar of anyone official. You guys head to the *Scoop* and be on standby. If all goes well, we'll see you there before we go back to the courthouse for the 2:45 press conference that ruins evil in Metropolis's day, week, month, and next few years."

My stomach sank as I realized that I'd overlooked an obvious element. "Except. I was planning for us to go wait across the street until the mayor leaves to hook up with Moxie. But how do we know he's there?" I paused, chewed on my lip. There had to be a way . . . I pointed to Devin. "Can you hack his assistant's computer or something?"

"I may be a rule-follower," James said, "but that's not necessary. The mayor's public schedule is posted on his website."

Devin whipped out his phone, but James held up a hand. "No need," he said. "I pulled it up this morning. He's chairing a meeting of the Neighborhood Revitalization and Waterfront Development Committee. It lets out in half an hour. He won't leave before then."

"Oh, the irony," I said.

"The committee meeting?" Devin asked. "Yeah."

"No," I said, "that James's knowledge of the rules has proved so helpful."

"Ha," James said.

"I meant it affectionately, *almost* like a compliment." I gathered my bag and slung it over my shoulder. "Let's get going, boy scout. Time to stake out City Hall and wait for our moment to strike."

Maddy sighed. "I really do wish we could watch this."

*

James and I sat on a bench across from City Hall, attempting to look casual about our surveillance. It was hard not to feel like spies on a mission—which I suppose we were. Well, James wouldn't like being described that way. So, *I* was like a spy on a mission.

The weather was as beautiful as had been predicted, and the sky above us was—I liked to think—the blue of victory.

Assuming so many things fell into place. And that I was not just a spy *for* good, but a good spy who could successfully retrieve the evidence.

What if it wasn't there anymore?

Stop thinking that way. You got this.

But I couldn't quite convince myself.

"I hope this works," James said, echoing my thoughts.

People—lots of people, people who were frustratingly *not* Mayor Ellis—entered and exited the building opposite us, taking the broad steps at varying degrees of speed.

James continued, "I don't know how the disappointment

would affect Dad. Now that he has the ability to rehab his image . . . If he loses that chance, he'll be shattered."

"One, he won't lose it," I said. "Two, you're wrong. I don't think he cares as much about the public as you think, not anymore—" James started to protest, but I went on. "I know he cares about his job, his duty, all that. But as far as image, caring what people think, all he cares about is that you and your mom will believe in him again. And that's settled, no matter how this goes. Isn't it? Your mom knows?"

"Yes, but she's skeptical," James said. "Like I was. She doesn't really buy the whole story, and not being able to talk about it makes it harder. But if we get this evidence, she will. Maybe you're right."

"Don't sound so shocked. Of course I am."

The doors swung open and a guy in a sharp suit wearing an earpiece appeared. A member of a security detail? James and I both leaned forward in anticipation.

Nope, just a guy with an earpiece talking on the phone, followed by no one.

"Could be a guy leaving the meeting Ellis's in," James said.

"Here's hoping. I was not born to wait." But there was no reason to sit idly. I had another piece of business to discuss with James. I could employ the same method Maddy had on me in the cab. "So, Maddy. Why the sudden paying attention to her?"

"Um, what?"

"You mean who. Our colleague, Maddy Simpson." I held out a hand in the air in front of me, "A few feet taller than this, has a streak in her hair, knows a lot about music. Style editor. Am I ringing any bells?"

"I know who Maddy is." James looked away and shifted uncomfortably on the bench. "But, what do you mean?"

So that's how he was going to play this. "James, she's had a crush on you this whole time, but all of a sudden she gets a boyfriend and you're interested. Not cool."

He turned back to me, happy surprise in his eyes. "Maddy likes me?"

"Yes, Mr. Oblivious, she does. Well, *did*. But she's seeing Dante now, and they seem into each other. And good with each other."

"I noticed," he said, glum.

I remembered something important: James was my friend too. My sympathies engaged. "Why the change? I thought you were into Melody before."

"Melody and I were just using each other." He watched closely as the City Hall doors opened and closed again.

"That sounds bad," I said. "And that isn't the mayor over there, so keep talking."

"I didn't mean it like that." He ran a hand through his still-mussed brown hair. "We were convenient for each other to be seen with. We were never serious. I mean . . . After Dad went away, I didn't know what would happen to me, to my place."

I knew what it meant to feel like you had a place. And it was easy to imagine what it would be like to feel it slipping away.

"Melody saw that," he said. "She made sure I still had a lunch table to sit at, that no one treated me any differently. I don't even know if she knows how much it meant. So my gratitude expressed itself . . . confusingly. But then, this week . . ."

The City Hall door opened again, and this time it was no false alarm. Two security detail guys came out first, followed by Ellis. Two more security guys followed them. A sleek car, no doubt bulletproof, pulled up to the curb, and the mayoral posse headed toward it.

James got up, and so did I. But I stopped him. "Hold on. This week?"

He shook his head. "This week, seeing Maddy and Melody together, watching them fight. It made me realize how much more to Maddy there was than I'd seen. How much we have in common."

I had no clue what Maddy and James had in common other than the *Scoop*, but I didn't go there.

"You still will, if she and Dante break up. I think you should wait and see if this sudden change of heart sticks." I paused. "She's worth waiting for, if what you feel is real."

He snorted. "I hardly think a mystery boyfriend qualifies you as an expert on these matters."

"Watch it," I said. "He's not even my boyfriend. Just . . . think about what I said."

Mayor Ellis climbed into the sedan, and so did two of his security detail. The other two turned as it roared away from the curb, heading back inside. *Please don't be going back to hang in his office.*

"I'll think about it," James said. "Okay. I guess it's time for us to do this. And by 'this' I mean something incredibly stupid, which might work or might get us in real trouble. I'm not sure this is a good idea . . ."

"And you've convinced me it is." I stepped behind him and gave him a little push. "Forward march. This is the only way you get your dad back for keeps."

CHAPTER 31

We exited from a semi-crowded elevator onto the slickly polished marble of City Hall's second floor. This was the same route Devin and I had taken to the property records office, around the corner from the suite that belonged to the mayor and his staff. That was why we'd encountered his clump of very important people during the other day's evacuation.

Our trip through security had been uneventful. We'd listed the hall of records as our destination again. No suspicions had been aroused. But the guard on scanner duty also hadn't seemed to recognize James, and from his expectant waiting for some hello and the way he trudged onto the holoscanner when none came, I thought that disappointed him.

"It must have been something, to have the run of this place as a kid," I said.

James's dad wasn't a first-termer. He'd been in office for six years when he got busted.

"'No running in the halls, James Worthington the Third!'" James responded, in what must have been an imitation of his mother. "'Let the boy have his fun.'" That one was his dad.

Two flags flanked the entrance to the mayor's office. The wide wooden doors to the suite were propped open, with a member of the security detail standing on either side. I smiled at the taller guard as we passed, and glimpsed somebody inside who must be the mayor's assistant. The youngish man with a buzz cut sat behind a desk in the outer office, the hallway that branched toward the break room opposite him. And behind him was the door to the mayoral HQ itself. It was closed.

We didn't stop, not yet. James touched a door we passed near the end of the hall. "This is the break room."

It was in the peripheral view of at least the closest security guy, which wasn't ideal. But they both looked pretty bored. The one I'd smiled at was now busy checking his phone.

We rounded the corner and I relaxed against the wall beside the entry to the property office. "I'll wait here. You text me when you get to the break room, not before. Open the door as quietly as you can."

"We'd better wait here a minute before I go, so it's not suspicious that I came right back." James spoke in a hushed rush. Nervous.

I kept my voice down, too. "You're going to be—so, *good* might be a stretch. You'll be perfectly decent at this. You said you stop by and talk to . . . what's his name?"

"Cal."

"You stop by to say hi to your pal Cal sometimes, and so this is all perfectly normal. You tell him you're here with a friend, working on a story, and want a snack from the vending machine like old times. Easy."

He shook his head wonderingly. "It sounds like it when you put it that way. No wonder your permanent record is the stuff legends are made of."

I straightened. "You've seen it?"

He adopted his usual air of superiority, which had been MIA of late. "Butler loves me, remember?"

"So unfair," I said, and kicked his shoe. "I never get so much as a peek. Does it . . . well, what I want to know is . . ."

A grin that I did not like crossed his face. "Does it make you sound like the kind of girl who strikes fear into the hearts of all who cross you?"

I wouldn't dignify that with a response. Out loud, anyway.

"Yeah," he said. "It kind of does."

I suppressed a smile. That was something, at least. And I gave James another push—he'd need it to get through this. "Go work your magic. I'll watch for the door to open."

I stepped over to the edge of the hallway's corner and waited. I had a perfect view of the door in question, and I would leap across and in, hopefully without anyone seeing me. James was about to leave cover, but I said: "Wait."

"Yes?" he whispered.

"If someone sees me, it's important I get into the ceiling before they can reach the room. So be ready to help."

Trepidation returned to his face, but before I could tell him to buck up or similar he was gone.

I didn't want to be caught loitering suspiciously if someone came up the hall, and so I removed my phone. Pulling up the app, I tapped out a message.

SkepticGirl1: *Don't text me back. I'm just staying occupied while James does part one. Then I go up into the ceiling.*

I pretended to look at the screen of my phone, but my focus was trained on the door. Until a reply came. I hadn't expected him to be signed in.

SmallvilleGuy: *Just pretend I'm there and you're flying. Don't fall.*

What a sweet response. Typically sweet. The kind of sweet that made me want to swoon, even if I couldn't seem to admit it out loud. My friends—and the taxi driver—were right. I should tell him how I felt. I vowed to consider the matter more seriously, stop agonizing and find a way—

I heard a hiss. "Lois?"

The door was already cracked open. *Whoops.*

I crammed the phone into my bag and glanced over—the closest security detail guy was *still* scrolling down his screen. James opened the door the rest of the way and I hurried through it.

It shut behind me with a bang. I'd almost missed my cue. I needed to get back into my game mindset.

The break room was standard issue. There were a couple of vending machines, two long tables surrounded by mismatched plastic chairs. A half-eaten box of cake that looked like it'd been there a week sat on one of them.

"Hurry up," James said, eyes pointing ceiling-ward, and I worried he might faint if I didn't rush.

"I'm on it." I looked up, too, and considered the ceiling. It was tall. James hadn't exaggerated.

Probably nine feet. Which meant the table wouldn't give me quite the launching pad I needed to get there.

But it was only a couple feet above the vending machine.

I pulled a chair over to the nearest machine, filled with bad-for-you snacks, and held a hand out to James. "Help me get up here and in I go."

Someone knocked on the door out in the hallway. Then again, more insistent.

"Tell them I handed you money and went back to do research," I told James, climbing on the chair. I stepped into one of his hands and he practically tossed me up.

I landed on the target—the gross, dusty top of the vending machine. Pressing aside the panel above me, I stuck my head through to check out the inside of the ceiling. Yes, in between the removable tiles there were some support beams that I could use to get me where I needed to go.

"Hello?" a voice at the door. "Is someone in there?" And after a beat, "We may need to call down for keys."

"I'm coming!" James called out.

I pulled the skinny flashlight out of my bag, then adjusted the bag's strap so it clung tight to me. "See you on the other side," I said. Then I put the flashlight between my teeth and climbed into the darkness above. I replaced the tile immediately, sliding it back into place and staying put. Listening.

I heard James open the door to the hallway and footsteps enter the break room.

"Do you have any change?" James asked, almost making it sound like he wasn't mid-heart attack. *Good boy.*

"Did we see a young lady come in here?" a man asked. "What are you doing in here?"

"Hey, I didn't recognize you before." That was a different voice. "You're Mayor Worthington's kid."

"I am," James said, donning his full-on snooty mode. "I'm here working on an assignment. I wanted a snack and to say hi to Cal. But I realized I don't have change. My friend—my *colleague*—passed me some and went back to work, but it wasn't enough."

"I might have some," one of the guys said.

I began to crawl as quietly and slowly as I could and still make decent progress. The important thing was getting to the evidence.

Unfortunately, it was beyond dark and dusty up in the ceiling. I couldn't see farther than my flashlight beam, and keeping it in my mouth wasn't exactly comfortable. I paused and removed it, swept the light around, and concentrated on memorizing my path forward.

And what was that? I strained to hold the flashlight farther in front of me.

Yes, there it was, a box, so dust-coated it almost blended in with its surroundings. It was far from me, but not *so* far. Just about right per Devin's estimate. Right over the mayor's office. I'd say I had about twenty feet to cover to get there.

"Should've worn fatigues and a face mask," I mumbled, and then I turned off the flashlight.

Completely in the dark, my progress wasn't any faster. And about halfway to the box—I thought—my nose decided it couldn't take any more dust and forcibly ejected a sneeze. A *loud* sneeze.

I expected the cool metal bar beneath my hand to shudder with the force of it.

I waited, afraid to move. But no one came, no alarm was raised. "Forward march," I said, repeating my command to James from earlier, blinking dusty eyelashes and moving.

And a few feet later, my hands blundered into cardboard.

I shifted to sit, facing the box, and took out the flashlight again. Holding it between my shoulder and neck, I lifted off the box top and nearly dropped the flashlight in the haze of yet more dust that shook into the air.

Inside were files. Many, many files. I flicked through a few of the neat brown folders, and they were exactly what James's dad would have put away. Receipts, two small audiotapes (one labeled: threat against family), lists of dates and times and requests—of the inappropriately corrupt variety—from Boss Moxie. There was a map with his high-priority property development projects marked. I saw Mayor Steve Ellis's name pop up here and there too. Back then, he'd been comptroller.

In other words, in the box? Paydirt.

I replaced the box lid, already skipping ahead to our triumph. Except . . . in all our talking about getting me up here and retrieving the evidence, there was one key thing we'd forgotten to discuss: How I'd get down. And transport a box this size out of this office.

"Sorry, James, I told you we might have to wing it," I said, scooting aside a ceiling panel.

Oh good. The mayor's desk was right below me. Making it only a six-foot or so drop. Ack.

I picked up the box, squinted to line it up as close to center as I could. "Bombs away," I said, then dropped it straight down. Where it hit with a *CRASH!*

It looked mostly intact, for all the racket. The mayor's desk . . . not so much. Papers had flown this way and that, displaced by the impact.

Now it was my turn. Helpfully, the door to the office opened, and James and the assistant burst in.

"James, I have no idea how I got stuck up here. Be a dear and—" I slung my bag down to the floor ahead of me, and then launched myself out of the ceiling—"catch!"

To James's credit, he rushed forward and managed to keep me from landing in a busted sprawl on the floor. But my impact knocked the wind out of both of us and nearly took out a leather wing chair.

"Thank you," I said, releasing him and straightening my dust-covered T-shirt, jeans, and boots ensemble. I gave the assistant a friendly smile, and held out a dusty hand. He blinked at it.

"You must be Cal," I said. I kept my voice low, conspiratorial. "Those two guys outside, I take it they didn't hear the commotion?"

Cal was tall, pale, and about as scared as James looked, contemplating the breaking of a rule. I'd have to be gentle with him. But I wanted—needed—to believe that given a clear choice between right and wrong, most people would choose right. Cal would be my latest test case.

He swallowed. "James told me it was nothing, not to get them. But . . ."

Cal took in the gaping ceiling, and the only slightly dented box on the desk, and my dust-smudged clothing.

"Cal, you trust James, don't you? And you trusted the former mayor? More than trusted, you liked him."

Cal seemed afraid to speak. He nodded.

"If you help us get out of here," I said, "he might be your boss again. And Ellis—who I'm guessing is an unappreciative jerk—will not be anymore. He'll get what he deserves."

Cal had begun to nod more at the jerk part. I was pretty sure he hadn't meant to.

"What if I get fired?" he asked.

"We'll never tell anyone you saw us."

His eyes went back to the box. "And you're taking that box?"

"Yes," James said, stepping in to take a more active role. He picked it up. "We are."

I fished around on the floor and came up with my bag. "We'll just need you to distract those two gents outside. We'll go out the break room door. No one will know anything about this. Where we got the evidence is immaterial. It belongs to Mayor Worthington."

"Evidence?" Cal repeated nervously. He added, "Mayor Ellis

was acting funny this morning. I think he's on to you." He hesitated, and then said, "You'd better go."

"Thank you," James said. "Dad will remember this."

At Cal's alarmed reaction, complete with scared, blinking eyes, I said, "But he'll never know about it. He'll just remember you are a good employee."

"Right," James said. "No one will ever know about your helping us."

Cal said, "Right this way," and gestured for us to leave. "I'll clean up the mess."

"I wouldn't bother," I said. "He won't be here much longer."

James and I lapsed into silence as soon as we left the extravagance of the mayor's actual office and entered Cal's domain in the reception area, not wanting to draw the attention of the security detail back at their posts in the hallway. We could see them stationed on either side of the entrance. They had returned to phone-checking.

But one of them lifted his head.

I ducked behind a bookshelf. James—bless him for thinking quickly—pretended to set the box on Cal's desk, like he was helping Cal out.

As soon as the guard's attention wandered again, Cal waved us toward an interior hallway I could only assume led to the break room.

James picked up the box and, when we were safely out of front entrance earshot, said low, "There are people in the offices, so move fast."

He didn't need to tell me twice. In the break room, the

woman I'd seen the mayor cursing at during the evacuation stood in front of the vending machine. I ignored her questioning look and opened the door to the main hallway.

She shrugged and put in her quarters. I peeked out, James behind me. The security detail wasn't in the hall anymore. Well done, not-so-cool Cal.

James and I scurried toward the elevators. As we passed the entrance to the mayor's office, I spotted Cal inside pointing at the top of the bookshelf, the security detail squinting up at it.

And then we were back at the elevators. James pressed the call button, and we both vibrated with tension, waiting.

I finished typing a quick message to Perry: *Headed to first floor.*

"Should we find the stairs?" James asked.

But the car arrived and the doors slid open. We lunged inside, somewhat freaking out an overly tan man in a polo shirt.

I forced myself to stand tall under his scrutiny, and only then realized what he was dismayed by was the state of my wrinkled, dusty outfit. My face was probably dirty too.

"It's a new style thing," I said. "Hobo chic."

He said nothing, but his face wore a "kids these days" look.

James pressed the button for the first floor until the doors closed.

The elevator stopped at the first floor. James had a death grip on the box.

The doors opened, but there was no rush of security to meet us. Instead, Perry and an elegantly dressed woman who looked a lot like Devin stood outside it. The polo guy excused himself, leaving fast as James and I stepped out of the elevator.

Devin's mom and Perry both absorbed my wrecked state. Perry asked, "What took you so long?"

CHAPTER 32

I gave Perry what I hoped was a withering look. *Way to take the wind out of a girl who just leapt out of a ceiling's sails.*

He held up his hands. "Don't shoot," he said. "I'm just kidding."

The main lobby was full enough that no one at the security checkpoint nearby was keeping a close eye on the elevator. All good.

James handed Perry the box of evidence. The woman said, "I'm Angela Harris."

"Devin's mother," I said. "Hi." I wished I wasn't meeting such an impressive person while I was coated in dirt. If there was ever a time to quote Dorothy Parker, it was now, so I did. "Excuse my dust."

"Pleased to meet you," she said. "Let's move."

No-nonsense. I approved. Boss Moxie wouldn't know what hit him until he was knocked off the perch of his lofty, illegal empire.

Devin's mother started walking, and Perry, James, and I followed her. Even Perry was deferential to her—that was a new look for him.

Oil portraits of important men and women from the city's past dotted the walls, nearly blurring as we took the hallway at all but a run. Ms. Harris moved fast, and she talked faster. "We had to bring your father in through an employee entrance," she told James, "but he's waiting in an office this way. If what he told me is in the contents of that box really are there, then this should be a slam-dunk. I've already taken his sworn statement, and I've got a judge on standby."

James caught up. "Wait. Dad's *here*? Already?"

"Seemed wisest," Perry said. And when Ms. Harris slowed for one brief moment, he added, "In Angela's opinion. And I agreed."

I had my doubts. "What if there's a rat in the home incarceration monitoring office?"

Ms. Harris looked at me with pleased surprise. "You're just as sharp as Devin says. We got a quiet—*very* quiet—judge's order to remove the monitor and leave it at the Worthington residence. No one will notice anything unusual."

Perry opened his mouth, but I anticipated his question. "Yes, Principal Butler is heading there shortly and should deliver the summons to Moxie and Ellis and the, er, twin right on schedule."

Ms. Harris paused in front of a door with a frosted glass window. "In here. This isn't my office, but it's one we're able to use. One of my most trusted staffers is keeping an eye on him. Getting Mayor Worthington in was difficult enough." I must have raised my eyebrows in question, because she said, "It's quieter to stay here than try to leave. And we need to keep this quiet."

Oh, did we. If Moxie or Ellis got wind of this before they were nabbed, chances were they'd flee the city—and probably the country. Our chance to nail them would be lost.

Ms. Harris whisked us into the office. James's dad was sitting in a chair at a small table positioned opposite a desk. A middle-aged man with a slight frame and his sleeves rolled up stood beside a corner chair. He nodded to Ms. Harris and sat back down.

Mayor Worthington rose to his feet and before he could say a word, James launched himself at his dad and they hugged each other.

Ms. Harris snapped her fingers and pointed to the table. Perry obeyed without question, depositing the box there. "Sorry to interrupt, Mayor Worthington," she said, "but the clock's ticking."

"Heartwarmingness aside, I couldn't have said it better myself," I said.

Mayor Worthington extracted himself from James's embrace, and I was happy that James didn't bother to be embarrassed at the display of affection. It was also nice to see his dad looking hopeful. His head was up, eyes clear (if a touch shiny from unshed tears), and he was dressed in an extremely mayoral navy suit. "Your mom's on her way," he told James.

I'd almost forgotten how blindingly white James's teeth could be until he smiled.

"The property documents and threat tape will do for the arrest warrants," Ms. Harris said.

"Of course." James's dad crossed to the box and removed the top of it, then began sorting through the files as Ms. Harris observed. After a moment, he passed one her way, and she flipped it open to read. She held out her hand and he passed her another one, and she repeated the process.

The atmosphere was as thick with tension as if the box contained a bomb while we awaited her verdict.

Finally, she looked up and half-smiled, probably at our laser focus on her. "You can all relax. It's good. I'll call the judge. Perry, you're going to take care of the presser invites in a bit?"

I cleared my throat. "Shouldn't Perry go write the story?"

Perry gave me a disappointed head shake. "What are you talking about? This is *your* story, Lois Lane. Never step aside and let someone have something you worked for. You earned this. So you'd better get back to the office and write it. The copy desk is on alert to get it prepped and ready to post when the press conference starts."

I was going to write the story?

I'd just assumed it would be Perry. "I . . . I don't know what to say."

"That's a first," Perry said, but I could tell he was suppressing some emotion. I thought it might be pride. "No stopping to take a shower and change clothes, either. You'll just have to live with your finest journalistic hour coming while you're in your Oliver Twist get-up."

Definitely pride. Despite the insult.

"Hey," I protested. Besides, he was right: my boots and jeans and top were still smudged with dirt, and my face likely was too.

Perry was not in the mood for niceties. "Go, little orphan reporter girl."

There was one thing I needed to do first. I grabbed a post-it from the desk and scrawled the address of Ismenios Labs on it.

Ms. Harris was on hold with the judge, so I gave her the note. "Unrelated, but something we found as part of our reporting—there's an illegal lab, no permits, shady business, the works, at this address. Can you have someone go check it out? Stat? We think they might try to move it."

She accepted the post-it. "Why not? I'll pass the tip to a cop I know." Then, a beat later, clearly not to me but to the person on the phone, "Oh, hello, Judge Watkins, it's Angela again. I'm about to make your day. Or vice versa." She laughed at the response, post-it still in her fingers, and I took that as my cue to leave.

"Lane," Perry said, "don't screw this up."

James was already waiting by the door.

"Likewise," I said.

★

There was a giddiness to our mad dash from City Hall to the Daily Planet Building. James and I bolted across streets and the concrete front plaza and through the revolving doors into the lobby without stopping for so much as a breather. Inside, we waved at the fresh-faced security guy, who knew us and laughed as we darted over to the grim gray elevator. For once, it came right away, the door sliding open to admit us. We were sweating and winded, but we were also still flying high, and so when the elevator stopped on our floor, we ran again, at top speed up the dim hall and into the Morgue.

Maddy and Devin were at their desks. Both jumped up, alarmed at our speedy entrance. "What's wrong?" Maddy demanded.

James bent, hands on knees, recovering. I slipped into my chair and moused my computer to life, breathing hard too. "Just a sec."

"No, you write," James said. "I'll fill them in."

"My mom already texted me that the warrants came through," Devin said. "She added that the press conference is at 2:45, don't be late."

I opened a new document on my computer before I looked over. James was gazing at Maddy in a way I couldn't interpret. He'd promised me he'd think about what I said. Maddy might not even be glad about my meddling.

I'd done all I could there. I was doing my best to be a good friend—and to be true to myself. The rest was up to them.

"Why is Lois covered in dirt?" Maddy asked.

I laughed. "I like to think of it not as dirt but as the layer of truly gross grime that accumulates in a ceiling no one has been in for *years*. James, come up with a headline while I do the honors."

"Got it," he said, pausing his Maddy-staring to go to his own desk. Maddy walked over and sat on the edge of it, and Devin joined them.

They murmured together for a few seconds. I heard James say, "Perry told Lois to write the story." That got a shocked coo in response, and he told them about our adventures in ceiling spelunking at City Hall. They kept their voices down so I could work, though. Which I appreciated.

I longed to check in with SmallvilleGuy, see if TheInventor was going to come through for us after all. But it would have to wait until I'd finished the story.

HEADLINE TK (Or . . . to come? Why is it TK? Am I spelling that wrong? Probably. Add the headline here.)

With unprecedented swiftness, the Metropolis Public Defender's Office moved today to expunge any and all corruption and embezzlement charges against former Mayor James Worthington, Jr., after providing evidence to the Central District Court of Metropolis of an elaborate plot to frame the former mayor uncovered by reporters at the *Daily Planet*. Arrest warrants were being issued Thursday afternoon for the architects of the plot, Mayor Steve Ellis and the well-known local crime family patriarch Moxie "Boss" Mannheim, who has evaded authorities for years.

The story unfolded quickly as I typed, in a way I was becoming familiar with. There was something about putting the truth on paper, bringing facts into the light of day where everyone could look at them, that made my fingers move faster—it was becoming one of my favorite sensations on earth.

"And . . . done." I had no idea how long it had taken to

compose the story, but no one had nagged me, so we must have been all right on time. "Saved in the edits folder. Add the headline and send it up to copy."

Devin was back at his desk. "On it."

"What headline did you choose?" I asked.

James stood. "Cleared Former Mayor Helps Send Crooks Who Framed Him to Jail, with the subhead: Mayor and Mobster Arrested."

"Nice. Factual, not emotional. I would have been tempted to go with 'See you later, suckers!'" I checked the clock on the wall. It was already nearing two thirty. I might still make it home for Dad's looming deadline. But, first, I wanted to watch evil go down. "We don't want to miss the press conference."

"Which is why we all have our things ready to go," Maddy said.

"Cheeky," I said, gathering mine. "I need a minute."

She opened her mouth to protest, then saw me lift my phone. She said, "All right, but make it quick."

When Devin and James chimed in with variations on "What? No, come on," she shushed them.

Of course, she couldn't know it was the thought of my dad's deadline that was prompting me to contact SmallvilleGuy. The next sighting was tonight. Had TheInventor gotten the info we needed to scare off the snoops? Had he figured out my dad was one of them? Even if he hopefully had no way of knowing General Lane was my dad.

And I wanted to share the victory high I felt from writing the big story.

SkepticGirl1: *You there?*

He responded immediately.

SmallvilleGuy: *I didn't want to bother you. But big news. He traced back Insider01's account to an NSA-issued computer, and the person trying to hack the servers is from the CIA.*

SkepticGirl1: *So no Army?*

SmallvilleGuy: *Nope, and this is enough. He's sending the IP addresses along with the message. In fact, he just sent it.*

SkepticGirl1: *Now we wait.*

SmallvilleGuy: *Now we wait. All good with you?*

SkepticGirl1: *The best—keep your eye on the home page. The press conf will be streaming.*

"Ah, Lois, we need to go?" Maddy said gently.

Devin said, "We needed to go five minutes ago!"

James said nothing, though he had the most invested in not being late.

SkepticGirl1: *Be in touch ASAP.*

SmallvilleGuy: *Proud to know you.*

It was unfair I couldn't take a moment to enjoy those words as thoroughly as I wanted to, but I put my phone away and hurried toward the others. Maddy thrust my bag at me.

"Is Dante coming?" I asked her.

"Not to this," she said, and we walked as we talked. "He's finishing the mural tonight and tomorrow. He wants us to come see it after school. All of us."

I couldn't help watching James for his reaction. "Sounds fun," he said. "That's probably why Lois hasn't filed her story on it yet."

"I've been a little busy," I admitted. "But I should have been more interested in it, in what happens in every part of our city. We all should."

And not only the stories that would hit page one—though I was some kind of proud to picture the story I'd just written there. Proud for all of us.

We headed back to City Hall. Not running, but not slacking off either, which left little room for conversation. Had the plan worked? It must be driving everyone in the press corps crazy, inviting them to a "major press conference" without saying what the event was about.

But there was always a chance someone would have managed to penetrate the secrecy and tipped off Moxie and Ellis so they could get out of Dodge before the cops could snag them. If my plans had gone right, a few minutes ago Principal Butler should have given them the vaguely sinister note to travel to City Hall, where Mayor Worthington would be waiting for their meeting.

I prayed the clone would be with them, *and* that he'd take me up on my offer for us to try to help him. Donovan's proclamation wasn't the only echo bothering me from that morning. There was also the clone's insistence that he was nobody.

City Hall came into view, the street in front partially blocked by a few police cars. There was a podium backed by flags at the top of the steps in front of the doors, the press gathered below it. I spotted Devin's mom nearby, Perry chatting in the crowd of press.

James's dad was nowhere to be seen.

The others started across the street and I made to follow them, when a voice at my ear stopped me. "You don't know me beyond my looking like him," said the double.

I whirled to face him. "What?"

"I am free of him, but I find I prefer the idea of a leash," he said. "Jail sounds nice."

He lifted his arm so I could see he wore the tracker no longer.

"You positive about that?" I asked.

"Yes."

I was about to question where Donovan was, but he spoke again.

"Oh, and they're about to get away." He extended a finger behind him, pointing off to the left.

A fancy sedan was stopped in the middle of the street on the other side of the cop cars. The driver threw it in reverse and began backing up, clearly intending to turn around and take off.

Oh no, no no no. Not so fast.

My friends had finally noticed I wasn't with them, and they came back to me. "Lois?" Maddy asked. She and Devin and James were frowning in confusion at the clone.

"One sec." I ran to the nearest police car and knocked on the window. The cop inside opened the door. "What's the problem?"

I pointed at the car. "Boss Moxie and Mayor Ellis are right over there, and they're leaving. I believe you have arrest warrants for them."

"So we do," he said, seeming unconcerned as he reached in for the radio.

"What are you doing?" I said.

"Northwest," he said into the radio.

Two more police cars screeched from an alley into the street, blocking any possible escape. The cops jumped out of them and ran over to the sedan. They had the doors open in seconds and were pulling two men from the back seat: the beefy, square-faced Boss Moxie and the tan, balding, soon-to-be-former Mayor Ellis. The driver got out with his hands up.

I couldn't help it—I grinned at them and waved. "Got you!" I called.

They may not have noticed, but it was still worth it. The *click-click* of camera shutters flashed as the reporters on the steps noticed the arrest, and then Devin's mom took the podium, tapping on the mic for attention. She nodded back toward where the arrests were happening. "I see it's time to get started. Stay where you are, and the reason for those arrests will be explained."

There was a pause, and she lifted her hand to shade her eyes and see better. I saw why.

The clone was leaving our clump, heading to the arresting officers. He held out his hands to indicate he'd accept the cuffs.

It was bittersweet, but I couldn't stop him. In a few seconds, the cuffs were around his wrists. He wanted them there.

Past the cop cars, a shiny shark-like gray Mercedes finished parking beside the curb. Who should climb out of it like a sleepwalker, but a stunned Principal Butler. He gaped over at the arrests happening and the press conference, wandering toward it.

"Good job, Principal," I said as he neared us.

When he saw me, he blinked and then exploded. "You! You sent me to talk to mobsters. And the mayor!"

"I did you a favor," I said. "Just listen to the press conference."

James was beside me and he chimed in. "Thank you. Dad won't forget this."

Principal Butler, his tie crooked, his shirt sweaty, swallowed whatever else he might have said to me.

"Lois is right. Go listen," James said, and he waved for him to go on past us. With one final shake of his head at me, Butler went to join the chattering crowd gathered for the event. We crossed and stopped on the sidewalk at the bottom of the steps.

Ms. Harris continued, and the conversation in the crowd died back down as she spoke. "That man being arrested is not who he appears to be. I think you'll do better to hear about all this from the person who brought forth the evidence, evidence that clears his name: Mayor James Worthington."

Once you were an elected official, you got to keep the title forever as a courtesy. But James's dad hadn't been called that in non-accusatory tones in far too long.

He strode out from the building's grand entrance, where he must have been semi-hiding. The collective gasp was audible.

"I am honored to be able to step in front of you today with evidence of my innocence. My only betrayal of our great city of tomorrow is that I was cowed into not bringing forth that evidence earlier. I hope the people of Metropolis can forgive me. I believed I was protecting my family, but I see now that the truth is better. It was a lie that allowed Moxie Mannheim and Steve Ellis to frame me. They found a brother I and my family never discussed . . ."

Okay, so he still had to conceal the truth about the clone. But that was a white lie, one that both protected Melody's involvement from coming out *and* allowed the public to know a more important truth. That he was innocent. And by the time he was done talking, I had no doubt he'd be mayor again as soon as there was another election. I also bet he'd be an even better one this time around.

The press corps started shouting their questions: "How long had Moxie been blackmailing you?" "What was your experience in prison?" "Will you run for office again?"

James's dad said, "We'll take your questions one at a time. Perry?"

Butler looked back at me, his anger gone, before launching himself up the steps to no doubt wait for a chance to glad-hand with James's dad and take credit for his role.

"Celebratory milkshakes?" James asked Devin, Maddy, and me. Soon enough the other reporters would be rushing away to write their stories, but mine on the *Daily Planet* had already gone live—the moment the press conference started.

We'd gotten the scoop.

"Not for me," I said. "I have a date with being grounded, and there's someone I need to talk to."

Maddy gave me a quick hug. "If you didn't before, tell him," she whispered.

But I didn't say one way or the other whether I planned to. It might depend on how the day wrapped up for the two of us. Would the threat to Strange Skies still be out there by the end of it?

Verdict unknown.

CHAPTER 33

I arrived home at exactly the time I would have if I'd actually been at school: 3:45 on the dot. *Take that, Dad.*

Surely he'd be proud when he heard about the story. But, of course, he wasn't home. He was off in Kansas, preparing to go out and try to catch the flying man.

"Hi Mom," I called. "I'm going up to my room!"

She called back, "Okay, dinner in three hours!"

I closed and locked the door to my bedroom, and opened my laptop. I hadn't had a chance to look at myself, and I shuddered at my reflection in the dresser mirror. Smudgy streaks slashed across my cheeks.

Oh well. No time for that. I didn't even log in to chat first, but pulled up a window and went to Strange Skies. There was a little number *2* over my private message box. I clicked it.

The first was a message from TheInventor to SmallvilleGuy and me, and it included the message he'd sent to Insider01.

I hope my friends approve. I felt there was no time to lose, so I have already sent the message. Now we hope it is properly received... A

Dear Insider01, or should I say, dear member of a secret interagency task force on which you represent the CIA: You have entered my house, which would typically not be a problem. My door is open for all who seek a place to share the truth of experiences they cannot explain, honestly and in safety. No one who would need such a place can be who you are seeking, and yet I find those who have relied on the haven I created terrified after being interrogated at fake sightings that are aimed to be the locations of . . . what? A flying man?

If you do not delete your account and leave my house well before this evening's sighting, I will be forced to share publicly the details I've been able to discover about your efforts. How embarrassing that would be! For you and your superiors, who no doubt feel untouchable. Know also that I have recently made the acquaintance of a journalist. But I have no interest in spilling secrets. Go in peace, do not return, and all will be well.

p.s. No matter how close you think you might be to finding my location, trust that you will not. You will have no way to prevent my actions, other than to make the retreat I've described here. I'll be watching should you attempt to return or make any further approaches aimed at compromising the security and privacy of my guests.

It was a thing of beauty—and slightly terrifying. Particularly the mention of a journalist, aka me. But had it worked?

I closed the message and opened the next, also from TheInventor to both SmallvilleGuy and me.

You can both relax. The previous posts and the user account were deleted approximately half an hour after I sent the message, and I did still have an open channel, so I watched enough traffic pass back and forth from Insider01's IP address to suggest a serious discussion behind the decision. The interloper trying to crack my firewall is also gone. In short: we did it. I hope to see you both back at Strange Skies soon. Best, A

Would we ever find out what A stood for? I had a shivery sense, almost like a premonition, that we would. Even if today's problem was solved.

I grinned.

Maybe I'd been wrong about Dad. Maybe his trip to Wichita was a coincidence all along. Maybe. I scrolled down the board to confirm that not only was Insider01's name no longer in evidence, the threads were gone. They were.

Already a new one had been posted by another user with the subject line: "What happened to Insider01?"

I clicked on it and noted the top reply.

Posted by **QueenofStrange** *at 3:31 p.m.*: Be glad he's gone. I know what I posted before, but I was encouraged to. The whole thing was a hoax.

After closing the window, I opened chat. SmallvilleGuy's name popped up immediately.

SmallvilleGuy: *I read your story. Congratulations.*

SmallvilleGuy: *James must be thrilled.*

SkepticGirl1: *You must be too. I just saw Strange Skies.*

SmallvilleGuy: *Yeah, relief, for both of us. And I don't think TheInventor has any idea your dad might be on the task force.*

It had never occurred to me to wonder if what we'd seen that night had changed the way Dad saw the world, like it had for me. Now that I considered it, he *would* want to identify what he'd seen too.

But he probably saw it as a threat. I saw that night and what we experienced as something wonderful. The people doing bad things were the ones to hunt down. Not people who could fly. Not people who saved you from getting hurt. Not people who opened your eyes and showed you the world had secrets. Some bad, worthy of being thrust into the public eye, but some good, worthy of keeping.

SmallvilleGuy: *That message was . . . I hope we never make TheInventor mad.*

SkepticGirl1: *You and me both. Although I'm confident we could take him.*

SmallvilleGuy: *Not that we would need to. He's our friend.*

SmallvilleGuy: *But we could. Only with you there to back me up. ;)*

I laughed.

SkepticGirl1: *The good guys won.*

SmallvilleGuy: *Yes, we did.*

I made a happy sigh, and I thought about what I was going to say to him. To tell him how I felt or not to tell him . . .

SkepticGirl1: *How about we catch up tomorrow night, in* Worlds?

Our maybe-a-date night. I would tell him. But not yet.

I knew I was giving myself time to chicken out, but I couldn't make myself do otherwise.

SmallvilleGuy: *I can't wait. See you then.*

I touched the screen with a fingertip.

★

The next morning, Maddy caught me as soon as I came in the school doors. Her T-shirt today was for Victory Nap—ha, we probably could all use one of those.

She wasn't alone. Melody was there too, along with James and Devin.

"What crisis is there now?" I asked.

"No crisis," Melody said. She seemed completely unconcerned with being seen with us. "I just wanted to thank you all, together. I'm going to be different from now on—I'm going to try to be myself. This has been the worst and best week of my life."

She looked at her sister when she got to the best week part.

"Mine too," Maddy said.

"You know, ditto," James put in.

"Not *that* notable a week here," Devin said, "but I'm happy for all of you."

I gave him a little punch.

"I'm kidding," he protested. "It was a big week."

I'd made it through this with my friendships intact, and managed to reunite a pair of estranged sisters. Still, I told the rest of them: "Our best times are still to come."

"After school, you mean?" Maddy asked. "Remember, Dante wants the whole staff to see the mural. He's freaking out about it."

James was the first to answer. "Wouldn't miss it."

This was worth pushing Dad's boundaries for. He hadn't mentioned Friday anyway, just Thursday. I expected to use how bad a mood he was in to try to determine whether he *had* been part of the interagency task force that suffered such a rousing comeuppance at the hands of a mere message board architect.

That wasn't the only loose end I worried over.

We walked up the hallway, about to head to classes. I asked Devin, "Did your mom say anything about the lab?"

He grimaced. "Bad news. The cops went to the building, but it was completely cleared out."

Somehow, I wasn't surprised. Disappointed but not surprised. "Donovan got away."

It was Melody who responded. "Karma has its way of coming around," she said.

Fair enough. I suspected at some point our paths might cross Donovan's in the future, no matter his statement that I'd never see him again. On a hunch, I'd Googled the words "Cadmus lab" and found it was a real company with a web presence and a reputation for being on the cutting edge of science.

We went our separate ways to go to class. The night before, I'd—the horror—mostly studied for the rest of the night. I planned to make good on my promise to Butler to get back on track with my grades.

So the only question remaining was whether I'd be brave enough to make good on my promise to myself to be honest with SmallvilleGuy later. But I had the whole day and the mural expedition before then.

I would spend it with my dear friend denial, who assured me the whole decision was no big deal.

★

We took the subway to the Suicide Slum stop together, the others laughing and joking and talking while I obsessed over how that night's "date" would go and whether I'd choke. Again.

The same old man was playing an enthusiastic guitar solo by the steps up to the street, and I paused to drop a few dollars in his hat. "If it isn't the famous lady and her famous friends," he said, pausing with his fingers on the strings. "Thank you."

When the others gave me questioning glances, I shrugged. I didn't know what he meant, and so we climbed on up the stairs, his music resuming behind us.

The meaning didn't remain a mystery for long. It was solved as soon as we got a look at the mural.

Dante stood below it, proudly, with one of those grand smiles of his, and flung out his arms. "Ta-da!"

"Holy moly," I said.

It was us. Not *just* us—younger kids and teenagers made up the entire swath of the wall now, but we were among a few figures that had been adjusted to be bigger than scale.

In the mural, we *Scoop* staffers stood at one side, the skyline and the globe of the Daily Planet Building behind us. Maddy was beautiful, her crimson streak a stark contrast to the pale yellow he'd done the rest of her hair in. James was noble, tall and serious, in his usual button-down style. Devin was coolly smart, a laptop cradled under his arm. And then there was me.

I was in front of them, with one leg slightly in front of the other, my black boot in the foreground, a notebook and pencil in my hand. I looked . . . fearsome.

"I thought about what I told you I wanted this to show," Dante said, "after we did the interview. I wanted it to be about how *we* can make change. How it's up to us, the new generation, to set things right. Watching you guys, what you did . . . I wanted to show that anyone can be a hero. We're our own heroes." He paused. "Give me something here. Do you like it?"

Maddy answered by smiling at him and giving him a quick kiss. "Very much. So much."

"We're speechless," James said. He shot the couple a thoughtful look, and then gave me a nod.

So, he was waiting. He wouldn't say anything to Maddy. Not yet. *Good decision.* Because Dante was a great guy.

"But can I have a crown?" Devin asked, half-kidding.

"You're only a king in the game," I said. "It's incredible, Dante. Thank you."

I pulled out my phone and moved back to snap a photo of the mural. I'd use it with my story. And I sent it—via the messenger app—so SmallvilleGuy could see it too.

"Speaking of the game . . . I have to go. I have, um, a date." I waved, and turned to head back to the subway. Their hooting calls after me made me grin, but I didn't let them see. I was still nervous, so nervous the trip home passed like I was in a fugue, only awaking for a message from SmallvilleGuy: *See you soon.*

Yes, he would.

Only not quite as soon as I wanted, because when I got home, Dad was in the study with Mom. Before they realized I was home, I overheard some of their conversation.

"No, my meeting didn't go well. It was a disaster. We're trying a different approach," he said.

Dad was careful not to overstep clearance by sharing things with Mom, but they talked about his work. Just in nonspecific terms.

"We still have a source monitoring the channel we were looking at. Though I'm not sure if I trust him anymore."

Sounded like Dad was on the task force. And wait a second. Talk about ideas almost as disturbing as that—was it possible their "source" was TheInventor himself? I didn't *think* so, but I couldn't help wondering. I might have to do some sleuthing in Dad's study soon. See if there was anything to indicate whether it was or not. I'd tried, but I still couldn't quite trust that guy.

A creak in the floor gave me away. "Lois, you're home," Mom said, coming out of the study. "Can you come here for a sec?"

Dum dum dum. I heard the sinister sounds in my head. "Sure thing. Though I'm supposed to meet a friend online in a few." I added, "Homework talk."

"That's fine," Mom said.

"It's not fine," Dad said, joining her in the doorway. "I hear you met the letter of the law yesterday, but I also heard about your story. You're busted. You want me to tell your mom or should I?"

I tried to decide which response would delay me the least, but Mom spoke first.

"You mean tell me she snuck out after our movie night and

came back home later? I knew the whole time," she said. "It wasn't a boyfriend. It was your story, wasn't it? The one that was tough. You'd said James was texting you, and then when it ran, I put it together. That *was* an important story."

Dad was gaping at her. "Why didn't you stop her?"

"Lois would never sneak out at night unless it was for an important reason. I trust her. You should too."

Dad's mouth was still wide open.

"Yeah," I said. "You should trust me."

Mom laughed. "Don't push it."

"Understood," I said, "I'm lucky to have you. Both of you." Dad deserved that, even if he was snooping where I'd rather he didn't.

I pecked Mom and then Dad on their cheeks and went upstairs. I heard the murmur of their voices behind me.

When I passed Lucy's door, I noticed she'd taken off her *Keep Out* sign.

I locked my bedroom door, though I didn't think anyone would bother me, then dug out my holoset and hooked it over my ear. I sat on the bed and thought about the past week. About how there are people we're meant to be connected to. About how easy it is to not let those people know that.

Then I pressed on the holoset.

He was waiting, a lanky alien with light green skin and blue eyes. It felt like ages since we'd seen each other. Whatever "seen" really meant.

The game always felt real. But today it felt even more real. Because I was about to try to make it that way.

"You are a sight for tired, finally-passed-a-test-in-bio eyes," I said.

He shook his head. "That mural was something."

I wasn't sure what he meant, good or bad, but when he held out a hand, I put mine in his. We floated up, over the green hills of *Worlds War Three* to our castle turret, but instead of going inside, he flew us up to the stone teeth around the top.

We sat on the wall beside each other. No spying bat was anywhere in sight. The sunset was again one of those insane game ones, many hues fighting each other across the skies and red winning, the giant moons illuminated gray and dipping low in the sky.

Our hands were still clasped together. I didn't want to let go.

"Your dad's back, right? Did you get in trouble?" he asked.

"No, but I don't want to talk about him right now." Dad would be a threat to us, even if he didn't mean to be, if he was still determined to find the flying man. Especially if my suspicion about TheInventor was right. But that discussion could wait.

He tilted his head, curious. His eyes were so blue. "So what did you want to talk about? The fact you lost the bet? I can send you links to the best Monarchs sweatshirt."

"I did lose, but that's not it. I wanted to talk about . . ." I paused. "This, us."

He didn't say anything, but he didn't let go of my hand. His finger traced a C on my hand, back and forth, back and forth.

I took a breath, and then began to talk before I could

chicken out. Again. And all the words poured out. "I just . . . is this a date? Is Friday our date night? Because I think of it that way. And I know we haven't met out in the world, and you can't tell me who you are yet for whatever reasons you have—which I'm sure are good, although really you can tell me—and that means we can't see each other. We live halfway across the country from each other, and so I know that none of this makes sense, but."

"But?" he asked.

I sighed. "I like you. More-than-a-friend like you. I worry about you. I look forward to talking to you more than to anyone else. I know we can't actually, like, go out on dates, but I would want to know. If you met someone else."

He started to laugh. The sound was nice. I loved his laugh. But I kind of wanted to push him off the turret.

"This is not funny," I said. "I'm pouring my heart out here."

He released my hand and touched my cheek. "I'm not laughing at you. Ever. I'm laughing at me."

"Explain," I commanded.

He dropped his hand to his lap. "I have been living in fear that you would tell me you were going out with Devin or James or some guy you met in Metropolis who I haven't even heard about."

"Shut up." I laughed. "I worry about that too. Well, not with me. With you."

"I don't want to see anyone else," he said. "I do think of this as a date. And I think all the time about when we'll finally be able to stand across from each other in real life."

"Wow." My heart was beating ridiculously fast. But I didn't feel like it was stupid anymore. My heart was smart. It had knowledge. "You totally stole my thunder."

"You know the mural?" he said. "That's how I see you. A hero. I want to be the kind of guy you deserve."

"I would tell you to stop," I whispered, "but I'm enjoying this."

I wanted to know what would happen next.

He reached out and took both my hands in his, and we smiled. Just like that, we were floating up from the turret, flying up into the red sky together, holding on to each other. I didn't know which of us leaned in toward the other first.

We kissed.

And I knew my feet wouldn't touch the ground for a week.

GWENDA BOND is the author of the young adult novels *Girl on a Wire*, *Blackwood*, and *The Woken Gods*. She has also written for *Publishers Weekly* and the *Los Angeles Times*, among other publications, and just might have been inspired to get a journalism degree by her childhood love of Lois Lane. She has an MFA in Writing from the Vermont College of Fine Arts, and lives in a hundred-year-old house in Lexington, Kentucky, with her husband, author Christopher Rowe, and their menagerie.

Visit her online at **gwendabond.com** or **@gwenda** on Twitter.